THE BUBBLEHEAD TRILOG

HIDDEN IN PLAIN SIGHT

A NOVEL

M. G. SELBREDE

STOREHOUSE
PRESS

VALLECITO, CALIFORNIA

Published by Storehouse Press

Storehouse Press is the registered trademark of Storehouse Press, Inc.

This book is a work of fiction. Names, characters, businesses, organizations, places, events, and incidents either are the product of the author's imagination or used fictitiously. Any resemblance to actual persons, living or dead, events, or locales is entirely coincidental.

Book design by Kirk DouPonce (www.DogEaredDesign.com)

Printed in the United States of America

First Edition

Library of Congress Cataloging-in-Publication Data is available.

ISBN-13: 978-1-891375-51-4

ISBN-10: 1-891375-51-2

The author wishes to thank the following individuals for their valuable contributions (inspirational, editorial, philosophical, and/or technical) to the manuscript during its protracted evolution: Susan Burns, Dean Davis, Lee Duigon, Ben Finklea, John Ford, Darlene Valerie Hall (who would have approved), Arnold "Eucatastrophe" Jagt, Joanna Jagt, Rosie Jagt, Chuck Johnson, Chris Kiick, Ron Kirk, William Leake, Kathy Leonard, Melissa Mara Rose Maschler, Bonnie Miller, Nina Rehburg, Levi Rouse, Andrea Schwartz, Diana Schwarzbein, Stiles Watson, and Lisa Young. Special thanks to Kurt DouPonce of DogEaredDesign for bringing a pivotal moment of the story to life so vividly on the front cover, and heartfelt gratitude to my beloved wife Kathy for graciously enduring the birth pangs of the upcoming novels in this series.

PART I

I

Jenna Wilkes pushed her glasses up on her nose to squint at the phony data on the screen in front of her, going through the motions expected of people analyzing real data. The junior researcher facing her from across the laboratory table looked up from his computer.

"Whatcha got, Jenna?" he probed, eyes locked upon her.

She fidgeted in her chair, chafing that she, a physicist, had been reduced to a thespian pretending to do physics. When she returned his stare, the overhead fluorescent lights caught her glasses just so, making her eyes over-bright disks. Jenna opened her mouth as if to answer, then closed it, brushing her long red hair out of her face. She was a bad liar. Her gaze shifted back to the screen to better avoid the wordless accusation she had seen in his eyes. His resentment at being excluded from her zealously guarded work was palpable.

"Don't make me come over there," he urged with a bit more force than he intended.

"You *know* I don't like sharing half-baked research with anyone, Bryn." As she turned in her chair, her eyes darted from Bryn to the screen to the massive titanium cube mounted behind her on its stainless steel frame. The matte black surface of the cube, measuring more than a yard on a side, bristled with copper tubing, wires, meters, foil, and thermal shielding. She didn't know how long she could keep the device from being pried out of her hands. Decoys, deceptions, and lies had their limits.

Bryn Zilcher smirked and called over his shoulder to a senior researcher. "Jenna's her usual talkative self again. Think she'll ever get around to documenting anything she does around here?"

The older scientist, Ron Bartleby, slowly swung his chair around to regard Bryn with an upraised eyebrow. "You want to hide some secrets too, Bryn? Then discover something of your own to hide. Leave the redhead alone."

Jenna cocked her head at her defender's comment. She could count on Bartleby to keep the newer researchers in line—another reason he had earned her trust over the last three years.

When Bartleby unexpectedly rose to approach her workstation, she knew her elaborate on-screen facade may need to come into play. She turned her monitor off and sorted through some papers. Bartleby came around her lab table and approached the room-dominating cube behind her. She pretended he wasn't there.

"Remember, Doctor Wilkes, a huge chunk of our division's 2024–2025 fiscal year budget was sunk into your isolator system here," Bartleby chided with undue formality, patting the titanium surface with a chubby hand.

"So I'm told," she mumbled.

Across the table, Bryn's eyes bored through her. He knew she had been working on the workstation just moments earlier. But Bartleby would assume Jenna's computer was turned off. Bryn tried to signal Bartleby, pointing at Jenna's screen. Bartleby shifted his eyes and caught the gesture. So did Jenna.

"Done for the day?" Bartleby asked her.

"Yeah, just looking for a journal article I'll need for tomorrow," she replied.

Bartleby reached over her shoulder and turned her computer screen back on. Her eyes narrowed at Bryn, who shot back a smug grin. She turned in her chair and looked up at Bartleby, who was leaning across her to examine her results. The decoy would prove more effective if she could feign some convincing anger.

"Great precedent. Thanks a lot, Ron. Tomorrow, Bryn will be doing that. Thursday, the grad students will check my work, and Friday, the cleaning lady will be running error regressions on my data."

"Temper, temper," Bartleby replied with a faint air of superiority, one she knew was rooted in experience, not condescension. Though technically not her superior, he was on much better terms with the lab managers than she.

"I'm not showing Bryn jack," he added decisively.

"Nice," Bryn fumed. "Great intramural data sharing. World class."

"Hmm ..." Bartleby dragged a finger down the column of data on her screen. "The same result as your other five prototypes."

She nodded, trying to push her chair out farther from him. Bartleby had no idea his older, heavier bulk was too far into her personal space. He kept his finger on the screen, his heavy-lidded eyes turning serious.

"Do you have any idea what it means?" he finally asked. "Without giving me your stock answer about it being too premature to draw any conclusions."

"I don't like ..." she began

"... to speculate," he finished.

"*Everything* she does is pure speculation," Bryn scoffed, knowing he wasn't being kept at arm's length from something trivial. "Our budget was torpedoed fabricating that mystery box."

Jenna ignored Bryn's barb and looked back up at Bartleby with renewed purpose.

"There's a way to know whether it's just a simple cryogenic effect, or something more," she whispered.

Bryn's ears perked up. She turned to glare at him, invisible daggers flying from her eyes.

"You heard that?" She wasn't whispering anymore.

"I don't like to speculate," he cracked.

Bartleby waved Bryn off, but looked at Jenna with concern.

"Look," he said, "I've done everything I can to keep management off your back. You're supposed to optimize existing products. If you keep stumbling on things by accident, that's bad juju in management's eyes. It proves you can't keep focus."

He looked across the lab table at Bryn, then back down at Jenna.

"You're the best researcher here, but they're pragmatists. They only care about tangible, marketable results. Period."

He released his fingerhold on her monitor and pulled up a rolling lab chair. Bryn tilted his head. Bartleby noticed and promptly ordered Zilcher downstairs on an errand they both knew to be meaningless.

Bartleby turned back to examine her data. "You said there's a way to know?"

"Yeah," she didn't miss a beat. "This thing might be a neutrino shield."

Bartleby stopped sipping his coffee, his eyes staring into hers. "You *do* know what you're saying, right?" They both understood that the subatomic particles called neutrinos were incredibly difficult to stop on their speed-of-light journeys through space, through matter, through anything.

She nodded, knowing she had just thrown him a bone, one calculated to divert attention from her bigger discovery.

"Are you proposing to test that?" he asked, a dark look passing over his face. Transporting the isolator to one of the world's underground neutrino detectors could bust their budget.

"How can we not?" she asked, naively surprised at his question.

For a moment, Bartleby embraced the spirit of her reply. He had cut his teeth on basic research like this. But the wave of nostalgia evaporated, and his face hardened.

"Easy there. We don't run the test unless you're willing to jeopardize your job again, Doctor Wilkes. That's a risk you're not taking seriously enough. Trust me."

Jenna dropped her gaze evasively, knowing Bartleby wouldn't stop staring until she acknowledged his concern.

"Ron, what would you do if you were sitting at your desk and got these results on the isolator?" she asked.

"You're changing the subject," he replied. "I'm not the one that management is thinking about firing every quarter."

Jenna brightened suddenly. "Then maybe *you* can sell the test to management!" She leaned forward. "Find some kind of value proposition they'll buy."

He regarded her warily. She was coming across as a daughter pleading with her father to let her do something ill-advised. Given their age difference, the comparison didn't lack merit: he was fifty-eight; she had recently turned twenty-nine, a year older than Bryn. Bartleby scratched his balding head and tried to reason with her.

"We've done that with every aspect of your project so far. So far, no tangible results, just anomalies like this in the wake of otherwise successful ignitions." He pointed an accusing finger at her screen. "I won't sell a string of empty promises that goes on forever. It's got to end, preferably before you lose your job."

Bryn reentered the room with the journal reprint Bartleby requested and settled back into his chair, clearly miffed with Bartleby's dismissive nod toward him.

"Look," Bartleby turned back to Jenna. "Just turn the isolator off and we'll track its behavior as it returns to room temperature."

Jenna stiffened in dismay, alarm rising in her eyes. She'd been caught. That was the last suggestion she wanted to hear, but there was no going back. She'd have to take Bartleby into her confidence immediately to have any chance at damage control. Whether his suggestion was innocent or intentional didn't change the crisis it would ignite—nor was there time to discern where Bartleby stood. Her gut knotted.

She grabbed a notepad from the table and scribbled furiously. She signaled to Bartleby to roll his chair farther away from Bryn, closer to the black cube. Once settled out of earshot, she turned the page toward Bartleby so Bryn couldn't see it. Bartleby silently read the chicken scratch, barely able to make out her frantic handwriting: IT CAN'T BE TURNED OFF.

"Really?" Bartleby whispered. "Why not?"

"I don't know. You turn it off, and it stays on. I've never been able to turn *any* of the six test isolators off."

"Are you saying they're self-sustaining?" he asked in bewilderment.

"No, no!" she hissed, pointing at the circuit boxes on the east wall of the lab. "If I shut down the switches and pull the plug, I show the meter *still running* in that local circuit box. The isolator is—was—the only thing on that circuit. I'm afraid of pulling the wall breaker."

"Why should you be afraid ..." Bartleby's voice trailed off in recognition of Jenna's fear. "Are you sure?" he asked again, grappling with the realization that this was no joke.

Bryn arose to leave. "I'll be back in the morning. It's so nice working with people who communicate openly with me. Wild horses couldn't keep me from enjoying such a synergistic work environment."

"You too, Bryn," Bartleby called the bluff.

As the door closed behind Bryn, Bartleby quickly put his finger across his lips, signaling for silence. He ambled around the lab table and examined the peripherals near Bryn's computer. He located a wireless microphone—its antenna was inserted into the workstation. He pulled the antenna out enough to deactivate it.

"Oh oh, I bumped Bryn's computer. I'm SO sorry."

Jenna grinned at Bartleby's overacting as he lifted up the now-dead microphone to indicate what their coworker was up to.

Bartleby kept an eye on the wall monitor that would alert him once Bryn left the building. Until then, small talk was the safer option.

"You know, Jenna, most of the crew would have been flattered that someone considered them worth recording." Bartleby brandished the microphone her way. "But not you. You, you don't much like Bryn, do you?"

"You don't either," she retorted.

"Irrelevant. I don't treat every newbie as a threat. You do."

"I have reason to distrust everyone in the lab."

"Do you distrust me?" Bartleby asked, setting Jenna aback momentarily.

"No, Ron, I don't distrust you, I guess." She looked vulnerable for a moment, but her anger quickly got its second wind. She pointed at the microphone.

"I won't let Bryn rip me off."

"I don't think Bryn is your problem," Bartleby suggested.

He was right. She was a stranger to her own greatest breakthrough. But the pit deep in her mind, the memory hole where she had buried her revolutionary ideas seven years ago at Stanford, wasn't a particularly secure place. Those ideas had crept into the six isolators she had designed, but she couldn't recognize or understand her own blueprints once she finished drafting them.

The green light on the personnel board in front of Bryn Zilcher's name winked out.

"Now is the time for answers." Bartleby remarked grimly. He walked back around to face the isolator and folded his arms.

Jenna didn't know what to expect. Though Bartleby was the closest thing to a friend to her at CryoMax, he was a company man under the skin. It was getting harder to reach the scientist lurking beneath the executive facade he was expected to maintain.

"This is the most expensive isolator ever prototyped," he asserted. "Solid titanium a meter on a side. A spherical control cavity, soccer-ball-size, in the middle … and *nobody can shut off the power to it?*" The demanding expression on Bartleby's face unnerved Jenna. He marched over to the circuit breaker on the wall.

Jenna tensed up in her seat. She wasn't sure she wanted to be in the building if the breaker were thrown. "You're just going to check the meter, right?" she asked anxiously.

"That … and turn off the breaker to the line." He meant it.

"That might be dangerous," she warned.

"It had better not be dangerous, Doctor Wilkes." Bartleby's words were tense and angry. "There's nothing in the research being done in my lab that could possibly be dangerous to anybody, ever!"

His unprecedented outburst stunned her—he was visibly shaking. She found her hands gripping the armrests of her chair so tightly they were almost bloodless. They stared at each other.

They said nothing, but her mind was racing, her eyes searching his eyes for answers that couldn't possibly be there …

Do you know what I'm really doing with this isolator, Ron? What I've been doing here for the last three years? It's driving me crazy, designing things I don't recognize or understand moments after the ink has dried. Am I going through someone else's motions—or are they my own? I can't push past the walls of pain to get at the answers I know must be in my head somewhere. I can't even tell anyone what I'm going through. Nobody ever invented the right words to explain it.

She squeezed her eyes shut with a pained expression; Bartleby knew nothing of her inner turmoil. But his expression relaxed, and he continued without missing a beat.

"Take your cell phone with you. Go downstairs to the maintenance room where all the electrical lines come into this building. Find the box for this lab room: it's marked 2130. Find the meter that matches the kilowatt hours being pulled from this isolator outlet, and then call me from there. I want you there watching that meter when I throw this breaker."

Now she understood. He was going to put himself in danger's way.

"I can't let you be the one to throw that switch, Ron," she insisted, rising to her feet. Realizing she had kicked her pumps off under the desk, she sat back down to recover them, interrupting her mock-heroic speech in midstream.

But Bartleby took charge. "Take your cell phone. You know my number. I'll be waiting here," he ordered.

"What if ..."

"Call 911," he shot back. "Get down there. Take a flashlight."

A flashlight? she wondered. "This can wait, you know," her tone as calm as she could muster.

"No, it can't. I'm hungry."

Hitting the speed bump of Bartleby's sophomoric humor was momentarily jarring, yet it encouraged Jenna to cooperate. Shoes back on, she paused at the door after pulling a flashlight out of the wall cabinet.

He called out after her. "Unless, of course, you want to stop testing your hypotheses in this lab!"

She let the door close behind her and made her way to the elevator, carelessly leaving her cell phone earpiece behind. It dawned on her that she'd never taken the stairs before. If the electricity were going to fail, she'd better know what to expect in the stairwell. She glanced at the flashlight in her hand, gripped it even more firmly, and walked resolutely past the elevator.

Her innocent decision to take the stairs, pragmatic in the extreme, changed everything.

2

Downstairs, division chief Bic Johanssen waited for an unwanted pest from headquarters to arrive. Such visits triggered reflections on the career-threatening conduct he'd been pushed into over the last three years. His thoughts took visual form, words on a computer screen that burned brightly in his mind's eye. He hoped the words, or more to the point, their absence, would never be detected. The day the deletions were discovered would be his last at CryoMax.

Jenna Wilkes is damaged goods.
Emotional baggage.
Big chip on shoulder.

Deleted. Bic Johanssen had long ago deleted those three negative evaluations of Jenna sent upstairs to him by her managers. That was the first time he had mutilated corporate data.

Rain Man. Except female, and less reasonable.
Motormouth last year. Lockjaw last eight months.
Promising initial results. Her project is still a money pit.

Bic had retained the one positive comment, striking the money pit assessment despite knowing in his gut that it was all too true.

Jenna's job interview from three years earlier hadn't escaped Bic's digital knife either.

Earned Ph.D. in Physics at Stanford, May 2018, age 22.
Denied opportunity for postdoctoral study.

Bic had deleted the denial. It would raise questions.

The four-year period between leaving Stanford and joining Cryo-Max bristled with red flags. She'd had fifteen jobs—*fifteen!*—which all ended prematurely. Therefore, no meaningful references. All she had was a powerful advocate upstairs, a bigwig on the CryoMax board, who chose to remain anonymous. A spook. Could be one of the good guys. Could be otherwise. Could even be a trap.

A spook. Bic didn't need one of his bosses complicating his life like this, but turning down an unknown board member could recoil on Bic's head in unseen ways. *Better to choose the devil you know,* Bic reasoned. *I can control something that's predictable.* It helped that the laundry list was limited. Her advocate had wanted Bic to get Jenna hired and to spiff up her records as needed—which was often. Bic hoped his rear was being covered, but the spook could have vulnerabilities of his own. Most board members did.

Jenna's psych file was a melting pot of pathologies, none of them certain—the grammar of trauma stretched beyond its legitimate reach. Bic had cleaned that up too.

That made for two strikes against him.

Yet Jenna had thrived working with Ron Bartleby, had managed to somehow transcend her past. Her dysfunctional family situation was only part of the story. Bic didn't know the rest. Stanford had done its own deleting, he had guessed. Something had happened back then. As long as Jenna's work passed muster, it wasn't Bic's problem.

Bic assumed that Jenna's selective amnesia was benign because she functioned in spite of it. But the void in her mind wasn't truly empty, and what hid inside it had taken concrete shape in Bic's lab, under his nose, with his approval, on CryoMax's dime, carved out of a primal block of titanium, a coiled spring poised to snap in half.

Bic's visitor arrived at the lab entrance. This was already a bad sign—the man didn't want to meet Bic at the admin building but here, where he could wreak the most personnel damage. Bic quickly put the disturbing reveries of Evaluators' Labor Lost out of his mind and stepped outside to intercept his visitor, greeting his guest with as much sincerity as he could possibly fake. From all he could tell, it was an unqualified waste of energy.

Bic didn't like *any* visits from corporate headquarters in Boston, but he positively despised the quarterly visits from the most caustic director, Niles Emmerich. Niles was in one of his cut-and-run moods, shaking things up by terminating a handful of researchers. The stock price had dropped again, but Wall Street would respond favorably to hard-nosed action by management. It was all Bic could do to retain his most promising researchers against his superior's ruthless pruning.

The two gray-suited men, briefcases in hand, walked down the first floor hallway bisecting Building F, the part of the Livermore corporate lab focused on isolator optimization. The late afternoon sun couldn't reach this deep into the facility; artificial lighting illuminated the walls, which were emblazoned with the italicized blue CryoMax logo, a stylized red snowflake boldly superimposed on top of the final X. Niles was droning on about the room service at the hotel just outside the corporate campus.

"... and that's why I hate coming out to the Livermore lab, Johanssen. Aren't there any better hotels here? Like we have in Boston?"

Bic was quickly wearying of Niles's endless stream of complaints. "Well, there's ..."

"I mean close by!" Niles cut him off.

"Well ..."

"See what I mean?" Niles finished triumphantly. "One day we'll move the lab to a better location."

"Wouldn't it be cheaper to build our own hotel?" Bic asked, but before Niles could answer, a side door in the hallway suddenly swung open, nearly hitting them, and a red-haired woman bolted out holding a flashlight and cell phone. Her lab coat had obviously never been washed: it was dingy gray and heavily mottled, not the bright white coats everyone else in the facility wore. Due to the angle the door opened, she never saw Bic or Niles and hurried away from them down the hallway, the sound of her shoes reverberating down the corridor.

Niles quickly set down his briefcase and purposefully put his hands on his hips.

"How rude!" he blustered. He called out more loudly. "Miss, come back here this instant!" The usual velvet tones of his English accent sounded shrill and brittle echoing off the hallway walls.

Jenna jumped when she heard the voice from behind her. She spun around in her tracks, now about eight yards from the two.

"I'm sorry!" she cried out, and turned back around and kept going.

She had recognized Bic Johanssen, but not the other man. She couldn't keep Bartleby waiting by the circuit breaker. She wasn't even sure she wanted to be in the *building* when he popped the breaker, but right now she was committed.

Niles ignored her hasty apology and called again. "Miss, come back here. Now!"

"I can't!" Jenna called back, nearly breaking into a run, forcing herself to slow back down to an urgent walk.

Niles's eyes narrowed to angry slits. He turned to Bic. "Do you know her?" he demanded, pointing at the receding figure.

"Yes," Bic answered glumly. "That's Doctor Jenna Wilkes. She is one of my best researchers." He looked down the hallway after her and was surprised to see her entering a maintenance room. "What the hell?" Bic muttered in surprise.

"Exactly my point," said Niles, his gray mustache and goatee framing a severe scowl. "What the hell is *with* your people, Johanssen? What kind of show are you running here?" He paused and pulled out his pocket digiscreen. "Did you say Wilkes?"

Bic nodded absently, then turned his head, eyes riveted on Niles's digiscreen. Niles only remembered the names of people he was planning to cut from the staff. Bic had insulated Wilkes so completely from upper management that they hardly knew she existed. Nothing negative about her ever floated upstairs. How did Niles get her name?

And what was Jenna doing in the maintenance room? The massive current pumped up to the lab provided power cushion to spare. What could possibly have triggered an interrupt? And Jenna wasn't even qualified to handle power glitches.

"Niles," Bic tried to excuse himself. "I need to see what Doctor Wilkes is doing. This should only take a moment of my time."

"Of *our* time," Niles tapped the stylus on his digiscreen decisively. "I want a word with her."

Bic groaned inside. The last two people he wanted to see cross paths were Niles and Jenna. Bartleby's recent reports had implied that she was finally onto something important—important enough to justify not having fired her ten times over since she came on board. But *Niles* didn't know

Bartleby from Adam, nor how an anonymous board member had covertly orchestrated her arrival and retention through Bic's ample distribution of lipstick on the pig. And given Niles's first impression of Wilkes ...

"Right," Bic sighed. "Of *our* time. Let's catch up to her."

Bic found the maintenance room door locked, so he knocked. Niles fumed impatiently. There was no answer, but they could hear Jenna talking inside to somebody.

"Liaisons in the maintenance closets, Johanssen?" Niles asked snidely.

Bic ignored the venom, knocked, and called out Jenna's name.

"I'm busy," came a muffled female voice behind the door.

Bic saw Niles turning bright red. *It's getting ugly fast*, he realized. Bic held up an index finger at Niles, signaling for him to wait. He then went to his wallet to find his passkey. He rarely used it: he was always expected by his employees, who always left their doors open for him. He didn't even take the passkey out, but just swiped the wallet across the sensor. The door buzzed, and Bic pulled it open. Niles followed him into the maintenance closet.

The room resembled a high-school locker room, except the lockers were electrical meters and modular interrupt boxes. Like Building H, this building used the older through-the-door fused pull-out disconnects behind panel door interlocks, instead of intranet-controlled power, ostensibly for enhanced current limiting, making the room a literal throwback to the twentieth century.

Jenna wasn't in the first row, but they could hear her voice to the right. They walked around the first rank of meters. Bic glanced around the corner of the next row and saw Jenna, or at least the bottom two-thirds of her. Her shoulder and head were blocked by an open circuit box panel; she'd obviously defeated the interlock to open it. She hadn't noticed them yet; the hum in the room had covered the buzz of the entry door lock and their footsteps.

"Okay, Ron, I'm ready," she said. "We're steady at 8.132. Throw the breaker."

Niles took a step forward to open his mouth, but was startled when Jenna's cell phone dropped to the ground and the shell split from the impact. Her hands dropped to her side.

"Oh my God," she whispered.

Niles didn't know why, but her words riveted him in place.

Bic recognized that this wasn't just a minor power problem. He pushed past Niles and walked behind Jenna. She was staring at the meter, turning only for a moment to recognize Bic before refocusing her gaze on the digital readout ticking off the power flow.

Now Bic was getting spooked. He muttered to her under his breath. "Look, Jenna, what's going on here?"

She just pointed to the meter, its display module showing a continual power drain of 8.132 kilowatts, and said, "It's not stopping."

"What's not stopping?"

She pulled herself together and quickly closed the circuit module panel. Bic saw the number stenciled on the galvanized metal: 2130. He pointed at the numerals.

"That's to the isolator lab, isn't it?" he asked.

She nodded, bending down to pick up the broken cell phone, cursing under her breath that now she couldn't talk to Bartleby, and even more upset that Johanssen and the stranger with an accent had been in the maintenance room with her.

Niles had had all he could stand at this point. He felt foolish standing there, poised as if something climactic were happening, and ... nothing. He felt she had made a fool of him.

"Doctor Wicks," he began angrily.

"Wilkes," corrected Bic.

"It doesn't matter," Niles shot back.

"Who's he?" Jenna asked Bic.

Niles stepped forward, coming within a foot of Jenna.

"I'm Doctor Johanssen's boss, Director Emmerich," he announced with pointed condescension.

Bic recognized this pattern all too well: in Niles's book, maximizing a target's discomfort was the obligatory prelude to being fired.

Jenna nodded, not entirely comprehending, her mind still reeling from the fact that in the circuit box she had just closed, power was flowing to the lab that had no business flowing *anywhere*. Her mind was racing to try to find any plausible explanation for it. All she could conclude was summed up in one simple phrase she'd been subconsciously repeating to herself since trying to shut down the first isolator months earlier: *the laws of nature require it.*

"Miss Wilkes," Niles started again, pointedly dropping Jenna's title. "You nearly slammed a door in my face, refused to stop when I called you, and now you play me for a fool with your little game *in this stupid broom closet*!"

"Niles," Bic began, "I think that was an accident. You know ..."

"If Johanssen isn't going to run a tight ship here," Niles sneered, "I know where to find someone who can."

Bic recognized he had no choice but to back down. Jenna was on her own this time; he'd try to pick up the pieces later when he was in a better position to do so.

"Look, I'm sorry about the door," she apologized, "but Ron was waiting for my call, and I had to ..."

"Is Ron a director of CryoMax?" sniffed Niles.

Jenna looked around, starting to feel trapped, desperate. *There's no place to go*, she thought. *These guys are blocking me in. Should I push past them to get to Ron? He must be freaking that my cell phone went dead ... Cell phone. Bic has one.*

She ignored Niles's question and turned toward Bic. "Doctor Johanssen, it's critical that I call Ron Bartleby up in the lab. May I use your cell phone?" she asked.

As Bic started to reach for his cell phone, Niles grabbed his arm and glared at Jenna.

"We weren't finished, Miss Wicks."

This time, Bic didn't try to correct him.

Jenna blurted out to Bic, "Just call Ron and tell him I'm okay."

Niles snorted. "Of course you're okay, for the moment. It's your job here that's not."

Bic saw Jenna's eyes boring in on him, imploring him to make the call. He backed away from Niles and pushed the speed dial to Bartleby's cell phone while Niles continued to berate Jenna.

Bartleby answered the phone, but Bic was stunned at what Bartleby said.

"Bic, I can't talk right now. I'm waiting for a very important call. Sorry." And the line went dead.

Bic redialed.

"Bic, I told you I can't ..."

"Jenna's with me," Bic interrupted. There was a pause on the other end of the line. "Did you hear me? Jenna's with me."

Bartleby could hear an Englishman yelling at someone through the line. "Where's Jenna?" he asked Bic.

"Here in the maintenance room."

Bic heard Bartleby curse.

"What's going on, Ron?" Bic was rapidly losing his patience.

"Oh, just some flaky power spikes messing with our amps, Bic." Caught unprepared, Bartleby had to improvise.

"Really." Bic knew Bartleby was hiding something. He'd only do that if it were important. Or if it were something that would hurt Jenna.

Not wanting Niles to overhear his call to Bartleby, Bic moved to the far end of the maintenance room. He spat his words into the cell phone in a loud whisper.

"Funny thing is, Ron, that Jenna thinks the problem isn't power spikes, it's the power being too constant. Would you happen to know anything about that?"

"What's wrong with power being too constant?" Bartleby's improvisation had just slammed headfirst into the wall.

"Must be *something* wrong with it. Jenna dropped her phone in a state of shock. Wasn't she talking to you at the time?"

Now Bartleby was stuck. He'd already said he was waiting for a critical call and had hung up on Bic after saying so. Bartleby had obviously forgotten all about that call after Bic mentioned Jenna. He was caught red-handed.

"Can you and Jenna come up to the lab and we can talk about it?" asked Bartleby.

"I don't know, Ron. Right now, Niles is having roast Jenna for dinner."

"Niles Emmerich?" Bartleby tensed.

"Mmm hmmm."

"Bic, listen. Don't let Niles come up with you. You and Jenna get up here."

"Niles may have different ideas. He's probably gonna can Jenna. She'll be the first researcher fired in a maintenance closet."

"Is that Niles talking to her in the background?"

"Yeah, it ... was ..."

Nobody was talking in the next aisle. Phone to his ear, Bic walked back to the aisle and saw both Jenna and Niles staring at the power meter, with panel 2130 reopened.

Bartleby was beside himself. "Bic, what's going on? You're not talking."

Bic spoke more quietly into the phone as he approached Jenna and Niles. "They're both looking at the power readout." Bic moved around to see what they were staring at.

"Bic, talk to me!" Bartleby wanted to leave the lab and get downstairs. He was running blind, with no idea what was going on, and with Bic saying nothing ...

"Ron, it's just a power meter. Same eight-kilowatt power flow as before. Nothing special."

Bic felt Niles nudge him. He looked down to see what Niles was pointing to. He followed Niles's finger to the fused pull-out disconnect module. Power only flowed to the meter if the module was wedged into its socket.

Only the module wasn't in its socket. It was in Jenna's hand.

3

Four hours later, Jenna sat on the edge of her seat in the corporate lounge staring at the floor. The smoke from the cigarette Niles had left in the ashtray snaked toward her. She barely heard the hushed conversation between Bartleby, Niles, Bic, and several other people from Boston headquarters on the treble-heavy speakerphone. She pushed on her cuticles and unconsciously bit her lower lip, barely making out Bic's voice above the chatter.

"Look, Niles, there's nothing of value here," Bic protested. "The isolator isn't creating energy out of nothing; it's just bridging energy from one place to another. Ron says it can't be controlled: it's like a hole in a dyke. You plug one hole; the water comes out another."

Niles would have none of it. "Just because Bartleby and Wick say it doesn't create energy doesn't mean it's so. Let's get some new researchers in here with a can-do attitude. To hell with this pessimistic rubbish."

Murmurs of approval burbled up from the speakerphone—Niles knew how to push management's buttons.

Bartleby stood up angrily. "None of the other researchers have a *clue* what Jenna's done. *She* was the one who designed and built this line of isolators. If anybody should carry this forward, it should be her!"

He stared defiantly at Niles, who turned away and lit another cigarette. He stuffed it into the ashtray next to its still-burning companion, the smoke from both wafting into Jenna's face. She was too deep in thought to even notice.

"Ron, nobody's trying to take anything away from Jenna," assured Bic.

"Right," agreed Niles, "you can't take something away from Jenna that wasn't hers to begin with."

Bartleby took a step closer to Niles. "Are you insinuating that this wasn't Jenna's work, Director Emmerich?"

Bic knew Bartleby was about to cross the line. Bic tried to shoot him a warning glance, hoping Bartleby would notice.

"Sure it's her work," Niles conceded testily. "A raise for her is obviously in order. But it's owned lock, stock, and barrel by CryoMax. And CryoMax can look after its interests quite aggressively, with or without her. I'll even add her name to my patent." Niles smiled his toothy grin at Bartleby.

Bic slapped Niles on the back, intervening before Bartleby could respond. "Ha! You've got your name on every one of my patents too, Niles. You're an equal opportunity parasite, by God!" Bic chortled and glanced at Bartleby. Niles glowered at Bartleby, then Bic, not knowing how to react, but then started laughing himself.

"Yes, yes, of course you're right. That's been policy here from day one: pay the piper. The question remains, though, what exactly *is* this invention?"

"It's an energy transfer device; that much is clear." Bic leaned back in his chair and sipped his drink, satisfied in that assessment. Bartleby shook his head slowly, but the next voice they heard startled everyone.

"That's not really what it is." Jenna looked up, still looking small and tired and weary, but her green eyes were glowing behind her smudged glasses.

Niles scoffed at her. "Of course it's an energy transfer device. Short circuits and backpaths have all been ruled out. We spent two hours confirming that it bypasses conductors over a hundred yards apart. It would do Tesla proud." Niles turned away from Jenna, but she spoke again.

"It's transferring energy only because it has to. That's strictly incidental to what it is. Its purpose is completely different." She brushed the hair out of her face to look directly at Niles. He saw something disturbing in her eyes, something matching the tone in her voice that had frozen him in place earlier today. He nervously lit a third cigarette.

A voice on the speakerphone crackled through. "Doctor Wilkes, are you saying then that this is an enhanced cryodevice like we've been building for the last two decades?"

Jenna didn't recognize the voice. She assumed it was another corporate director who had swooped down on her research. "No," she answered, "it's not a cryodevice either."

Bic reacted with annoyance. "Of course it's a cryodevice. It's operating near absolute zero at its core. You're not making any sense, Jenna."

"Doctor Johanssen, I admit it's cold inside the unit." Jenna took a deep breath. "But not because it's a cryodevice. That's also incidental to its design."

Niles slapped both knees with his palms and exclaimed, "That's good enough for me. If it's cold in there, I don't care how it got that way. A rose by any other name."

Jenna shook her head. Bartleby could see she was aiming at something more. He only had an inkling of where her research was headed, but he could tell she was too stressed to maintain any mental discipline under interrogation. He was too curious to stop her, but lamented the total loss of project control her letting the cat out of the bag would trigger.

Bic turned to her, met her eyes, and pointed at the speakerphone while holding her gaze. "The man on the speakerphone is our chairman, Jenna. Could you explain what you mean to him in layman's terms?"

Jenna's heartbeat quickened. Chairman Eckhardt? He had been a Nobel laureate for his cryogenics work in 2020. *Why layman's language? Was Bic trying to say something without saying it?* Her mind tried to focus. Everyone in the room fell silent.

"Chairman Eckhardt," she began in earnest, "in the simplest possible terms, the isolator core is frozen." She heard a couple of guffaws over the speakerphone.

Niles rolled his eyes and lit a fourth cigarette.

The voice that was Eckhardt's crackled through the speaker. "We do that all the time, Doctor Wilkes."

"Not like this we don't." She looked at Bartleby, who nodded back at her.

Bic drummed his fingertips on the lounge table and stared at Niles, who had laid the fourth cigarette, also still smoking, in the ashtray. Bic knew Niles never took more than three puffs on a lit cigarette—the smoldering butts were simply his way of staking out territory.

"So, is it a new way to make things cold?" asked the voice of Eckhardt. The voice had a metallic German tint over the speakerphone, a voice softened by age.

"I'm not trying to make things cold," she explained. "I'm trying to actually freeze them."

"You're saying there's a difference?" asked Bartleby, trying to head off another round of scoffing by Niles.

She nodded.

Bic spoke into the speaker, "She's nodding yes, Chairman."

Bryn's tall, black-haired figure had sauntered into the room during the exchange. Bartleby got up to challenge him, but Niles waved him back down.

"I've asked my nephew Bryn to join us," Niles said slyly.

Bartleby's eyes widened.

"Nephew?" asked Jenna.

She watched Bryn sit down. He sniffed disapprovingly at the smoking ashtray and pushed it across the table closer to Jenna.

Bic looked back at Niles as if seeing him for the first time.

"I didn't know Doctor Zilcher was your nephew, Niles."

"Bryn is my sister's only child." Niles nodded toward Bryn.

Bartleby figured that Bryn must have pushed his siblings out of the nest to their deaths like a cuckoo bird. He could see Bryn acting the part of a brood parasite with Jenna's work as well. Was Niles really that calculating?

Bryn contradicted Jenna outright. "It's just cold inside that box, that's all. Frozen, cold, they're all the same. Doctor Wilkes is wasting Boston's time playing her silly word games."

Bartleby could see Bryn deliberately pushing Jenna's buttons, but there was nothing he could do about it. In this situation, nepotism was a better shield than merit.

But Eckhardt spoke again from the speaker. "Doctor Wilkes, I finally understand what you've been trying to say here tonight. I'm diverting my personal jet to Oakland to fly you to our East Coast offices. We will speak in private. Emmerich, see that the lab is locked up. No access to anyone except Wilkes, myself, and anyone whom I authorize. Is that clear?"

Niles shot up to his feet (his custom in board meetings when Eckhardt issued orders), but the gesture was wasted over the phone. "Chairman, we will seal the lab tomorrow morning as you ordered."

"Director," Eckhardt corrected Niles, "I want the lab sealed *immediately*, not tomorrow morning. No exceptions on access."

Niles looked crestfallen. Bryn smiled an uncharacteristically crooked smile and clicked his pen, watching Jenna's reaction. Bic reached over to turn off the speakerphone.

Niles shook his head. "The chairman *never* flies anybody in to see him. He's virtually retired."

Bryn pursed his lips, then whispered under his breath, "Lab, schlab. I can find out what you want to know, Uncle."

Niles stared blankly at him, wondering what Bryn had in mind.

But Bic and Bartleby locked eyes with each other, each thinking the same thing. *When is freezing something different from simply making it cold?*

4

"You told Jenna to use layman's language to explain her work to Eckhardt?" Bartleby settled behind his desk, regarding the guest seated in his office expectantly.

"Yes, I did." Bic put the paper latte cup down on Bartleby's desk and flexed his hands. How long had he been holding that cup in a death grip, anyway?

"That instruction was bizarre," Bartleby persisted.

"Was it?" Bic regarded the hand he was flexing, ignoring Bartleby's stare for the moment.

Bartleby kicked his chair back and tapped his lower lip with a pen. He envied Bic the clout he had with management. They had worked together at another research lab before coming to CryoMax. Bic was eight years younger than Bartleby, an inch shorter, and fit and trim. His close-cropped blonde hair mercifully drew attention away from the unibrow he inherited from his father. Before CryoMax, Bartleby's seniority meant something: he had always outranked Bic. But at CryoMax, Bic had somehow risen in the ranks past Bartleby. The corporate culture simply favored Bic's style (or so Bartleby had always rationalized their reversal of fortune).

Well, good for Bic, reasoned Bartleby. *I wouldn't want to have to give Niles Emmerich a quarterly tour of the lab to hunt down people to fire without cause. You can keep that buzzkill job ... I'd rather keep my integrity.*

Bic explained himself. "It's only bizarre if you don't know what it means."

Bartleby nodded for Bic to go on.

"Niles doesn't know that Eckhardt keeps an invisible finger on all his labs. Niles *thinks* he's the only liaison between management and the senior research staff. Having carte blanche to fire people at will, or stick his name illegally on their patents, reinforces that illusion."

"Didn't know," said Bartleby blankly.

"Yeah, and you still don't know. Right?" Bic wanted Bartleby's silence on the matter.

"Cut the dramatics. I know what not to say to Niles."

"To *anyone*." Bic picked up his cup again.

"Fine," Bartleby answered. "Get to the point. Why layman's language?"

"It's one of several signals Eckhardt developed, allowing senior research staff to communicate to him without eavesdroppers detecting the real message."

"Kind of like hiding something in plain sight?" Bartleby found the idea intriguing.

"Yeah." Bic sipped from the straw again, and his expression soured.

"So Jenna knew to talk in code to Eckhardt, eh?" Bartleby mused.

"No, she didn't," Bic shook his head. "She's not senior research staff. She had no knowledge of the code." He tossed the paper cup in Bartleby's filled wastebasket. It tilted sideways; cold coffee trickled out, soaking the papers wadded up inside, but Bartleby was too surprised at Bic's comment to notice.

"How can that be?" Bartleby wondered. "She obviously got a message across to Eckhardt."

"Yeah, she did," Bic agreed.

"Well, what was the message?"

"I don't know. I thought you could tell me. That's why I'm in *your* office." Bic wished he hadn't tossed the coffee now. He had nothing to do with his hands.

"You're kidding me."

"I wish I were."

Bartleby didn't know what to do or say. He tried to sum up what Bic was getting at.

"You're saying that Jenna explained what the isolator does to Eckhardt, and nobody else in the room understood it. Only Eckhardt and Jenna."

"That about sizes it up, Ron."

"If Eckhardt can figure it out, why can't we?"

"Probably for the same reason he's a Nobel laureate and we're not."

It then dawned on Bic that Bartleby hadn't been forthcoming about Jenna's work. That was something Bic needed to nail down before leaving Bartleby's office.

"I just want to confirm something here, Ron. Jenna didn't build a do-it-yourself black hole, did she?"

"No. No, she created something infinitely worse."

"Worse? Why worse?" Bic was riveted by Bartleby's grave tone.

"Black hole theory is something that a multitude of scientists understand, Bic. They know how one would behave, and they could make intelligent predictions about it."

"So? Jenna understands her isolator design."

"Don't bet on it." Bartleby looked directly into Bic's eyes, unblinking.

"*What?*" Bic couldn't believe what he was hearing.

"Well, something deep inside her understands—or used to. But she has no idea how it works. She can't remember how or why she designed it that way."

"You're not serious."

Bartleby had to look down at his shoes, unable to meet Bic's eyes as he continued.

"Look, Bic, you haven't seen the closed circuit video of her coming into work the morning after she modifies a blueprint. Those first three smaller isolators she designed? She was frantic to recall them from the fab vendors. She was sure she'd be fired for garbling a good design with gibberish that made absolutely no sense."

"But those designs performed beautifully. I signed the approvals to build larger ones based on those initial results, Ron."

"Nobody was more shocked at getting a green light for those monster units than Jenna herself."

Bic's feathers were ruffled at Bartleby's having hidden such crucial details from him.

"You didn't think any of this was important enough to mention to me?" Bic railed. "All this time I thought the only odd behavior associated with her amnesia concerned that stupid lab coat. I find out only now that the Jenna who might actually understand these unstoppable devices is only a sporadic blip on her mental radar? That we're sitting on powder kegs designed by Sybil the Oracle?"

Bartleby could only hold up his hands helplessly, eyes still averted downward. "I gave Jenna her space, and that's why she finally opened up some. It was a calculated risk. Weren't her results sufficient to keep the board happy?"

"Yeah," Bic shot back, "only, I'm not happy to learn about these critical details so late in the game. No more secrets up your sleeve, okay Ron? I shouldn't have to tell you, of all people, to keep me in the stinking loop."

"Of course, Bic. You're right." But it had slipped Bartleby's mind that weeks earlier he had stuffed a wadded up data printout in his wallet, a printout that recorded an anomaly in how Jenna's isolators ignited. And in Bartleby's wallet the forgotten printout stayed, a smoking gun both out of sight and out of mind.

After a long pause, Bartleby looked up from his shoes into Bic's eyes and broke the uncomfortable silence in his traditional way. "Well, there's one good thing about Jenna's project."

"What?"

"There's no way Niles can pull the plug on it."

Bic hated Bartleby's inane puns with a passion, but he hated even more being unable to resist smiling at them. "Don't you have enough disciplinary actions against you for inappropriate use of corporate humor, Ron?"

"Is thirty-eight enough?"

Bic shook his head helplessly, his temper having cooled some. He rose to depart.

"Leaving?" Bartleby asked in surprise. "Don't you want to stay and decode Jenna's statements to Eckhardt together?"

"That's not the best way to find something that's right under your nose," Bic answered. "You need to back away from it to see it better." He took another step toward the doorway, turned on his heels, and said something utterly superfluous. "Of course, the true meaning must be pretty damn important to provoke Eckhardt to fly Jenna out to our Boston offices."

"I wouldn't have guessed," said Bartleby, sinking fitfully back into his chair.

"Well, you were the last one to talk to her in the lab before she was spirited away. Maybe she said something that could help you figure it out."

"Yeah, maybe." Bartleby held out little hope of *that* happening.

An hour later, Bartleby phoned home to have his wife keep dinner warm, then extracted a large chocolate bar from his desk. He tapped the wrapper indecisively, still wracking his brain about the events of the day, when the missing piece suddenly came to remembrance.

Neutrino shield! Jenna had said the isolator might be a neutrino shield!

Bartleby had initially dismissed the idea on both scientific and business grounds. But with the developments of the last twenty-four hours, he could dismiss nothing. Was that the clue? What did it mean, anyway? How did it connect with Jenna's comment that making something cold and freezing it are two different things?

Bartleby picked up the phone to call Bic … then thought better of it and put the phone down, hesitant to cry wolf.

"I'd better think about this before telling Bic about her neutrino shield comment." Bartleby had said it out loud, but a second later wished he hadn't.

Bryn walked into the room breezily and flopped himself down in the guest chair.

"Neutrino shield, eh?" probed Bryn coyly. "That sure took you long enough."

Bartleby knew he was in trouble. He had a terrible poker face and wasn't going to be able to take back what he had just said. "It doesn't mean anything. A stray comment." Bartleby tried to sound calm.

"A stray comment picked up by my microphone." Bryn examined his fingernails closely, sitting sideways in the chair, flouting all professional protocol in Bartleby's office.

"Your microphone?" asked Bartleby.

"Yeah, the one you cleverly took out of commission a few minutes later. It was still running when Jenna told you that the isolator might function as a neutrino shield."

Bartleby exhaled in defeat. He had pulled the plug on Bryn's bug before Jenna had talked about being unable to turn the isolators off. But that was now common knowledge. The key to unlocking the puzzle might have been the previous snippet of conversation. And Bryn had known it long before Bartleby had remembered it.

"Bryn, were you coming here to share that information with me?"

"Sure, Ron, sure. Just like you and Jenna share with me all the time. Who *wouldn't* return such generosity in kind?" But then Bryn leaned forward in the chair, his voice suddenly taking on a threatening tone. "Watch your back, Ron. My uncle didn't get to fire anybody yet, you know. Jenna's out of reach now that Eckhardt's taken her under his wing."

Bartleby stared in open disbelief at the brazen taunt.

"In fact," said Bryn, leaning back and folding his hands behind his head, "I think your job security might be improved if you help *me* crack the puzzle for my uncle. To hell with Bic Johanssen. He can't stop Niles from firing anybody anyway."

"Maybe integrity is more important than job security, Bryn." Bartleby heard his own teeth grinding.

"If you believe that, you'll deserve what you're gonna get."

Bartleby leaned forward, conspicuously pulling his shirt lapel out toward Bryn. "Could you speak a little more loudly into my microphone, please?"

Bryn rose with a start, then realized Bartleby had no microphone in his lapel. He chuckled viciously. "Good one, Ron. Had me going there. Only problem is, my microphone was real. Your job security's not."

Bryn made a point of knocking Bartleby's wastebasket over as he stepped toward the door. "Oops. Pretty crowded office, Ron. That won't be a problem anymore once security helps you clean it out." He slipped out the door.

Bartleby cursed Bryn. With the acid dripping in his stomach now, he could look forward to a nice dinner at home, replete with reflux.

Why didn't I keep my mouth shut? he asked himself. *Bic would have never ...*

"Bic!" Bartleby knew he'd have to share the clue with Bic, now that Bryn knew.

A few minutes later, Bic was sitting across from Bartleby. He had been briefed about Jenna's neutrino comment, but he couldn't make heads or tails out of the clue either.

"Is it really connected to the power transfer?" Bic wondered out loud.

Bartleby knew it must be, but he didn't yet know why. "Well, all I know is that we'd better find out what it takes to shield neutrinos if we don't want to see Eckhardt and Jenna publish their findings and win the Nobel Prize with us'ns left in the dark. Besides which, Bryn ..."

"Bryn?" asked Bic suspiciously, immediately forgetting the moronic Nobel Prize comment at the sound of that name.

Bartleby's eyes dropped to the desk. "Yeah, Bryn." Bartleby couldn't bring himself to admit his gaffe, so he only shared the fact that Bryn's microphone had captured Jenna's conversation with him.

Except for Niles and Bryn remaining oblivious of Eckhardt's coded dialogue with Jenna, they were all on a level playing field now.

But Bryn was determined to tilt the playing field to favor Niles. He spent the night poring over the electrical blueprints for the power grid feeding all the buildings on the CryoPlex grounds that encompassed CryoMax's Livermore holdings. Bryn was sure the answer was there.

"So Jenna says that power transfer is only incidental to the isolator's purpose," he said to himself grimly as he drove back to his condo just before daybreak. "We'll just see about that."

5

Jenna couldn't remember the last time she had dressed so neatly. Most days she barely had time to shower and throw some suitable lab clothes on. She was glad there had been a corner of her closet where her fancier clothes, dry-cleaned four years earlier, still hung in unopened plastic overwraps.

The blue and gray business outfit she picked out today made her appear more officious than she really was. Jenna had always been uncomfortable around anyone in a higher social echelon than she occupied. Her intelligence had been her ticket out of the miserable existence her two sisters lived in, but Jenna had to fund her schooling herself. Her alcoholic mother wouldn't lift a finger to help, but later took all the credit for Jenna's achievements.

Jenna had allowed the corporate cosmetologists to do her hair, but as they started to apply acrylic nails, she balked.

"Oh no. Just file my nails so they're a bit more even," she instructed.

They gently argued with her.

"Look," she explained a bit too harshly, "pretend I'm a nurse—someone who doesn't want or need long nails. Okay?"

They looked at her in dismay, and did so again when she declined their offer of nail polish. Even when she tried to be polite, she rubbed people the wrong way. She failed to mention that short manicures were more sensible for cello players like herself.

Jenna had arrived the previous afternoon and had yet to meet the chairman. At least the meeting was now imminent. She was finally seated in the anteroom of his home, which was gorgeously appointed, but surprisingly modest in size. "Quality, not quantity" came to her lips silently as she rotated her chair slowly, studying the elaborate cornices and valances above eye level.

As she finished her circle, she was startled to see an old man standing only four feet in front of her with a highly polished dark cane in his left hand. He had penetrating black eyes and a thin but gracious smile that gave him an almost impish expression. He was obviously in his seventies or eighties, his white hair neatly groomed, but apart from the cane, there was no evidence of age in his physical bearing. He wasn't stooped over in the slightest, but stood bolt upright.

He looked like the figure depicted in the big painting hanging in the CryoMax lobby.

She rose right away, but he waved her back into her seat without saying a word. She bowed awkwardly as she sat back down. He said nothing. Several seconds passed.

"Chairman Eckhardt?" she asked, now wondering if this was indeed the chairman.

The man nodded, waited a few more seconds, and only then gestured for her to follow him. She rose to do just that.

He suddenly handed her the cane, saying quietly, "You'll need this."

She had no idea what he meant, but followed him with growing curiosity. She could now understand how he had appeared before her without making any sound. He surely didn't need the cane. Why then did he have it? And what would she need it for?

The dining room was richly furnished. She felt out of place and was surprised when Eckhardt himself pushed her chair in. What was she doing here anyway? She didn't rub elbows with dignitaries like Eckhardt. But his gentle manner was so disarming, she found herself relaxing. He settled down across from her.

"Please," he said, "let me pour you some wine."

"Thank you, but I don't drink."

"Neither do I." His eyes twinkled. His hand uncovered the label on the bottle: it was high-end filtered grape juice.

Her eyes brightened. She looked up and nodded. He filled her glass and sat back down. She sipped it; it was indescribably good, like nothing she had ever tasted before. "Wow!" she finally said, trying hard not to gulp it down.

Eckhardt nodded, his hands folding together after sipping his own glass. There was still no food on the table. But she could smell something delicious.

"Come," he said. "In my home, Thursday nights are smorgasbord nights." She stared blankly at him. "Buffet style," he added. She nodded slowly. "All you can eat," he continued.

"Got it," she answered, cursing herself for being so socially dense in front of him.

Others were in line ahead of them in the kitchen buffet.

"More guests of yours?" Jenna asked.

"My household staff," he answered, standing in line behind her with his plate in hand.

"They eat before you eat?" she asked in wide-mouthed surprise.

"He who is last shall be first, and vice versa," he replied.

"That sounds terribly familiar," she mused.

"No wonder. It's been around a while," Eckhardt acknowledged.

"Who said it?" she asked.

"I could tell you. I could even give you chapter and verse." He leaned over and whispered into Jenna's ear. "But it's more important to live it than to know its address."

She looked at him curiously. This was not what she was expecting from a multibillionaire Nobel laureate.

Their plates filled with food, they reseated themselves. Jenna eyed the bottle of grape juice. Eckhardt noticed and refilled her glass.

"You don't see it because of where you sit," he remarked, "but your hair has the same color as the juice from this angle."

She nodded politely. But Eckhardt did something unexpected. He repeated the same sentence, but more intensely, looking directly at her.

"You don't see it because of where you sit, but your hair has the same color as the juice from this angle." He then put his finger to his lips and pointed to the walls. She suddenly grasped what was going on.

He was speaking obliquely, in code, using clever circumlocutions to communicate. Was his own house bugged? She'd heard Bartleby once mention that modern man's reliance on hi-tech had rendered bugs virtually ubiquitous, that only low-tech tactics could hope to provide secure communication. The business of America was no longer business, but spying on other businesses.

Thinking quickly, she improvised. "That's much better! I was able to hear you clearly the second time. Sorry for chewing food while you were talking to me, Chairman."

Eckhardt winked at her subtly. She had understood what he was doing.

What she didn't know was what Eckhardt meant. His twice-repeated comment about the color of the juice surely pointed to something beyond its surface meaning. She had suspected something like this was afoot, seeing as how Bic made her deliver a layman's explanation to a Nobel laureate. But how would Jenna distinguish encoded messages from mere small talk? Was the comment about "living it being more important than knowing its address" also code? How would she keep any of this straight? She wasn't trained as a cryptologist. She was trained ...

"I was trained as a physicist," she said out loud, looking directly at Eckhardt.

"Me too."

Now she knew: it wasn't code if it didn't deal at some level with physics. The "living it/know the address" comment didn't qualify as code for something else. Right?

Eckhardt raised his glass and added, "But not everything qualifies as physics, does it, Doctor Wilkes?"

She raised her glass, realizing he had anticipated her reasoning and was confirming this first clue to his obscure code. "No," she answered softly, "but physics is the key to knowledge."

Eckhardt nodded as they clinked their glasses. "Amen to that," he whispered.

One hundred thirty miles away, two U.S. military operatives, both army captains, were huddled in a cramped surveillance van, a military vehicle camouflaged as a disabled UPS delivery truck. The two men concentrated hard, jotting down occasional notes as they kept their headphones cupped to their ears. The secure field phone rang, startling them both. One of them answered the call, gesturing to the other to keep listening.

"Sorry, Colonel, but there's nothing but small talk so far. Sir." He shot a glance at his companion. "Yeah, we're getting it all down digitally, but they're not talking shop yet. I've got a live feed streaming into headquarters.

If they say anything relevant, we'll capture it. Sir." He listened for a moment, gave out a clipped "Yes sir!" and hung up the field phone.

He looked back at his partner. "So, is it a full-fledged romance yet?"

His counterpart stared at him as if he'd gone nuts. "Mike, he's old enough to be her grandfather. Maybe her great-grandfather."

Mike eased back into his seat, putting his headphones back on. "That's what's gonna make *this* detail interesting, Richard, my man."

Richard stared at Mike for a moment, then turned back to the control console, muttering, "That's what happens when your headphones are worn too tight."

Mike turned back to Richard in mock anger. "What did you say, Soldier?" he demanded.

"I said, 'That's what happens when your headphones are worn too tight—*sir*!'"

Mike couldn't help but laugh. "That's more like it. Colonel Riesen would be proud."

Except that Colonel William Riesen was anything but proud of the intel efforts to date. He was going into his Monday morning briefing with General Stall virtually empty-handed. He paused at Stall's closed door gathering his thoughts, but the door opened to let Stall's private assistant out into the Pentagon hallway, allowing Stall to glimpse Riesen standing outside. Riesen sighed. He needed to burn his old Boy Scout uniform; he had so dishonored the dictum to *Be Prepared* during the last six days of working the Livermore situation. Stall waved him in, bidding Riesen to close the door behind him.

Aside from his uniform and posture, Harrison Stall didn't look like a general. At five foot four inches and thin, he looked more like a flyweight boxer. He disliked ostentation—he preferred not to wear his medals at all if he could help it. His blue eyes transfixed Riesen from across the wood desk.

"What have your boys pulled out of the static, William?" Stall began.

Riesen shifted uncomfortably in his chair. They both knew that Dr. Wilkes wouldn't spend four straight days talking with Jonas Eckhardt, with every word painstakingly recorded and sifted, without their pulling at least something meaningful out of it.

"To be honest," Riesen replied, "the only thing we can be sure of is that she likes grape juice. Sir. The rest ..."

Stall nodded his head soberly.

Riesen decided not to stand to present his portfolio to Stall, given how much taller he already was to his superior. He knew Stall wouldn't have minded—it was Riesen who minded. Apart from their height, and the fact Riesen's hair was black and balding while Stall's was white and balding, they might have been taken for twin brothers. Riesen was in his green Class A uniform this morning, but Stall was sporting his preferred low-key battle dress uniform.

"I had our crypto guys look at what they're saying," Riesen explained.

"Go ahead, Colonel."

"If it's encoded, it's at some higher level of abstraction. That would mean you could get more information across than meets the eye ... or ear, in this case."

Stall immediately understood what Riesen was driving at. He had already arrived at the same conclusion after listening to the first five minutes of the Eckhardt-Wilkes dialogues.

"All right, Will. Anything else?" Stall asked.

Stall never accused in speech or posture, but Riesen was disposed to read disappointment back into the general's words. The general was what he appeared to be: a good man who treated everyone well. This triggered cognitive dissonance in Riesen because Stall was his first superior officer who didn't browbeat him at every opportunity. Riesen compensated by mentally beating himself up on Stall's behalf.

The colonel chose his next words carefully. "Sir, we've had two overlapping shifts in the main surveillance truck, but we've been unable to move the truck. The meteor burst com signal is too weak elsewhere."

Stall chuckled quietly to himself. He looked across at Riesen, smiling. "I'll bet UPS can't contain their joy at having a disabled delivery truck stuck in the same spot for an entire week."

The corners of Riesen's mouth turned down. "Sir, that's exactly why FedEx wouldn't let us use their truck style as camouflage. Courier services don't want their customers to see a broken down truck on the road. It sends the message that your package may be inside that truck going nowhere."

"Going nowhere for four days and counting."

"Yeah."

Stall overlooked Riesen's faux pas in omitting the "sir." His eyes glinted mischievously. "Well, Colonel Riesen, I guess it's a good thing the current CEO of UPS is an ex-paratrooper who bleeds red, white, and blue."

Riesen nodded. Stall gestured for him that the meeting was over.

As he started to pull on the door handle, Riesen turned and added, "There may be one more thing, General."

Stall stopped writing on his notepad and looked up. "Go on."

"Doctor Zilcher has been quite active at the lab building, sir."

"Zilcher?" mused Stall. "Emmerich's nephew?"

"Yes sir."

"But nobody can get into the lab."

"Nobody can get into the second floor isolator lab, sir. But that's not where Zilcher has been working."

"Where has he been working?"

"In the downstairs maintenance room."

"Is it directly below the lab?" Stall inquired. "Is he trying to tunnel up into the lab?"

"No sir. No evidence of that. The two rooms are eighty meters apart laterally, so you can't tunnel up into the second floor lab that way. Zilcher just keeps working on a set of unused spare capacity circuit boxes one rank over from the one Doctor Wilkes's prints are on."

Stall wondered why Riesen didn't refer to circuit box 2130 by number. Maybe Riesen realized that Stall's office was itself bugged.

"Does Zilcher suspect you're watching him?" Stall asked.

"No. We can see him put his telltales out to detect anybody tampering with his work space, so we know how to return the room to the condition it was when he left."

"And you always know his comings and goings."

Riesen nodded at Stall's assertion. Spying on the spy was a skill the Pentagon had long ago honed to a fine point.

Stall nodded approvingly. "Thanks, William. Keep an eye on Zilcher."

"Yes sir." And with that, Riesen closed the door behind him.

Stall put his pad down and pondered this last revelation. Did it mean anything? The intel he had so far pointed at the second floor lab as the focal point. Circuit boxes don't exhibit anomalous behavior all by themselves. Was the first floor activity a ruse?

What was Zilcher really up to?

Stall pushed himself away from his desk and leaned back in his leather chair, contemplating the pictures of Civil War generals on the walls of his office. Once having confirmed the report of the phenomenon reported at CryoMax, he had sold this surveillance effort to the Joint Chiefs with glowing talk about getting remote power out to battlefield forward area outposts. Leave the generators behind and pack more munitions, food, whatever. That wasn't a hard sell, considering what was indisputably happening in circuit box 2130.

But Stall knew instinctively that something else was at play here, something even bigger than pumping huge amounts of electrical power wherever the military needed it.

"Hell," he said out loud to himself. "Nobody's really pumped any energy anywhere yet. It goes where the hell it wants to in that damn building." He thought a moment. Even if you could direct the energy transfer where you wanted, he was certain that wasn't what made Dr. Wilkes's work interesting to so many people.

Interesting? The better word to use was *dangerous*. He coughed nervously. *Dangerous* was the more appropriate word, if the self-serving Niles Emmerich was anywhere in the mix.

He started to write some more notes on his pad, but suddenly laid it down to pick up the phone. Maybe there was another way to get intel, a back door that hadn't been tried yet. He dialed a number he hadn't dialed in years. He knew his line was bugged, so the best he could do was arrange a meeting in a noisy venue if he wanted to speak confidentially.

"Maybe," he grunted. "Just maybe." He heard the phone ring, and then the click of someone picking up.

6

Bic's right forefinger worked a hangnail on his thumb. He sat in his office like a man doomed, knowing Niles was on the way up to see him. Why oh why did he and Niles have to be in that hallway the same time Jenna Wilkes burst through the stairwell door? Niles normally would have flown back to Boston last Wednesday. Now it felt like he'd never leave.

Niles opened Bic's door without knocking, without saying good morning, and sat down across from Bic.

"Well?" asked Bic.

"You tell me, Johanssen."

Bic could see that Niles was already in a bad mood. *Guess he didn't forget to take his nasty pills—the high potency ones marked For Mondays Only.* Bic shrugged.

"First things first," Niles began. "Wilkes was on the list of techs I was going to purge last week. I trust you knew that."

"Only because you mentioned her name and looked it up on your digiscreen."

"That's not the truth." Niles poked a finger across the table at Bic. "In fact, lack of truth is the big problem here, Johanssen."

What was Niles talking about? Bic glanced furtively around the room.

Niles pointed at Bic. "You were protecting her, weren't you?"

"Doctor Wilkes?"

Niles's eyes narrowed. Bic knew not to play cute when he was like this. But he couldn't tell whether Niles had any hard evidence—he may just be fishing.

Bic decided to play dumb. "You saw her evaluations, Niles."

"NO!" Niles caught himself. "No," he repeated more calmly, "I saw the evals that *you* deodorized with your itchy delete-key finger."

Bic realized that he had just ripped the hangnail off his thumb, only to leave a painful tiny laceration in its place. Perfect. He tried to relax as he answered Niles. "Those *were* the evaluations." Bic hoped Niles didn't have anything up his sleeve.

"Oh, they looked like they were, Johanssen. Even the digital seals were correct … or engineered to look correct."

Niles had a triumphant look on his face. Bic started to realize that Niles wouldn't go this far unless he really had Bic dead to rights.

"Go on," Bic said without emotion.

"I had my nephew find the original emails in the backup archives."

"What backup archives?" Bic knew that the server archives had also been carefully adjusted to keep Boston headquarters off Jenna's back.

"Not the archives you're thinking about," Niles said, enunciating each syllable distinctly. "The archiving spybot I had Bryn place on your networks; *that* spider archived the original keystrokes from Doctor Wilkes's various superiors these last three years. About the only evaluations that weren't doctored were the ones you wrote over your own signature." Niles paused. "But in a very real sense, you wrote all of her evals, because the words in the sealed records aren't the ones that *should* be there, are they?"

Bic knew he had played a dangerous game by protecting Jenna. Even if she became a corporate hero, Bic was completely vulnerable. Niles could terminate him on the spot for tampering with sealed evals. The company never turned a blind eye to insubordination.

Damn that Bryn! Only network administrators could unleash that kind of spybot. Bic remembered that Bryn had started in the IT department before being kicked up to the isolator lab. Niles was playing a shell game with his versatile mole.

"But to be honest," Niles continued, pulling out a cigarette, "I got alerted to the possibility of data tampering by quirks we would have filtered out, like an employee who'd rather pay monthly disciplinary fines than wear a clean lab coat. That's when I risked putting a spybot out there, keeping it one step ahead of your spyware filters."

Bic pointed to the No Smoking sign on his wall, but Niles lit the cigarette anyway. One puff and into Bic's coffee mug it went. The fizzling sound as it hit the coffee mirrored Bic's career trajectory right about now.

"And so …" Niles continued, "I want to talk about the new leaf you're going to be turning over. A new era of cooperation. With me."

That was the knife, the sword of Damocles, that Niles was now hanging over Bic's head. Bic nodded dumbly.

Niles knew to make blackmail sound inviting, even gracious. "Let's let bygones be bygones, right, Johanssen?"

"Yeah, bygones." Bic couldn't have been any less enthusiastic.

Niles paid no attention. He launched into an extended soliloquy, the relevance of which Bic didn't at first grasp.

"You know, CryoMax goes way back. We had a checkered past, especially in the early years." Niles pulled out another cigarette, but it slipped out of his hand. It rolled under Bic's desk. Niles looked down at it for a moment, then fixed his gaze on Bic. "Some would say our origins aren't terribly legit. What do you think, Bic?"

Bic was surprised to hear Niles use his first name. It didn't sound natural. For a second, Bic thought he'd ask Niles to call him Johanssen, but swallowed that arrogant urge. He didn't have the upper hand in this room at this moment. *Just let Niles rave on. You'll get through this …*

"Well," Niles prodded, "what do you think?"

"I think that freezing terminally ill people while harboring the delusion they could be reanimated once medical science learned to cure their condition ranks among the worst business plans ever funded."

Bic's answer wasn't diplomatic, but he delivered it calmly, not knowing what Niles was after. In any event, it was the official corporate line. CryoMax was now a leader in semiconductor fabrication using low temperature techniques nobody else could replicate. Bic summed it up simply: "What's past is past. It's a dead past. We've moved on."

Niles looked curiously at Bic. "Funny you should say it's a dead past," he mused. "We still have almost a thousand corpses in deep freeze in San Diego. The courts ordered us to honor those early contracts and maintain those bodies in cold storage."

Bic knew the story, knew the one thing worse than being fired was being shipped out to the San Diego facility to monitor row upon row of those brushed aluminum tubes.

"Niles," Bic interjected, "I thought all of those people in the tubes were declared legally dead. That's the only way their survivors could collect the life insurance payouts."

"The dead live ... at least in legal theory. As we grew, our legacy operation became a smaller piece of the pie and fell off of Wall Street's radar."

Bic nodded, but still didn't know what Niles was driving at.

Niles stood up and moved to look out Bic's fifth-floor window to the flagpole quadrangle below. Employees were still filing in across the lawn, most equipped with umbrellas. The sky was unseasonably overcast, and it drizzled intermittently.

"Do you remember our company's original name?" Niles asked.

"Maximum Cryo?"

"Yes, Maximum Cryo." Niles gave it a Shakespearean flair. "Of course, we've gone through several name changes before becoming CryoMax." He turned around to look back at Bic. "What do you know about the company's founders, Johanssen?"

Ah, good. He isn't going to keep defiling my first name, Bic thought. Niles had reverted back to impersonal form. Bic again offered up the official answer to Niles's question.

"We're taught not to mention them. They were ... shysters." In any other setting, Bic wouldn't have hesitated to lump Niles in with the founders.

"Well," Niles replied, "I've been scanning the premerger data files and recordings."

Bic wondered how Niles had found that material. When Eckhardt International merged with the troubled CryoMax, the internal databases had been ordered purged. Then again, Jenna's original evals weren't supposed to resurface either. Thanks to Bryn, the figurative bodies Bic had buried at sea had abruptly turned into flotation devices.

Niles continued. "I think Wicks might have figured out how to make good on our company's original business plan."

Bic swallowed wrong, gagged momentarily on his own saliva, and began coughing violently. Niles was annoyed at the interruption, but there was no point talking to Bic while he was coughing. But the first to speak was Bic, between the last coughs he emitted.

"You're ... joking ... Right?"

Niles lit another cigarette. Bic finally regained his normal breathing.

"Wicks ..." Niles began.

"Wilkes. Doctor Wilkes." Bic was tired of Niles's rude refusal to pronounce Jenna's name properly.

"Fine, Wilkes. Bottom line, when Wilkes spoke to Eckhardt in the corporate lounge last week over the speakerphone, that conversation was recorded."

"So what?"

"I compared what she said to the statements made by our founders." A crafty look spread over Niles's face as he settled back in the chair. "Wilkes used similar lingo."

"Pure coincidence," answered Bic with resolve. "She's only been here three years. She never met Brinkman or Wallace. Hell, she was eleven years old when they died in that car wreck."

"Is it coincidence?" asked Niles. "What about the neutrino shield?"

Had Bryn shared that factoid with his uncle? Of course he had, Bic realized—that's what moles do. The neutrino revelation rankled Bic, and he quickly became testy.

"Again, Niles, so what? What does a neutrino shield ... assuming her isolator can even shield neutrinos ... have to do with corpses? We'll never reanimate the bodies in San Diego. That's why we write off those losses, why we depreciate them over the length of those idiotic contracts."

"Bic, I know we can't reanimate *those* corpses. Their cell membranes were all ruptured by the expansion of freezing water."

"Then whose? We're not freezing bodies anymore, and haven't for years."

"If Wilkes figured out how to do it right, why not start it up again?"

"Well, let's see." Bic put a finger to his cheek mockingly. "Hmm. Because it's illegal? How's that for a good reason? Because we don't want to all go to jail? That'd be number two on my list." Bic was unable to hide his exasperation.

"Not funny." The lit cigarette went into the coffee mug filter first, the smoke clarifying who had the upper hand. "Think this through, Bic. Ionizing radiation takes a pretty dangerous toll on our cells, our genetic code. Do you disagree?"

Bic shook his head. "No. You've got that part right."

Niles leaned forward several inches. "What's the hardest radiation to stop, taking miles of lead to even perturb a tiny bit of it?"

Bic knew the answer, but didn't like being led by the nose, least of all by Niles. Something wasn't right here.

"Neutrinos, right, Bic?" Niles tapped the lip of Bic's new ashtray for emphasis.

Bic just nodded, knowing that Jenna's shielding hypothesis had never been tested. What was Niles driving at?

Niles spelled it out for Bic. "So, if you can shield something from neutrinos, you can shield it from just about anything, right?"

"Well, maybe."

Niles leaned back and put his fingertips together, contemplating Bic's cautious reserve. "Why maybe?" he demanded.

"Why couldn't something exist that shields neutrinos, but not other things?" Bic reasoned. "Scientists consider all possibilities."

Niles's lips tightened. He checked his watch and rose from the chair.

"We'll speak later. I need to talk to the board right now. We've been unable to get Eckhardt to brief us about his conversations with Wicks, and with the lab still sealed, nothing's going forward, so ..."

"So you wait for Eckhardt, right?" Bic looked up as Niles took a step closer to his desk.

"Waiting might be dangerous." Niles's eyes met Bic's for several seconds. Neither blinked. Niles then added, "Saying certain things can also be dangerous. Vocationally dangerous. Right, *Bic*?"

Bic stared after Niles as the director departed, leaving the usual moral disaster area in his wake.

7

Philip Hernandez pulled his trench coat more tightly around himself as the wind, laced with drizzle, whipped past his body. He stood outside a sports bar in Fairfax, Virginia, trying to stay far enough from the curb to avoid splashback, while avoiding the press of pedestrians noisily clogging the sidewalk in interwoven two-way chaos.

He wasn't particularly happy about having had to fly into Reagan National Airport on such short notice. The secretary at the Pentagon could only get him a middle seat on the flight, and that was located in the last row. The seat couldn't even recline. The plane's malfunctioning rear toilet made a racket louder than the rear-mounted engines. Philip didn't know how long it would take to regain his normal hearing. He had trouble understanding the cab driver, a soft-spoken man with a heavy accent. Philip had probably over-tipped him.

Someone tapped him on the shoulder from behind. He turned to face a short man in yellow foul weather gear, dark sunglasses peering out from under the bright-colored rain hood. They were out of place under the sunless gray sky.

"Good to see you again, General," said Philip. He thrust out his hand.

General Stall took Philip's hand in both of his and pumped it firmly. "Don't call me that, Phil. You know me as Harry, remember?"

Philip smiled. He surely did remember Harrison Stall as Harry. They'd kept in intermittent touch ever since graduating so long ago from the Claremont Colleges.

They stepped into the sports bar and were quickly immersed in the noise of two hundred patrons trying to simultaneously cheer on teams for five different sports playing on twelve different television monitors. Most of the games were delayed broadcasts, but nobody in the sports bar cared. The two peeled off their rain gear, slid into a well-worn booth, and placed orders for iced tea.

The general was dressed in modest civilian clothing. As he pulled off his sunglasses, Philip noticed the piercing blue eyes that brought back memories from their college years. He looked down at himself. His rumpled shirt and tie were the result of being pulled out of work to hop on an eastbound plane several hours earlier.

After exchanging pleasantries about their families, the general got down to business.

"Look, Phil, I've got a real sensitive intel situation at CryoMax I think you can help me with."

"I don't work at the Boston headquarters anymore, Harry."

"I know you don't. It's not Boston I'm interested in."

Philip's brown-hued fingers circled the iced tea glass, drawing random circles in the condensed water droplets forming on its outer surface. "Not interested in Boston? But everything at CryoMax happens in Boston."

"Not everything, Phil."

"San Diego then?"

Stall looked startled. "The body shop? No, no, not that. The research lab in Livermore. That's what interests me."

Well, that made more sense from one angle, since that's where Philip actually worked. But it didn't make sense from another. Philip pointed out the mismatch. "Nothing's going on in Livermore, Harry."

"Not even in Building F?" the general asked.

"Nothing." Philip paused. *Building F?* He glanced at the menu again. *The Building F guys only do incremental enhancements to the existing product lines.*

He looked back at Stall, who next posed an unexpected challenge to him.

"Phil, when you go back to Livermore, try to get into the second floor isolator lab in Building F."

"Okay."

"Phil, I'm actually kidding. Don't try it. That lab has been totally sealed. Nobody can get into it."

"Why? Who sealed it?"

Stall tore open two packets of sugar and dumped them into his tea, stirring it quietly as he continued. "Someone developed something ... unexpected. Something unexpected and very, very significant."

Philip knew that Harry wasn't given to hyperbole. Ever. The general's *very significant* was the average man's *earth-shattering*.

Had Stall said *very* twice just now?

The general continued in earnest. "Look, Philip, I know you don't know what's going on in Building F, and I can't get you up to speed on all of it. But you do know the person who made the ... discovery."

"Discovery?"

"Well, what else to call it? We don't understand what happened in Building F. We only have shadowy details, but no clear picture." The general waved away the waitress with a curt "We're still looking." He looked back at Philip.

Philip decided to bite. "Okay, who's this person that you think I know?"

"The best researcher you ever taught at Stanford."

"Brevard Mays?"

"I didn't say the most recognized or credentialed researcher, Philip."

Philip thought a moment. Surely he couldn't mean ... Was *she* working at CryoMax and he didn't know it? How could she hold a job anywhere with her approach to science? Philip looked up at Stall. "If you're going to say Jenna Wilkes, you've wasted my time and yours, Harry. She can't conduct real research. Her mind won't engage long enough on any one thing."

The general leaned forward, bidding Phil to do the same, and whispered. "Maybe that's because nobody ever bothered to give her something meaty enough to sink her teeth into for more than a day or two."

Philip was nonplussed. He hadn't seen Jenna in seven years. She had earned her doctorate at age twenty-two, but she had had to defend her dissertation nine times. Nine times ... over thirteen days. Grueling ten-hour sessions that strained the committee to the breaking point, triggered only in part by the burdensome new national accreditation standards imposed on all universities, public and private, in 2015. Philip still wasn't on speaking terms with the department head in the wake of that fiasco.

Jenna's work was undoubtedly brilliant, but she couldn't focus long enough to make her own case. Philip knew there was no way she could survive in the real world, and her attitude meant she'd even wear out her welcome with institutions friendly to basic research. How in hell did she end up at CryoMax? Even more to the point, how could she not have been fired within the first evaluation cycle if she'd gotten past the hiring interview? *He* wouldn't have even tried to hire her if she had shown up at his door in Livermore.

But Philip couldn't argue against Stall's sober gaze. Stall wasn't kidding about Jenna. "Harry, are you saying that she stumbled on something?"

"You could say that."

"How long was she at work on … whatever it was. Was it two weeks, or a mind-boggling three weeks?"

"This may come as a shock to you, but she was on one project for *three years.*"

"Well, there you go, Harry. You've got the wrong lady. The real Jenna Wilkes is obviously the victim of identity theft. There's no way …"

"It's Wilkes, Philip. Do you know anyone else who won't launder their lab coat?"

Philip leaned back in the booth. *Jenna*? How? He met Stall's eyes again. "All right, fine, Harry. Someone must be lacing her milkshakes with Ritalin. What do you want from me?"

"I want to find out what really interested her when you were her advisor."

"She was interested in her dissertation topic, like anyone else spending that kind of cash to get a sheepskin at Stanford."

"I don't think so, Philip. You, of all people, know her mind wouldn't be reined in by that kind of tunnel vision."

Philip recognized the truth in Stall's statement. He tried a different tack with his old friend. "Harry, have you met Jenna Wilkes?"

The general rearranged his silverware and spoke without looking up. "No, I've not. And I probably won't be scheduling a meeting, either."

"Well, then, you don't know what you're getting into. She can't hold a conversation like normal people."

"She's been holding conversations in person with Jonas Eckhardt for more than a week."

Philip opened his mouth in disbelief. He didn't know what was more shocking: that Jenna was with Eckhardt or that she could stay on topic for an entire week with *anybody*.

"All right," Philip conceded, "you've got my attention. I'll go over my notes."

Stall raised a forefinger, the signal that he was going to make an important point. "I want you to look at *all* the disciplinary actions against Jenna. Everything her professors complained about. The ugly details. That's where the truth lies."

"Can't you just interrogate her?"

"Not while she's with Eckhardt. I respect him too much to pull that on him."

Philip knew that Stall was almost alone in the Pentagon in holding Eckhardt in high regard, but Philip didn't know why the others saw things differently. Stall's colleagues distrusted Eckhardt, projecting their own predilections for power abuse onto the elderly billionaire-scientist.

"Well, Harry, you're bugging Eckhardt's house, right? Just listen to what they're saying."

"They're speaking in code."

Again, Philip caught his mouth hanging open. "You guys know about Eckhardt's code? Only the regional managers are supposed to know it."

"We only know that they're speaking in code. We haven't cracked it yet. They're talking in quote layman's language unquote."

Philip nodded. That told him something about what was going on, but the resulting high-level linguistic chess game being played could get heady enough to challenge an army of Noam Chomskys. And if Jenna had picked up on Eckhardt's intentions ...

"She's been talking to him for a week?" he wanted to confirm.

The general nodded.

"Eckhardt's not known to waste time with trivia," Philip added.

"Well, not for an entire week. That's for certain. But it's hard to know if she's giving him information, or if it's the reverse."

It suddenly dawned on Philip that the general had missed something.

"Harry, maybe it's not a case of either-or. Maybe it's a case of both-

and. They're sharing information. Two ways. You know, synergy. She might find talking to a Nobel laureate stimulating enough to not lose interest after a week."

Stall nodded thoughtfully, then looked down at his watch. "I've gotta run, Philip. It's been really great to see you again. Say hi to Graciela for me. I'll pick up the tab for the iced teas."

"And," he continued, "don't forget to dig up all the disciplinary complaints we talked about."

"Sure, Harry. They're all on record. Somewhere, anyway. I'll get back to you."

"Soon, Phil, soon. This situation is barely under wraps. I don't want the wheels to come off without us knowing what the hell it's really all about."

They shook hands outside, and the general strode down the street, a receding column of bright yellow against the massed crowds.

Philip maneuvered himself into position to hail a cab. As he tried to flag one down, he kept thinking, *Nothing like tearing a scab off an old wound.* And then another, more sobering possibility hit him. *I wonder if she resumed working on the idea the committee told her to abandon.*

He dropped his hand momentarily at the thought. An empty cab whizzed by. He raised his hand again, cursing, but resumed his ruminations. *If that's why the isolator lab was sealed, maybe our department was wrong in holding that her proposal violated the laws of physics. Jenna always insisted her device conserved the laws of physics better than the status quo theories did. Is this all happening because her dissertation committee was wrong, and Jenna, the heretic, was actually right?*

Philip shuddered as the rain doubled in strength. It would be a fitful flight back to Livermore.

Jonas Eckhardt decided to share his deepening concerns with Wolf Borse, the technical director he had handpicked for his in-house team. Eckhardt arranged to meet Wolf under the mansion's main floor in a room the two men designed to defeat surveillance efforts using stochastic decorrelation techniques. They stepped inside, sealed the door, and Wolf tested and activated the decorrelator.

"Well?" Wolf turned toward Eckhardt. His large mustache crinkled with every word he spoke.

"It's worse than I thought," Eckhardt answered. "She remembers nothing about her original dissertation research."

"How's that possible?" asked Wolf. "Her device is based on that work."

"Exactly. Her ideas are only present subconsciously. When she designs her isolators, she slips into a kind of mental autopilot. She creates blueprints that she cannot defend or explain consciously—the ideas are coming from some deep recess in her mind, squirreled away even from herself." Eckhardt shook his head in frustration. "I'm certain now that her ordeal with the dissertation committee was more severe than originally reported."

"I didn't believe the official reports anyway," Wolf scoffed, his intense eyes radiating compassion for Jenna's situation. "There's no way the committee would spend two weeks on a dissertation defense without an explanation. The whole episode stinks to high heaven."

"I'm thinking, Wolf, that her mind may have responded to the ordeal the way oysters respond to irritants. Put a jagged pebble inside an oyster and it coats the pebble to protect itself, creating a smooth pearl. Cut through that coating and the pebble's jagged edges are exposed again. For Jenna, that mental pearl has started to crack open."

Wolf dared to ask the question that hung heavily in the air between the two men.

"Then how are we going to get Doctor Wilkes reconnected to her own past? How long can she be expected to function mentally if she's unconsciously blocking memories of her breakthrough?"

"I'm afraid she'll have to make that voyage of discovery on her own," answered Eckhardt. "Self-discovery is always the most difficult journey. If we're going to salt the mine to nudge her along, we'll have to be very subtle about it."

Wolf's eyebrows knitted in anger.

"Subtle." He all but spat out the word. "The opposite of her dissertation committee's approach."

Eckhardt looked into Wolf's eyes, nodding.

"Wolf—they didn't know what they were doing."

"That's not much of an excuse. We're left picking up the pieces seven years later. Imagine where we'd be today if they'd just listened to her."

"It's too late for that. That's water under the bridge." Eckhardt pointedly turned off the decorrelator system that had protected their conversation from external probing. "But it's definitely not too late for Doctor Wilkes."

Wolf's eyes narrowed in determination. "Good. I can hardly wait to see her come out on top after all that's happened to her."

Eckhardt allowed himself a faint smile, knowing full well that the moral outrage Wolf had vented had just passed into the public domain.

8

Bryn was working in the third row of breaker boxes and meters in the maintenance room, one row over from box 2130, where Jenna had all but won the lotto jackpot and the right to seal the upstairs lab from everybody, even Bryn's powerful uncle. He closely examined the customized high-current wiring harnesses he had ordered. They appeared long enough to do the job.

As he strung the multicolored harnesses over the top of the circuit box to fall to the ground in the adjacent row, the row where box 2130's digital readout was unaccountably pegged at 8.132 kilowatts, he kept being stung by twinges of conscience. And he knew exactly why he was hot and bothered.

He resented being the beneficiary of nepotism.

He'd always wanted to crawl up the ladder by merit, but he knew he was merely a good researcher, not a great one. But his uncle's continual intervention—and *quid pro quo* list of guerrilla tasks he expected Bryn to perform in return—made him rethink his envy of the better researchers. Even of Jenna. He knew he didn't hate her, or Bartleby, or Bic. He was simply self-centered. But recognizing that same trait in his uncle was slowly sickening him on this defining aspect of the family gene pool. He figured he wasn't likely to rise above it, least of all if he wanted to get promoted as high as his uncle, or inherit the chairmanship from Niles after he took over for Eckhardt.

He looked down at the harness.

That's okay, he rationalized, *I'm not stealing from Jenna. I'm just building on her work.* He wasn't completely convinced by the words, but he was in too much of a hurry to whip up anymore salve—real or bogus—for his conscience. Niles would not be kept waiting.

Bryn tried to work up a sense of humor over his exertions. *It isn't every day you get to perform for the Pentagon,* he thought. He knew they were entering the room while he was away, but they weren't aware that he had busted them. He laughed inside at all the pains they took to restore his telltales, which he deliberately made outrageously intricate just to spite them.

The only telltale he really cared about was one that gave them away so completely it was laughable they hadn't foreseen it. They focused on Bryn's placing a human hair across a door lock and other tactics. They never knew he was taking a thermal snapshot of the room with a pocket analyzer he borrowed from the cryogenics lab. He knew exactly what the thermal signature would look like if he had been alone in the room, and how long it took for it to decay in the laminar flow hugging the circuit boxes.

Bryn knew exactly where he walked inside the maintenance room. His secretive guests weren't so circumspect. He calculated that there were usually three intruders in the room at night spending more time restoring his decoy telltales than studying his handiwork.

One day the Pentagon suits will be home watching a show about how astronomers mapped temperature variations in the microwave background radiation and will yell out, "He knew!"

Bryn threw the last wire harness over the wall of circuit boxes. In the third row, he had wired up three of the circuit/meter modules to match the box at 2130. He even took pains to calibrate their meters, which he recognized as overkill, but what the hell, he was on Pentagon TV. He was going to look like a great researcher even if he wasn't. Let them marvel at his thoroughness.

He approached box 2130, pulling on his safety gloves and lowering his goggles over his eyes. Nobody had ever tried this before. He didn't know whether it was safe or not. But he figured that no more than about eight kilowatts were going to transfer anywhere, if at all, so his measures seemed reasonable. He'd been planning this for days. The test was letter-simple; preparation was minimal, apart from having the harnesses wired correctly. He'd verified that four times. Maybe five.

Bryn opened up the interlock panel. He was tempted to look back at the Pentagon camera hidden in the ceiling behind him but quickly dismissed that frivolous notion.

The digital readout held steady at 8.132 kilowatts—a monotonous result that Bryn intended to subvert.

The pull-out disconnect module that Jenna had yanked out in front of Niles (*why had she done that anyway,* Bryn wondered) had been sealed inside the upstairs lab, but such modules were interchangeable. He reached into his utility pouch to retrieve a new one and positioned it over the empty socket. It looked like a battery pack with a metal handle. When in position, it bridged the power through the entire box, completing the circuit to the upstairs breaker in the now-sealed lab.

Bryn took a deep breath and pushed the disconnect module into the socket. He gritted his teeth and looked up at the readout.

It showed a power consumption of 8.132 kilowatts.

His heart skipped a beat.

"Damn," he growled. Then he realized how premature his excitement was. *This is the way it's supposed to work, Bryn. Just like all the other circuit boxes in this room. In this world. This isn't anything special.*

He pulled the module out. No change. That was the 2130 miracle: power flow without continuity, even flowing past the panel safety interlock. Bryn inserted and withdrew the module several times, convincing himself that the readout wouldn't change. *This doesn't prove anything yet,* he reasoned. *The next step is what counts.*

He left the module in place and attached the override harness to the breakout connector used by service techs to crowbar the inputs to another source. They could bring up a bad box using a good box in parallel or series with it, depending on the philosophy *du jour* of the attending electrician-schlub.

Once the override was attached, Bryn returned to the third rank of boxes where he had configured the three surrogate systems. He intended to move the source for the upstairs lab to a circuit box without an ID number stenciled on it. The harness was configured. He simply had to punch the digital multi-throw switch.

As Bryn reached up to touch the button, he realized how much sweat had accumulated in his safety gloves in only a couple of minutes. He shrugged and punched in the override.

The meter came to life, reading 8.134 kilowatts.

Close enough, Bryn thought. *The difference probably arises from thermal dissipation in the harness conductors.*

He walked back around to box 2130 for the first of two acid tests. Nobody had ever stopped a running current draw this way before, at least, one exhibiting power transfer across absolute nothingness. There was no spark arcing across the gap, and tests conducted the previous Tuesday night, before the lab was sealed, showed that yanking the conduit out of the upstairs walls and circuit boxes couldn't stop the flow. Would Bryn alter the power path? Or was box 2130 the irrevocable pathway for the energy flow going into the isolator upstairs, the one he had taken for granted as a piece of JennaJunk just one week earlier?

He grabbed the disconnect module handle and pulled it out.

The digital readout flickered. Zero kilowatts. Bryn let out a long slow whistle. The power had never stopped flowing with the disconnect module removed since Jenna had pulled it. Bryn had obviously altered the setup. Had he altered it enough to control it?

He circled around to the third row again, glancing up at the digital readouts. *Why didn't I use the mid-level boxes instead of these top boxes?* he now asked himself. *There's nothing special about them. Just because 2130 is a top box doesn't really mean anything.* He felt stupid for being so unscientific and, in his view, superstitious. He had made himself more work using the topmost boxes.

"All right now," he said more firmly, and he looped his gloved fingers around the handle of this box's disconnect module. He looked up at the power readout, still holding steady at 8.134 kilowatts. Then he yanked the disconnect module out.

"Yeahhh!" he tossed his black hair defiantly. The meter readout was still pegged at 8.134 kilowatts. He had moved the energy transfer effect to a different circuit box. The effect had no memory of where it came from at this branch in the power tree: it didn't care.

Bryn smiled slyly. Earlier tests had shown the effect couldn't be moved back upstream, but he had gone one step further, moving it from one circuit box to another. This *was* significant.

He had no intention of ever connecting the adjacent second and third boxes he had painstakingly built. They were decoys to throw the Pentagon off the track. He planned to leave the one overridden box as it was. Would it make Jenna or her handlers angry? Too bad: this room wasn't off-limits. Let them move the signal back over if they wanted. They had the whole method down on video.

"My Nobel-winning video. Paid for by Joe Taxpayer," he whispered in triumph. He pulled off the safety gloves and goggles and dropped them on the floor. Bryn never intended to return to this room. His next destination: the power distribution station that fed these facilities.

He deliberately left the door ajar to show his love for the intel boys.

9

Jenna stood patiently in the anteroom. She pushed the wall button again to call for assistance. The sweet older housekeeper, Katherine, hurried to her side.

"What can I do to help you, dearie?" she asked with a quick curtsy.

Among Eckhardt's staff, Katherine was Jenna's favorite. Jenna loved her quaint English accent and the gorgeously coiffed gray hair that supported the black and white maid's hat so primly. Katherine didn't really remind Jenna of her own mother, but rather what she might have wanted in a mother.

Katherine alone referred to Eckhardt as the master, a title so over-the-top that Jenna couldn't help but ask her about it once. An impish play on words fueled the feisty housekeeper's decade-old habit. There had been a medieval theologian named Meister Eckhart, and *meister* was German for *master*. When Eckhardt pointed out that the theologian's surname lacked the letter *d*, that the Nobel laureate was therefore not a real Eckhart, that clinched the deal for Katherine: "That's okay, Doctor Eckhardt, you're not a real master, either." The title stuck, there being no court of appeal high enough to revoke it so far as the housekeeper was concerned.

"Katherine," Jenna explained, "I've been gone from my home for more than a week, and I really need to take care of some of my bills. I wasn't allowed to bring my digiscreen with me because of your security policies. Are there any computers I can use around here to do some online banking?"

With a wordless smile Katherine turned around to lead the way, Jenna in tow.

As they walked, Jenna considered how wise she had been to board her cat before leaving for Boston. That kind of planning in advance wasn't her strong point. She could easily imagine coming back home to a lifeless ball of fur due to her inattention. But Pinball was holed up in a friendly place. Pinball wouldn't think that, though: the boarding facility planned to bathe her.

Katherine led Jenna into a part of the home she didn't recognize. *I've never been in this room before,* Jenna realized. It was filled with glass cases, floor-to-ceiling bookcases, and a small rank of surprisingly ancient Macintosh computers on a long, stained-wood desk.

Katherine pointed to the computers. "Any one will be fine, dearie. They're already logged in—you won't need a password, or so Wolf assures me," she said pleasantly. She left the room as quickly as she had led Jenna into it.

The staff apparently trusted Jenna—or, perhaps more accurately, were monitoring everything she did and said from a dozen different angles. In light of the exposure she was getting on that many video cameras, she wasn't so upset anymore at the steps they had taken to freshen her up for her now nine-day-long stay with Eckhardt.

Except Jonas Eckhardt didn't actually sleep here. He arrived every day on the helipad just before lunch, joined her for both that meal and dinner, and talked with her in between. He usually left an hour or so after dinner. Jenna had no idea where he came from, or where he went. She gathered the topic was taboo, so she didn't indulge her curiosity in his presence. She had asked Katherine once about it, who simply said, "Too many places to count, dearie." So Jenna had left it at that.

A few minutes later, Jenna had all her financial affairs squared away. There was nothing worse than coming home to a house with the utilities turned off ... especially if the return were to fall on a weekend.

The vividly appointed room invited further exploration. The nearest glass case protected photographs of Eckhardt receiving his Nobel Prize. The original award check was also in the case, the check that Eckhardt had famously declined to cash. Other glass cases served to display prototypes of his pioneering work. One of the cases was empty, but a placard occupied the dais inside it. Jenna inspected the words printed on the placard: *On Loan to the Smithsonian.*

"It must be nice," she said wistfully. "Maybe one day an isolator I designed might be missing from my house too." She moved over to the bookshelves.

On closer inspection, she saw that only one of the shelves contained actual books. All the rest had bound copies of doctoral dissertations. Jenna started thumbing through a few. They hailed from all over the world, and not all were in English. She'd see an occasional annotation in what she took to be Eckhardt's distinctive handwriting, written in English on English dissertations, but in French on the French ones and German on the German ones. She knew he spoke German, and now it was evident he could speak French. Perhaps he spoke even more languages.

As she went from row to row pulling out dissertations, she was nagged by a pattern that became evident by the time she got to the third row. The authors' names were in alphabetical order.

I wonder if my dissertation is in his library, she mused.

She had to walk to the opposite side of the room to find the *W*'s. From what she could tell, she'd need the ladder to reach anything she had written. *Wilkes, J. A.* would be on the top row, more than twelve feet off the ground. She rolled the library ladder along its guide rail and climbed four steps up to face the dissertations that started with *Wi*.

"Ah, here's mine!" she crowed, delighted it was actually in Eckhardt's collection. She pulled it out, but several other dissertations fell to the floor, being yanked off the shelf by friction with the volume she wanted.

"Shoot, I'm so lame," she groaned. She tucked her dissertation under her arm and stepped back down to pick up the ones she had knocked off the top shelf. One had splayed open on the floor, title page up. She started to reach for it, but was surprised to see that it also had her name on it.

"Multiple copies," she muttered. Then she glanced at the revision number. It should have been revision nine—the one that had been accepted by the committee after her defense was finally accepted.

She found herself frozen in mid-reach for the bound document. It was *revision six*! That had never, ever been published! By anyone. She finally picked it up and straightened herself out. What was under her other arm, then? She opened it to its title page. Revision eight. *What's going on here?* she asked herself.

A minute later, she had collected nine different copies of her dissertation, the bona fide one the committee had accepted, and the eight she'd had to voluntarily reject and formally repudiate before being granted her Ph.D. There was no copy of the so-called revision zero, the original, uncontroversial work she replaced with revision one and its successors.

Jenna had rewritten the dissertation—virtually all of the foundational theory parts—almost overnight after every single rejection during that grueling dissertation defense. She had barely slept during those hellish two weeks. She knew that hadn't been her advisor's fault. She hadn't really listened to him, but put what she wanted in each revision, trying to stay the course with her initial convictions.

She laid the nine volumes out on the computer table. The rich fragrance wafting up from their leather covers was intoxicating. As she stood over them, Jenna began flipping through the pages of the final one. It was sparsely peppered with Eckhardt's comments. She lifted it up closer to her eyes to read several of them, but was shocked to see that he was disappointed in her work. From all that could be seen, he thought she didn't deserve the doctorate for the work the committee had approved, that it was subpar.

Jenna swallowed hard. She thought Eckhardt had respected her. Losing her one thread of validation reawakened every insecurity she harbored. Her face quickly reddened.

God, I'm such an idiot. What could a Nobel laureate ever see in my work? Hello! Earth to Jenna! I can't believe I let myself think I'm anywhere near this guy's league. I've gotta get out of here, gotta get back home, today. It was stupid to come. Stupid, stupid, stupid. He was playing me. I'm so out of here.

She scooped up the dissertations with considerable roughness and hurried back to the ladder, beating back the urge to fling them in the trash. She stuffed them under her right arm to free her left hand for climbing.

The nine-high stack of volumes was heavier than she anticipated. Her personal copies were never bound in leather like this. *This is how all these rich people order up their review copies. Pretty outsides to cover the putdowns inside. They might as well have just bound this junk in cardboard.*

As Jenna reached the final rung, she crossed her left hand under her right arm to start pulling out volumes to return to the shelf. Her hair, wedged between her clothes and the unwieldy stack, caused the inmost volume to slip out, bounce off the ladder, and flop noisily to the floor. She grimaced, shoved the other eight volumes onto the shelf, and descended the ladder.

The stray dissertation had also splayed open, but face down. She picked it up and turned it around in her hands. The open page spread caught her eye: it was filled with Eckhardt's annotations. *But more than just short comments.* He had penciled in equations and apparently had corrected some of her work. She examined his remarks and suddenly realized that these notes didn't read anything like the annotations she had just been so hurt and humbled by. If anything, this page reflected Eckhardt's excitement over something.

She started flipping through the pages and could see that virtually every page was heavily annotated. She even found several additional pages of equations and notes that Eckhardt had stapled into the volume—he didn't have enough room in the margins to write what he wanted. It was as if he was rewriting and expanding her dissertation.

"But what revision?" she now wondered, and turned to the title page.

Revision one.

A wave of emotion overcame Jenna. She remembered it now, how she had stood there for hours, not even taking a restroom break, being methodically excoriated by the committee on every single point of her dissertation. Her communication skills weren't good enough to top their rhetoric—not to mention their open contempt. But as she looked through Eckhardt's notes strewn throughout her work, it was obvious that *somebody* not only thought she was right, he thought the subsequent revisions were pale shadows of the first version.

She barely recognized her first set of equations and diagrams from seven years ago because she had unconsciously formed a mental block in response to the ordeal. She had been *so* mercilessly coerced into repudiating her work, which the committee had unanimously held to be nothing less than scientific heresy. But Jonas Eckhardt—the Nobel laureate—held the opposite conclusion. *Why wasn't someone like Eckhardt on that committee?*

Jenna read a few sentences of her work and unexpectedly became nauseous, hitting the wall of pain in her mind. She closed the volume quickly, not grasping the significance of her visceral reaction: the writhing of a butterfly caught inside its chrysalis. It took her nearly a minute to recover her composure. She dismissed the nausea as a fluke.

After retrieving the other volumes, Jenna laid all nine out on the table as before. She called for Katherine, knowing she wasn't far.

Katherine appeared in the doorway with a feather duster in her hand, smiling. "All done with the computer, dearie?"

"Katherine, what do you know about these documents?" Jenna ran her fingers over their leather covers and looked up at the housekeeper.

"What do you want to know?" Katherine asked sweetly, walking up to the desk.

"Why are they here?" Jenna asked.

"Why, I don't know, dearie. The master loves to read from these things." Katherine glanced down at the volumes. She tapped the open page of the first revision with her knuckles. "Oh, this I know is one of his favorites."

"How would you know that exactly?" Jenna asked.

"Well, that's the one thing I *can* tell you about these documents, dearie."

"That they're all his favorites?"

"No, not all. I can tell which documents are his favorites by what's in them."

Jenna did a double take. How can a housekeeper know what's *in* these documents?

"Katherine, you mean, like stapled papers and such?"

"Well, yes, there are those—where the master wrote his quaternion solutions to your tensor formulations. He didn't have room in the margin, you know."

Jenna stared at Katherine, speechless.

"Dearie, can I put these back up on the shelf for you?" Katherine asked, gently running the feather duster over the books under Jenna's hand.

"One more question, Katherine, if you don't mind."

Katherine nodded imperceptibly, one by one picking up each volume from the desk separating the two women and carefully dusting the leather bindings.

"Are *you* a scientist?" Jenna asked, taking a deep breath. This was getting creepy.

"Oh no, dearie, I'm no scientist." Katherine collected the volumes and carefully put them in order. "I just archive for the master. The master likes to hire help whom he can converse with at his level, or at least close to it. It's not easy to get a job here."

As she turned around to walk the books up the ladder, Katherine stunned Jenna with another casual observation. "Anyway, according to the master, *you're* the only living scientist today, dearie."

Jenna sat down like so much deadweight and stared at, or rather through, the computer screen in front of her.

Katherine cheerfully pushed the last dissertation into place, dusted the entire top row, and descended the ladder. As she started to leave the room, she stopped at the threshold, an apologetic expression crossing her face. Jenna noticed it and gave Katherine her attention.

Katherine then said something to Jenna before departing, something so disorienting that the inner demons she'd held at emotional bay for seven years busted loose in full strength.

"Well, I shouldn't have said that, dearie. Master actually said that the woman who wrote that first revision was the only living scientist today. He said the other revisions just document how that was completely beaten out of her."

IO

Bic and Bartleby had studied the diagram on the whiteboard until their eyes were sore. The red and green lines and rectangles showed the original and altered power flows to the isolator still running upstairs. The diagram reflected the conduit torn out of the walls before the lab had been sealed, but not Bryn's unnoticed handiwork.

Bic grabbed a black marker from the conference table.

"What if the circuit were broken here?" he asked, starting to draw on the whiteboard. The dried-out marker only squeaked. Bic eyed the nearby wastebasket and attempted a free throw. Missed. It joined three other markers on the floor, all equally desiccated.

"What if the black marker were broken where?" Bartleby quipped.

Bic wasn't amused. "Ron, the circuit. Not the marker."

"What's the difference? Neither works." Bartleby sat down at the conference table to take another bite out of a sub sandwich.

"What's the difference," Bic repeated. He said it again more slowly. "What's the difference."

"You're repeating yourself."

Bic began paging through one of the transcripts in his digiscreen with urgency. "Wasn't that the question Eckhardt and Jenna touched on over the speakerphone?" he asked.

Bartleby blinked. He'd made a lame joke, nothing more.

"Yeah, here it is," said Bic. "Listen. WILKES: I'm not trying to make things cold; I'm trying to actually freeze them. BARTLEBY: You're saying there's a difference?"

Bartleby shrugged. "I don't get it. How is that like comparing a dried marker to a broken circuit?"

"It's not like it. Not exactly. No analogy is perfect, remember?" Bic sat down next to Bartleby, envying him his sandwich. Why hadn't Bartleby alerted him when the grad students were collecting takeout orders?

Bic tried to explain his point. "It's like this. Jenna and Eckhardt seem to think that making something cold and freezing it are two different things."

"Yeah, and Bryn says they're playing with words. I'm inclined to agree with Bryn." Bartleby bit into his sandwich, leaving a smear of mayonnaise on his chin.

"Think of it this way," Bic continued, ignoring the mayo. "*We* think they're the same thing. Jenna and Eckhardt don't. Is there a sense in which the broken marker and the broken circuit could mean the same thing?"

Bartleby stared, uncomprehending.

Bic tried again. "If I'm unable to draw the line to reconnect the circuit on the board, does the whiteboard show a broken circuit?"

"Sure, Bic, but that's only true for the symbols we use to draw circuit topologies. That doesn't apply to the actual circuit." Bartleby still hadn't wiped his chin.

Bic pointed back at the board. "But what's the *actual* circuit when we're talking about freezing and making something cold?"

Bartleby looked from Bic to the board and back again. He extended the rest of his sandwich out toward Bic, saying, "I think you've got some kind of malnutrition-induced dementia. You need this worse than I do."

Part of Bic wanted to accept the sandwich, but he was too intent on getting his argument across. "That's my point. There's the symbol, and there's the thing symbolized. Which is which?"

"Well, we know that. The diagram we drew is the symbol, and—"

"But what's the symbol when we're talking about freezing something and making it cold?"

Bartleby opened his mouth to reply only to realize he didn't have an answer to Bic's strange question. Was something symbolic going on here? Was one thing a symptom or consequence of another?

"Bic, does that have anything to do with Jenna's comment that all the things we think are central to the isolator's function are only incidental to it?"

Bic nodded somberly. "That's what she was driving at, Ron. She regarded those behaviors as mere side effects of something more fundamental."

That struck Bartleby as almost reasonable. He bit down on his sandwich again. Two streaks of mayonnaise on his chin. "Still," he kept chewing, "the isolator was designed to make things cold. That's beyond question."

"You think so?" Bic shook his head. "Think again, Ron. I shouldn't be doing your physics for you—I'm in lab management now."

"Think what through?"

"Why Jenna made *her* isolators out of titanium."

"Well, she chose titanium ..."

"Yes?"

Bartleby looked back at the whiteboard. Every other isolator built at CryoMax used Thermos-style vacuums to insulate the cryo-cores. Nobody questioned the first isolators built to Jenna's specs because they were small and cheap. Due to their superior performance, her designs were green-lighted all the way up to the two-million-dollar monster that precipitated the lab lockup two weeks earlier.

Bic became impatient. "Tell me, Ron, when do you design an isolator with a thermally conductive metal?"

"Well, you don't."

"*She* did."

"Aren't we going around in circles here, Bic? The damn things work. What's to know? The walls are pretty thick."

"Thermodynamics, Ron. You know this. Why aren't you thinking this through?"

Bartleby knew the answer. He *had* thought it through, several weeks ago. Jenna's isolators were the only ones ever built that could be safely touched while running.

Even though you were separated from a core of absolute zero by about a foot of thermally conductive titanium.

Even though you were pumping about eight kilowatts into the cube.

Bartleby walked Bic through this concession, but Bic recognized there was more to it.

"Well," Bic objected, "that isolator is loaded to the gills with convection tubes to spare to carry away that heat, Ron. There's no mystery there."

But Bartleby just started laughing; he could hardly control himself. Bic waited him out. Did Bartleby know something more than what he had just revealed?

When Bartleby had recovered, he simply said, "One word, Bic. Cosmetics."

"Cosmetics?"

"Yeah." Bartleby laughed again but caught Bic's disapproving frown. He cleared his throat. "I discovered it by accident after hours. I was walking by the isolator right after the Monday evening cleaning crew passed through. I slipped on a wet spot on the floor and slammed into the thing."

"Yeah? So?"

"Guess what fell off her isolator."

Bic couldn't imagine what Bartleby was getting at. He was agitated by the secrets his people had been keeping from him and was about to react when Bartleby answered his own question.

"Three of the convection tubes fell off."

Bic stared in disbelief. "Ron, convection tubes don't fall off, they're woven through the cryodevice shell to maximize transfer efficiency."

"Not if they're fakes glued onto the titanium exterior."

"Fakes?" Understanding was starting to dawn for Bic.

"Yeah, fakes. After I glued them back on, I thought about the end run that device was making around the laws of physics. It was so hard to believe, that I made a point of putting my hands on it for a few moments every day, just to remind myself that the exterior was at room temperature despite the tubes being fakes."

"You're sure all the convection tubes are fake?"

"Yeah, all 128 of them. I did an ultrasonic test one night, and all exhibited the same resonance of the fakes I glued back on. A tube going through the shell takes on the rigidity of its encasing matrix." He shook his head. "No, they were all fake. The foil is just camouflage. Her isolator doesn't need it. It just keeps other lab rats at arm's length because nobody wants a cryo-burn touching it. She knows that's our industry's version of Don't Tread On Me for open-air prototypes."

"Ron, I've got documentation *certifying* that all the convection tube holes were drilled into that titanium block!"

"She faked that too—got the vendor to go along with an undocumented engineering change. Less work for the same price. What vendor would squawk at that?"

"When were you going to tell me any of this?" Bic demanded.

Bartleby shrugged. "Never."

Bic started to get hot, but Bartleby quickly explained.

"Never, because it was Jenna's to explain. She had something going there, but she was always so insistent on finishing her tests before reporting anything premature."

"Yeah, and look where *that* got us," Bic snapped. "Now who's got control over the isolator division? Niles is circling like a vulture, his nephew the Mole-Man is digging into our backside where we can't see it, and Eckhardt's too old to stop a corporate takeover."

"What about Jenna?"

"You think Niles is going to keep her on board when he finds out she hand-glued 128 fake convection tubes to the most expensive isolator ever built to keep her work hidden from the people who were paying for it?"

"You've got a point." Bartleby paused. "But you're missing *my* point. Let's talk about the new isolator and what it's really doing. Or, maybe more interestingly, what it's not doing."

"What's it not doing?" Bic asked.

"Well, for one thing, it's continually taking in eight kilowatts and not getting any warmer."

Bic did some quick math in his head. "That's completely impossible."

"It's worse than that," added Bartleby, wadding up his sandwich wrapper noisily. The mayonnaise streaks were still on his chin, but Bic wasn't noticing them anymore.

"How is it worse?"

"It's keeping the core at absolute zero while eating up those eight kilowatts."

Bic nodded. It was common knowledge that refrigerating things was never a zero-sum game, that entropy always extracted a price. Cooling the core required a bigger heat rise elsewhere. *What was Jenna's isolator doing?*

Bic tilted his head toward Bartleby. "I know why you protected her. She's out there breaking the laws of physics left and right."

"She'd never admit that." Bartleby knew how tenaciously Jenna defended her designs, designs that she seemed unable to actually explain. Bartleby never dared tell her he knew about the fake tubes, not knowing how she'd react. She was lucky Bryn hadn't slipped on the floor.

"Ron," Bic asked, "are Niles and Bryn aware of this?"

Bartleby shook his head. "Right now, only three people know those convection tubes are fakes. Not counting the possibility this room is bugged."

"Well, it's bugged alright," smiled Bic, "only, it's bugged by me."

Bartleby's eyes drifted back to the whiteboard. "I guess we never solved that problem either," he winced.

"But you did solve it." Bic ran his hand over his chin stubble. *Was it after five already?* His expression clouded over.

"No," Bartleby corrected, "I didn't even get close to solving that puzzle. And I still think you're nuts comparing crapped-out markers with real circuits."

But Bic was shaking his head. "It has to do with the *sense* in which something is the same or different. If the words *cold* and *freeze* were taken in the same sense, then there'd be no way they could be different. They'd be synonyms."

"That's the point that Niles lost it over."

"Yeah, but what Jenna was getting at is that she's not seeking to freeze something *cryogenically*. Her low temperature is the result of freezing something in a non-cryogenic way."

"You're just reading that into her statement."

"Only if you admit *you're* reading something into my statement when you say a dried-out marker isn't equal to a broken circuit."

Bartleby was genuinely confused. "I don't do well with brain twisters."

"Actually, you've already solved the problem," Bic explained. "Or, more modestly, you've discovered the key to solving it. We just have to work out the possibilities. Like Sherlock Holmes said, the last remaining possibility, no matter how improbable, must be the truth."

Bartleby was skeptical but started thinking out loud. "Well, you'd have to go back to fundamentals, to first principles ..." he remarked. "There'd be some other sense of the word *freeze* that entailed cold, but strictly as a side effect."

Bic listened intently as Bartleby started to follow his intuition.

"Okay ..." Bartleby paused again. "Let's pick a place to start. Here we go. Police yell *freeze* when they want to stop a suspect."

"Yeah," answered Bic. "It's a synonym for *stop*."

"Let's begin there," Bartleby suggested. "Did Jenna mean she wants to stop the molecular motion in the isolator core?"

"I don't think so. That makes it a synonym for *cold*. We're back where we started."

"But the molecular motion in the core would have to be stopped for the core to be considered cold, which Jenna never denied. That's something the indirect measurements have confirmed since day one."

Then a strange look came over Bartleby. He realized he'd have to be careful how he communicated his next idea in case Bic had been overly confident about the room being bug-free. He hunched over, signaling for Bic to do the same, then removed the watch from his wrist.

"This can go one of two ways," he said, pointing at the watch now in his palm. Anyone bugging the room would be unaware of the gesture and its significance. "We can stop its molecular motion. Or ..." He pulled the watch stem partially out, stopping the second hand in mid-tick.

Bic looked from the wristwatch into Bartleby's intense gaze and then back to the watch. A faint smile spread over his face. "Cold either way, right Ron?"

Bartleby restarted the watch and fastened it back onto his wrist. "Colder 'n hell, Bic. Maybe literally."

Bartleby's eyes widened suddenly as he realized something else. He reached into his back pocket and pulled out his wallet. Bic watched with curiosity as Bartleby extracted a wadded up piece of paper and unfolded it.

"She didn't know I had turned on the remote sympathetic temp monitor the day before she ignited her fourth prototype," Bartleby whispered, "and I've been holding on to the resulting printout ever since. Until just now, I thought the sensor had failed. Look at this."

He handed the crumpled readout to Bic, who glanced at the temperature curve. Ignition always followed a gradual curve as the temperature dropped inside the core. But there was no curve on the printout. At the ignition event, there was just a black vertical line diving straight down to absolute zero. Instantaneously.

"You've got to be kidding me!" Bic whispered hoarsely, stupefied.

Bartleby shook his head slowly, retrieving the sheet and hiding it away again.

Neither spoke for several minutes, but their minds were racing.

Bic finally rose to leave the room. As he reached the door, he turned and called out, "Yo, Ron. One more thing."

Bartleby looked at him expectantly.

"You've got mayonnaise right ... about ... here, on your chin." Bic circled his forefinger around his own chin, deadpan.

"How long has it been there?" Bartleby asked, starting to reach up to correct the indiscretion.

"About two hours." And Bic disappeared through the door.

Bartleby rubbed the mayonnaise off his chin and regarded his now-shiny fingertips. He gazed at the slowly closing door, pondering how long Bic had allowed him to twist in the wind.

"Long-term facial mayo," he muttered. "Again."

But Bartleby had stumbled upon a versatile new context for Bic's smackdown. He looked up at the wall clock.

Two hours on my chin, sure, he thought. *But those same two hours have yet to happen inside the upstairs isolator core.*

II

Jenna looked out the window of the CryoMax jet that was taking her back to Oakland. They'd only been aloft for an hour, and she was already exhausted.

She turned and glanced over at her neatly stacked luggage in the seats across the aisle. The cane protruded from her gym bag. *It looks so out of place among my things.* She trusted that she would one day need it but had no idea when, where, why, or how to use it. Maybe it would become obvious when the occasion arose.

Worst case, if I miss my chance to use it, I can give it a good workout when I turn eighty, she mused. *I'll probably need it then for sure.*

She flipped topics mentally—something she had been adept at as a young doctoral candidate. Too adept, her advisor, Professor Hernandez, had kept drilling into her. He wasn't here to object, well above the clouds. At least, not in person, but his stark warnings still rang deep in her memory. The recollection of it made her shudder. The flight attendant stepped up to her right away.

"Are you cold, Doctor Wilkes? Can I get you a blanket?"

"No, no, I'm fine. Thank you though, Karla."

The attendant smiled and went back to her seat. Jenna figured that with only one person to serve, Karla would probably be overservicing her the entire flight. Her small diet soda cup had been refilled five times in the first hour alone.

Jenna turned back to the window, staring at the passing cumulus clouds, thinking through the background science behind her dissertation work.

Mainstream physicists after Einstein understood relativistic time dilation. The faster you traveled, the slower time passed in your frame relative to a chosen inertial rest frame. Measurements had long ago proven that muon lifetimes got longer when those subatomic particles were accelerated to high speeds. There was an untidy dispute about interpretation, but the effect was real enough. If muons could reach the speed of light, they'd never decay. Time would allegedly stop for anything moving that fast.

High speeds had other consequences. The faster that objects traveled, the more massive they became and the more they flattened in the direction of travel. A sphere traveling near the speed of light relative to an inertial observer flattens to a disk as seen by that observer. If it could ever reach light speed, it would flatten completely, exhibiting zero thickness and infinite mass.

Jenna's work began where those distortions of time, space, and mass left off, veering into controversy with a set of axioms that sideswiped accepted thinking. The only thing her model had going for it was internal consistency.

She had intuited the axioms on a whim, as geometric games in her head with no apparent physical meaning. But the more she developed them, the more she came to see that her games were describing nature as it really was, and that modern physics had missed the boat, had been stranded on shore with nowhere to go.

Jenna reached up and pulled the pins out of her red hair to let it fall naturally. She was going back home, back to work, back to normal. No point dressing up for Eckhardt anymore. He hadn't seen or spoken to her the last two days she was at his manse. He hadn't even given her any warning that this was his plan. She had awakened expectantly those last two mornings, only to be disappointed by word from Katherine that he wasn't flying in to see her.

She never got to talk with him about his annotations in her dissertations, nor how he had acquired copies of the first eight unpublished iterations.

Why didn't I ask to borrow that copy of my first revision to take back with me? I could just kick myself thinking about it. She wasn't sure where she had stashed her own copy of that version—assuming she hadn't long ago destroyed it along with its seven unloved siblings.

She shook her head to let her hair take up its natural position—right over her face, which felt liberating after two weeks of formality. She twisted her now-unleashed hair around her fingers while gazing at the clouds floating by below, but she just couldn't relax.

Her thoughts kept returning to her first dissertation revision.

She tried to remember back seven years. *What had the dissertation committee first gagged on again?*

It soon came back to her.

All of it.

Jenna felt she could even replay the scene in her mind. But hers was an emotionally charged recollection far removed from objective truth. The reality of that day was radically different and pregnant with consequences ...

She was standing in the newly completed science rotunda, her red hair in a ponytail and a hard-copy printout of her dissertation in her left hand. She was wearing thick-rimmed black glasses, unlike the wire frames she could now afford. A long-sleeve denim jacket, unbuttoned, framed her white turtleneck, with her denim jeans partially covering white tennis shoes.

Those were the best clothes she owned. She had no friends from whom she could borrow anything more formal. It had only been three days since her twenty-second birthday. She was still fighting acne on her forehead, which was mottled with too-obvious dabs of Clearasil—not the transparent kind.

Her advisor, Professor Philip Hernandez, had been stuck in traffic, arriving late and seating himself directly in front of her, with the other six committee members arrayed on either side of him.

Jenna was apprehensive. The version of the paper she had been defending in her advisor's absence wasn't the one he had approved—and he didn't know that yet.

Time was at a premium, so the proceedings had begun before Philip arrived. The line of inquiry that Sexton was pursuing with Jenna didn't immediately register with Philip because he was focusing on style, not substance nor the numbing jargon that infested such proceedings.

"Miss Wilkes," Sexton asked, "are you trying to tell this committee that there's actually a way to take a velocity-flattened disk and re-expand it to its full original dimensions in the frame in which it is flattened due to its motion? And that the dilated time in that reconstituted sphere holds the same value the sphere had while completely flattened at light speed? And that in the process of re-expanding and retaining that infinitely dilated time dimension, the disk, or sphere, whatever shape you're proposing for it, no longer needs to be moving at or near light speed in the system in which the sphere had been reconstituted?"

"Yep," she said brightly. "A time bubble. It's retroflexed through the fiducial world plane. The inertial coordinates are only first-order projections intersecting that plane."

Sexton, born with a scowl, the sixty-three-year-old head of the Stanford physics department, slowly put down his copy of the paper. Jenna was oblivious to the mounting animosity in the room. This was her first doctoral defense, and she naively expected to breeze through it.

Philip put his head in his hands. *Yep?* he thought. *Yep?* Hadn't he drilled her on protocol and etiquette so she could keep her trailer park persona on ice for a few hours?

And what was Sexton talking about, anyway? That's not what Philip had in *his* copy of her dissertation. He started flipping through his copy hunting for the axioms Sexton just mentioned. *I thought she had removed that speculative section about expanding world lines into world planes. How'd that arbitrary extension of standard 4-space geometry get back in there?*

The committee member to Philip's left, Dr. Cynthia Carter, unceremoniously tossed her copy of Jenna's dissertation on top of Philip's copy. Startled, Philip looked up at Carter. She didn't look happy.

"You've got the wrong copy, Philip. Your student exchanged dissertations with all of us before you walked in the door. Which," she added ominously, "isn't really allowed. At least, not without express prior written permission."

Jenna had seen Dr. Carter toss her dissertation copy in front of Professor Hernandez but didn't grasp the gesture's significance. Jenna piped up. "Shall I continue?"

Carter rose from her chair, a short stuffy matriarch who also had red hair tinged with gray. "No, young lady, there's no reason to continue. Your subsequent axioms are even more counterintuitive than the ones Professor Sexton just read from your preamble. What, pray tell, do you think you are doing with the education we've given you these last six years?"

Flinching at Carter's harsh tone, Jenna lifted up her dissertation copy to respond. "Why, this is what I've been doing." She patted the pages of her work. "I'm really excited about this stuff, and so I'm here to walk you guys through it."

"Walk *us guys* through it?" Sexton harrumphed.

Carter tucked in her chair and took a step to her right, bending down to whisper to a quickly reddening Philip Hernandez.

"I'm coming back in a few minutes, as will my colleagues, but right now I'm recommending everyone leave so you can talk to your young charge one-on-one about what she's doing, switching dissertations like that. Especially," she glared at him, "substituting a muddle that makes no sense to anybody on the committee. Except maybe you, Philip. Only I doubt it." She nodded at the other committee members, who rose and started to file out the back door.

Jenna was bewildered. What was going on here? She looked at Hernandez, who was slumped in his chair.

Philip rubbed his face with both hands. They were supposed to be in the middle of a run-of-the-mill dissertation defense, and within minutes of his arrival, everybody on the committee had bolted. Only he and Jenna remained in the rotunda.

"Where did they all go, Professor?" she asked Philip.

"Bathroom break."

"Really?"

Philip grabbed the dissertation Carter had flung at him and slammed it on the tabletop. Jenna jumped.

"Did that startle you?" he asked her with rising anger in his voice.

She nodded timidly.

"Not as much as I was startled three minutes ago," Philip pointed out. "In fact, not even close! Jenna, what the hell are you doing?" He knew where this was going, though. He'd seen this same thing happen with her master's work two years earlier.

"I'm defending my dissertation. You told me to write the best dissertation that I knew how to write, and to go for it."

He saw that her eyes were beginning to glisten, her chest starting to heave with the labored breathing of someone trying to control her emotions.

"What was wrong with this one?" he asked, holding up the work he thought she was going to defend.

She waved the pages in her left hand. "This one's a hundred times better."

He had to force himself to lower his voice. "Jenna, even if that were true, if you can't get your work past this committee, what good is it? You want an M.S. behind your name for the rest of your life?"

She stared straight at him, nearly motionless, still breathing rapidly, still holding out the copy in her left hand. Her right-hand fingers were twiddling. He knew she was typing something mentally, her fingers unconsciously tapping an imaginary keyboard.

"Okay, look," he said, "They're coming back here in a minute or two, but you're going to have to decide, right now, which of these two dissertations to defend today."

"I already know which one I want to defend," she cried out.

"The one that will get you your Ph.D.?" he asked.

"The one that speaks the truth!" she shot back. "You just told me that it could be true, and the committee still won't give me a pass here. Right?"

"That's kind of my point."

She clutched her revised dissertation to her chest protectively, as if she were protecting scientific truth, even Science itself, with her gesture.

"I'm defending this one," she answered with determination, suppressed tears reddening her eyes. "This is the dissertation where I did actual science."

"And this one?" asked Philip, holding up her original dissertation.

"That? That one?" She pointed at the copy Philip held. "That's the one where I caved in and didn't do science. I only followed the leader."

Philip heard the cloister door open behind him. He knew his colleagues were filing in.

Jenna wiped her eyes on her denim sleeve. The wet spots on the blue fabric were dark and conspicuous. She backed up several paces, by chance to stand directly under the rotunda's acoustically perfect ceiling dome.

As Carter settled down next to Philip, she turned her head to whisper to him. “I had a doctoral candidate like that once too. You need to guide yours like I guided mine, Philip.”

Philip’s brow crinkled, and he tilted his face up to look Professor Carter in the eye. “Did your student follow your advice?”

“Yes, she did,” Carter answered with obvious satisfaction.

“What was your advice to her?” he was curious.

“Be a hairdresser.”

The committee couldn’t see it, but Jenna, overhearing their whispered comments with crystal clarity due to the overhead dome, gripped her dissertation even more tightly in her left fist. So tightly, the cover tore under her fingers.

Philip noticed the warrior-like look spreading over Jenna’s face. This had the makings of a long day. *Well, at least she’d get this nonsense out of her system by the end of the day and come back tomorrow to finally defend the first version,* he thought. *This circus can’t possibly go on past tomorrow.*

But looking at how Jenna had unconsciously spread her feet out, as if she were trying to amass enough strength in her stance to defy the world itself, he wondered.

No, he thought. *Two days, max.*

12

For the first time in nearly a week, the Bay Area rains had stopped. Philip pulled his car up to the curb, confirmed the address, and parked. He noticed how the Saturday morning sunlight glinted off the modest older home, making it look inviting, as if freshly painted, preserved in time from the 1950s. Philip sat in the car adjusting his tie, inspected the results in the visor mirror, then reached into the backseat for his briefcase.

Last stop, he thought. *At last. That'll be it for helping Harry out. Not that I've got anything to give him.*

He climbed out of his sports car and walked up the brick pathway to the front door. A quaint hand-painted sign hung under the doorbell. *The Sextons.* He knew he'd find only Wallingford Estes Sexton and the live-in nurse inside; Sexton's wife had died two years earlier.

Sexton was on an IV and oxygen, his prognosis guarded. The nurse was being code-compliant down to a gnat's eyelash. Philip knew the truth could either be a lot worse or better than the picture the privacy laws allowed her to paint over the phone.

It had taken Philip only a few days to collect Jenna's disciplinary records and the review sheets from the committee members other than Sexton. The disciplinary records General Stall had keyed in on turned out to be irrelevant. The dissertation reviews followed a grim pattern: thoughtful comments restricted to the morning of May 10, 2018, followed by terse condemnations of content like *rubbish* and *we awarded her a master's?*

The tide didn't turn until Jenna defended her ninth revision on May 22, when the committee had to grudgingly admit she had satisfied its requirements, meaning her heresies had been expunged. The May 22 evaluations looked a lot like what Philip had been expecting on day one, except it didn't work out that way—Jenna had her own agenda.

Philip had found Sexton's notes for everything but the first day's defense, and for that, only the first page was found in the campus archives. Sexton's records should have been on campus, but the missing pages made the house call necessary. Philip hated having to visit Sexton, but his commitment to Stall coaxed him out of his comfort zone.

Sexton had conveyed through his nurse that he wouldn't discuss anything with Philip over the phone. That was a relief: at least Sexton *was* willing to talk in person. Maybe he had forgiven Philip for the gaffe that turned Jenna's dissertation defense into a two-week circus. Nine consecutive weekdays, nine different dissertations, all because of Philip's loose wording of the agreement the committee adopted after Jenna's first defense had imploded.

Sexton had been the committee's secretary, charged with capturing the wording on that ad hoc agreement. He didn't catch the discussion quite right—it was late, everyone was tired—but Sexton did catch the "So moved" comment from Shumerian. Sexton had asked Philip for the wording of the resolution under his breath, but Philip misunderstood and only paraphrased the agreed-upon wording. Sexton transcribed it, then circulated the unproofread document for signatures. The committee then summoned Jenna from the anteroom and compelled her to sign it, citing sanctions for the unauthorized dissertation switch if she wouldn't.

That act was their undoing thanks to Sexton's misunderstanding.

The committee thought they were extending the testing window for one more day so that Jenna could defend her original work, the one she had exchanged for the heretical new dissertation they'd wasted the day arguing over.

Due to the miscommunication between Philip and Sexton, the compulsory agreement actually stated that Jenna could continue rewriting and defending the dissertation on each subsequent weekday until the committee finally accepted it. When Sexton had stamped the copies with the physics department seal, he was simultaneously sealing the committee's doom.

The error didn't come to light until the next morning, when Jenna showed up with a freshly drafted new dissertation to pass out—revision two, not the expected revision zero original.

"What's this?" asked Philip. "Where's the original we agreed to retest you on?"

"That's not what the agreement you made me sign said!" Jenna protested. "I rewrote my work, like you said."

A dark cloud hung over the rotunda. None of the professors had bothered to bring a copy of the sealed agreement, having filed them away in their offices the preceding evening. Everyone had expected things to return to normal this bright Friday morning.

Philip motioned to Jenna to approach him with her copy of the agreement. She extended it to him and waited patiently.

She was still dressed in the exact same clothes as yesterday. He was certain she hadn't even slept all night to rewrite her dissertation and get the copies made at the campus services center. What they saw was what they were going to get.

He eyed the contract, convinced that Jenna had misread it, but then realized the grave mistake that had been made. He stared at the slip of paper in consternation, knowing he had bad news for his associates.

Cynthia Carter reached over and took the agreement out of Philip's hands to scrutinize it. She curled her lips and glared at Sexton, then Philip, then Jenna. She handed the paper back to Jenna, adding,

"Well, young lady, this committee has just managed to make itself look like total idiots. According to our mutual agreement, you're to keep presenting dissertations to us, *ad infinitum*, until we accept one. *Except* ... " Her eyes fixed knowingly upon her fellow committee members. "Except that you must present the new version of the dissertation on the next weekday morning."

"That means, gentlemen," she said, rising, "that if we reject a defense, she has till the next weekday morning to submit a new revision. If she fails to appear with a new dissertation, her denial will be final until the next testing season. She must be prepared to defend each dissertation for the maximum allowed ten hours every weekday."

Carter was belaboring this point for a reason. If the committee used up all ten hours of its allotted challenge time, there'd be little time left for Jenna to draft a new dissertation. She needed sleep, and had to be mentally alert to handle the committee's sustained attack on her positions.

"And so, my esteemed colleagues, we can thank Sexton here for putting us in this unprecedented position. I suggest that we begin the defense immediately. The sooner we begin this process," Carter looked directly at Jenna, "the sooner it will be over."

Jenna nodded, not realizing that a clerical error had just pitted her against the entire committee for a war of orthodoxy that would rage over the next week and a half.

"Oh," Carter added, "I don't need to remind the committee that while Miss Wilkes is here to defend her dissertation, we are here to defend the integrity of the doctorates that Stanford issues. We owe our forebears that much."

As far as anyone knew, the whole fiasco would be over by the next weekday morning. She simply *had* to buckle under and submit the originally planned paper, or else abandon any hope of receiving her degree until the next testing season.

Except there was a catch.

"Of course," Carter continued, "If she fails to earn her Ph.D. in this testing season, the committee reserves its sovereign right to expel her from its doctoral studies program in physics altogether."

Philip knew what this meant. Either Jenna got her doctorate here and now, while this ill-worded agreement was in effect, or she wouldn't receive a Stanford Ph.D. at all. He explained this to Jenna to make sure she understood. The message was clear: abandon this nonsense and go forward with something defensible.

"So," Carter added after Philip had spoken to Jenna, "it is understood that you, Miss Wilkes, are either going to earn your Ph.D. under that sealed agreement in your hand, or you won't earn one here, period. Do you understand?"

Hunching over, Sexton had a whispered cell-phone discussion with the dean to see if the agreement could be overturned. Bad news: if the student fulfilled her end of it, the university would be liable for breaching its end. Any student willing to fulfill such onerous terms wouldn't hesitate to seek justice, and Wilkes had a history of filing protests with the Office of the Dean, prevailing on all of them.

Sexton snapped the cell phone shut and returned Philip's stare. Philip looked at Jenna.

Jenna looked back at Philip Hernandez for support, but realized there was none there to be found in his eyes. One look at Sexton told her the whole story. *Sexton looks like he could kill Professor Hernandez,* she thought. And that didn't look to be too far from the truth.

She was now caught up in an academic war that the committee was resolved it wouldn't lose. She was facing the stiffest academic penalties they could impose. She was either hours away from a Ph.D.—or years.

Jenna's right fist was balled up now, slippery from sweat. She pulled off her denim jacket, dropping it behind her, standing now in the white turtleneck she had worn yesterday. She had sworn to herself to stick it out with her new dissertation, the one with the insights her research had inexorably led her to.

The professors facing her had no idea that the garbled agreement they had unwittingly signed had chartered a war of attrition between them and the iconic redhead in a white top. She was going to go to the mat with all of them. It boiled down to a test of strength.

Philip cleared his throat and addressed the committee with more resignation than actual hope. "Well, my esteemed colleagues, let's not underestimate the candidate and her obvious resolve."

That prophetic understatement had haunted Philip for the rest of his career.

And here he was, seven years later, in front of Sexton's home.

Philip hoped against hope that time had healed this wound. If not, this was going to be painful. He'd keep things straightforward: just ascertain the whereabouts of the missing pages, acquire them if they exist, close the case if they don't, and wish Sexton well. He rang the doorbell.

The nurse answered. "He's expecting you," she said.

She was dressed in street clothes; Philip expected someone in hospital greens. He didn't know why. She led him down the main hallway. The walls were plastered with photos of Sexton and his family. Family-only shots—nothing related to his illustrious career. Philip expected otherwise.

Sexton was lying in a tilted-up hospital bed, its metal-tube safety rails retracted. The IV was in place, as were the tubes in his nose to keep him oxygenated. He waved Philip over, indicating the chair next to the bed. Sexton's hand showed blue bruises, probably from various shunts his treatments had required. He was alert but gaunt, far weaker than when Philip had last seen him—the outward sign of the cancer within.

Philip was surprised when Sexton spoke first.

"She built it, didn't she?"

Philip had no idea what Sexton was talking about. He hadn't told the nurse why he was coming because he didn't want to upset Sexton in advance of revisiting so divisive a topic.

Philip leaned in closer and spoke quietly. "Wally, I'm trying to get some old paperwork in order here, that's all. For the Pentagon." He opened his briefcase, Sexton eyeing him with a rheumy gaze.

Philip handed Sexton the first sheet of his notes covering Jenna's first day before the committee. Sexton held it in his right hand; his left hand lay at his side. Philip saw it was even more bruised than the right.

"Wally," Philip explained, "this is the first sheet of ..."

"I know what it is, Philip." Sexton's voice was breathy, but strong. "You want the rest of it, I take it."

Philip nodded. Maybe Sexton had something he could use after all.

"Philip, I'll give you the other sheets, but I need to know if she built it."

"Built what, Wally?"

Wallingford Sexton reached for the bed control and tilted the bed forward a full two feet closer to Philip. Sexton was looking down at Philip at this angle.

"The storage cell." Sexton looked straight at Philip. "Did she build it?"

"Say again, Wally?" Philip figured he had misunderstood.

"The storage cell. To store energy and return it to our frame." Sexton handed the sheet back to Philip. "It's implicit in the energy transfer equations in her first dissertation."

Philip leaned back in the seat. He wasn't expecting the conversation to take this turn content-wise or with respect to tone. He had come expecting to be chewed up, but Sexton was all but coming to *him* with hat in hand.

Philip decided he could trust Sexton. "Well, all I know is that she had worked on some cryogenic isolators for CryoMax and the lab she had been working in is now sealed tighter than a drum."

Sexton fiddled with the knob on the oxygen tank. "You know, *I* thought it was a storage cell. Her equations exhibited enough symmetry to allow the energy flow to be reversible. I wanted to expand on that idea on my own. I kept seeing people like Eckhardt and Mueller winning Nobel prizes in the same field I'd worked in for forty years. I wanted to do something unique, some actual science, but I didn't have the sharps up here ..." he pointed at his temple, "to pull it off." He sighed. "I'm never going to do anything like that now, am I?"

Philip looked at the IV drip and back to Sexton, nodding. He wondered if Sexton had used the term *actual science* on purpose—those were Jenna's fightin' words.

Sexton turned to pull a tiny envelope off his nightstand. "Hold out your hand, Philip."

Philip complied, a little nervous at the formality of the request. Sexton pressed the envelope into Philip's outstretched palm but didn't release Philip's hand. Philip looked up into Sexton's eyes.

"Tell her I'm sorry," Sexton whispered. The bruised hand that had lightly locked Philip's hand in place trembled for a few seconds and finally released its fragile grip.

Philip glanced down at the envelope. A bank address and some codes were written on it. *He's giving me the key to his safe deposit box?* Philip closed his fist on the envelope.

"One more thing," Sexton added.

Philip nodded for him to go on.

"This ..." Sexton pulled a larger envelope off the nightstand.

Philip wondered what this one was. It couldn't have required security, or it would also be in the safe deposit box. He took it from Sexton.

"Open it now, Philip." Sexton smiled weakly.

Philip pronged a finger and slid it across the sealed end. He pulled a single piece of paper out, one he didn't at first recognize.

His signature was on it.

"Wally, this is the original of the agreement we signed with her. I thought everybody agreed to destroy their copies."

"We did all destroy the copies. This isn't a copy," Sexton snorted.

Philip looked back down at the slip of paper in his hand, and there they were: the original seal, the original signatures, dated May 10, 2018, the day when everyone involved had unwittingly enlisted for two weeks of hell.

"Why would I want this?" Philip protested. "It's nothing more than a painful memory."

"Come on, Philip. You should know what to do with it. When the time is right."

"What?"

"Why, give it to the Smithsonian, of course."

Philip wasn't amused. Was this just raw sentimentalism on Sexton's part? Philip tried to reason with him. "It has no scientific meaning. It's just an administrative mistake, like a fly caught in amber, Wally. Again, who'd want it?"

But Sexton was shaking his head vigorously. "No, Philip. You've got it backward. If you're talking science, I mean really talking science, *this* will be the most important document in the Smithsonian."

"You're kidding. Why would you think so?" Philip regretted getting testy with a dying man, but Sexton met him head-on.

"See these signatures here?" Sexton pointed to the document, to Jenna's signature on the left side, and the signatures of the gathered academics on the right.

"So?"

Sexton leaned back. "This document answers the question, *Where can we expect to find truth?* An object lesson ..." he searched for the right words, "on institutional power and authority...," he bent over to run his fingers over the sweeping signatures of the seven professors, "and truth." His wrinkled fingers lightly loitered over Jenna's tiny signature in pencil.

Philip left Sexton's home deeply shaken. He always thought Sexton was bitter toward Jenna, Philip's prize researcher. If anything, it was Philip who had remained bitter toward Jenna.

Sexton had made his peace with the past.

Philip looked down at the safe deposit key in his hands.

A key to what? he asked himself.

13

Jenna's eyes flew open with a start. It took her a moment to realize where she was and what had awakened her. Karla was tucking a blanket around her as she slept in her seat on the flight home.

"Karla, are we almost home?"

"We still have ... mmm ... about three more hours, Doctor Wilkes. Can I get you something to drink?"

Jenna laid her head back against the headrest. *I've only been asleep an hour?* It obviously wasn't possible to nap that easily in this jet.

"No, Karla, I'll pass. Thank you."

"Would you care to read a magazine? You might like to try one of the chairman's favorites."

Jenna shook her head.

As she readjusted her blanket and closed her eyes once more, she made a mental note how attentive Karla had been during both flights, the one to Boston and this return flight home.

But something was nagging at Jenna's subconscious, something she couldn't put her finger on.

Several minutes later, she finally got up, disentangled from the blanket, and looked for Karla. She found the flight attendant cleaning the aft bathroom.

"Excuse me, Karla, where would I find the magazine rack?"

"It's forward of the bulkhead, on the left side, Doctor Wilkes. You'll see the sliding door marked Magazines. You can't miss it."

Jenna thanked her and walked back to the front of the jet and found what she wanted. She slid the door open.

The magazines were in the old-fashioned binders that airlines and doctor's offices use to protect them from heavy wear, and what few this aircraft had were standing upright, like books in a library. She ran her finger over the white block-letter titles stamped on the binder spines to see if she could find something of interest. They were all dusty. Hadn't anyone ever read any of them? The variety was also lacking.

"What, he only likes *TIME* magazine?" she complained. "Maybe he owns stock in the company." She figured she'd pick the most recent one, but his stock of magazines was ancient. All the binders were stamped May of 2018. Wait. No, it looked like each was marked with a different *date* in May of 2018.

They don't publish TIME *daily, do they?* she asked herself. Then it dawned on her.

She had defended her dissertations in May of 2018.

She counted the magazines.

Nine.

Jenna pulled out the earliest one to make sure she wasn't dreaming. It *was* the dissertation she had defended on May 10. The inside pages were freshly printed, and Eckhardt's stapled notes had been reproduced and bound into the binder. It was all here … nothing was missing. It was a faithful copy of the leather version in Eckhardt's library.

Jenna noticed Karla coming back up the aisle and pushing her hair back in place.

"Did you find one you like?" Karla asked.

"Yes. Yes I did. Doctor Eckhardt knows how to stock a magazine rack."

Karla smiled innocently, stepped into the galley behind Jenna, pumped a dollop of hand moisturizer on her palms, and rubbed her hands together.

"Karla, passengers can take these magazines home, can't they?"

Karla paused to consider Jenna's request. "I guess you'd have to call Doctor Eckhardt and ask him, Doctor Wilkes. Would you like me to get him on the phone for you?"

"Yes," said Jenna, fully galvanized now that she had her first revision back in her hands. "That would be very nice of you, Karla."

"I'm afraid this jet's long-distance phones use those old-fashioned cords," Karla apologized. "You'll need to sit in your seat."

Jenna all but flew down the aisle to take her seat. Karla detached the phone from the bulkhead caddy and placed the call. Jenna was still examining one of Eckhardt's notations in the "magazine" when Karla succeeded in raising Eckhardt.

"Doctor Eckhardt, this is flight attendant Karla Maseri aboard CM-2-B en route to Oakland. Doctor Wilkes is on board and wants to ask you something about your magazine rack. May I put her through to you?" Karla paused to listen. "Okay, I'll put her on." She smiled and handed Jenna the phone.

Eckhardt spoke first. "I hope Karla is keeping you comfortable up there, Miss Wilkes."

Jenna smiled at Eckhardt's perpetual congeniality. Since she planned to ask a favor, she decided not to complain about his recent absences. "Yes, Doctor Eckhardt, Karla's been just great. Listen, about your magazine rack."

"How can I help you?"

"Do these need to stay with the jet, or can I take one or more home with me?" Her eyes were still scanning his equations, her mind multitasking, processing each step in his derivation while exchanging pleasantries.

"I don't see why not," he answered her.

She breathed a sigh of relief.

Then the other part of her brain, the one scanning Eckhardt's equations, blurted something out before she could edit it. "You switched the tensor indices inappropriately." Jenna groaned inwardly for having just insulted Eckhardt so indiscreetly.

"I did?" he asked. "Are you sure?"

Now she was apologetic, more for being distracted while talking to him than for saying he had erred in his work. "I'm sorry, but yes. But I'm sure it's nothing."

"Looked at slantwise, I'm sure it is," he assured her.

It dawned on Jenna that this wasn't a secure phone line and that Eckhardt was speaking the contrived pseudo-language they had evolved. *Slantwise, nothing.* That meant the tensors would have zeros along the diagonal.

She scanned the page again. "I'm not sure I see it," she said.

"Really? Hold on a sec."

Jenna figured he didn't have the page in front of him. He'd probably need to ask Katherine to fetch it from his library.

As she waited, eyes glued to Eckhardt's notes, she could hear Karla opening the door to the flightdeck. A shadow crossed Jenna's peripheral vision—Karla had been leaving, not entering, the flightdeck. Jenna, still engrossed, could hear Karla clear her throat close by. Did Karla have a cold? Jenna looked up …

… right into Eckhardt's eyes.

"Doctor Eckhardt!" she exclaimed, dropping the phone.

He nodded, bending down to look at the page of equations. Her eyes followed his finger as he explained the flow of his ideas.

"I think this was really your main point," he said, "because the transverse and longitudinal waves are reversed on the other side of the fiducial world plane. So you have to conduct separate analyses for both before you see covariance conserved in the overlapped manifolds. Hence the indices being reversed. Contra Carter."

Jenna's head snapped back at him. *Contra Carter!* Professor Cynthia Carter? Was that one of Carter's challenges to her so long ago?

Eckhardt continued, still moving his finger across the page, never really looking at Jenna.

"Cynthia did what I did here and came to the conclusion you just came to during our long-distance phone call. That's why she rejected your model. But she neglected the polarity reversal across the fiducial world plane, which not only conserves covariance, it preserves Maxwell's equations. Lorentz invariance, though, was never in question. She threw that out there just to see if she could spook you. You were wise not to take the bait."

He straightened, turned around, and was apparently heading back to the flight deck.

Jenna called after him. "Doctor Eckhardt."

He turned and looked back at her. Karla was working in the galley near Eckhardt. He tapped Karla on the shoulder and extended his hand out toward her, his gaze still fixed on Jenna. Karla handed him a small green bottle with a blue stick protruding from its open mouth.

"Thank you, Karla," he nodded, and pulled the blue stick out of the bottle.

Were Jenna's eyes deceiving her, or was he holding a child's bubble-blowing toy? A second later her suspicion was confirmed. He blew through the ring to form a plum-sized bubble that gently floated through the vestibule where Eckhardt stood.

When he started to speak, Jenna knew to pay close attention. He tended to make every word count.

"There's more than one way to make a bubble with this," he pointed out, holding up the plastic bubble maker—a plastic stick with an open ring. He dipped the bubble wand again and held it out. "Normally, the soap film forms this flat plane inside the ring. And someone with the breath knocked out of him would have to do it this way ..." He wafted the stick through the air in a wide arc, leaving a trail of bubbles erupting to life in its wake.

"But you can save a lot of energy doing this ..." And he once again blew a bubble using his breath. The new bubble was as large as the first one still loitering near the floor. "And at my age, that's probably best, wouldn't you think?"

He suddenly turned serious. "Anyway, about your question yesterday."

Jenna caught the significance. She had asked no question yesterday. Whatever he was saying was designed to throw eavesdroppers off the scent in case the plane was security-compromised.

"Up until now," he affirmed, "there really hasn't been any archaeological evidence for the existence of unicorns and gryphons. So, case closed."

"It figures," she answered.

Eckhardt smiled, his frail frame still bolt upright in the vestibule. He scratched his head in mock-confusion as a puzzled expression crept onto his face.

"I wonder what the best way to burst your bubble might be?" he wondered.

He again dipped the wand and extended it toward Jenna, his eyes telling her to take it. Jenna took it and raised it up to her lips, but was startled to see Eckhardt step over to her gym bag to extract the cane. She blew a large bubble that wobbled through the air into the vestibule.

Eckhardt approached it with the cane.

Jenna expected him to use the cane either as a baseball bat to smack the bubble or as a cue stick to poke it. He did neither. He held the cane upside down, not unlike a really tall letter J. Held this way, she could see that the curved handle ended in a metal cap. Eckhardt positioned the J so that the slowly descending bubble would land on it like a worm on a hook. It seemed an awkward way to pop the bubble, but Eckhardt's next words made it clear this was intentional.

"There's always a right way to do an-y-thing."

On the last syllable, the bubble hit the cane and softly plopped into nothingness. He pulled a handkerchief out of his vest pocket and gently wiped the sticky soap film from the metal cap. He then handed the cane to Jenna.

She tried to accept it from him, but he didn't immediately release it. She looked to see what he intended by this, but he kept his eyes on the cane, explaining something that Jenna gathered was important.

"You don't have to be thick-skinned to live in the land of unwalled villages."

"That sounds like Zen philosophy," Jenna countered. In their code, if clarification about a statement's status as real or decoy were needed, she'd make a non-Biblical religious allusion. If he replied by repeating the questionable statement in different words, it was real—and important. Any other construct meant the sentence was a ruse.

"When was the last time you saw elephants in Jerusalem?" he asked.

"Never been there," she had to admit. "Wouldn't know, Doctor."

"You should consider a visit some time, Doctor Wilkes."

The last two comments meant nothing. The encoded message stopped at elephants in Jerusalem. This was a serious clue about releasing the core from its titanium prison. The clue was secure—the interlacing of the encoded meanings made it impossible to crack the grammar the two had evolved.

Eckhardt released the cane and slowly tapped his temple with a forefinger. She nodded. He returned to the flightdeck.

When the plane landed, Jenna stepped out onto the tarmac, her gym bag literally overflowing with *TIME* magazines. Walking through the charter flight terminal, she stopped at an ATM. Putting down her gym bag and suitcase, she hunted through her purse for her bank card.

The lady in front of her had just finished an ATM transaction and was starting to walk away when she paused a few feet from Jenna. She pointed at Jenna's gym bag, with the airline magazines sticking out of it.

Jenna looked up at her to see what she wanted.

The one word the woman uttered before departing dripped with contempt.

"Klepto!"

14

Colonel Riesen recognized that General Stall may not approve of his new tactic, but the failed surveillance of Bryn Zilcher was too humiliating to ignore. After the fiasco in the maintenance room had been uncovered, and one lieutenant's promotion reversed on account of it, Riesen realized that conventional techniques would never get the job done. And getting the job done was what he was determined to achieve for Stall.

Riesen strode up to the flagpole, taking his cap off and bowing his head for a moment before walking into CryoMax Livermore's administration building. He was in his Class A uniform, making no attempt to hide his affiliation as he walked through the spacious atrium toward the reception desk.

"Who are you here to see, sir?" a bespectacled receptionist asked.

He rested his arms on the countertop and glanced at her security badge: Eva McMillan.

"Colonel Riesen to see Doctor Bic Johanssen, Eva." He slid a business card across the counter toward her.

She looked at the card, then her computer screen, clicking around the daily schedule hunting for his name. "What time was your appointment, Colonel Riesen?"

"I don't have one."

She stopped clicking and looked at him more closely. He didn't look like someone she should turn away, and he seemed to know her somehow. She inspected her digital switchboard.

"Sir, he has no appointments until after lunch. He's in his office but on the phone. I can't buzz through to him until he releases."

"I should have had an appointment in your system. I only came here because he needs to see me." Riesen delighted in using technically true statements with flaky syntax to mount clever deceptions.

"Sir, I'm not sure ... without an escort, I mean ..."

"Miss, you need to know how important it is that Bic and I went to different schools together."

"You did?" she brightened. "Let me print you up a badge, then." She pulled his card off the counter.

Several minutes later, Riesen was on the fifth floor, walking toward Johanssen's office. He'd never been to this admin building before, and he planned never to be here again. But he had every intention of becoming familiar beyond reason with the building six hundred yards to the east: Building F. This was the first critical step.

Bic's office door was open, and Riesen could hear Bic talking on the phone. He breezed straight in and sat down on the lone chair across the desk from Bic.

Bic saw the colonel enter and seat himself, but kept talking as if nothing had happened. Riesen waited patiently.

Bic ended the call and started jotting on a notepad while ignoring the colonel.

A minute later Riesen decided to break the ice. He had expected a different reaction to his unannounced appearance.

"Don't mind me."

"I won't," snapped Bic. He kept writing. *First the spook, then Niles. Now the U.S. Army is piling on. I've about had it.* Bic couldn't remember ever harboring such bitterness before.

Riesen didn't think the relationship between the services and industry had deteriorated this far. *It must be Johanssen's personal style I'm confronting. Or else he's bent out of shape by our ongoing surveillance.*

"I know you're busy," Riesen apologized, "but I figured you'd want to see my latest home movies. They're pretty hot." He held his iPod Peta out and pushed the play button.

Bic didn't intend to look up, but he couldn't resist a glimpse at the screen.

The video the colonel was playing showed Bryn Zilcher in the maintenance room tampering with the disconnects. As far as Bic knew, nobody had ever entered that room since the day Jenna, Niles, and Bic had witnessed box 2130 become a power bridge to nowhere back on August 12. This video was time-stamped August 20—only five days ago.

Twenty seconds later, Bic realized that he hadn't even taken a breath while watching the footage. He reached out and took the iPod Peta out of the colonel's hand, who willingly released it. Bic watched the rest of the video in silence. Riesen said nothing while Bic studied Bryn's activities.

The video ended seven minutes later. Bic handed the unit back to the colonel and folded his hands on the desk. The colonel slipped the iPod Peta back inside his briefcase and slid his business card across the desk toward Bic.

Bic studied the card, wrote something on the back side of it in pencil, then wrote a few words on his notepad using a light blue marker. He went to the window, wedged Riesen's card into the frame, and walked past Riesen toward the door. Stopping there, he leaned on the doorjamb and addressed Riesen a bit more respectfully.

"Four things, Colonel," Bic began.

Riesen nodded.

"First," Bic explained, "I only have one reason to trust you. Second, I'm going downstairs to fire the receptionist who let you in here. Third, if I like the deal you're bringing to the table, you can have your business card back."

Riesen smiled. "Fine. I'll just end up hiring Eva and paying her twice what she makes here at CryoMax."

Bic adjusted his tie. "She doesn't deserve double pay. She needs to be taught a lesson, so she's staying here with me. That'll teach her."

"What value is my business card?" Riesen asked.

"Because they don't take American Express," Bic said without a smile. He turned to leave, but Riesen spoke up again.

"What reason do you have to trust me?" the colonel asked.

"You buy products from Apple."

"What's the fourth thing?"

"I don't remember. But thanks for asking." And Bic was gone.

That's about as cryptic as I can take, Riesen thought. It was evident that everyone operated under the suspicion that their offices were bugged. Riesen knew that was a safe bet for this particular office, knew it was bugged by Emmerich, Eckhardt, three competitors, and Riesen's team. And those were just the readily detectible bugs his people had discerned. Someone outside the building was bouncing light off the window to pick up sympathetic vibrations induced by people talking near the glass.

He rose to his feet, trying to decipher Johanssen's comments, when something on the desk snagged his attention. He was meant to see it: Bic's notepad, turned to face him, with a message in large pale blue letters—a message for Riesen.

So, Riesen thought, *he wants to meet me in the cafeteria. And he wants me to take my card off the window and put this message in my briefcase.* Riesen wondered if the scientists here had been able to make a listening device that looked like a sheet of notebook paper. The convoluted web of countermeasures wasn't getting more sophisticated so much as it was turning into a giant Mouse Trap game.

That's because this is a race. Because Riesen felt he was losing the race, the race to solve a mystery important enough that everyone involved spoke in cryptic, annoyingly stilted words, he had dared to come here. Stealth hadn't worked, so a new tactic was called for. *If you can't acquire information directly, get it by sharing.*

Riesen grinned for a brief moment, wondering how Bryn Zilcher would respond to this new tactic. He knew that Bryn's performance in the maintenance room was just one big *In Your Face!* directed at Riesen's intel operation. The colonel was now returning the favor.

15

Bryn tapped the steering wheel in time to the Shostakovich Fifteenth Symphony playing over the car stereo. The Lone Ranger theme was embedded in the first movement, so he had adopted it as his personal theme music for driving through the sparse chaparral. His eyes continually scanned the high desert brush that marked the outskirts of Livermore.

He'd been taking this untraveled road out to the remote power distribution station for nearly a week now, satisfied that the physical layout there made it impossible for anyone to sneak up on him undetected. He had set the station up to reveal the presence of trespassers. His detectors even sensed the large sea of jackrabbits that often surged through the station.

The station was the odd man out in an otherwise uniform row of skeletal towers stretching north and south to connect the horizons with power lines. But by the time Bryn had approached to within a mile of it, he knew something was different. A dark rectangle was in front of the power distribution station, obstructing the entrance to the station's phalanx of gray transformers, insulators, wires, and weathered meter cabinets.

Was it the right day for the monthly maintenance crew to visit the station? He blanked. It must be, though. Maybe this was a leap year or something.

The closer he got, the more the rectangle morphed into something he didn't expect out here, where the nearest building was six miles away: a UPS delivery truck. Who gave them the access code to open the security gate?

Must be a drop ship of something ordered by the head engineer, Bryn reasoned. *Nobody trying to install bugs would do it in broad daylight.*

It wasn't until he parked nose-in, perpendicular to the UPS truck, that Bryn noticed the red reflective road-hazard triangles set up around the truck. This wasn't good. Could spies be that obvious? As he opened the car door, he was even more surprised. He smelled something burning.

It didn't smell like arc welding or any other maintenance work he could imagine being performed at the station. Trying to place the smell in context kept leading him astray but realization finally dawned on him.

"A barbecue?" he asked out loud.

Bryn walked to the other side of the truck, the sand underfoot making him sound like a trudging soldier. He couldn't have been prepared for what he saw.

Two twenty-something men dressed only in cutoffs, sandals, and sunglasses sat in lawn chairs under a large beach umbrella with an ice chest between them. The one on the right held a bottle of beer in one hand and a cell phone in the other. His partner to the left was reading *Sports Illustrated*. A hibachi barbecue was several feet away with burgers cooking on it. A portable table with an umbrella was set up adjacent to it, a plaid tablecloth cheerfully slung across it, configured with place settings and a central lazy Susan filled with condiments and fixings. There were three chairs distributed around the table.

"Bryn's here. He's late, though. I hope the burgers aren't burned," said the beer drinker into his cell phone. He was making no effort to hide anything he said, but Bryn wasn't thinking at this level. He was still struggling to process the displaced scene.

Mr. Beer snapped his cell phone shut and turned to his partner.

"We now return to our regularly scheduled program," he announced.

The other man reached down and fiddled with a plastic yellow box. A garbled sports broadcast became instant background noise for the absurd scene.

Bryn didn't move, but he did finally speak. "You guys aren't with UPS."

Mr. Beer laughed. "Yeah, you've caught us red-handed. We're with FedEx. We hijacked this truck and disabled it to make UPS look bad. Dirty tricks work in politics, why not in shipping, right? Keep our secret and you can help yourself to any package inside that has a corrosive liquid sticker on it."

The other beachcomber chuckled.

"There aren't any packages in the truck," Bryn said. "Who are you guys, and what do you want here?"

Mr. Beer's companion started applying suntan lotion over his arms and finally answered Bryn, sounding all the world like a surfer dude out of a movie.

"I'm Mike Boudreaux, and my esteemed colleague here is Richard Alan Green, or Rag for short. Or Ragman for longer. And I'm insulted that you think we didn't bring you a package in our oh-so-fine truck." He reached into the ice chest and pulled out two bottles of beer. He extended one to Bryn, who wasn't sure what to do.

"The beer is the package?" asked Bryn, finally reaching out to take it. His mind kept screaming *What am I doing talking to these bozos? I've got work to do.*

Mike extended a large padded envelope toward Bryn, explaining, "This is the package. We didn't have time to wrap it properly, but we're still pretty proud of it."

Mystified, unopened beer still in hand, Bryn awkwardly tore into the envelope. Inside was a large glossy photo of Richard and Mike staring like zombies.

Bryn handed it back unamused. "Who do you work for?" he demanded.

Richard brought a shiny object up to his face while simultaneously pulling off his sunglasses. A bright flash emitted from it. Bryn couldn't react before Richard spoke to Mike.

"Looks like I got a shot of Doctor Zilcher drinking on the job," Richard gloated. He held the digital camera out toward Mike, who peered with interest into the viewfinder.

"Well, Richard, normally I'd say that'd be worth about five hundred dollars in blackmail, but you failed to set the date and time on your trusty camera, bud. This picture proves ol' Bryn here was drinking a beer at midnight on January 1, 1980, about a decade before he was even born."

"Aw, I can't get five hundred out of it? How much, then?"

"Maybe a ten-spot," Mike speculated.

Bryn recovered from the camera flash and surreal antics seething with anger.

"Look, *who do you work for*?" he demanded.

"Easy, ranger, easy," said Richard, slipping his sunglasses back on and shooting Bryn a toothy grin. "Your grammar bites. It's whom, not who. Anywhom, we work for you. Or, more accurately, for Joe Citizen. *You* pay our salaries. We thank you kindly."

Mike's head spun around in mock surprise. "You're on salary, Ragster? Damn. I'm not even on hourly wage. They put me on commission only."

"That's because you're a putz," Richard asserted. He looked up at Bryn and folded his right leg over the left, bouncing his sandaled foot, clearly enjoying his role in this exchange.

"But *you* want me to say I work for the Pentagon, which would be true indeedy. We're army. Boo-yah!"

Bryn scanned the scene before him for a moment. "This doesn't look like a military operation to me."

Richard tapped his beer bottle on his forehead. "Stealth, Bryn, *stealth*. We learned this from *you*. Hide things in plain sight. You've had *your* fun," he looked at Mike, "and now it's our turn."

Bryn suddenly realized what this was about. "You guys are going to camp out here and never leave, aren't you?"

"Never say never," said Richard, noisily cracking open a bag of potato chips. "I've got cruise tickets to Alaska in a couple of months. I'm going AWOL if they think they can make me cancel my vacation."

Bryn shifted uneasily.

"Actually, yeah," Mike added. "Colonel told us it was time to literally shadow you, except we're going to watch your every move by being inches away, photographing you, shooting video of you ..." He poked a thumb toward Richard. "And Ragman here will accumulate even further proof of what you've been up to at midnight, January first of 1980."

"Damn right," mumbled Richard, his mouth completely full of chips.

Bryn spun about and walked away, thinking furiously. He stopped and turned back.

"I'm just going to go to another power station."

"You can't," said Richard.

"I can't?" Bryn asked, surprised his ruse had flopped so quickly.

The two seated men shook their heads slowly in synchronization.

Mike pointed at the station. "*This* be the spot through which the power passes back to ol' Building F. The only place in the entire world where you can reroute the flow is right here. You're stuck here as much as we are. So stop being so bogus, Zilch. The burgers are gonna get burned."

"I'm not hungry." Bryn spun around to leave.

"Liar!" Mike yelled after him.

Richard turned to Mike. "That's pretty harsh, bromo. Don't be harsh with civilians."

Mike's expression became apologetic. He shouted back out to Bryn. "Teller of untruths!"

Bryn sighed. What could he lose? He had acquired his own personal peanut gallery, two ticks sent by the Pentagon to burrow under his skin so deep they might never be dislodged. He hadn't expected anything like this.

And, he had to admit, he *had* lied. He was quite hungry.

Bryn turned back around in resignation, twisted the cap off the cold bottle and tried the beer. It was exceptionally good. What brand could it be? He checked the ornate label.

Corrosive Liquid premium beer.

He pointed at the label, but Richard was shaking his head vigorously.

"Sorry, Bryn, that offer about the packages on the truck is, like, so five minutes ago. You lose."

In short order they were all seated at the table, Richard laying down the steaming cheese-covered patties onto the buns stacked on their plates. Bryn started to reach across for the ketchup bottle when Mike smacked his hand away.

"What the hell!" Bryn pulled his hand back in shock.

Richard put his hands on his hips and rebuked Mike in mock disappointment. "Mike, I'm surprised at you. Haven't I taught you how important it is to share?"

"Sorry, Ragman," said Mike sheepishly. He looked at Bryn. "Sorry, Bryn. I won't do it again. I didn't know that applied to civilians."

Richard pointed at the ketchup. "Damn right it applies. We're here to play nice. It's important to share. We all have to learn to share, Mikey." He popped open another beer, took a slug, wiped his mouth, and looked directly at Bryn. "*We all have to learn to share.*"

16

Bic's office door exploded open with enough force to drive the doorknob through the drywall. The sharp noise was so unexpected, Bic yelped and cringed at his desk. Bartleby stood in the doorway, breathing hard, what hair he had a windblown shambles.

"He's been in the room for two whole hours already!"

"Who? What room?" Bic demanded.

Bartleby coughed raspily, trying to talk through the paroxysms. "The lab! He's ... been in there ... and we didn't even know it!"

Bic shook his head, uncomprehending. "Ron, *nobody* can get in the lab. Did Niles knock out the guards and break the seals to get in?"

Bartleby stopped for a second, not processing Bic's reply. "Niles?"

"Yeah, Niles," Bic replied.

Bartleby realized he hadn't made himself clear. "*Eckhardt* is in the lab!"

Bic's heart skipped a beat. "Is Jenna with him?"

"Not that we can tell. The guards said only Eckhardt was allowed in."

"We've got him on video the last two hours?" Bic asked.

"You bet! He was busy with the isolator for the first few minutes, then spent the rest of the time entering stuff into his digiscreen."

"You couldn't just phone me with this?"

"Not all bugs are created equal."

Bic wasn't sure he understood what Bartleby was saying, but he let it go. "Let me pull up the video camera feeds, Ron. Come around so you can watch too."

Bic immediately regretted the invitation. Bartleby was sweating profusely, and his deodorant had given up the ghost hours ago.

After studying the video clip of Eckhardt's activities at several different magnifications, Bic was even more confused. He logged off his workstation and looked at Bartleby. He then decided to literally clear the air.

"Uh, Ron, please, sit down," he pleaded, gesturing to the chair across from the desk. Bartleby ambled over and slumped into it.

Bic breathed easier. "Ron, do *you* know what he was doing?" he asked.

"I know *what* he did; I just don't know why, or what it means," Bartleby answered. "You saw it as clearly as I did."

Bic rubbed his upper lip thoughtfully.

Eckhardt had counted down the ranks of convection tubes on the isolator's face with his index finger. Finding the ones he was interested in, he snapped them right off the isolator. He knew they were fakes. The tubeless region he left behind looked like a diagonal island just above the cube's center.

Eckhardt had then laid the tubes he had removed on the table, arranging them to form a rough-hewn letter J. And that was the end of his actions. Fast-forwarding through the rest of the video proved he had remained seated, working with his digiscreen, up until the present.

Bic couldn't stand it anymore. "Let's get over there. Maybe Eckhardt will talk."

"You're just going to go and knock on the door?"

"Why not? It's worth a try. Let's get there before he up and leaves."

They both ran to Building F. Bic realized that he'd soon end up smelling as ripe as the out-of-shape Bartleby—business suits made poor running clothes. Out of consideration, Bic didn't outrun the older man.

They arrived on the second floor of Building F, Bartleby wheezing from the exertion. They approached the guards at the lab entrance at a more casual pace. The senior guard saw them coming and calmly opened up the lab for them. Bic looked at him in confusion.

"He said to let you in," said the guard curtly.

The two men found Eckhardt still in the same position, legs crossed, tapping his chin with the digiscreen stylus. Eckhardt looked up, his black eyes shining, penetrating as always.

Bartleby had never met Eckhardt, but Bic had done so twice. Bic always felt inferior in Eckhardt's presence, not because Eckhardt paraded superiority, but because he didn't but could have. Power under restraint, the classic definition of meekness: Eckhardt radiated it.

"Doctor Eckhardt ..." Bic began, but Eckhardt interrupted him.

"This," the chairman waved at the isolator, and then at the fake convection tubes carefully laid out on the table, "is just for Doctor Wilkes, so I won't speak about it with you. She'll tell you about it once she sees a bit deeper into her own work."

Bic and Bartleby both nodded dumbly.

"But I do have some comments for you and Doctor Bartleby," Eckhardt continued, pointing at some lab chairs nearby. The three men quickly formed a tight huddle.

"Doctor Eckhardt," Bic warned, "this room is probably bugged. You surely know that."

"I know," said Eckhardt. "A mild inconvenience. I know what I'm saying, and who my audience might be."

Bic and Bartleby were all ears. Eckhardt was apparently going to speak straight with them.

"First," Eckhardt began, "this isolator can't be used for what Niles envisions, though I'm personally sorry for him that this is so. CryoMax will never revive its founders' folly because these isolators can't provide for resuscitating somebody who is terminally ill.

"Second, everybody but Jenna Wilkes is barking up the wrong tree regarding the energy transfer issue. She told everyone plainly what was going on, but your tunnel vision is getting in the way."

Bartleby chafed at the criticism. "I don't see what we're missing. There's no question the electrons are quantum tunneling where they shouldn't, right past open circuits of incredible size."

But Eckhardt was shaking his head the entire time Bartleby was talking.

"No, Doctor Bartleby, you're only correct because of an historical accident. You're hung up, as they say, on the fact that the energy flow is electrical at this point in the chain. You have to follow the chain back to understand the significance of this phenomenon."

Bic was starting to catch on, but couldn't get past his fear of bugging. "Doctor Eckhardt, loose lips sink ships. Is it really prudent to speak candidly?"

Eckhardt nodded. "Bic," he used Bic's first name, "I'm pretty disgusted with information asymmetry, the enabling root of information crimes."

Bic knew that maximum freedom entailed information symmetry. He felt that such idealism only worked if nobody harbored wicked intentions. “There’s no possible downside, Doctor Eckhardt?”

“There’s a time to open the kimono, and a time to play things close to the vest,” Eckhardt looked back at the isolator. “About certain things, I’ll remain as inscrutable as a statue of the Buddha. But not about this.”

Eckhardt’s meaning dawned on Bartleby. “You’re saying that if you keep trying to shut off this isolator and work your way back to the coal-burning plant or hydroelectric dam, coal will burn hotter or gravity will pull harder to make up the difference?”

Eckhardt turned to Bic. “I always knew you’d figure out whom to keep away from Niles’s axe, Bic.” He looked back to Bartleby. “Correct. If the chain extended to the sun, the laws of nuclear fusion would shift slightly to make up the difference. Those eight kilowatts are going to flow into this isolator no matter how you try to confound that process—until you turn the isolator off the correct way.”

Eckhardt’s eyes flitted momentarily toward the J he had made on the laboratory desk. Bic noticed, but kept his suspicions to himself.

Bartleby’s excitement mounted. “That means Bryn’s wasting his time,” he rejoiced. “He can’t measure a delta of only eight kilowatts passing through that distribution station. The further up the chain, the tinier the fraction of energy that flow becomes. A change in the gravity near the dam would be too tiny to detect. This effect is obliterated in the noise.”

Eckhardt chose to correct him on one point but not the other. “The gravitational constant wouldn’t just change at the dam. It would be a cosmic-level change. Because this box,” he pointed at the isolator, “is actually leveraging cosmic effects.”

“Cosmic?” asked Bic. “A change transmitted instantaneously from one end of the universe to the other? That won’t sit well with most physicists I know.”

“From one standpoint, it’s a local phenomenon,” Eckhardt continued, “but the universe keeps score. When you detach a part of the universe from the rest, the conservation laws kick in. You have to rob Peter to pay Paul.”

“Doctor Eckhardt,” Bartleby became thoughtful now, “there’s no way that anyone can increase that energy flow to huge terawatt levels, is there?"

"Not at present," Eckhardt replied, picking at some lint on his suit. "The energy flow is a strict function of the volume of the core. It's a linear correspondence. These thick titanium walls will limit the core size until Doctor Wilkes comes to realize two things I've tried to get her to key in on."

"What two things?" asked Bic, enthralled.

"First, you can dispense with these titanium walls. Second, if you can manipulate one dimension as she has done, you can manipulate the others."

"Do you know how to do these things?" asked Bartleby. "Are you just playing some sort of all-knowing guru to Jenna, and you've already worked it all out?"

"No," Eckhardt replied, "I'm only parroting Jenna's dissertation work. She's the original thinker here. I'm the captain of a fishing boat, I know where the fish are biting, but I don't have a fishing pole, at least not one worthy of the name. *She's* got the intellectual fishing pole, and I'm taking the boat back out where she landed her first big whopper seven years ago. But I'm no genius, gentlemen."

"Could have fooled me, Doctor Nobel Laureate," Bartleby shot back.

Bic had forgotten how undiplomatic Bartleby could be, socially and in respect to the corporate pecking order. But Eckhardt didn't seem offended. He even smiled.

"Doctor Bartleby, I guess it's relative. To most people, I have a first-rate mind. And I work hard at it. But nobody *works* their mind as hard as Doctor Wilkes does, even when she's daydreaming. In that regard, she's something of a force of nature. And she continues to pay a high price for it without griping."

Eckhardt reached for a Biblical allusion to summarize his strategy. "Saul chose valiant men; David chose loyal men …" He paused for effect. "Solomon chose industrious men. Solomon was a pretty bright guy. I've just put a tiny twist on his strategy."

"A twist?" asked Bartleby.

"I also chose someone who's industrious." Eckhardt rose from the chair with difficulty. "Only, the person *I* chose doesn't happen to be male.

"Now, gentlemen, I hate to do this to you, but I'm going to reseal this lab. Doctor Wilkes will return in a day or so. If she lets you in here, fine. If not, let her be. If she lets someone in that you don't think should be here, that's her business, not yours. No corporate interference. I wear several hats, but the most important one does not involve this corporation."

Eckhardt motioned them both to the door, adding a final aside, his eyes sparkling.

"Well, to use Doctor Wilkes's terminology, any benefit to CryoMax stemming from my actions is strictly incidental to my actual purpose."

But the sparkle quickly faded. Eckhardt suddenly looked old and weary, as if the only thing animating him was the eleventh-hour quest that Jenna had set in motion.

Twenty seconds later, Bic and Bartleby were standing outside the lab, their minds still spinning at Eckhardt's revelations. The guards again blocked the door, their eyes daring any would-be intruder to just try to breach the entrance. Eckhardt had already disappeared into the elevator.

Bic looked at Bartleby. "I don't even know what to say."

"Well, *I* sure the hell know what to say," Bartleby replied.

Bic waited for it. "Well?"

Bartleby sputtered and sighed. "No, you're right. I don't know what to say either." He glanced down at his sweat-stained business shirt. "You don't think he noticed I was a little bit sweaty, do you?"

"We can only hope."

17

Philip Hernandez left the bank with the item retrieved from Sexton's safe deposit box, a bulging gray 9x12 envelope crudely sealed with layers of tape. There was clearly far more stuffed into it than the missing notes.

Philip had intended to take the envelope to his office for inspection before remembering the precautions Stall had taken in Virginia against snoopers. Now he had to wonder whether he could even trust his own automobile, which could be riddled with micro videocams hidden God-knows-where.

He headed instead to a local restaurant. After settling into a corner booth and ordering coffee, he pulled out his pocketknife and began to cut into the tape protecting the envelope.

It took some doing to get the envelope open. Inside was another gray 9x12 envelope; the outer one had merely been a protective shell. Philip turned it around and noticed a white mailing envelope taped to it face down. He peeled it off to examine the front. The top left corner bore Sexton's name and return address. The addressee's name was centered in large block letters:

Dr. Philip J. Hernandez.

Interesting. And unexpected.

Philip unfolded the single sheet stuffed inside the envelope with mounting fascination. The handwritten message was brief and disconcerting, even more so when Philip noticed the date of the document. It was written several weeks after Jenna's dissertation fiasco, filling half a sheet of graph paper.

Dear Philip,

Please forgive me for letting you take the blame for the garbled wording on the Wilkes Agreement. You should know that the wording was no mistake. I knew what the agreed-upon wording was, but I didn't want the committee to quash Wilkes's research. I also needed to know how willing she was to defend her ideas against opposition, to get a taste of what price the iconoclast pays. I therefore chose the wording in the Agreement deliberately. I don't know if you'll ever get this letter, but if you do come to read this, know that privately I have always held you blameless. Science is too often done by cowards. No one could accuse your student of cowardice. She might end up shaming us all. Good for her.

Peace,
Wally Sexton

Philip didn't know whether to consider this turn of events comic or tragic or both. He folded up the graph paper and put it back in the envelope.

His cell phone signaled an incoming text message. He took another sip of coffee and checked to see what it was.

It wasn't good.

Sexton's nurse had sent it. Sexton had suffered a stroke shortly after Philip's visit. He'd had three minor ones in the preceding two weeks. This one appeared to be more serious. An ambulance had taken him to Metro. He was in stable condition.

End of message.

Philip clicked his teeth together nervously. *Should I visit Sexton at the hospital?* he wondered.

He wasn't sure he could handle that. Reminders of mortality made him uncomfortable. He steered clear of funerals, and on the rare occasions he attended them, he avoided looking at the recently departed if the ceremony were open casket. He couldn't help picturing himself lying peacefully in the white cocoon-like lining. He shook himself back to reality with a shudder.

"Okay," Philip cut open the bulging gray envelope, "What've you been hiding, Wally?"

He pulled out a half a ream of handwritten notes and equations. On top he found the second page of Sexton's notes on Jenna's defense on that portentous day in May 2018.

Philip counted forward to see where Sexton's notes ended. The other professors facing off against the red-haired doctoral candidate generated no more than a dozen pages of notes each. After thirty pages of counting Philip began to wonder where Sexton's review actually stopped.

Philip soon realized that the entire stack constituted Sexton's notes. The dates sprinkled throughout stretched between May 10, 2018, and March 29, 2019. Sexton had labored ten months on this material.

Philip turned back to the earliest notes to see what the gist of Sexton's comments were. There was a steady progression in the first three pages, from *She couldn't possibly be right about conducting the derivation using this formalism* to *What if she IS right?* At the top of the fourth page, Sexton let the cat out of the bag. *We can't award a doctorate for something this speculative, but this is too important not to put to the test. Time to make her put up or shut up. I'll need to goose the Agreement a bit.*

There it was: the reason Sexton had pulled out these notes and kept them secret. Jenna must have swayed him over the course of that first brutal day, but Sexton didn't have the confidence or ability to work the issues through himself. He came to realize that Jenna could actually visualize manifolds, fields, even what tensors represented, that he himself could not.

But Sexton couldn't determine which of the two was truly blind: Jenna, or Sexton and his colleagues.

Philip turned to the final page to see why Sexton had discontinued this line of inquiry. Had it fizzled out?

It *had* fizzled out, but only for Sexton. He could understand some of what Jenna had written but not the things that were counterintuitive. His final comments were disturbing.

I am now certain that if Wilkes is right about the stuff I agree with her on, there's no question she's right about the stuff I don't agree with. The laws of nature require it.

Philip recognized that last line all too well.

It was Jenna's mantra.

Part II

18

The sunlight had traveled 93 million miles on its glorious cosmic journey to finally pass through her bedroom window, illuminate some swirling dust particles, and extinguish itself forever by warming the plush carpet near her bare feet.

It was a strange way to look at everyday things.

Jenna's way.

Other scientists had seen further by standing on the shoulders of giants.

She had seen further by opening her eyes wider.

This morning, back in her own home, she took a moment to savor the simple pleasure of digging her toes deep into the soft warmth of the carpet.

She sat on the edge of her bed, freshly showered, wearing a terry cloth robe with her hair wrapped turban-style in a fluffy white towel. Jenna's tortoiseshell cat Pinball purred contentedly on her lap. Pinball had grudgingly forgiven Jenna the transgression of placing her at the mercy of nutcases who relished making cats and water meet.

Jenna was relieved that Eckhardt had arranged for her to be completely unharassed, without obligation to her superiors. She'd been given the ultimate Get Out of Jail Free card. Eckhardt had even sent a contingent of guards to her house before her trip to prevent the planting of bugs and secure her privacy.

She had a hard time accepting the new car he provided her, but Jenna's Toyota had become compromised at the airport lot. Jenna had received keys to a new vehicle parked near her own. She wasn't allowed to transfer any of her effects out of her Toyota because bugs could be placed on or in anything. Shopping, or doing anything that meant leaving the new car unattended in a security-compromising place, was forbidden.

Knowing that Eckhardt rarely did anything without a reason, she wondered why he chose a white Volkswagen Beetle for her. She figured that Eckhardt had added features to it far beyond her ken. His actions were always fraught with deeper meanings that kept her mind engaged. So far, the only hidden meaning appeared to be the personalized license plate. ACTS2624 seemed to refer to a passage in the Bible. She looked it up online, having no Bible of her own.

The relevant part of the verse appeared to be *much learning doth make thee mad*. Perhaps Eckhardt was saying that someone of great learning could be regarded as insane despite speaking the truth. Jenna assumed the reference was intended to offer comfort, but being compared to an apostle of the Christian religion seemed over-the-top to her.

She recognized that Eckhardt was an exceedingly moral man who took the Bible seriously, although only his inner circle openly acknowledged it. She came to peace with the strange dichotomy he embodied: he was old enough to be her grandfather, but they were able to talk as peers and equals. Formally speaking, she wasn't Eckhardt's protégé, she was Dr. Hernandez's, although Hernandez had long ago repudiated her and abdicated his mentorship.

Hernandez had been instrumental in insuring she'd get no postdoctoral research opportunities at Stanford, immediately forcing the inexperienced woman into the commercial world. She didn't blame Hernandez, knowing how much she had disappointed him. But Jenna was sure she'd done the right thing, and in retrospect wouldn't have changed anything she'd done so far in her life ...

Except maybe for having yanked out the disconnect module in front of Niles as she had foolishly done.

That impulsive act was done in a moment of irrational panic. The fear that Niles was then and there terminating her research, that she'd never get to know if the energy transfer went any further, that others would take over her work, drove her to seize the handle, her hand completely unprotected with the safety interlock defeated, and rip the module out of its socket.

Dumb. Jenna had crafted an entirely different plan of attack for developing her isolator work, but she had promptly sent that ship to the bottom with her action. Still, getting to interact with Eckhardt seemed to mitigate the folly of that fateful day.

But deep down, grabbing the disconnect module was symbolic of her ultimate intentions. She wanted to track the energy bridge all the way back, not just to the power station or the generators or the fusion in the stars, but to the first cause, to the ultimate seat of energy in the universe.

She knew that following the rabbit hole she had opened would lead there if she could just measure the energy transfer points along the way. If Jenna could work out that key detail, she would peel back everything in the "universe that mankind knows" to reveal what was driving it from underneath.

Or as Eckhardt had once told her, "Remember humility, Miss Wilkes. That's what you'll need the most if you intend to touch the face of God Himself."

She scooted Pinball off her lap and started dressing. She felt ready to reenter the lab this morning.

Because Eckhardt's security staff could protect her car at home and work but not in an uncontrolled situation, she was warned not to park at sit-down restaurants. She had to use drive-thrus, a different one for each meal. There were strict rules about how to eat, when to talk, and how to dispose of trash. This being her first foray out, she was scrupulous about each "best practices" security precept they'd drilled into her.

Grocery shopping was out. The only food entering her unbugged home was cat food, which was flown in from a known, safe source.

Jenna didn't care for all these precautions. On the plus side, her weakness for fast food could now run riot without guilt. Orders are orders, after all.

She had just placed a fast food order on a particularly distorted speaker system. It took five attempts to get her order right, or so she hoped. *These security guys are barking up the wrong tree,* she thought. *You want ultimate encryption? Send your message through a drive-thru intercom system.*

She pulled her VW up another car-length; she was next in line to collect her food. Her eyes wandered to the driver-side newspaper convenience rack.

What *was* going on in the world? She didn't have a television in her home, considering the diversion a waste of time. She pulled a couple of quarters out of her purse and bought a paper. *I hope I'm not breaking the rules by doing this,* she thought. *This ought to be safe though. Somebody would have to bug every San Francisco Chronicle for this to be dangerous.* She set the newspaper down on the passenger seat.

She noticed that the order handed into the car in front was being sent right back. The person at the register had gotten most of it wrong. That would likely be her fate too.

Realizing she'd be sitting there for a while, she picked up the paper and scanned the national headlines. *Same-old, same-old.* She pulled out the local news section and flipped through a few pages before recognizing a name. She looked up ahead to make sure she had the time, then let her eyes fall back on the story.

The brief article concerned the hospitalization of Dr. Wallingford Estes Sexton, professor emeritus of physics at Stanford and former department chairman, for a moderately severe stroke the previous day.

Jenna realized the hospital he was at was two miles away. She laid down the paper.

She had a hard time coming to grips with her reaction. Jenna stared into space, only to jump when a car honked from behind her. She had missed seeing the SUV in front drive off.

She hastily pulled up and collected her order, then drove across the street to an empty parking lot to eat. Jenna was relieved to find her order was correct. Between bites of the egg and cheese croissant she could feel her eyes continuing to drift toward the squib about Sexton. She kept coming back to the possibility that he may not be around much longer. Did she owe him a visit before the inevitable happened? He had surely wielded the heaviest axe against her during her dissertation defenses.

Had he really, though? She tried to remember.

Wasn't there something different about his attacks, versus the savage criticisms from the other professors? Or was she imagining things here?

Jenna finished her juice and prepped her garbage as instructed. She drove by the dumpster behind the strip mall and flung the bag at it. Missed. She knew not to get out of the car, but she hated littering.

She drove across the lot and entered traffic, still thinking hard about the defining events in her past, turning left to drive to her intended destination, CryoMax Livermore, and away from Metro Hospital.

Halfway to CryoMax, Jenna changed lanes and looked for a place to do a legal U-turn. She was remembering more of the details now, details clearer today than they were seven years ago. Back then, she only remembered that Sexton was the loudest, angriest-looking professor in the rotunda. But now she was remembering his *words* and not how he said them.

There was something different about what he was saying and what the others were doing.

The others were pushing her to alter her position, which they were ultimately successful in doing by her ninth defense. They engineered her retreat in the face of relentless pressure, compounded by the lack of sleep their strategy had imposed on her. She had actually collapsed on the sidewalk on the way to her final defense. Two undergraduates had helped her back up and wanted to call an ambulance, but she waved them away. The good Samaritans persisted, but she lied about having tripped, assured them her bloodshot eyes were due to conjunctivitis, and pressed on grimly to the rotunda with copies of her last, most severely compromised dissertation in her backpack.

But Sexton? Was he really pushing her to peel back her ideas, or to clarify them, strengthen them? Was he trying to get her to repent, or make her position more rigorous, more robust?

She replayed back the first day's defense in her head over and over, and increasingly realized that she wasn't imagining things. Sexton wasn't playing the same game as the others, notwithstanding the snarl in his words. He was apparently acting that way in front of the committee to save the appearance of solidarity with their paradigms.

She unconsciously pressed down harder on the accelerator.

She hoped the hospital staff would let her see Sexton. She at least wanted to apologize to him for not recognizing his intentions at the time. Back then, Jenna was reacting emotionally to what Sexton had said, or rather, how he had said it.

The space of seven years had cleared the fog of faulty perspective, and it finally dawned on her that Sexton must have actually understood her theory.

She didn't even notice that she had run a stop sign.

19

Jenna knew never to leave her car in a public space such as this hospital parking structure. She also knew she might end up compromising security and still be turned away from the hospital, never getting to see Sexton at all.

She parked on the third floor of the structure, turned off the engine, watched the rearview mirror, and weighed her options in the shaded concrete cavern through which cars spiraled up and down behind her. She knew once her car had been bugged, there'd be no chance to undo it.

Once Sexton had died, there'd be no chance to talk to him.

She stepped out of the vehicle, paused a moment, then decided to lose her lab coat. People with fixations on hygiene would not approve of the condition she kept it in. And virtually nobody understood her reason for never laundering it, and she planned to keep it that way. At CryoMax she put up with reprimands and paid the inevitable fines rather than wash it.

But when in Rome ...

She learned from the information desk that she'd need to go up to the third-floor nurse's station. There she'd find the gatekeepers who determined who could see Sexton. Jenna rode the elevator up, trying to remain optimistic. She felt comfortable in the hospital, perhaps because the smell reminded her of her own laboratory. Had she shared this observation with anyone, she knew they would have thought her demented. Who'd enjoy strolling down these hallways?

She approached the nurses' counter. Five female nurses were being kept busy with phone calls, chart updates, and scheduled rounds. Jenna waited patiently until one was able to acknowledge her presence. The young Asian nurse seated directly in front of Jenna filed one last chart and then looked up with a smile.

"How can I help you?"

"I'm here to visit Doctor Sexton," Jenna said.

"Are you family?" the nurse asked.

"I'm his daughter," Jenna lied.

The nurse pulled a chart out and examined the instructions written on the folder. "Miss, Mr. Sexton only had sons. I'm sorry, family only. The orders are strict."

"But I was hoping to ..."

"What part of *family only* do you not understand?" the nurse asked sharply.

Disappointment crossed Jenna's face. She suddenly felt a deep bitterness in her stomach. What if Sexton died here, in this cold sterile place, and she never had a chance to talk to him one last time?

She walked back to the elevator. She couldn't explain why the tears started to slowly form in her eyes. The perceived injustice of the situation was difficult to accept.

Jenna reached the elevator but didn't press the button. She stood there for several minutes, as elevators came and went, and people walked around her to enter or exit them. Anyone watching the situation would have thought it a pitiful spectacle.

At last, Jenna walked back to the nurse and waited for her to become freed up. But when the nurse was finally free to speak, she did not acknowledge Jenna's presence.

Jenna addressed her in a small, shaky voice. "Nurse ..."

The nurse looked up, unsmiling, but noticed Jenna's tear-filled eyes. Her disdain for Jenna's blatant lie evaporated.

Jenna saw the nurse's expression soften, so she continued. "I'm sorry for lying to you like that. I just wanted to see Doctor Sexton very badly. I only had him for one class at Stanford, so I honestly was never close to him, but he was on my doctoral dissertation committee, and I wanted to talk to him one last time."

But the nurse was shaking her head slowly. "Miss, I'm sorry ..."

"My name is Jenna Wilkes," Jenna interrupted, "But if I could change it legally to Jenna Sexton to get in there, I think I would. But I know you're just doing your job. Thank you, though."

And Jenna turned on her heels quickly, not wanting the nurse to see her shaking with a grief she hadn't realized was pent up inside. She didn't recognize it for what it was—an emotional catharsis, a bittersweet realization that part of her ordeal seven years ago wasn't all horror and humiliation. She may have had a hidden advocate all along.

And now, she may never even get to see him face to face to thank him.

As Jenna disappeared around the corner, the nurse looked back down at the manila folder. The instructions were clear: nobody but family, P. Hernandez, and J. A. Wilkes could see Sexton.

The nurse tapped on that name, Wilkes. The gender was ambiguous. Was that the name the redhead had given? She had lied once, maybe she'd lie again. But the nurse had to be sure, so she got up to find the woman.

The elevator doors were nearly closed when the nurse shot her hand through them to stop the car. As the doors reopened, the nurse saw Jenna in the corner of the car, both hands covering her face, sobbing quietly.

"Miss," said the nurse, "I have to ask you a question."

Jenna looked up; she needed to wipe her nose but didn't know it.

"What's your middle name?" the nurse asked.

Jenna wiped her eyes trying to collect herself. The nurse punched the Open Door button to keep the elevator from sending them both downstairs.

"My middle name?" asked Jenna. "It's Angela. Why?"

The nurse reached out to take Jenna's hand and led her out of the elevator. As they passed down the hallway, the nurse snatched a green cloth surgical cap off a supply rack and handed it to Jenna.

"I'm supposed to wear this?" Jenna asked.

"It's to wipe your nose and eyes," the nurse replied.

Jenna studied the nurse's nametag before blowing her nose into the cap. "Thank you, Nurse Takashi," she said, now wondering what to do with the mucked up cap in her hands.

Nurse Takashi guided her to a biohazard container along the wall, and Jenna figured out the drill.

"You can see Mr. Sexton," Takashi announced as they approached the nurses' station.

"Oh God, thank you, thank you!" Jenna whispered to her in gratitude. "I know how much trouble you could get into by bending the rules for me."

"I'm not bending the rules," Takashi informed her. "You're one of two people, other than immediate family, specifically mentioned on the orders who are allowed to see Mr. Sexton."

Jenna didn't comprehend what Takashi was saying at first. "My name is on a list of approved visitors?"

Takashi nodded.

"Who put my name on the list?" Jenna asked.

"Mr. Sexton requested it be placed there. J. A. Wilkes. That must be you. If you hadn't lied, we might have saved a lot of trouble, Miss." But Takashi's tone and expression were devoid of harshness.

When they arrived at the door to Sexton's room, Takashi advised Jenna what to expect. "He's got a roommate, but his roommate is usually so heavily sedated you won't notice him unless he snores," the nurse explained. "Mr. Sexton is in the far bed. The nurses on the last shift say he's able to talk, but he's very weak. It'd be best if you kept it short." And Takashi was gone.

Jenna pushed the door open and slowly passed by Sexton's sleeping roommate toward the man behind the partition curtain, the man she hadn't seen in seven years. She heard the gentle beeping of monitors recording Sexton's pulse and respiration. Two more steps and he came into view.

She hardly recognized Sexton, but the analytic side of her mind told her it was irrational to think people looked their best under these conditions. The patients here were fighting for their lives, a difficult fight to wage when deprived of your strength. *Making bricks without straw* came to mind. Something Eckhardt had said one night in a different context, but this place made an equally strong claim on that image.

Sexton was sleeping, so she pulled a chair up close to him, eyes widening at how bruised the tops of his hands were. *Human beings revered life so highly that they'd willingly undergo the most frightful indignities to fight for it.*

She pondered the parallel with her own life.

There *was* something that she had been willing to suffer nearly inhuman hardships for as well. In fact, it had landed her in an institution not unlike this one, when she had collapsed the morning of the ceremony to receive her doctoral degree. She awoke in a hospital the next day and spent a week recovering from the effects of sleep deprivation and malnutrition. When she finally arrived back home, she found her doctoral degree in a mangled envelope wedged into her mailbox. That was the insult. The injury was the other letter in her mailbox: the rejection letter, signed by Professor Hernandez, ruling out her chance to do postdoctoral studies at Stanford.

"I'm glad you came."

Jenna was surprised to hear Sexton's voice. It was quiet and weak, the opposite of her last experience of it in the rotunda. He had even been bombastic in the one class she took from him as an undergrad. Was this the same man?

She bent forward so she could hear him better and instinctively took his hand. She tried to avoid the bruised spots, but they were too extensive. Sexton squeezed her hand weakly and didn't let go. He rolled his head straight for a moment, then turned back to face her, his eyes weary slits.

"You've done well," he finally said.

She nodded, not knowing how to respond. Any words she might choose to speak would be woefully inadequate, a circumstance she hadn't anticipated when she purposed to see Sexton.

"I wanted ... to have my cake and eat it, Jenna," he said slowly. "I wanted to believe in you, and I wanted to be respected as a staunch defender of modern science, the established paradigms." He spoke with considerable effort, so much so it alarmed Jenna.

"Doctor Sexton, please relax. You don't have to talk right now. Save your strength."

He tightened his grip on her hand and asked her a question. "If you had one last breath left, how would you use it? Would you want to say something important with it, or just let it slide out of your lungs quietly?"

Jenna searched his face, the eyes that had widened with life, and was struck by the fiercely burning core of humanity inside this frail figure.

When she had entered the room, she honestly thought the only brightness in it emanated from the flowers on the nightstand. She had completely misjudged the situation.

His words were coming out ever more slowly, sometimes spoken one at a time. "Jenna, allow me this opportunity to speak. I'll stop speaking soon enough."

Jenna felt her cheeks becoming streaked with tears. She reached over with her free hand for some nearby tissues and tried to collect herself emotionally. He noticed and didn't speak again until she was able to listen.

"You know," he started, "you reminded me a little of my wife Rowena when she was your age. Well," he chuckled quietly, "except for the hair. And she kept her lab coat cleaner than you did yours. She also ..." Sexton trailed off, thinking about the distant past. "She also was a fighter. At school, like you. The glass ceiling. And later, against cancer. She fought until her last breath ..." He turned his head away.

Jenna waited patiently, squeezing his hand gently.

He rolled his head back to face her. "I asked Professor Hernandez ... a few days ago whether you ... had built your device. It sounds like you have. Did it work? How much power ... is being transferred?"

Jenna now wondered if she should speak candidly. Could this hospital room be bugged, or was she becoming too paranoid? Sexton may be dying. Who'd trawl for information that heartlessly?

She decided to open up to Sexton. "Eight kilowatts," she said. "Just eight kilowatts. Electric. It's too small to see if the effect will migrate across a conversion point, say to a hydroelectric plant. One is upline from us, but we'd be unable to detect the transfer at the distribution station, let alone the dam. Eight kilowatts is just a drop in the bucket."

Sexton nodded. He spoke again after a minute of labored breathing. "I know ... you were going after ... much bigger fish than energy transfer, but I spent about a year ... working through that section of your dissertation." He moved his left hand across his frail form to cup her hand between his own. She moved to do the same.

Sexton then strained mightily to tilt his head forward several inches. This allowed him to speak easily for a few pivotal moments, but it cost him his consciousness, being so weakened by the exertion that he afterward let go of her hands and fell back asleep.

"Don't be the Jenna who handed in that ninth version. *Think*. Archimedes said he could move the world with a lever if given the right place to stand." Sexton's eyes opened as wide as she'd ever seen them, boring right into her. "You said it yourself. *A drop in the bucket*."

While speaking his last three words, he squeezed her hand so tightly she thought the force was coming from somewhere else than his fragile frame.

"*Drain the dam*."

20

Katherine breezed into the manse anteroom to alert the guest that Eckhardt's helicopter was only a minute way. He nodded politely as she left through the other hallway.

He had no way of knowing he was seated in the same place where Jenna Wilkes had first waited to meet Eckhardt. But there'd be no chance of Eckhardt surprising him as had happened to Jenna. He was a tight ball of concentration solely focused on the mission that brought him here. That mission caused him no end of frustration, which was unacceptable considering what his superiors expected of him.

He sat motionless, not crossing his legs or trying to get comfortable, even though the beautiful leather chair invited such indulgence. He could make out the sound of the chopper in the distance as it neared the helipad.

And then he jumped when greeted by a voice behind him.

"Good morning, General Stall."

Stall whirled around and saw it was Eckhardt sitting in a wheelchair. "But Katherine said your helicopter was only a minute away," the general sputtered.

"It is," Eckhardt replied. "I only hire honest people here, General. I hope the armed forces can make the same claim."

Eckhardt rose out of the wheelchair to come forward, hand outstretched. Stall rose to accept it, straightening his uniform and recovering his normally unflappable demeanor.

"Doctor Eckhardt ..." Stall began.

"Please, call me Jonas," Eckhardt replied, giving the general one of the firmest handshakes he'd ever had.

Is this guy ex-army? Stall wondered, finding himself further engrossed by the enigmatic octogenarian.

"A wheelchair?" Stall pointed at it, his tone telegraphing sincere concern.

"My doctors want me to use it 24-7, but I'm stubborn. That'll probably come back to roost soon enough. Come, let's go into the study."

"Is that an unbugged area?"

"Probably not."

Stall shook his head at this.

"For the record," Eckhardt explained, "I'm not hiding anything, contrary to the impressions floated in the media. Come. I have Katherine preparing some tea."

They were soon seated in a room that Stall, scanning the walls, would have called (a more descriptive term being impossible) The Valley of the Books.

The general scrutinized the small teak coffee table situated between the two men. There were several notepads, photos, paperbacks, and a heavily worn Bible stacked on it. He leaned over and opened the Bible, flipping through several sections while Eckhardt watched quietly.

Stall figured he shouldn't have been surprised by what he saw between the cracked leather covers. The margins were filled with notes written in Greek, Hebrew, and Latin. There were virtually no notes in English.

Well, this was Eckhardt after all. A scholar. A polymath. A fellow Christian. And at this particular moment the biggest thorn in Stall's side.

Stall carefully closed the Bible, straightened up, and stirred his tea some more.

They sipped from their cups, acclimating themselves to this first meeting, a meeting of two individuals who respected each other from a distance but had never spoken to one another.

Eckhardt seemed to be completely unfazed at Stall's unannounced arrival. Stall considered this circumstance carefully. *Perhaps he knew I was coming,* he thought.

Stall was the first to speak. "Jonas, I'll be frank. My superiors are concerned about what is going on in Livermore."

Eckhardt nodded, looking directly at Stall. Stall had to admit that he knew few people whose gaze was more authoritative, yet unthreatening, as Eckhardt's. Although he had only seen Eckhardt in photos before, he had always harbored that peculiar notion. In the military, authority and threat were correlated. In Eckhardt, they weren't. They didn't need to be. His authoritative bearing was rooted elsewhere than in posing a potential threat. *A strangely beautiful antinomy.*

Stall went on. "I need you to assure me that you plan to use what you're developing over there for the good of America, that you have America's best interests at heart. I'll believe you if you tell me."

"I can't do that, General."

Stall put down his teacup and stared directly into Eckhardt's eyes. "Why not?"

"I'm determined solely to do what is good *considered absolutely*. Whether it is good for America is up to America. She has her destiny in her own hands on this count."

"You don't care about the good of our country?" demanded Stall.

"Oh very much. I work and pray for it every day, General. But I think you have to come to grips with your allegiance. Do you come here serving king and country?"

"President, Constitution, and country," Stall corrected.

"You have no king? Think hard about this one."

Eckhardt signaled for Katherine to refill Stall's teacup. Stall glanced at Katherine, then looked back at Eckhardt, finally relaxing a bit.

"Yes, Jonas, I have a king. King with a capital K. You've done some research, I'll give you that. It's not relevant to this situation."

"That seems to be a prevailing problem in our world, don't you think?" Eckhardt licked the teaspoon and tapped the Bible on the coffee table. "Mixed allegiances."

"Anyway," he continued, "I'm afraid that the situation in Livermore is going to make it relevant. I know what side you'll take, but I can't promise you won't be torn over it. I was, myself, for many years."

"You sound like those guys who think they'll find Noah's Ark on Mount Ararat," Stall remarked.

"General, what would impress you more—a dried out, mounted skeleton of a T. rex or a living, breathing one towering over you?"

"Stupid question."

"The Livermore discovery makes Noah's Ark, even if they found it, look like a dried out fossil by comparison."

"You're talking some kind of miracle?" Stall asked.

"No, not a miracle. Merely proof that God governs the world by law."

"Everyone knows the world is governed by law. Natural law. Physical law. You got your Nobel prize working with those laws."

"Granted."

Stall put down his cup to use his hands for emphasis. "That's the point. If natural law is involved, you don't need a God. The explanation is already covered. You'd need a miracle to show there's a God. People will only acknowledge God when natural law is suspended, not when it's conserved, when it's business-as-usual."

"A common misconception."

"You'll need to unpack that for me, Jonas. By the way, call me Harry."

Eckhardt nodded politely. "Harry, she doesn't really know it yet, but Doctor Jenna Wilkes is on the verge of doing exactly that. Do you read science fiction?"

"Some." Stall shifted in his chair, mystified by the abrupt change of subject.

"Do you know this book?" Eckhardt held up one of the paperbacks.

Stall looked at it, recognizing the cover art. "Yeah, I read *Ringworld* a long time ago. Larry Niven. Great writer. People living on a giant ring the size of a planet's orbit, living on the inside surface of it while it rotated around a central sun."

"Do you remember the name of the biggest mountain on Ringworld?"

Stall had to think a second ... it had been so many years since he had read it. He shook his head. "Sorry, no." He tapped his right temple to make his point. "Too many leaks over the years."

Eckhardt smiled. "Well, they called it Fist of God Mountain. Some of the inhabitants attributed it to God's fist smashing into the underside of their world, raising the mountain up from underneath. The reality was, a big asteroid or meteor had hit the ring, denting it, creating the mountain."

"I'm starting to remember it now. What's the point of this discussion?"

"There was a perfectly good naturalistic explanation for the phenomenon that had the name Fist of God. The name perpetuated an illusion, or a polite fiction, shall we say."

"So?"

"*This* situation might be the exact opposite. There'll be no plausible natural explanation for it, denying science a rational basis for dealing with it. But science will refuse to acknowledge the finger of God ... or, perhaps more accurately, the palm of God. Figuratively speaking, the very stones will shout. Actually, they've been doing that all along. Jenna's work is going to allow everyone to at last hear it."

"But it's not a miracle?"

"No. It's not a one-time suspension of natural law, as if God were knocking at the door of the universe and playing a brief prank to get our attention. This will be a continual 24-7 witness to the absolute authority of law."

"Natural law," Stall affirmed.

"No, just law. The foundation, the ground, on which natural law rests."

"What, like divine law? Law incarnate, or something like that?"

Eckhardt leaned forward and spoke with quiet intensity. "I think Jenna will soon peel back the stuff that hides the foundation on which natural law stands. She'll show that natural law cannot be anchored in a sea of chaos or a vacuum of meaninglessness. The impact of that will be overwhelming. The old chestnut about the Word of God being the solvent of all institutions not based on itself will apply forcefully to the work she's been given to do."

Eckhardt ended with the kind of Christian allusion that seasoned his speech when waxing theological. Stall noticed it, and called to remembrance Kepler's edict *to think God's thoughts after Him*. Applying that edict seemed to come naturally to Eckhardt, although Stall didn't accept stretching theology into places it clearly didn't belong.

But Eckhardt's views commanded the utmost respect, and though Eckhardt might be deluded on this, he was no idiot. A Nobel laureate's opinion on what Wilkes was doing had to be given due weight. How would one define *due*, though?

Stall leaned back in his chair. "Jonas, that's pretty heady stuff. You've turned this visit into some kind of high-end Sunday school session, not that I mind. I know enough about you to not write off anything that you're saying, although I find the philosophy obscure and eccentric, to say the least. But why so candid if you suspect this room is bugged?"

Eckhardt picked up three photographs from the table and handed them to Stall.

The first showed Babe Ruth pointing his baseball bat at the bleachers.

The second showed Minnesota Fats leaning over a pool table about to take a shot, the caption saying *Six ball in the side pocket.*

The third was a snapshot of a Bible page with part of a verse highlighted. Stall squinted to read it. *My Word shall not return unto Me void.*

Stall returned the photos understanding why Eckhardt didn't mind whether they were overheard. Whatever was going to happen out on the West Coast was inexorable. What was that Biblical phrase Stall had recently heard? Something about *groping after God*? Was that what Jenna Wilkes was doing without knowing it?

Stall was shocked to see Eckhardt become woozy for a few seconds. The scientist rubbed his temple with one hand and tried to get a hold of himself, his other hand gripping the armrest tightly.

"Are you okay, Jonas?"

"I'll be fine," Eckhardt shook it off. "It comes and goes. Age, you know. I'll leave you with some final thoughts because that helicopter you heard was coming to pick me up, not bring me here as you assumed. I appreciate you taking the risk coming here to meet me, and I'm glad I was actually here for this encounter.

"I know you'll keep your men spying on me, and I intend to keep my people spying on you, although I take no joy in the necessity of it. But I'm relieved you and I are clear about what's truly important.

"I never expected to meet you in person, Harry, and I'm guessing you never expected to come out here like this either."

"You'd be quite correct in guessing that," Stall acknowledged.

"Which proves that this is an extraordinary thing, Harry. It is big, complex, and will get messy before it becomes clear. But I want you to know what *I* consider to be the most extraordinary thing about this whole matter, which I hope I live to see through to the end."

"What would that be, Jonas?"

"We've seen a lot of countermeasures and hijinks since day one. Even before, if you consider the diversions Doctor Wilkes plastered over her device. In studying the summaries of my intel reports I noticed a recurring phrase, one that you and your friend Colonel Riesen probably know."

"A phrase? What recurring phrase?"

"Hidden in plain sight."

"Yeah, I've heard it." Stall's expression turned sour. "It applies to things we do, and it's a major pain when you do it to us."

"Sorry about that part," Eckhardt smiled. "Can't be helped in a fallen world, at least, not for a long while. Anyway, do you want to know who is the master at hiding in plain sight?"

"Who?"

Eckhardt regarded the Bible on the coffee table for a moment.

"God."

21

The Volkswagen's wipers were losing the battle against the heavy rain. The downpour fell in relentless sheets from a gray, angry sky while lightning bolts occasionally knifed to the ground in the distance.

The weather had changed quickly, slowing her progress between Metro Hospital and CryoMax. It was Jenna's first day back to the lab, and she was dreading the new security measures Eckhardt had imposed. They'd be a major hassle for her. And others.

The four guards assigned to her car waited in their rain gear in an empty parking lot quite some distance from Building F. Nobody could park within seventy-five yards of her Beetle. Only she was allowed to enter the circle of traffic cones defining the security perimeter. Not only would Jenna's walk (now in heavy rain) be longer than ever, but other employees would be unable to park anywhere near their buildings. She realized her popularity among the rank-and-file, nonexistent before, had just plummeted through the floor.

She pulled the VW up between the guards. One moved to open her car door, but she shook her head. He knew she wanted him to wait. He backed off and resumed sweeping the horizon with stern eyes, his standard-issue rifle's shiny barrel reflecting flashes from the electrical storm strobing across the southern sky. Jenna sat quietly with the engine running, collecting her thoughts before she would leave the safety of the car.

And ...

And running through the events of the previous hour at Metro Hospital.

When Sexton lost consciousness, Jenna buzzed the nurses' station, not sure whether something was seriously wrong or not. A male nurse she hadn't seen before popped his head in quickly, letting her know *Mr. Sexton was fine, his vitals are fine, he slips in and out of consciousness pretty easily especially when exerting himself.*

Jenna was relieved. After the nurse left, she decided she'd say a little prayer for Sexton; having no experience forming such an entreaty, she made it brief and simple. She rose from the chair and was halfway out of the room when she reconsidered, returning to Sexton's side.

Jenna twisted her hair up in a bun to keep it out of the way, lest she disturb his sleep, then bent over and gently kissed his forehead. He still slept peacefully.

She felt she had closure here, and hoped he felt it too. Maybe he'll recover and they could talk again sometime, especially about the unorthodox proposal he'd made.

But her brain was on overtime, a recklessly overclocked thinking machine probing the implications of Sexton's last instruction to her at lightning speed. By the time she had walked back to the nurses' station, Jenna had resolved to do something she would never have dreamed of earlier.

Jenna scanned the faces at the nurses' station looking for Nurse Takashi. To her relief, Takashi was still on duty. The nurse turned and smiled at Jenna's approach.

"How did it go?" Takashi asked.

"I'm glad I came," Jenna answered, undoing her hair bun to let her distinctive mane fall over her shoulders. She shook her head to loosen the tresses a bit more. "Thank you again for chasing me down in the elevator. I'm sorry I was such a wreck. I'm afraid that I'm battling some demons from the past, and it just poured out of me." Jenna didn't mention that she had misjudged one of those demons.

"That's all right, Miss ... Wilkes, wasn't it?" Takashi guessed.

Jenna nodded. "Listen, could I borrow a pen and paper? I need to leave Doctor Sexton a note, and I'm hoping you can give it to him when he wakes up."

"Sure, hold on a sec."

After finishing at the nurse's station, Jenna returned to her Volkswagen, hoping that nobody had tracked her to the hospital and hidden bugs in her Bug. She laughed at that odd symmetry, but then realized it wasn't a laughing matter. If she were to have followed best practices, Jenna should have asked Eckhardt for a new vehicle. Embarrassing. She'd only had this car for three days, which meant she held the world record for fastest security breach in a Volkswagen Beetle.

A quiet knock at the window aroused her from her memories, pulling her back to the present, back to the peculiar transistorized sound of her car's engine. One of the guards was checking on her; she'd apparently been sitting there, windshield wipers pumping ineffectively, for longer than they expected. She signaled A-OK with her left hand, and then turned off the engine with her right, pulling out the key. She watched the rain, her fingers fiddling with the key chain for a couple more minutes, still thinking.

She couldn't have known it, but at that moment Sexton was conscious, had just finished drinking some juice, when Takashi handed him the folded note from Jenna.

Sexton fumbled for his reading glasses and dropped them on the floor. Takashi retrieved them and turned the lights up so he could read the note.

He unfolded it and held the note before his eyes for some time, utterly transfixed. Takashi found this curious, since Jenna had taken only ten seconds to write it. Sexton dropped his hand back to the mattress, still holding the note. He squeezed his eyes shut, and tears started oozing out of the corners.

He was emotionally shaken, and Takashi wondered what had upset him. His heart rate and respiration even rose moderately. She glanced down at the note: the wording was facing up. She hoped she wasn't intruding overmuch, but she bent over to see what it said. Having read it, she didn't understand Sexton's reaction, but his sobs were deep and intense.

What was so disturbing about that note? Takashi adjusted the pillow behind Sexton's head, now growing angry with Jenna. *One more stress this patient didn't need.*

Still steaming inside, the nurse gently removed the glasses from Sexton's face, folded them, and put them on his nightstand, then began drying his eyes and cheeks with a tissue. She attempted to switch the note in his hands for some Kleenex he'd soon need, but was shocked at how forcefully he held on to the note. She relented, leaving the Kleenex box on his lap.

As Takashi left the room, she continued to ponder the cryptic words the redhead had written.

I swear it WILL be drained, and if it works and they allow me to name it, I'm calling it the Sexton Effect. With gratitude, Jenna.

She snapped her cell phone shut and stepped out of the VW into the driving rain. The closest guard rushed over to extend his umbrella over her head. Jenna had the cane in her hand. He gawked at it in confusion.

"What happened to your umbrella?" he asked, pointing at it. "Half of it is missing!"

"It's a cane."

"Oh. Oh, here, sorry!" He again tried to protect her with his own umbrella. She was wearing no rain gear to speak of, just a dingy lab coat over a white pants suit.

"No, I'm okay, thanks!" she turned down the offer.

He looked at her like she was crazy. Already her hair was plastered down on her forehead, looking more black than red under the dark stormy sky. *She was going to walk nearly a half mile in this weather without an umbrella?* The guards exchanged glances in disbelief.

As she walked away, briefcase in one hand, cane swinging in the other, she let the rain, now blowing in diagonally, thoroughly soak her lab coat. It was really the only way it was ever washed. She knew she'd be a sopping human sponge once she got to the entrance, but it couldn't be helped. *One more eccentricity of mine for them to shake their heads over.* She smiled weakly and kept walking. It was invigorating.

On the fifth floor of the admin building, Bic was calling Bartleby with excitement, phone in one hand, binoculars in the other, watching her through the window facing the distant lot.

"She's finally gotten out of her car, Ron. God, what took so long? She was in it for nearly a half hour with the headlights turned off."

"Is she walking to Building F?"

"Yeah. No umbrella. As usual."

"I'll alert custodial." Bartleby was resigned to the inevitable. "They'll have to put the wet floor signs out. Again."

"Yeah, *Piso Mojado* to you too. She's got Eckhardt on her side now.

I suggest you don't chew her out or lobby me to dock her pay to cover janitors' overtime like you usually do."

"Bic, to hear you tell it, she could afford to get docked now."

Bic had to agree. Eckhardt had instructed him to wire Jenna two hundred thousand dollars and issue her a company Visa card with a credit limit five times larger than his own.

"Wait a minute," Bic said, "it looks like she's got a tire iron with her."

"She's coming to *my* building with a tire iron?"

"Looks like it."

"Does she look upset?" Bartleby panicked.

"I can't tell. Maybe you should send Bryn down to greet her."

"He's not here."

"Then buy her off with one of your chocolate bars."

"I'd rather be clubbed with the tire iron."

"Hold on, she's swinging it funny. Sorry, false alarm. It's not a tire iron," Bic apologized. "I'd better get over there. Maybe she'll let us in the lab with her. Maybe not."

"Bic, just remember. This has all got to be very new and disorienting to Jenna too. Go easy on her."

"Do I have a choice?" asked Bic. "She's the gatekeeper now."

He hung up and considered that statement. *Better her than Niles, though.* He donned his raincoat and headed for the elevator, wondering about the next twist in the Cinderella story of Doctor Jenna Angela Wilkes.

Bic thought the comparison to the fairy tale was somehow apt.

22

She saw that someone was holding the door open for her. Bartleby. Absolutely soaked, she smiled as she walked through. "Hi Ron."

"Hi Jenna. Welcome back." He looked at her with curiosity. What was with that cane?

Behind Bartleby, she saw three custodians armed with mops and buckets; yellow Danger Wet Floor signs lined the entire hallway down to the elevator, where a fourth custodian was posted.

"Expecting me?" she grinned.

"You might say that." Bartleby laughed.

Without warning, she dropped her briefcase and cane and gave him a brief hug. He cleared his throat and didn't know what to say, miffed that his shirt was now quite wet. She seemed to be a bundle of energy this morning, which made that damn cane she carried all the more incongruous.

Jenna approached the custodians sheepishly, trailing a path of water. "Please believe me that I'm sorry about this mess, and I'd clean it up myself if I had time. Honest."

They looked in her eyes and knew she truly meant it, although no one could comprehend why she made these puddles in the first place.

The older custodian was bemused. "That's okay. We were starting to miss this part of our job."

Jenna walked with Bartleby toward the elevator, a train of custodians following her, mops a-swishing. Bic entered the building moments later to witness the comical procession from behind. He called down the hallway.

"Jenna, wait up!"

Bartleby and Jenna stopped. The water pooled around her bare feet; she had taken her shoes off to avoid slipping on the tile. The custodian at the elevator started mopping around her feet, the mop head brushing against them, tickling her. She laughed.

Bartleby turned to criticize the custodian sharply. "Why don't you just wait until she's gone?"

The custodian backed away, clearly stung by the reprimand.

Jenna quickly intervened. "It's okay, Ron. I thought it was funny. He's just doing his job."

"I don't think Bic included this kind of thing in his job description, Jenna." But Bartleby was smiling again. A moment later Bic had caught up to them.

"Good morning, Doctor Johanssen," Jenna said. "I'm glad to be back."

"Good to see you too, Jenna," Bic beamed, hoping that they'd finally get some answers and make some progress on this project. But he had to admit he was also pleased to see her. The lab wasn't the same without this eccentric redhead stirring things up with her antics. *That's a stupid cliché,* he caught himself. *In truth, she drove us crazy.*

"Can we enter the lab with you?" Bic asked as the elevator doors closed on the three of them and the custodian, who continued to mop around their feet. The cadence of water dripping off Jenna's clothing punctuated the ensuing silence. Bic glanced at Bartleby's wet shirt. *God, I swear this guy wakes up sweating,* he thought.

"I have a few things I need to do by myself," Jenna finally replied. "Give me a half an hour and I'll let you two in. Is that okay?"

"Sure, that's great. Get yourself settled, back in the swing of things," Bic replied.

The four of them walked toward the lab door. The guards parted for her, the taller one unlocking the new mag seals that fortified the original passkey system.

Jenna shocked Bic with her next instruction. "Guards, the custodian can come in. Doctor Johanssen and Doctor Bartleby can come in later once I give the word."

The custodian took this in stride, unaware of the shock on Bic's face.

"What's this all about?" asked Bic.

"I'm still dripping," she replied.

"Oh, he can come in and we can't?"

Bartleby grabbed Bic's arm. "Give her some space, Bic. I'm sure it's not personal. It's not as if Gomez here is a spy." The custodian was no such thing, but planting that thought only made it harder to shake.

Bic quickly recognized his overreaction. "Sorry, Jenna, it's just that it feels like we've waited an eternity to get you back in there. A half-hour wait is fine."

Jenna suddenly laughed in his face, then apologized in embarrassment, pointing to the mop sliding between her feet. "Sorry, he tickled me again."

Bic heard the nearest guard snigger at the sopping wet redhead being shadowed by the aggressive mop wrangler.

Bic let it go and addressed Jenna. "Okay, I'll be in Ron's office. Buzz us when you're ready for us to come back."

"Okay." Jenna was oblivious to Bic's angst over Gomez. To her, requesting custodial help was reasonable.

The door closed behind her and the custodian. He kept mopping as she walked up to her "old" desk (had it really been that long?). Jenna set the briefcase down and opened it, laying the cane down next to it.

She called out to the custodian. "In a few minutes I'm going to need to turn the lights off in the lab. Do you mind just waiting in here with me until I can turn them back on?"

"Sure, sure, I can wait. You need to do something in the dark?"

"Yeah, for a little bit. It's an experiment."

"Sure, you tell me when. I'll turn off the lights for you."

"Thank you. Your name was Gomez, right?"

"Yes. Gomez Mejia."

"Thank you, Gomez. I'm Jenna."

He smiled at her, then sniffed the air, realizing that the trashcans hadn't been emptied for weeks, smelling of food that had spoiled. "I'm going to bag the trash, okay? Then I'll mop some more for you."

"That's fine, Gomez. I need to focus on something now. Do what you need to do."

The physical resemblance between Gomez and Professor Hernandez pricked her conscience. She wondered if her old advisor was aware of what was going on here in Building F. Jenna knew that Hernandez worked at CryoMax Livermore, in the west side enclave, but she never had the guts to visit him, assuming he'd want nothing more to do with her. She wasn't sure she wanted anything more to do with him either.

She pulled a box out of her briefcase and opened it—special auto-sensing night vision goggles that Eckhardt had given her. She turned to regard the isolator, noticing the diagonal area where someone had snapped off the fake convection tubes.

She knew only Eckhardt had been in this lab since it had been sealed.

Jenna saw where the chairman had laid the tubes on the adjacent table, immediately noticing the shape they had formed: the letter J. She stepped up to the table and ran her fingers over the tubes. Grasping their significance, she collected them and intercepted Gomez.

"Throw these away too." She dumped the tubes into the plastic bag he held open for her. "I won't need them anymore." As she turned to walk back to the desk, her bare feet padding more quietly as less water dripped off of her, she was thinking about her next move.

Time to put the worm on the hook.

She paused at her desk, staring hard at the cane she'd laid on it, her jaw muscles unconsciously flexing and tightening. Jenna knew the inner core was sealed from the outside world by an incredibly massive wall of titanium about a foot thick. Eckhardt had shown her how to burst a soap bubble on this cane. The bubble was meant to represent the core. How could you possibly get the cane into the right position to touch the core behind that solid titanium?

She carefully placed the night vision goggles over her head, turned them on, and approached the isolator.

In Bartleby's office, Bic and Bartleby were watching Jenna on closed circuit TV.

"What's that she's wearing?" asked Bartleby.

"I've got no idea." Then it dawned on Bic. "Those are night vision goggles. We're not going to see a thing! Damn it!"

Jenna pulled a special marker out of her lab coat and knelt in front of the isolator, outlining the tube-free region Eckhardt had made. She regarded the diagonal rectangle she had just drawn, satisfied that she'd be able to see the special ink in the dark. It was time.

She placed her right hand on the cane lying on the desk, ascertained the position of the key objects she'd be working with in the dark, and called out to the custodian.

"Gomez, could you go ahead and turn the lights off now? And please, don't turn them on until I say so. It would ruin the experiment."

"Okay, I'll turn them off for you."

Three seconds later, one floor above Jenna, two men began cursing up a storm as their video screen went blank. Once their tirade abated, the one with the blonde unibrow looked at his balding, older compatriot.

"She might as well have let us in there. We don't have any night vision goggles."

"Nice."

Viewed through the goggles, only two things were visible: the cane and the diagonal "slot" drawn on the isolator. Everything else was in utter darkness. It was surreal in the extreme, but Jenna was focused and didn't consider the oddity of what she was doing, nor could she know how her associates upstairs were reacting.

She felt for the top edge of the titanium cube with her left hand; finding it, she kept herself positioned. Holding on to the isolator was somehow comforting in the dark, despite its being cold and hard. A safe, solid anchor, anyway.

A thought flitted across her mind. *Safe?* Standing here barefoot in a puddle of water with eight kilowatts at high amperage possibly arcing through the titanium, or the cane, or both, to send a fatal electrical current through her heart? Had Eckhardt figured on her using the cane while soaked with water?

She gripped the cane, thinking about the story of the sorcerer's apprentice. Mickey Mouse had swiped his master's enchanted hat; *she* had a cane and night vision goggles. Would she unleash something that made Mickey's descent down the maelstrom—*death by broomstick*—pale in comparison?

But the scientist in her wasn't having any of it. She knew there was only one way to get the end of the cane to touch the core, and that was for the cane to go through the titanium.

This isolator, the largest one constructed to her specifications, weighed just over three tons and required a massive steel frame to support it, replete with forklift anchors and custom casters for moving it.

But going *through* the titanium? A three-ton block of it?

In the dark, two voices in her mind were screaming contradictory things at her. One voice considered only what her left hand told her about the irrevocable solidity of the isolator. The other voice considered what her right hand told her about the cane that, she just knew, *had* to be able to get through to the core somehow.

Because her hand covered up its soft glow at the point where she was gripping it, the cane appeared to be in two pieces. She lined it up, hook-end first, with the diagonal rectangle, like aligning a key with the slot of a keyhole. She bit her lip in concentration.

Jenna first touched the cane lightly to the region Eckhardt had cleared off, orienting the hook diagonally while keeping the shaft parallel to the ground. No go: the cane bumped hard, stopping abruptly at the surface. Her heart sank: the titanium *was* impenetrable.

She pushed a bit harder just to see, and was shocked to feel the titanium give a little, like a hard rubber. She swallowed and pushed harder. It went in an inch. *Unbelievable.* She wasn't even breathing as she inched the cane farther in. It took some force to get it to go, as if pushing it through sand, as if nature were resisting this interpenetration but only modestly.

And nobody in the world is seeing this, she thought. She rubbed one foot over another to deal with a sudden itch that arose, glad she had kept one hand on the isolator to steady herself, then pushed the cane two feet farther in.

She knew from its depth that the cane had passed over the core. The next step was to rotate the cane to get the "hook" centered, and then pull the cane back out a few inches until the hook penetrated the core.

If *penetrated* was even the right word for anything touching the core. Because few people knew what Jenna had actually captured inside this black cube of titanium. Ironically, what she had captured was clearly marked in big block letters on the isolator itself, right on the label glued to it. To her knowledge, only Eckhardt, Sexton, and she knew how literally accurate her label was.

Perhaps the ink on the label had enough trace fluorescent dye in it to be visible through the goggles. She looked upward and strained to see. It was faint but legible.

The label read simply 11:08 AM 8/2/2025.

Hidden in plain sight, she thought. Because inside this core, it was, and always would be, about 11:00 AM on that date, the date she threw the switch to turn it on. That's when the core had instantaneously sliced off a piece of the universe and frozen it in time while the rest of the world moved on.

Except that the rest of the universe noticed something was missing. The mass, the energy, in that spherical volume, were missing. And the universe of inviolable conservation laws, the everyday universe that kept its appointed rounds with the sweep of the world's clocks, watches, and chronometers, triggered its own version of double-entry bookkeeping to compensate for the hole Jenna had gouged out of the fabric of reality. It did this by adding 8,132 joules of energy debit to balance each complementary energy credit with every single tick of the clock. Exactly 8.132 kilowatts for this size core. Like money in the bank. It was the way the cosmos took back its pound of flesh.

And Jenna was about to do what modern science would have regarded as utterly impossible. She was about to make a withdrawal from that energy account, tearing it out of nature's hands across the pages of nothing less than the calendar itself. With an old man's cane. In the dark. Barefoot. In a puddle of water. It was absolutely insane.

Of course she knew this to be no ordinary cane. Despite its unexpected shape (*why did Eckhardt think this shape important?*), she knew that under its shell it embodied an elaboration of a proposal she made seven years ago, an idea she bled for, that was struck down by the dissertation committee as total crap. And here she was, holding the actual device in her hand, embedded in a three-ton block of titanium, slicing through spacetime convolutions no one else had ever conceived.

Jenna had to grip the cane with both hands to twist it around because she now had considerably less leverage to rotate it through the molasses-thick titanium.

Molasses?

Too curious to not check, she felt with her left hand around the point where the cane entered the titanium and tried to dig in with her nails. It was absolutely solid. *Astonishing.* Despite being a macroscopic structure, the cane was quantum tunneling through the titanium due to the proximity of the core's overlapped spacetime manifolds. In this darkened room, quantum theory and relativity had at last kissed after a century of failed dreams of unification, all because a young woman had dreamed dreams and seen visions.

She was now certain she had turned the cane the required forty-five degrees. Jenna didn't have to be exact—just close enough to *get the worm on the hook,* a phrase she kept repeating to herself in a fruitless effort to calm her own breathing.

She said the next words out loud, although only Gomez heard them. "This is for you, Doctor Sexton." And she pulled the cane toward her about six inches.

A low-intensity red laser beam came out of the cane and hit the far wall.

"What's that?" Gomez yelped, startled.

"It's okay, it's okay!" Jenna assured him. "That's part of the experiment."

She let go of the cane, which remained rigidly in place like the sword in the stone, only horizontally oriented. Eckhardt had enabled her to manipulate the core, extracting energy in forms other than the electricity used to ignite it. Jenna was tapping only a tiny piece of the available energy stored in the core, converting it directly to the photons composing the beam. The resulting laser differed from conventional lasers two ways: this beam would never diverge, nor would it exhibit the fluctuations known as speckle contrast.

Jenna knew the emitted photons were constrained in a tight beam on purpose. Only then was momentum conserved as the returning energy passed through the inertial frame origami she had crafted inside the core. *An exchange that literally piped energy between today's date and a small chunk of the second of August.*

Jenna now wished she had been timing how long the laser beam was emitting. The beam represented a leak—the core was slowly moving forward in time to catch up with the present so long as the cane hooked the core. Given how little energy the laser radiated, the forward time creep couldn't have been more than a few milliseconds. *There's probably no need to draw up a new label,* she thought, chuckling at her misplaced pragmatism.

Upstairs, Bic and Bartleby were all over themselves, pointing at the screen and trying to make heads or tails out of the red beam bisecting the darkness.

"What the hell is that? What's going on?"

"I don't know. Is that coming out of the isolator?"

"I think so. Wasn't it around that position before everything went dark?"

"Damn it."

Back in the dark, Jenna pushed the cane deeper into the isolator, which caused the red laser to disappear as the hook was pulled back out of the worm. She twisted the opposite direction this time, again with both hands, then pulled hard to ease the cane back out of the metal, choosing a wide stance to prevent falling backward when it came free.

Once Eckhardt's cane was out and safely in her hand, she reached down to feel the titanium again. The surface was solid with no hint of an opening. The only clue left behind of the cane's penetration was rainwater clinging to the isolator, water that peeled off the cane during insertion. She hastily dried the spot with a still-moist sleeve and made her way back to the desk, laying the cane down gently. Jenna slowly ran her fingers over the cane to remind herself it was real, that she hadn't imagined what had just transpired. She could hear herself breathing hard, so hard her lungs ached. She had no idea she'd been doing that the entire time.

Finally taking off her goggles, she called for Gomez to turn the lights back on.

The custodian was happy to see once more, although both of them winced at the sudden brightness. The darkness had bugged Gomez, but not as much as seeing the laser firing across to the far wall against the pitch-black background.

He lumbered around the table to toss the trash bag by the door and then resumed his mop duty where Jenna was working. When he realized that she was about to sit down, he stopped her. "Wait, I'll get a towel," he offered.

"Thank you, Gomez."

He was back momentarily with a towel collected from the lab's supply closet, draping it carefully over her lab chair. He even picked up her shoes and dried them. While he plugged away, she stood wordlessly in front of her briefcase with a faraway look in her eyes. If her brain had had any meters attached to it, they would have been pinned, pegged, and snapped off.

She asked Gomez to call one of the guards in while on his way out and settled herself in her chair. Jenna rolled it back to her briefcase, which she closed after slipping the goggles inside. She rotated around to face the main door.

When the guard entered the lab a few moments later, she told him to let Dr. Johanssen and Dr. Bartleby in once they arrived.

"They're already here," he explained.

She nodded, then took off her glasses, pocketing them with care.

The two men all but ran up to her. There she sat, one leg crossed over the other, wiping some lab floor dirt off her left foot with the towel.

Bic couldn't get the words out fast enough. "Jenna, what the hell just happened in here?"

She looked up innocently, her green eyes sparkling, and brightly answered:

"Nothing."

23

The three knocks at the door were brisk and decisive. Riesen, seated at his desk, didn't look up from his laptop as he responded. "Come in. It's not locked."

General Stall walked through, wearing his Class A uniform.

Riesen glanced up and rose immediately, throwing a crisp salute. "Sir!" *Stall never comes here,* he thought. *I always go to him. Why isn't he wearing his BDUs?*

"Colonel," Stall acknowledged, returning the salute, then bidding Riesen to be seated.

Riesen was openly surprised at the visit. "I thought you were out of town, General."

"I was. Got back just now. A short trip." Stall removed his cap and sat down across from Riesen, who closed his laptop to give Stall his full attention.

Stall was direct. "William, I want to check with you on the situation with Doctor Zilcher out at the power station. Have you come up with a way to know what he's doing without him seeing us?"

"No."

"So we're still screwed."

"Not exactly. We've got him under surveillance. My two best guys have been on him for a couple of days already."

General Stall shook his head. "So you're saying he's going to catch on sooner or later."

"More sooner than later. In fact, he caught on pretty quickly, you might say." Then Riesen explained to Stall what he had done to confound Bryn Zilcher's countermeasures.

Stall listened intently, then spoke gravely to Riesen. "Son, if you were still working for General Melliton, he'd have busted you down to buck private for violating every military protocol in the book." The general stared at Riesen. Riesen licked his lips, wondering if he'd gone too far.

"Good thing I'm not General Melliton." Stall rubbed his chin, a bemused look crossing his face. "I, for one, like creative solutions. And paybacks. But next time, tell me first."

Relieved, Riesen nodded. "Yes sir."

Stall leaned forward in his chair. "So, tell me, have your guys Hawkeye and Trapper John come up with anything?"

"Yeah, Zilcher has set up a series of bypasses and voltage dividers inside the station. He can't do anything without us knowing. And my two boys pretty much don't do anything without Zilcher knowing. But it seems a fair price to pay for the information we need."

"So who's paying for their beer?"

"That's classified." Riesen tried to hold his poker face for as long as he could.

General Stall nodded with a faint smile. He briefly indulged his acute sense of sarcasm.

"That, Colonel, is probably the only part of this operation that isn't completely exposed naked for the whole damn human race to see."

"I believe it's important to keep a little bit of mystery in every operation," Riesen shot back. "Can I ask, by the way, where you've been? Your secretary didn't even know."

"I guess you can say I talked to my counterpart."

Riesen understood that Stall meant Eckhardt and was stunned that a meeting had happened. "Face to face, General?"

"It seemed to make sense, Will."

"Do you think he'll make sure this stuff doesn't fall into the wrong hands?"

Wrong hands. Stall now questioned whether that idea had universal validity. It was clear that nuclear power falling into Soviet hands and proliferating beyond that was a bad idea, given mankind's penchant for corrupting things. Scientific knowledge could always be parlayed into things harmful to people. Stall had always assumed that knowledge was essentially neutral, that how something was used made all the difference.

"William, I don't think this thing can fall into the wrong hands."

"Eckhardt assured you of this?"

Stall frowned at Riesen's open mention of that name in the bugged office. The damage now done, he went forward, figuring the Joint Chiefs would soon confront him with a recording of this conversation.

"He can't assure anybody of anything," Stall replied.

"Well, then, *we* will have to take steps to ensure that."

"Colonel, I already told you it *can't* fall into the wrong hands. It would be impossible. It doesn't need to be protected, although I'd bet my bottom dollar that we're going to spend billions turning it into a political football anyway."

Riesen was astonished at what Stall was saying. "Do you trust Eckhardt, sir?"

"Yes."

"Is he going to keep this technology secure?"

"No."

"I'm afraid I don't understand."

General Stall slowly polished the brow of his cap with his right sleeve, answering without looking up.

"When science discovers some application of physical law, people come at it with different agendas, different moral standards, and develop something beneficial or dangerous out of it. Weapons, say, which can be used for good to defend against aggression, or which can wreak havoc on the innocent. Sorry for that academy lesson on doctrine, you already know all that, but trust me when I tell you that if I thought what Cryo-Max was doing only involved a new application of natural law, I'd be on board with you one hundred percent. But this situation is different."

"How can that be? This is a scientific matter from the get-go, sir."

"That's how I viewed it too, Colonel. But I've since changed my mind."

Riesen was both confused and concerned.

Stall looked back up at him, blue eyes as intense as ever. "In short, Colonel, since time immemorial mankind has been able to manipulate physical law to overturn moral order, moral law, enabling evil and extending its reach. A bigger bomb, a longer missile trajectory, a more poisonous gas."

"How is this any different?"

"I just said it. People manipulate natural law to undermine moral law, ultimate law. But Eckhardt believes Doctor Wilkes is going to peel away the last layer of natural law to expose something more fundamental, some bedrock underneath the sand. I'd guess he'd call it the raw face of ultimate moral law. And you can't manipulate that moral law to undermine moral law. It can't contradict itself. It's an impossibility."

"With all due respect, sir, you're not making much sense." Riesen felt Stall was blurring some important distinctions. "I don't want to question your allegiance," Riesen glanced at the medals on Stall's chest, "but I don't think we can take *any* chances, especially not based on some kind of philosophical mumbo-jumbo. Sir."

Riesen was bewildered. This entire discussion was uncharacteristic of the general. He only talked up a streak like this during the quarterly prayer breakfasts which bored Riesen to tears, but which he attended out of deference to his superior.

Stall resumed his explanation. "I'm not going to pretend this is easy to digest. As for myself, literally up until the time I was pulling up in the parking lot here, I would have told you that anyone saying what I've just told you had lost it. So ..." he said, rising from the chair, "give it time to sink in. Who said everything had to be instantly understandable, anyway? Where is *that* written?"

Cap back in position, Stall reached for the door, then turned to consider the black wrought-iron sculpture on top of Riesen's classified material file cabinet.

"See that statue, Colonel?" he pointed at it.

"Yes sir?"

"Something for you to consider, if I'm not overstepping my bounds. Your statue: there's a defect in it. It shows the wrong person doing all the work." He closed the door behind him.

Riesen looked across at the file cabinet, uncomprehending.

"What, that statue of Atlas holding up the earth?"

24

Today was Friday, Jenna's third day back. All but one of the things she had set in motion for today would be done according to plan. It would look like any other workday, not that this meant a lot. She knew her plan would set off a host of nasty repercussions, but she had her reasons for going down this path.

Jenna was forthcoming with Bartleby and Bic, although she wouldn't discuss what she had done in the dark. Further interrogation was fruitless. She was as tight-lipped now as she was loose-lipped when she joined the company.

She was surprised both men had correctly speculated that time itself was stopped inside the core, an assertion they communicated in longhand to her. Bartleby had done the heavy lifting, solving the puzzle under Bic's prodding. She was pleased Bartleby was following in her footsteps, even if she wasn't wearing shoes at the time she made some of those tracks.

The expected message came in from the shipping dock. A large crate and several smaller boxes from General Dynamics had arrived for Jenna. They would need to be moved by hydraulic dolly up to the second floor using the special elevator for heavy loads. She asked for the boxes to be sent up. When the men from General Dynamics arrived upstairs, the guards had to open both doors to get the crates and boxes through the entryway. Bic and Bartleby watched with interest on the video feed in Bartleby's third floor office.

"Do you know what she's bringing in?" asked Bic.

"Yeah, she needs some metrology equipment."

"Must be heavy stuff. Those guys are following the reinforced flooring marks."

Bartleby's phone rang. It was Jenna.

"Ron, can you and Bic come down right away?" she asked politely. "It's important."

"Be right down!" said Bartleby. "Bic's right here with me."

They were headed down in the elevator when the power went off, sinking them in darkness.

"What the hell?" Bic groped for the faintly lit emergency phone and raised the operator, who found herself inundated in a flurry of calls.

"I'm sorry, Doctor Johanssen, there's a power failure throughout most of the building. We'll get you out of the elevator as soon as power's restored. If necessary, we'll take you out through the shaft or crank the car down manually."

Bic and Bartleby waited in the darkness for about two minutes before the lights came back on and the control panel booted, resetting itself. Bic pressed the button for the second floor.

When they arrived at the isolator lab, they saw the General Dynamics techs pushing their boxes back out the door while Jenna excoriated them.

"I expect a hefty discount for having to wait an extra two days for you to get your act together," she raged.

One of the engineers was wringing his hands apologetically, trying to make whatever mistake had occurred right. "Look, I don't know how your rush PO got misinterpreted," he pleaded. "We'll try to get the right caliber tube in here on Monday. I'll call the main office right now and make sure you get what you ordered."

"Please do," she insisted. "Your guy Nelson promised these to me for this morning. I was expecting to get these units calibrated and online this afternoon, and now my entire schedule is pushed out again. I thought General Dynamics of all people knew what they were doing."

The poor man was beside himself and ordered his coworkers to remove the faulty items on the double.

After the guards had closed the doors and Jenna had settled down, Bic and Bartleby approached her.

"Sorry we were late," Bic began, "but we got stuck in the elevator during the power failure."

"Yeah, it hit us here too. That spooked everybody in here." Jenna turned around to go back to the isolator.

"Why did you ask us down?" Bartleby wanted to know.

"I wanted you here for the unpacking of those units, to explain how I wanted them set up, but then I saw the freight manifest was screwed up. Please insist on a discount because I'll be too busy to deal with it. Blame General Dynamics for your coming down for nothing."

When the two men returned to Bartleby's office, they sat down to collect their thoughts. Bartleby punched the video button to rewind what had happened in the lab downstairs. As the digital frames rewound, all seemed to be in order. The screen winked out. He bent over to tap on the monitor, but the image came back on before he touched it.

"Hmmm …" Bartleby wondered.

"What?"

"Oh, right. That would have been when the power failure hit the building."

Bic was still radiating incomprehension, so Bartleby elaborated.

"There are a couple of minutes of black when the lights were out and the camera's backup batteries took over."

"Oh, yeah, right." Bic was satisfied with the explanation.

But something in the back of Bartleby's mind, on the edge of awareness, was trying to call attention to a parallel circumstance that, had he grasped its significance, would have changed his assessment. This was not the first time the lab's lights had been turned out this week.

Jenna jotted down a few more notes—handwritten, as Eckhardt insisted. It was too easy for spies to electronically snag what she entered on a digiscreen or laptop. She laid down the notepad and approached the isolator, reaching up to feel along its top edge.

It feels just like the real one, she thought. *You can hardly tell it's a fake made out of aluminum.*

No one would expect an isolator to be moved, not only because of its size and weight but because of the supposition they needed considerable power to run. But *her* isolators didn't need to be plugged in once started, and Jenna decided to leverage that unexploited portability.

Driving away from the loading dock, the General Dynamics truck departed CryoMax about two tons heavier than when it arrived. It was manned by Eckhardt's people, all of whom had night vision goggles stuffed into their utility pockets. Jenna's six isolators were safely on board, to be dropped off in the specific locations she had directed. Six isolators with hollow cores each uniquely preserving a different, frozen piece of yesterday.

The big one was going to her home. She was hoping its weight wouldn't crack the foundation under her living room.

She grinned, remembering how Eckhardt had dubbed her little heist Operation House Call. Eckhardt was impressed how she had thought out every detail of the plan herself. He only changed one thing—Jenna had wanted to use TRW, not General Dynamics, to botch her order.

"Oh no you don't," Eckhardt quipped, "I own stock in TRW."

The elaborate plan was communicated via handwritten notes exchanged in the plane, the safest way to communicate anything sensitive. This caper qualified.

Jenna worried how haggard Eckhardt seemed to appear. He didn't rise to greet her when she boarded, nor when she disembarked. Moreover, he had a looming boardroom battle with Niles that couldn't be postponed indefinitely.

Niles Emmerich. How would he react to Operation House Call?

I hope Mr. Emmerich doesn't get too mad at me about this, Jenna thought. *That guy has major temper issues.*

She knew that Niles had canceled a Boston meeting with Eckhardt to see what she was up to on the West Coast. This was the last time Jenna could run interference for Eckhardt now that she had raided the lab and would go AWOL shortly. She hoped Eckhardt would prevail in that corporate struggle.

Jenna slid both hands along the top of the black aluminum fake, precision-simulated down to the faux convection tubes glued onto its surface. It wasn't a perfect copy because of Eckhardt's sense of humor. The big label bearing the ignition date of the core had been changed to read midnight of January 1, 1980, what programmers consider the presumed dawn of time for computing. She relished the irony of the temporal reference.

Then she noticed something else. Underneath the date, Eckhardt had added the word PLACEBO in smaller type. She couldn't help but smile at that discovery and addressed the isolator mock-formally in unspoken words.

Well, Mister Bogus Isolator, no one's gonna push a cane into your innards anytime soon. I'd love to see them try it, though. Then they'd know how it feels to bang your head against the wall for years.

The elaborate ruse would only last a few hours. She herself was going to expose it by calling Dr. Johanssen and informing him she wasn't returning to the lab on Monday. They could have their parking lot back. All the guards would be decamping because the only isolators remaining were fakes swapped in under their noses.

As Jenna saw it, she needed more elbow room and less scrutiny than the lab could offer. Revealing the scam would seem pointless, but Jenna knew what she was doing. She was manipulating the chessboard to create the impression she made a grave tactical error, knowing full well how admitting to the swap would ultimately work to her advantage.

Several hours later, Bic received that call from her. Jenna had hung up before he could answer her a word. He just stood there, cell phone still glued to his ear, as if he had heard a parent had died.

Bartleby recognized from Bic's expression that something had gone awry. "What? What'd she tell you?"

Bic looked at Bartleby. "I'll be damned."

25

Bryn was busy deep inside the power station, Ragman keeping with him every step of the way, shooting video constantly. Bryn figured this was how nature videographers got their shots: the herds simply get used to an intruder's presence in their midst.

He *had* gotten used to these pests. In fact, at meal times, Captain Boudreaux and Captain Green generously provided the food and brew, presumably unspiked, and they all three spoke amicably, if somewhat sophomorically when the soldiers pushed the shtick.

Only when Bryn went back inside the station did their adversarial relationship resurface. Real life mirrored a Warner Brothers cartoon—sheepdog and wolf locked into a universe where civility and hostility were gated by the blowing of a time-clock whistle—except that Bryn's tormenters maintained the hip demeanor tirelessly. Bryn figured this was a new way the Pentagon had hit upon to wear down surveillance targets.

Richard and Bryn both heard Mike call out to them. "Woohoo, I hope you boys brushed your teeth this morning. We've got company for lunch."

Bryn didn't welcome that news. *A third army lug nut getting in my face? Perfect.* He unfolded stiffly from his hunched-over position working on the voltage divider and stretched his back, which cracked twice. "Has your superior officer come out to visit the station, Ragman?"

"You don't brush your teeth for them, Bryn. You're ignorant, you civvies are. You know, enlisting in the service might do you a world of good. Look at me, being all I can be!"

Bryn regarded Ragster standing there with his arms spread wide, a beer in one hand, video camera in the other, sandals, cut-offs, a torn Led Zeppelin T-shirt, sunglasses, an admittedly decent tan, and an ugly straw hat.

"Can't fathom why I haven't already busted their doors down," Bryn said. He dusted his hands on his jeans. "Isn't it early for lunch?"

"Can't be. If it's not too early for beer, it's not too early for lunch." Richard took a hit from the beer bottle, gargled, spit it out, mumbled something about that having to do, then put down the camera carefully and trudged out. "Come on, let's not keep our guest waiting."

As they walked, Bryn turned serious. "Are you expecting anyone?"

"Honestly, no," Richard replied. "I only know one thing about our guest, based on what Mike said."

As they were about to round the corner and come out into the eating area, Bryn asked, "What's that one thing?"

Richard threw the beer bottle far into the distant brush. "Our guest doesn't have a Y chromosome."

And then Bryn saw her.

The redhead seated at the table with Mike pouring her a diet soda. He couldn't believe his eyes.

Richard, of course, reacted predictably.

"Not bad, not bad at all. I must say, it's nice to know that *somebody* drinks something other than beer around here. I told Mike buying those sodas was a waste of good beer money, but I stand corrected. This is worth giving up an extra six-pack for." He elbowed Bryn in the ribs, causing him to cough several times.

"Dear lady," said Richard, approaching Jenna with arms outstretched in welcome, "Welcome to our crib. I'm Rag ..."

"I already told her who you were," hissed Mike, still maintaining the outrageous shtick.

"She needs to hear it from me, Mike. Let's try again. I am the esteemed Ragman, you've already met Mike, my valet, and this here," he slapped Bryn on the back, "is Mark."

"Mark?" Jenna asked, unhappy to recognize Bryn. "Trust me, I don't think his name is Mark."

"Not his name, his definition. He's the mark that we're spying on. His name's immaterial."

Bryn interjected quickly before Mike could speak. "Don't say it, Mike. Don't turn every conversation into a Who's on First freak-out."

"Wha?" Mike wailed. "What was I gonna say?"

"You were going to say something like *I didn't know his name was*

Immaterial, making a smart-ass play on words."

"No I wasn't. I was going to say your name was Bryn."

"No way you were."

"Uh huh!"

"Really?"

Richard broke in. "Really, Mike, you weren't going to say his name is Immaterial?"

"No ... well, maybe. Yes. Okay, yes."

Bryn addressed Jenna directly, ignoring the other two, exasperation in his eyes. "It never stops with these two idiots! Day and night!"

Jenna reached up and touched Mike by the arm. "Before I sit down and eat with you men, can I speak with Bryn alone, please?"

"Sorry," Mike said in all seriousness. "Not without authorization. We're to shadow Zilcher anywhere near the power chain to the dam."

"Can you get authorization?" she asked.

It was a question Mike didn't expect. He looked at Richard, who shrugged.

"Miss, we can try," Mike replied. "I'll be right back. The com center's inside the truck. Just wait here at the table. Richard, why don't you adjust the umbrella to keep the sun out of her face?"

Richard reached out and cranked the umbrella over, which squealed and complained, causing jackrabbits nearing the edge of the camp to bolt away. He sat down next to Jenna and spoke seriously with her.

"I've never met you, miss," he began, "But I know a certain redhead is supposed to play a part in all this. I suspect that's you. You're Doctor Jenna Wilkes, yes?"

She nodded. She'd already told his partner who she was earlier.

"Why are you here?" Richard pressed.

She didn't answer him.

"Did you come to see Bryn?" he asked.

"No. I didn't know he was here, and had I known, I probably would not have come."

Richard looked sarcastically at Bryn. "See, Bryn, you're a stinkin' buzzkill. Driving all the ladies away. Jeez. Then who'd there be to drink all this soda?"

Bryn ignored the wearisome comedy routine. He was about to say something when Mike popped his head out of the truck's rear door.

"Colonel says it's fine," Mike called. "They can take a walk out there in the brush and talk privately, but not inside the power station." He sprinted back toward them, hurdling over the ice chest and settling down at the table, adding a spin to what he had just said. "Now, mind you, Colonel gave *permission*, meaning it *could* happen, but I'm in command of this detail, so I'm adding a condition before I let you two disappear."

"What?" demanded Bryn flatly.

"Keep it quick. I'm starting the burgers."

The unlikely pair walked out about two hundred yards in silence, Jenna moderately angry and resentful, Bryn unhappy yet mystified by her presence.

She pulled up short. "Bryn, what are you doing out here?" she demanded.

"Same thing you were doing back at CryoMax."

"I don't think so. I wasn't there doing your uncle's self-serving bidding."

Bryn let that sink in. She was right, but he refused to give her the upper hand. "Jenna, you do know what I did in the maintenance room, right?"

"Sure."

"I came up with that all on my own," he explained. "I wasn't doing Niles's bidding there."

"Except that I came up with that seven years ago. It was one of eighteen tests I had written into my dissertation. Where were you?" She was getting angrier, starting to see Bryn as part and parcel of the second darkest episode of her life.

Bryn's shoulders slumped. He had overheard Ron Bartleby talk some about Jenna's past, not that he had the whole picture. But he recognized that he had to treat her more gingerly until he could figure out what was going on.

"Jenna, let's walk and talk. I think better when I'm walking." He took a few steps forward, but she didn't follow, but just looked at him expectantly.

He figured it out. "You want an answer, don't you?"

She nodded.

He sighed. "Okay, you're right, Jenna. You came up with these tests and got absolutely killed for it. I came up with same tests seven years later and got attaboys and backslaps by the CryoMax board. The world's not fair, but you move on. You want to keep reliving your doctoral testing season over and over again, like you're stuck frozen in those two weeks forever?"

She started to answer and couldn't. Something he had just said resonated with her. She started walking by him slowly, and he sensed that she had agreed to walk with him after all. But they again walked only in silence for dozens of yards.

She spoke first. "I have absolutely no reason to trust you, Bryn. None. From the first day you showed up in the lab, I had to protect my work from you."

"Must be nice having work worth protecting," he grumbled. "I was the junior researcher, and you gave me nothing worthwhile to do. I ended up getting crumbs from the table out of Bartleby, if I was lucky."

"You were hired to just do incremental enhancements to the existing product line. What did you expect?"

"Wasn't that what you were hired for too?" he pointed out.

Jenna winced. At CryoMax she had worked on unauthorized material constantly, choosing to work on isolators because her project could be disguised as one. She spent months learning how to make something look and behave like a cryogenic isolator when it wasn't.

"Okay, Bryn, you've got me there. I admit spending more time on my side research project than on my chartered task."

"I'd say you've never put in an honest day's work at CryoMax, Doctor Wilkes. Small wonder Niles was going to give you your walking papers," he scoffed. "On the other hand, some good is obviously coming out of this for CryoMax. But I suggest you consider your own hypocrisy before accusing me concerning who—uh, whom—I work for. At least I give my employer what he's actually paying for."

"Ron was supporting my work. So was Bic."

"They could have gotten fired for it. You shouldn't be bragging about that. You should be saying that with remorse, that men with families could have lost their jobs over you and your damn wild goose chases."

"Jackass, *I caught the wild goose*!" She was steamed at him.

But Bryn would not relent. "Jenna, you're nothing but a rebel, pure and simple. Never did what your advisor at Stanford said. Never did what Bartleby asked you to do. Johanssen got caught doctoring your evals, and now Niles has got him by ..."

"Stop! Stop it!" Her face was red with embarrassment, anger, and other emotions she knew not what. She was seeing Professor Hernandez in Bryn right at this moment.

"Answer me this," continued Bryn more quietly. "Have I said *anything* right now that isn't completely true?"

She couldn't answer him.

Bryn was disgusted with her sanctimonious attitude. "Fine. Let's walk back. I think I've said my piece, and you've said yours. I guess that's all that can be hoped for between us."

He turned to walk back. She waited about twenty seconds, then did the same, walking about ten yards behind him the entire way.

Which was *not* lost on Richard and Mike. Richard pointed a forefinger toward the approaching figures; his other fingers were wrapped around another beer.

"Mike, I hate it when I'm right. I told Brynster there that he was a buzzkill for da ladies, and looky what we got here."

Mike regarded the scene. "Well, Rag, maybe they exchanged Middle East-type wedding vows and she's following him like a good submissive wife."

On hearing that, Richard popped open the ice chest and pulled out as many beers as he could hold in his arms. "I'll bet you this much beer you're wrong!"

"That's my ice chest you grabbed those out of."

"Picky picky. Hey, here they come. Are those burgs ready?"

Mike went up on tippy-toe. "Hard to tell. I'd better check. I think Doctor Wilkes needs a refill on her drink. She'll probably be thirsty."

A minute later, Bryn and Jenna sat opposite each other with Richard and Mike on either side of them, the burgers all served up. Everyone began eating but Jenna, who hadn't had anything to drink either since Richard refilled her glass.

"Aren't you going to eat?" Richard asked.

"I don't belong at CryoMax," she said flatly to Bryn. "Never did."

Question marks flew across his face. He wasn't sure what she was saying. Mike and Richard looked across at each other—they could sense the conversation veering into the ditch.

"I thought I belonged at Stanford, but I didn't even belong there," she continued. "I come out here, and I see you hijacking my ideas. And you two guys," looking at Richard and then Mike, "are trying to steal from the guy stealing from me. I'm the little fish being eaten by a medium fish being eaten by a big fish being eaten by Godzilla. Bottom line, I'm at the bottom of the food chain, and all three of you are here to pick my bones clean, and I've absolutely had it up to *here* with this crap!"

She touched her right hand to her forehead at the word *here* to show how fed up she was. The two captains immediately saluted back, breaking her concentration.

Jenna pushed away from the table and marched out of sight behind the truck.

Mike and Richard huddled and whispered in front of Bryn.

"Think she'll come back?" Mike asked Richard.

"I'll bet you that armful of beer I had that she won't."

"I told you, that was my beer."

Bryn went after her. He reached her just as she closed the car door and was firing up the engine. He pointed at his watch and raised his forefinger vertically: he just wanted one minute.

She didn't look angry anymore, but beaten up, vulnerable. He signaled for her to lower her window.

She did so without enthusiasm. "What?" she asked.

"I just wanted to tell you that, one, I'm sorry, and two, I think you're a hell of a scientist. That's all."

"Bryn, why won't you leave this power station and get back to what you're supposed to be doing at CryoMax?"

"This *is* what I'm supposed to be doing. And you don't own this power station, the state of California does. It's on public land, it's leased by CryoMax and jointly co-managed by us and the state, which means I have every right to be here, and so do those two goons who keep burning my cheeseburgers. What makes you think *you* own this power station?"

"I *don't* own it, and what's more, I don't even need it!"

"Then why are you here, Jenna?"

"I can't tell you that."

"Can't or won't?"

"Both."

"Same old Jenna." Bryn threw his hands up in disgust and stalked away.

She put the car in reverse and backed out, then moved onto the road to leave the station. A minute later her cell phone rang. It was Bryn's number. She picked it up.

"What?"

It turned out not to be Bryn.

"Good lady, I've confiscated that cad's cell phone to let you know you don't want to miss today's hibachi special. In fact, I will banish said cad so you can talk to us righteous dudes in the complete comfort of our family-friendly enclave, with all the Southern Comforts of home in your disposal unit."

"Is this Ragman or Mike?" she wanted to know.

"Mike."

"Captain Boudreaux ..."

"Yes, Doctor Wilkes?"

She thought a second. "What kind of cheese do you put on your burgers?"

"Today our chef has gone pedal to the metal with jalapeño jack."

"Don't like it, too sharp."

"Ragman can pick the jalapeños out for you with his Boy Scout knife. Be nice and he'll even clean it first."

"Really. Why are you guys acting like rejects from a fraternity?"

"We *are* rejects from a fraternity."

She considered his reply and could feel the corners of her mouth turning upward.

"Good answer. I'm coming back. Bryn can stay. There'll be a small condition, but I'll come back."

She heard Mike shouting to someone in the background.

"Ha! I won the bet. Pay up. Gimme every bottle of beer that I store in my own ice chest, Ragamuffin!"

She could just make out Richard's outraged reaction.

"That's no fair, man. No fair. She's been manipulated to abandon her original plan, dude. It's not fair." And the cell phone went dead.

As she drove back to the station, those words, meant in moronic jest by Captain Green speaking through his alter ego the Ragman, kept ringing in her head. It sounded like the story of Jenna's life at Stanford. She felt the pressure of pent-up tears begin to mount, but fought them back.

Her past was a vise much easier to tighten than loosen. She gripped the steering wheel in a moment of vivid recollection of her dissertation ordeal.

It *wasn't* fair.

26

Jenna's "small condition" took some readjusting. Mike and Richard originally balked at it, calling it bogus, but when she started marching back to her Beetle, they capitulated.

"Fine," Mike conceded. "No more surfer dude talk. But it's going to be tough."

"I'm doing you a favor," she pointed out. "Once this is over, you've got to go back to wearing uniforms and yes sir, no sir, as you wish, sir. You're better off getting this crap out of your system sooner rather than later. Besides," she added with a smile, "it's not very professional, and I suspect I'm honestly not catching either of you two at your best."

It took a conscious effort for the two captains to hold their tongue. Maybe she was right. The last thing they needed was to blurt out the wrong thing to a superior officer.

Mike decided to act preemptively. "Hey, Richard, incinerate those videosticks of me, okay? I don't want one to accidentally get in front of the colonel."

"Good point." Richard then turned to Jenna. "Except I do have to disagree with *you,* miss. There is one thing where you *are* catching us at our best."

"What's that?"

"Cooking."

Bryn leaned over to Jenna. "Jenna, it boils down to a scientific equation, really. Burger equals food."

"It tastes fine." Jenna licked her fingers and looked up at Mike. "I must be really hungry, I guess."

"Hear that?" Mike chided Richard in triumph. "I win the bet. I *told* you the food would taste better when you clean the knife."

"You *lose* the bet," Rag retorted. "I didn't clean it."

Mike shrugged and turned back toward Jenna apologetically. "Excuse the clothes we're wearing, Doctor Wilkes. We had considerable freedom as to how to conduct this operation, and we were just paying back Doctor Zilcher for making us look like a monkey's uncle in Livermore."

She nodded, knowing the story and having figured as much. She finished off her soda and requested a refill, then glanced around. "Mike, how did you contact your colonel to get his permission for Doctor Zilcher and me to take a walk out there?"

"We used meteor burst technology, triple encoded," he explained. "There is no safer way to send data securely. You can't see them, but there are ultra-thin wires radially staked out around the truck to form the antenna."

"It's secure?" she asked.

"Yes."

"Absolutely secure?"

"Absolutely secure. Secure enough for the president to use, if he didn't mind typing his message rather than speaking into a mike. The system has bandwidth limitations, so voice doesn't really do well. But short messages, highly compressed, are its strong point."

"Interesting."

Her mind was working hard. Bryn knew this because he'd known her long enough to recognize it, but Mike and Richard just kept eating.

"How about cutting a deal with your superior officer?" she asked.

Bryn almost dropped his beer on hearing the question. "What?" he seethed. "You're going to work with these dimbulbs and not CryoMax?"

"I'm biting my tongue here, Bryn, biting my tongue," Richard warned in mock-ominous tones. "I told Doctor Wilkes that while she was here, we'd cut the corn, but there's a limit to how much provocation I'll take."

But Mike met Bryn head-on. "Why work with CryoMax? We're all sitting here, eating under this umbrella, out in the high desert surrounded by bunnies and bushes, having a damn Yalta Conference, and why? All because CryoMax goes out and starts building the next nuclear bomb."

Jenna took immediate offense. "First, Michael, it's *not* a nuclear bomb. Second, if the army wants its own technology, why doesn't it pay its researchers to storm the heavens instead of circling me like a hyena? I'm like the Little Red Hen: nobody wants to help me sow the seed, or water the rows, or harvest the wheat, or grind it into meal, or bake it, but you all want to eat it."

"We do pay for research. Tons of it."

"You'd have never arrived at my invention that way. You pay people to do research to make weapons. Since this isn't a weapon, all you can do is steal it because you don't make things like this by design."

Bryn put his hand up to prevent Mike from replying, then looked across at Jenna. "I don't want to upset you again, knowing you'll storm out of here if I do, maybe for good cause, maybe not, but I have to say I find it interesting that you use the story of the Little Red Hen."

"Why?" she demanded.

"Because I've heard Niles describe your supposed motivation for what you're doing."

"What would Niles know about it?" She didn't even try to hide her sarcasm.

"Eckhardt does talk to him. They may not agree on much, but my uncle does listen to Jonas Eckhardt. He respects him. They just don't see eye to eye. That's not a crime."

"I don't get your point. What did Doctor Eckhardt tell Niles about me?"

"That your entire motivation is to do something for the good of mankind."

"So what? I don't see the connection."

Bryn nodded to Richard to slip him another beer. He looked back at Jenna. "Jenna, what did the Little Red Hen do at the end of that story?"

"She gave the bread to her own family, and the rest of the animals had nothing, like they deserved."

"Yeah, she did. She kept everything and gave nothing to anyone else. It seems to me that if you honestly want to contribute something lasting to mankind, the Little Red Hen story is the wrong model. To help mankind, you need to plant the seed, with or without help, water the rows, with or without help, harvest, grind, bake, all with or without help, and then give the final loaves of bread to everyone. Maybe Eckhardt thinks you're selfless, but you sure talk a different line out here."

"I just want the credit for the work," she protested. "In fact, Niles wants his name *over* mine on the patent, if there's gonna be any. Do you approve of *that*?"

"Probably not," Bryn admitted. "But what you're telling me is that there are conditions on how you spread some lasting good to mankind. You want to leave a positive legacy for the world, but only if you get the credit. So, is your motivation the good of mankind, or getting credit for your work?"

"Why can't it be both?"

"What if it can't be? What would you do? Sit and pout because you're an unsung hero without a medal, take your ball and go home, or work sacrificially, unacknowledged, just because it's right to do it?"

Mike cleared his throat. Jenna and Bryn stopped their bickering and turned to consider his raised hand.

"Well, for what it's worth ..." he said slowly, "The services *have* provided for exactly that issue—the issue of honor when it's impossible to bestow it."

"What are you talking about?" Jenna asked, unhappy at the apparent diversion.

"The Tomb of the Unknown Soldier. For all those who fought for us, whose names we don't even know. They have no credit. And you know what?"

"What?" she asked.

"For most of us," Mike continued, looking across at Richard, "although we regard all our soldiers' graves as sacred, we regard *that* shrine as the most sacred of all. In fact, there's no comparison. There is no higher honor that the military gives than in that place, and we've done so twenty-four hours a day since 1937."

"The Tomb of the Unknowns," Richard clarified. "Mike used the popular name for it."

Jenna slowly twirled her empty glass, considering Mike's words carefully.

"I need to think about what you're all saying," she finally remarked. "In fact, I promise I'll do that. My earlier question still stands, however. Can we cut a deal concerning use of your com center? Perhaps in exchange for something else?"

Bryn knew the situation was mutating before his eyes, but he wasn't sure he liked it. He was aware that Niles may object, and Bryn was supposed to be there to press Niles's interest in it. "Do I have any part to play in this proposal, Jenna?" he asked.

She looked up at him. "I'll have to think about it. Maybe."

Richard started to clear the table and pointed to the horizon. "Storm's a-coming. It'll probably get here by three o'clock. If you want to do any more work, Bryn, it'd be safer to do it before it rains."

"I'm finished for the day." Bryn sounded tired. "I need to meet my uncle for a five o'clock pre-brief at the admin building before our meeting with Eckhardt tonight."

Jenna heard but tried not to react. She wiped her mouth with the plaid paper napkin and politely thanked Mike and Richard for their hospitality.

Richard leaned backward and lifted a paper grocery bag onto his lap. "I just want to show you what you were missing by making us talk like military professionals."

She nodded for him to go on.

He pulled out some paper party hats, noisemakers, and a pin-the-tail-on-the-donkey game. A photo of Bryn's face was pasted over the donkey's behind.

"You've got to be kidding." Jenna's eyes crinkled in delight.

Bryn rolled his eyes.

Richard explained the setup. "Mikey found a rusty old tub out there in the desert. We were gonna set up a bobbing-for-prickly-pears competition with Bryn."

Jenna giggled. "What makes you think anyone would stick their head into a tub with prickly pears floating in water?"

"It's all in the motivation," Mike interrupted. "You don't use water, you fill the tub with corrosive liquid. Do that, and I guarantee that faces and prickly pears will meet."

Jenna turned to Bryn, who pointed at the label on his bottle of beer. She caught on and laughed out loud. "I'm surprised you've lasted this long out here, Bryn. Thanks to these two guys, you've actually earned a smidgen of respect from me."

Richard eyed Bryn slyly. "Toldja we'd be indispensable to ya, brutha!"

Late at night, Jenna sat in her bed, chin on her knees, arms clasped around them, holding her legs tightly to her chest. She slowly rocked back and forth without being aware of it, alternately stretching and wrinkling her nightgown. The lights were on, and Pinball had given up her grumpy protests for attention once it was obvious the human was breaking covenant with her species.

In the far corner of the room, her cello was lying sideways on the floor by the music stand. She tried to play it for distraction, but the C and A strings refused to stay in tune: the tuning pegs kept loosening. She simply couldn't play anything while the strings drifted away from the pitches foundational to the music.

The cello was mirroring the dissonance in her mind.

To say she was conflicted was an understatement. Although she kept it bottled up, everything Jenna seemed to do or feel was larger-than-life, and her emotional turmoil—no, her guilt—was no exception.

She couldn't reconcile the fact that on one hand she had been the object of praise by Nobel laureate Jonas Eckhardt, and on the other hand the object of the sharpest moral rebuke by Bryn.

Bryn! Of all people!

She was angry that Bryn had gotten under her skin with his words.

But she was even angrier at the ring of truth in his accusations. The person she had up till now held in moral contempt had shown that she was actually worse than he was, in ways she had been blind to, had deliberately blinded herself to, out of pure self-absorption.

And she kept coming back to something she never considered before Bryn brought it up. *How many people got fired who would still have their job had I not been protected? Which scapegoat got the axe Niles intended for me? Who had to find other ways to feed their families while I kept playing games at CryoMax?*

She knew that her firing would have meant only one other person being spared. But because she was not in the lottery for firing thanks to Bic and Bartleby's stealthy interventions, she couldn't help visualizing a small sea of faces, faces of people who took the fall for her. The cumulative effect was oppressive.

She didn't know how to make things right. Jenna was confronted with something she had no answers for. She reached for the cell phone.

She remembered that Eckhardt had been in town to talk to Niles Emmerich in advance of next week's board meeting, a meeting concerning her discovery and its significance to the stockholders. She hoped Eckhardt could spare some time to talk to her right now, tonight. She intuitively felt he might be able to assuage her guilt, or guide her in some respect. That vague sense prompted her to make the call. It was already 11:45 PM.

Jenna was ecstatic that Karla actually picked up. Eckhardt may still be in town.

"Miss Wilkes," Karla said, "we're still preparing our flight plan to leave Oakland. What is your call in regard to?" This question was to trigger a figurative secret-handshake, Jenna's encoded response alerting Eckhardt, through Karla, what she needed.

But there had been no settled code for this circumstance, so Jenna answered straight up. "It's something personal and very important to me. Can I see him tonight?"

Karla was silent for a moment. She knew that this wasn't one of the agreed-upon responses to the question. "It must *really be* personal, then, Miss Wilkes."

"Yes, I'm afraid it is."

"Let me call you back in a minute."

"Thank you."

They hung up. Jenna grabbed Pinball, an animal who thought 24-7 attention still constituted gross neglect. Jenna cuddled her cat with affection, pressing her face into Pinball's warm fur. Her kitty was comfort food for her soul.

The cell phone rang. It was Karla. "You'll need to come down right away. We need to be wheels-up in less than three hours. There's a second storm front approaching, and the chairman doesn't want to be stuck here if we can help it."

"I'll be right down!" Jenna hung up and stuffed her feet into her slippers, quickly wrestling her lab coat over the nightgown. Grabbing her keys, she hurried to the garage.

She waved to the guards as she backed down the driveway. She could see their surprise in her headlights, but one waved back. *They probably think I've got a midnight urge for a Big Mac or something,* she thought. She had a hard time sticking to the speed limit barreling down the highway to Oakland Airport.

This time, Karla had Jenna sit in the back lounge area of the plane, where the front-facing seats had been torn out to make room for facing leather sofas, the walls beautifully appointed. All the comforts of home—only the fireplace was missing.

That's because the fire is in the engine nacelles two meters farther down the fuselage, she mused. She stirred the hot chocolate Karla had prepared, cooling it by blowing on it and by lifting up spoonfuls to pour back into the mug. All the cooling techniques she had picked up as a kid—her first experience with cryogenic science.

Jenna soon grew self-conscious at how she was dressed. Maybe she *did* have time earlier to throw some actual clothes on. *Stupid, stupid, stupid,* she groaned, *I'm going to talk to a Nobel laureate in my nightgown.* She closed her lab coat more tightly to hide the gaffe, but her fuzzy slippers simply turned their silent screams up a notch.

She peered down the aisle and saw Eckhardt in a wheelchair, pushing himself her way.

The meeting lasted nearly two hours, and they had to hurry the final part of it. She sailed down the gangway, nightgown flapping in the wind, with three things: some critical paperwork in her hands, a cleaner conscience, and a sense of purpose.

A sense of purpose that cracked the Richter scale in half.

27

She thought she heard something, but she couldn't tell over the noise from the hair dryer. She turned it off and listened again. It *was* the doorbell.

Jenna had arrived back home at 3:30 AM, just a few hours earlier, so exhausted she had fallen asleep with her slippers and lab coat on. She was pleasantly surprised that her morning shower was more refreshing than usual. She casually ran a brush through her hair as she walked to the door in her thick white shower robe, figuring that with the guards in place, it couldn't be anything dangerous.

She wasn't so sure of it when she opened the door.

The guards were there, but so were the police. And Niles.

"Jenna Wilkes?" asked the detective, pulling out some papers from his back pocket.

"Yes, I'm Jenna Wilkes," she replied, her mind racing.

"I have a search warrant for your home, in regard to some stolen property."

"There's no stolen property here, but you're welcome to come in."

"Miss Wilkes, Niles Emmerich here from CryoMax will be joining us. As the owner of the stolen equipment, he's here to help us identify it if it's on the premises."

"Okay," she answered. "Like I said, there's nothing stolen in here, but please, search all you want."

Niles followed the detectives in without a word, shooting a withering glare at Jenna. Before closing the door she glanced outside. Behind the police cars she saw a CryoMax truck with a work crew prepping a forklift: just what would be needed to retrieve an isolator and return it to the lab.

Jenna closed the door and went to the kitchen, putting some frozen waffles in the toaster and humming the Bach cello suite she had tried to play last night. She sat down at the table and pulled Pinball into her lap. Pinball didn't care for company; she was skittish around men in particular.

Jenna heard Niles shouting.

"It's right here in plain sight! She's not even *trying* to hide it. Right in her living room! I can't believe it!"

The two detectives entered her kitchen. "Miss Wilkes, Mr. Emmerich has identified the stolen property. We're placing you under arrest."

"It's not stolen, and I can prove it," she replied. "Please, have a seat. I'll show you." She put her hand on a manila folder resting on the table. The detectives looked at each other.

"You wouldn't want to wrongfully arrest anyone, would you?" she asked. "You should look at this."

They sat down. She could hear Niles running out the front door, yelling for his crew to drive the forklift up to the door. He slammed the door behind himself. They ignored the concussion.

"This," Jenna said, sliding a document toward the detectives, "is the bill of sale for that isolator. Three million five hundred thousand dollars, paid in full. And these ..." she gave them several more sheets, "are for the other five that I bought."

They stared at her in disbelief. "Where'd you get this kind of money?" the taller detective asked.

"In a plane."

They looked at her incredulously. "Really," the shorter detective said without emotion.

"Mm hmm," she replied. "Call CryoMax accounts receivable and see if these bills of sale aren't genuine." She smiled and arranged some silverware around her empty plate.

The shorter detective bent over to whisper to the other. *Check that out, Johnny. I don't want to make a mistake if this is just some pissing contest between these people.* The man she now knew as Johnny got up from the table, pulling his cell phone from his belt as he stepped out of the kitchen.

The first detective stared at the bills of sale and handed them back. He then pulled out his card and extended it to her. "Detective Bruce Edgar," he said tersely. She nodded, taking the card, and he continued.

"If Detective Court's call confirms these are real, and everything checks out, I'll have to apologize for my people having bothered you this morning, Miss Wilkes. On the other hand," he added, "If these are fraudulent documents, I don't have to explain to you what's going to happen."

Her waffles popped up. "Excuse me a second," she apologized, rising to collect her breakfast.

Johnny breezed into the room and spoke directly to Edgar. "Let's get out of here. That thing belongs to her, not CryoMax."

Edgar nodded, taking it in stride. He rose as she sat down. "We'll see ourselves to the door, ma'am. Please don't let us disturb your breakfast any further."

She rose again, extending her hand toward him. "It's okay. I think it was just a misunderstanding, Detective Edgar. Could you ask those people outside to move that CryoMax truck out of the way? I'll be late to work, and they're kinda blocking my driveway with it."

"A pleasure, ma'am." He shook her hand briefly and turned to leave.

"Thank you, Detective Edgar," she called after him. And she sat down, reaching across the bills of sale to grab the syrup.

Outside, Niles was directing the forklift to approach the double-door entrance to Jenna's home. The crew wore the kind of leather back brace belts used for protection when grappling with heavy machinery.

Edgar slipped outside and whispered to the taller guard. The guard nodded. Edgar walked up to Niles, interrupting his delivery of instructions to his crew.

"Mr. Emmerich, you're going to need to clear this driveway. Miss Wilkes needs to go to work, and you're blocking her road access with all this stuff."

Niles thought he had heard wrong. "*What* did you say?"

"Clear the driveway. Get this crap out of here."

"We're going in to claim our property! Haven't you arrested her?"

"No, she's not under arrest, and that piece of modern art in her living room apparently belongs to her."

"That's CryoMax property!" Niles bellowed, turning beet red. "She stole it!"

"Not according to your accounts receivable department. You know..." Edgar continued as he stepped inside a police car, "for a director of a major corporation, you're awfully out-of-touch with what's going on in your company. I'm surprised that Miss Wilkes isn't pressing charges against *you,* charges which I'd think may actually have merit." He slammed the car door shut.

Niles did a slow boil watching the police drive off. He gestured to his own crew to leave as well, recognizing he'd been temporarily beaten.

When all was clear, Niles approached Jenna's door, the two guards standing beside it. "Can I ring the doorbell?" he asked. "Or are you instructed to break my arm if I even look at her?"

"Ring all you want. It's for her to answer. Our orders don't concern any of that."

"Tell me, do you work for CryoMax or Eckhardt?"

"Neither. Miss Wilkes pays us directly."

"Really? When did *that* start?"

"This morning."

"That's what I thought." He reached over and pressed the ringer.

By now Jenna was fully dressed, trademark lab coat in place, cane in hand. She answered the door. "Good morning, Mr. Emmerich."

"Can I come in?"

"Sure."

He entered. "Is there a place to talk?"

"The kitchen table. That's where the detectives talked to me." She led him to it, and they both sat down.

Niles was furious but kept his anger under control. He noticed the bills of sale strewn across the table and guessed what they meant.

He started in on her. "That large isolator was worth more than two million."

"I know. That's why I paid three and a half."

"Three and a half?" he asked.

"See?" She pulled the first bill of sale out and showed it to him. "I compensated for its actual value, not the book value. No depreciation factored in."

Niles followed her finger to the bottom line. He furrowed his brow in dismay and looked directly into her eyes. She didn't even blink, let alone back down. Niles wasn't used to that. What was she trying to pull? She wasn't playing the game he'd been expecting.

He tried another tack. "You resigned all your positions yesterday."

"Yes. Sorry about the lack of notice, Mr. Emmerich. I couldn't get any work done in your lab."

Niles tore into her. "You may have the isolator, *Wicks,* but the *technology* still belongs to CryoMax. Lock, stock, and barrel. You have obligations written into your employment contract regarding that. The intellectual property rights are ours. You're trying to steal from us, and I'll sue you till you can't see straight."

"Mr. Emmerich, the technology *is* yours, and I fully intend to keep my obligations to CryoMax and to help you with the preparation of the patents. On my own time, in fact. I'm no thief."

Niles leaned forward and spoke more quietly. "Are you trying to tell me that you bought this isolator, obviously with Eckhardt's help, and yet are going to meet your obligations to CryoMax anyway?"

"Yes. You have my word on it."

"You'll do as I say then?"

"No, I simply said I'd keep my word and honor my obligations. You'll lack for nothing that you have a legitimate right to, but I won't be under your thumb. Besides, my contract only protected work done on cryogenic devices, and this isolator isn't cryogenic. Plus, I'm not doing commercial development, only pure research, so I'm exempt from those restrictions as well."

Niles pondered this all with a profound frown, stroking his goatee slowly. "This morning has not turned out as I had planned, Miss Wilkes. And I meant Wilkes, not Wicks. Dyslexia. Well, not really. I'm not sure whether to be happy with this arrangement or furious. Know this, that I'll check every damn thing out with my attorneys—if you've left one *t* uncrossed, you'll be landing in court with everything I can throw at you."

"I expected no less from you, Mr. Emmerich. But everything is in order."

"Yes ..." said Niles, his gaze drifting off. "Yes, I suppose it would be, if Eckhardt's behind this. I'm probably dealing with this at the wrong level. *You're* not the problem; you're just a symptom of the problem." He abruptly rose from the table to leave and marched out of her kitchen.

Jenna heard him call from the door before he slammed it shut.

"Enjoy your isolator!"

She collected Pinball in her arms and walked into the living room to watch as sun and shadow danced on the isolator's matte surface. The shifting kaleidoscope of shades, choreographed by the breeze through the tree outside, drifted hypnotically across the dark metal.

"Boy," she said to the isolator, "you sure seem to cause a lot of problems."

She stroked Pinball's head while she watched the shadow ballet. "Hmm. Like parent, like child."

She got ready for work ... except that as of today, work no longer meant employment with CryoMax.

28

Driving to the power station, with one stop to make first, Jenna replayed the meeting with Eckhardt again in her mind, letting it sink in. The memory was vivid, as if she were still on the plane in her nightgown.

She had helped him out of the wheelchair to take the leather sofa across from her. He looked weaker than before.

"What's on your mind?" he began, his eyes as clear and intense as ever.

"I ... I've done things at CryoMax that were wrong, that have, I think, hurt people, or hurt the company, or at least, I've fraudulently ripped off the company. Doctor Johanssen and Doctor Bartleby were protecting me from being fired, even though they knew I was doing G-jobs on the side all the time and neglecting a good chunk of my assigned work."

She couldn't believe she was revealing this to anyone, let alone Eckhardt, but she was now committed. "Somebody else got fired, lost his job, in my place. I should have been axed, but someone else got axed for me, and I was the cause of it. I don't even know which of those poor people who were fired were the ones *I* was responsible for. I now think I was responsible for *all* of them. And I don't know how to make things right. All I know is that I want ... I want to make things right. I just don't know what to do."

They sat in silence, Jenna agitated as her conscience raged within her, now accusing, now excusing, now bringing unflattering details to remembrance. Karla came in to check on them, but both Jenna and Eckhardt assured her all was well, they needed nothing right now.

Eckhardt finally began questioning Jenna about what she had confessed. "At what point would you know that you'd done enough to make things right?"

"I'm not sure I understand, Doctor Eckhardt."

"Let's say there were four families affected, to varying degrees, by job termination at CryoMax. How would you know how much compensation to pay to make things right?"

"I … I'm not sure."

"You have no standard, no criterion, to measure justice?"

She thought about that. "You just kinda have to feel it."

"And if you feel wrong, did those people get justice then? Isn't justice independent of your feelings, not subordinate to them, or defined by them? You felt differently before today about this—maybe you'll feel differently tomorrow. Your yardstick shrinks and expands like the tides of the sea. Not a very good way to measure anything, Miss Wilkes, least of all justice."

"So, what *would* be a way to tell if things had been made right or not?"

"You mean, how does one know restitution and justice have been fully satisfied?"

"Yeah."

"Well, in one case about twenty centuries ago, a Jewish man named Zacchaeus returned four times what he had stolen, and deliverance from guilt was proclaimed upon him and his family for it."

"Four times the stolen amount?"

"Restitution was scoped to the nature of the thing stolen and to whether there was premeditation or not. If a theft was inadvertent, what's called an unwitting trespass, you still had to pay one-fifth more, over and above restoring the amount lost on account of your actions."

"Why should there be a penalty of *any* kind for causing an accidental loss?"

"Because accidental or not, the fundamental law of the universe, its ordained order, has been violated, and it needs to be restored. Not unlike the way your cores work. Law is law. It's irrevocable. That's its nature. Otherwise, it's not law at all.

"The question, Miss Wilkes, is this: *by what standard* do we judge a thing. I use the Bible. The ultimate law, the ultimate authority, that it images."

"How do you know that's the right standard, Doctor Eckhardt?"

"Ultimate law says that about itself."

"That's not good enough to accept it as a standard. You'll need to prove it was the ultimate standard."

Eckhardt was visibly wearying from this dialogue, but drew himself up to continue. "If you use *anything* to prove the Bible is the standard, that other thing becomes your actual standard. If the Bible were ultimate law, any external standard of proof used to support it becomes more ultimate yet, because ultimacy is implicitly shifted from the Bible to that standard. Tell me, Miss Wilkes, why isn't it possible to appeal a decision by the U.S. Supreme Court?"

"Well," she thought, "if you could appeal its decisions, the Supreme Court would no longer be supreme. It's supposed to be the final court of appeal."

"Exactly. If there were a higher court you could appeal to, the Supreme Court could not possibly be the ultimate arbiter. Its authority has been trumped. An ultimate authority is always the final court of appeal. All that to say, you undermine ultimate authority if you don't treat it as ultimate."

"I'm sorry, Doctor Eckhardt, but I'm no theologian, and I honestly don't intend to be one."

"Everyone is a theologian, Miss Wilkes. Most people are simply very bad theologians."

"That's pretty judgmental of you to say that of other people." She was genuinely surprised at his evident intolerance.

"Actually," he answered, "you've just proved my point for me. *Who told you* that something is judgmental? Where did that value judgment come from, where did it arise, what did that discriminating engine in your head use to determine if something I said was judgmental? Where did that standard you're applying to me come from?

"You see, Miss Wilkes, you can't say you created it yourself because it was here before you were born. You've accepted a definition that originates from outside yourself. You've tacitly adopted a prefabricated theology. It wasn't homespun. You cobbled it together from preexisting theologies that struck you as what you wanted to hear."

"Maybe, but I pride myself on critical thinking," she affirmed.

"Wonderful. You pride yourself on consistency too, yes?"

"Absolutely."

"So, what did you learn when you applied critical thinking to the whole idea of critical thinking itself?"

"What?"

"You did apply critical thinking to critical thinking to see how it measured up to its own standard, right?"

She paused, uncertain of herself. "Why would we bother to do that?" she wondered.

"Isn't the principle behind critical thinking this, that nothing should get a free pass, that all hidden baggage needs to be exposed?" Eckhardt tilted his head inquiringly.

"Yes ... That *should* be applied consistently. Kind of like how my work exposes hidden baggage in modern science. Right?"

"Well, you certainly can't call it critical thinking if it gives something, even itself, a free pass. Pop the hood on your worldview and you'll find you're chained down by hidden baggage you weren't even aware of."

"What about *your* hidden baggage?" she challenged.

"It's not hidden. It's open." Eckhardt spread his hands out. "But most people have a strong aversion to examining the foundations of thought. It might expose their hidden subjectivity, might blow away any pretense to logical objectivity. You dig down deep enough into something, like logic or science, and what you find can really rock the boat."

She was starting to see the connections between what Eckhardt had said and her own work in the sciences. She dimly understood *some* of it, enough to prevent her from rejecting everything he said out of hand. They talked at length about justice and how to make things right.

At the end of the evening, she had a nine-million-dollar consulting contract with Eckhardt International, paid in advance for one year's research. But the money had strict conditions: she was to pay every tithe in the Bible, or she'd receive none of the cash, and without that cash, all six isolators would summarily be confiscated by CryoMax because Niles always made sure to press the company's legal rights to the limit.

She had no idea what these tithes, these three different Biblical taxes, were all about. There was a Levitical tithe to the Levites (Eckhardt explained who functioned as Levites in the modern world), the poor tithe, and a rejoicing tithe. In the coarsest possible terms, the three tithes subsidized education, charity, and vacations.

This was radically peculiar thinking.

Jenna was particularly surprised at the poor tithe. "So, I just give this part to United Way or to some other charity?"

"No, Miss Wilkes, the poor tithe is administered personally. It's a one-lump sum, given with you looking the recipient directly in the eye, which meaningfully lifts them out of poverty. This isn't like our welfare system, which dribbles things out to keep people on a bare level of subsistence, dependent on the state. This will be a very personal decision for you. You must *not* delegate it to a faceless institution, least of all the state …

"Speaking of which," he remembered, "you'll need to pay all your taxes in advance with an absolutely honest income tax return. You're to get out of debt as well, mortgage, auto loan, credit cards, student loans, everything. Owe no man anything. I'll tell you what the isolators are actually worth, which you'll buy from CryoMax, and I'll give you the names of everyone fired under Niles's watch so you can deal with them as we've discussed. You'll pay back every cent of time you defrauded CryoMax out of by pursuing your side projects. You'll return the credit card and cash you received from the company last week.

"After all that, you'll have an absolutely clean slate through God's provision, a conscience clear before God and man, with ultimate law being fully, objectively satisfied.

"But remember this …" A pained expression crossed his brow. "After you've done all these things, you'll have very little of this money left. In fact, you'll probably be significantly poorer than you are right now. Apart from meeting your basic needs, you'll have nothing left … except a clean conscience and the certainty that ultimate law, at least as touching the matters you've confessed to me, has been satisfied."

He handed her the bank wire documenting the nine-million-dollar transaction.

She looked from the paperwork into his eyes. "Doctor Eckhardt, I didn't work for any of this money."

"Oh, you're going to, Miss Wilkes. *You're going to.*"

29

At the power station, Mike had taken over for Richard, training the video camera on Bryn. Bryn had been thoughtful about the previous day's encounter with Jenna. Apparently, the army brats had been affected too. They had lost some of their interest in the shtick they usually smothered Bryn in. That didn't mean they were entirely humorless, but their true personalities came out rather than mock-heroic glorification of slackerhood.

"Are you getting this on your camera, Mike?" Bryn asked.

"Yeah, I see it."

"The meter numerals are visible?"

"Yep, as long as you're standing there shading them."

"Good. Hold on a second." Bryn threw a switch. Nothing appeared to happen. "Well, we're done here, Mike. We're going to the next power station."

"Done?"

"Yeah, I just finished my job. I've rewired this station so that the only way the eight kilowatts delta could be conserved would be if the power was leaping from the station upstream from here."

Mike let the camera hang limply in his hand, surprised. "I heard that wasn't possible."

"I thought that too. But never say never. Didn't Richard say that a few days ago?"

"Yeah, I suppose so. But I expected this to be something dramatic or climactic. With some kind of ceremony, you know?"

"It's been that way from the beginning." Bryn began packing up his toolbox. "Every time the power leaped, it was uneventful. Nothing miraculous. That's why this whole thing sneaks up on you."

"I guess so. You're literally serious. We're all leaving for the next power station."

"Yep."

"You know the colonel will make sure you never return here without us in tow."

"I know. Guard this all you want, though it'd be a waste of time. The reality is, the real work is upline. Oh, one more thing ..."

"Yes?"

"Take good care of the videostick you just shot. Between that and the videos you took of me at Building F, you've got a great future filming Nobel Prize-winning work. Anyway, Jenna will want to see that video. Make a copy for both her and me, could ya?"

"Sure, no problem, Bryn."

"Let's get something to drink."

"Beer?"

Bryn considered the suggestion. "Nah, actually, having had beer nonstop for all this time, I'm kind of sick of it."

"Me too."

"Really?" Bryn was surprised.

"No, not really. I really love beer. I won't be unfaithful to my first love. I think you're a traitor, saying you're sick of it. I'd keep that under your hat around Ragman."

"Why?"

"Beer is his religion, and he's its chief apostle."

They began to break down the video setup together, Bryn helping Mike with the tripod. That would have been unthinkable for Bryn not too many days earlier.

The oddball spirit of cooperation went against the grain of Bryn's abrasive approach to other people, but he couldn't help but acknowledge the gains it delivered. Always excluded from work of interest, Jenna's in particular, here he found himself on the ground floor of the project's extension. That would have been impossible without the peculiar glue the captains seemed to provide. How they disarmed Jenna so quickly was nothing short of astonishing to Bryn. He could never have approached her that way, but neither could he argue against the weak but growing cohesiveness that had since arisen.

We've all got to learn to share. He remembered the look in Richard's eyes when Richard had chewed Mike out for swatting Bryn's hand away from the ketchup bottle. *Maybe I'm learning,* Bryn thought. *At least, I've learned enough to let Mike use the ketchup first.*

30

She had just missed the *up* elevator, and based on the floor indicators, she'd have a bit of a wait before she'd catch the next one. Jenna turned around to study the hospital lobby, observing the families gathered together fearfully, or with hope, to support their sick and injured. As she considered the vivid contrast between broken bodies and burning familial love and compassion, she recalled an old quotation Eckhardt had cited: *man was a strange creature, a ray of heaven united to a clod of dirt.* She could see both elements in the lobby. Her roaming eyes focused on the entrance to the hospital gift shop.

Why not, she thought.

She soon left the shop with a small vase of flowers and a get-well card in her left hand, the cane in her right. The cane was now festooned with a blue ribbon she had just purchased. As she returned to the lobby, both elevators opened simultaneously.

Lucky. She thought again about that word. *Eckhardt wouldn't say that, though. He'd call it providential.* She ducked inside the left elevator and selected her floor.

Minutes later, she was back at Sexton's side. He wasn't awake, but he definitely looked stronger, and the oxygen tubes were no longer in his nose. That was a relief. She opened the drapes to let more light in and arranged the vase she brought next to another pot of flowers—not the one she'd seen before. Evidence his sons were visiting him faithfully.

She pulled up a chair and called his name softly. "Doctor Sexton … Doctor Sexton …"

He opened his eyes and turned. A smile formed on his dry, cracked lips. "Miss Wilkes. You've come back."

She nodded back with a smile, pleased that he was speaking with greater strength today. She placed the cane on his lap.

He examined the ribbon on it with sadness. "I'm sorry, Miss Wilkes, but the last stroke has paralyzed both my legs. I appreciate the thought, but I think I'm going to find wheelchairs more useful than canes from now on."

"It's not for walking …" she said, visibly shaken by the news about his stroke.

Sexton saw compassion in her eyes and nodded for her to finish her thought.

She swallowed and tried to keep going. "I very much wanted you to see and touch this. It's a frame shunt, the one I described in section four."

He reached for the cane with both hands, lifting it up before his face to regard its significance. The sun coming in through the window hit the cane square on. "Jenna, how could you know that?"

"I used it to drain an active core, removing a tiny bit of its energy as low frequency photons. It shunted right across the frames through the folded manifold, deep inside a big block of titanium. I wished you could have seen it. Actually, nobody could have seen it. I did the whole thing in the dark to mess up their spy cameras."

"Are you saying you actually tapped the energy that arises from the time differential between the core and the present?"

She nodded.

He thought about that a moment, then asked another question of her. "Have you already discerned that it takes ongoing energy input to sustain the universe in existence, that the conservation law isn't ultimate, that there's something more ultimate behind it?"

"I don't think I know what you mean by that, Doctor Sexton."

He shook his head in mild disappointment at her confusion. "I'm sorry, you're probably not that far along in your research. You'll bump into that soon enough. You've already drawn the map, after all."

He coughed a bit and shifted in the bed, pushing the controller to raise himself a bit higher. He ran one hand through his oily gray hair. It had been some time since his last shampoo.

"So, Jenna, you're saying that *this cane* quantum tunneled into the titanium *while you were holding it*? Amazing."

She nodded again.

He pointed to the end of the cane. "How far did you stick this end into the core?"

"I didn't stick *that* end into the core, but the curved end up here," and she pointed to the hook of the cane.

Sexton started to laugh at this. Jenna had no idea why.

"Is something funny, Doctor Sexton?"

"You could say that, Jenna Wilkes, you could say that. Who built this curved frame shunt?"

"Doctor Eckhardt did."

"Well, he's a very smart guy, Nobel Prize winner and all, but I'm not surprised he failed to see the right way to build the shunt. He looked at your work and concluded that without having half an Amperian loop in place to normalize the momentum, you couldn't guarantee photons in the shunt process but would get a less controllable form of energy. Hence this awkward toroidal crook in the cane, where he had to twist the fused silica core at great expense and time."

"How would you know that, Doctor Sexton?" She was bewildered by his revelations.

"Because I figured out how to build these things *without* the curve, simply following your dissertation with a little imagination. But nothing came of it."

He coughed again and handed back the cane. "I gave all my derivations to Professor Hernandez, Jenna. You'll need to see *him* about this. Let me try to write a note for you … hand me that pad of Post-its. Give my note to Philip. He'll turn my papers over to you. You can share my material with Eckhardt if you'd like. He'll then see what he overlooked, which gave rise to this ham-fisted architecture of his. He made his job harder than it had to be. Here, take this cane … I mean, your frame shunt … back.

"And thanks for letting me hold a piece of history. Truly. Thank you."

Her eyes were wide with excitement. She could never have imagined this outcome from her visit.

He slipped her a neatly written note, which she stuffed into her lab coat pocket without reading. She looked back at Sexton's now calm features. She saw that his gentle eyes were actually brown. She'd never noticed that before.

"Young lady," he concluded, "maybe we can make a little more history before we're through, eh? It's time for you ..." he winked, "to turn the world upside down."

She rose to thank him, ended up kissing him on the forehead again, her red hair falling all over his face. He chuckled at the mild impropriety of it.

As she departed the room, she overheard him say something to himself.

"God bless that girl."

31

Wolf Borse pulled the hard copies out of the printer and quickly stapled them, knowing that Eckhardt would be heading to the helipad by now. As he hurried through the manse, Wolf saw he was right. Katherine was already pushing Eckhardt, bent over in his wheelchair, toward the back door.

"Katherine, wait a minute." Wolf closed the distance.

"Yes, Wolf?"

"These are for Doctor Eckhardt."

She turned the wheelchair around, and Eckhardt looked up at Wolf and accepted the papers.

"Wolf, tell me ..." Eckhardt began as he scanned the printouts. "Do we have a consistent anomaly in these readings?"

"Yes, Doctor, just as you predicted. I don't think any of these three research groups even realized it was statistically significant. The standard deviation can't be run unless you have all three of their datasets in front of you."

"The amplitudes checked out as well?"

"Within about 5 percent. It's in range. It's consistent with a spherical shock wave of neutrinos emanating from Doctor Wilkes's core two days ago."

Eckhardt managed a weak smile. "Thank you, Wolf. I appreciate the good work on this."

"Have a safe flight, Doctor Eckhardt." Wolf turned on his heel and returned to the IT room.

Katherine continued wheeling Dr. Eckhardt toward the door. "It looks like you got what you were looking for, Doctor." She had a smile in her voice, a smile Eckhardt could hear but not see.

"Very much so." He spindled the printouts into a cylinder and tapped his knee with them as they moved along.

The three underground neutrino detector arrays across the globe provided regular printouts of activity. Eckhardt wanted to see what they recorded when Jenna penetrated the core with the cane. Each of the three labs showed a spike.

Considered individually, the spikes weren't statistically significant against the noise floor. But the three detectors showed the same spike at the same time, which *was* statistically significant. There was a detectible burst of neutrino activity at the precise moment Jenna touched the cane to the core.

Eckhardt knew that the core's ability to shield neutrinos was incidental, a side effect. It was more accurate to call the core a neutrino red light, where neutrinos striking the outer sphere of the core simply stopped, frozen in their paths. Any breaching of the core manifold, allowing time inside to slip forward even a microsecond, was long enough for neutrinos loitering on the surface to cross through the core and continue out the other side. The cane's touching the core was a green light, releasing an immense spherical shock wave of neutrinos. Once Jenna pulled the cane back out, the green light turned red and neutrinos started accumulating again.

Wolf's other point clinched it. As the neutrino shock wave spread, the inverse square law altered its intensity as distance from Livermore increased. The evidence was incontrovertible.

"What are you thinking, Doctor?" asked Katherine. "Are you thinking about the board meeting you're flying to?"

"No, Katherine, no." He turned to look up at her. "I was just thinking how that girl has never ceased to amaze me. These papers virtually constitute a second Nobel Prize, really, in the same field."

"She's a very sweet girl," Katherine replied in earnest. "I miss her, and I miss hearing you get excited talking to her."

"Well, Katherine, it took me a while to find her because like everything else she's doing, she was hidden in plain sight. If I hadn't had a standing arrangement with the copy centers at institutions like Stanford to collect digital copies of students' dissertations, I'd have never run across her."

"What caught your attention?"

"Let's just say that the amount of times that poor girl tracked back to her copy center was ... statistically significant to me." He smiled and Katherine beamed back. As soon as the back door of the manse had opened, it became too loud to hold a conversation at normal volume while the waiting chopper's blades bit the air.

Eckhardt tried to raise his voice above the noise. "Still, Katherine, pray all goes well at the board meeting! I expect some resistance!"

She pushed the wheelchair out toward the helicopter.

32

Jenna arrived at the power station to find Captain Mike Boudreaux collecting the red road hazard triangles hemming in the UPS truck. Bryn's sports car wasn't here. Mike walked up to the VW as she stepped out into the brisk morning air.

"Good morning, Doctor Wilkes," Mike greeted her. "I'm afraid the show is moving upstream nearly seventy miles east of here."

"That's what I figured, Captain. I just wanted to see how he had done it."

"I have a video of it. Would you care to step into the com center and watch it? It'll make more sense if you watch it first before walking blind into the station. Besides which, Bryn explained as he went along."

"I just want to know why he didn't just cut the power to the whole station." She pointed to the overhead cables threading through the line of towers into the distant haze. "Why not just cut those down?"

"We asked him the same thing," Mike explained. "He had a pretty good answer, something about not wanting to risk having three hospitals lose power. You cut those lines, it'll take some time to restore this part of the grid. This station services more than just CryoMax. I have to give him credit for showing some responsibility."

"Yes," she said thoughtfully, "yes, that would be something of a surprise for him, wouldn't it? I'd like to see that video."

Jenna stepped out of the bright sunlight into the dimly lit truck. As her eyes adjusted, she began to marvel at how cramped the layout was. The com center was bristling with electronics she'd never have imagined. There was little room for people inside it. It looked more cramped than the submarines she'd seen in old movies.

"You don't find this a little *too* cozy, you and Captain Green together inside this tiny thing?" She banged her knee trying to sit down on the wheeled stool.

"Beats a foxhole, ma'am."

"I see."

"Here, you'll be watching the video on that monitor to your left. I even have a videostick of it for you to take back."

"Bryn probably wouldn't like that one bit," she warned.

"Giving you your own videostick was his idea, not mine."

She looked at Mike with curiosity. "Where's Captain Green right now?"

"He's riding with Doctor Zilcher to the new location to scout it out. It's very close to the dam. That upline station apparently does the main distribution coming off the generators, if I understood Zilcher correctly. We drew straws to see who cleans up here, who gets to ride with Zilcher. I drew the short straw. Ragman gets to do cleanup when we pull up stakes at the dam. Fair's fair."

"People still draw straws?" she wondered.

"Technically, we didn't draw straws for *that*. We threw playing cards into a hat," Mike replied.

That sounded wrong to Jenna. "Bryn says he's seen you guys sitting around throwing playing cards into the fire you built outside."

"Shows what he knows. The hat's in the fire."

"Whose hat, exactly?" she grinned.

"That's where drawing straws comes in." He handed her a videostick.

She nodded and turned toward the screen. "Let's see what Bryn's got here," she said, leaning back with interest. She glanced at her watch, worn on her right wrist facing down. "Looks like I have time to check this out before I head back to Oakland. I've got a plane to catch."

"Sounds good."

"Oh, when you see Captain Green again, tell him thank you for making the arrangement with your meteor burst system."

"Thank Colonel Riesen, ma'am. He was the one who accepted your proposal."

She turned back to the screen.

"Lights, camera, action ..." Mike announced, and pushed the play button.

Jenna watched the video with new eyes.

33

General Stall picked up the phone. It was from the main entry desk at the Pentagon.

"General, we have two people requesting permission to see you. A couple of Ph.D.s from Stanford. Philip Hernandez and an associate of his. He says it's important. Would you want me to clear them and send them up?"

"Hernandez?" asked Stall. "Sure, if it's Hernandez, send him and his associate up."

Stall hadn't expected that news. Why would Hernandez be here? Maybe the material he dug up on Wilkes couldn't be trusted with a courier. But they certainly couldn't discuss things in Stall's office with any safety. Maybe the material was self-explanatory.

He got another call.

"Everything checks out with these two, General. I'm sending them up with an escort."

"Thanks, Lieutenant." Stall hung up and filed some items away on his desk. *I guess we'll learn whether that was a wasted trip to the sports bar or not.*

Several minutes later, there was a knock at his door.

"Come in," barked Stall to the escort.

The escort, a corporal, entered the room and saluted sharply. Stall snapped a salute back.

"Sir," said the corporal, "I'll be outside the door to escort them back when you're done speaking with them."

"Fine. Send them in."

The corporal left the room, and Hernandez walked in.

"We needed another chair," Hernandez told Stall as they shook hands. Stall looked to the door to see a desk chair being rolled into the room …

… by a redhead in a dirty lab coat.

Several hours later, Jenna's cab dropped her off at her next destination. She walked deep in thought, taking in the sights and the atmosphere of this place. She watched the guards, remembering what she'd been told about why they held their rifles so as to stand between any possible threat and the object they were guarding:

The Tomb of the Unknown Soldier.

She didn't even get that close to it, not daring to dishonor it while wearing her lab coat. Just seeing the Tomb from a distance moved her to emotions so deep she sank to her knees and sobbed quietly. The people honored here had lost their *lives*—she had nothing on them in regard to sacrifice. And as she wept, her heart received instruction from the silent white edifice, sealed by the solemn gravity of the guards as they rotated duty every half hour.

People passing around her assumed she was a bereaved war widow, a wife of a recently killed soldier, or perhaps a daughter of one killed in an earlier conflict. Perhaps she wept for one missing in action, coming here because there was no other place to go. They gave her space to mourn. Everyone coming here had a different reason. And the same reason.

When she had finally risen to her feet, the seeds that Eckhardt had been planting in her mind, and ultimately her heart, had germinated and burst into burning bloom. She made her way to the chapel, privately thanking Captain Michael Boudreaux for interfering with her spat with Bryn. She'd never have come here, never have known, never have found a context for her struggles bigger than herself, because until now it was all about going it alone, about being a rugged individualist. She was still that, of course, but now she was something bigger as well. Still Jenna Wilkes, yet something ineffably more than Jenna Wilkes.

The dawning of understanding had come. And with it, a measure of solace and peace she didn't honestly have before.

And like Zacchaeus, salvation had finally come to her house. Eckhardt's wiping out of her worldly debts was an intended symbol of another wiping out of debts, debts that no human being could ever pay.

She remembered a Scripture that Eckhardt had quoted. *Lebanon is not sufficient to burn …* She now found her sufficiency outside herself, knowing that only then would it be in safe Hands. She could no more have satisfied ultimate law than she could have come up with nine million dollars on her own.

Eckhardt knew what he was doing, she thought. *He never once preached the gospel to me. He simply lived it, was an ambassador for it, embodied it. Never applied psychological thumbscrews, like some people kept trying to do to me, however politely, at college. I was able to see God reflected in Eckhardt's deeds, rather than having religion stuffed down my throat.*

In this place, in her heart, she had at last come running into God's outstretched arms, knowing she had been pulled all the way.

As the cab shuttled her back to the airport, she leaned her head against the driver's side window vacantly scanning the passing landscape. Something caught her attention, and she lifted her head to look back. A park. With swings, grass, and trees. She checked her watch, then tapped on the glass dividing the backseat from the driver's compartment.

"Could we turn around? I saw a park back there I'd like to stop at for a bit."

"Sure," the cabbie replied. "There's a place up ahead I can turn around."

"Thanks." She settled back down. She needed this.

She paid the cabbie for the time he'd be cooling his heels in the parking lot while she recharged her batteries walking in the park. No one was in the sandbox, which included the traditional swings, merry-go-round, slides, and monkey bars where children can indulge pure innocent pleasure.

She kicked off her shoes and entered the sandbox, feeling the warm sand between her toes. *I'd better get this out of my system before I turn thirty.*

She closed her eyes and let the sun hit her face full on. It felt wonderful, like a gift that she too often took for granted. Her tread was steady as she walked toward the swings, choosing the closest to sit on. It creaked under her weight, but she soon had it gently swaying.

The arrival of an African-American family interrupted her silent reverie. Four children, ages four to eight, Jenna guessed, with their mother, who sat on the park bench to supervise while sorting through some papers. She looked like a proud woman, protective of her children yet firm with them.

The children, two boys and two girls, dropped a grocery bag in the sand and started extracting pails, shovels, metal trucks, and other toys from it. The four-year-old ran up to the swing next to Jenna.

"Can you push me?" he asked excitedly.

She smiled and nodded.

The mother called out, "Don't bother the lady, Michael!"

"It's okay," Jenna called back. "I'll be happy to give Michael a push." She obliged the bundle of energy as he kept asking to go higher and higher.

Several of the other children milled around, also wanting to be pushed. She soon had four children in the air at once, walking from swing to swing trying not to get knocked down by an ill-timed step between the human pendulums. Jenna found herself laughing and enjoying the encounter immensely.

She finally begged off after her arms began to ache, declined to push the merry-go-round for the same reason, then collected her shoes and went up to speak to their mother. As Jenna approached, she caught a glimpse of a logo on the papers the woman was sorting through. Jenna knew that logo and the government agency it represented, knew it by heart—a logo Jenna had seen far too often years earlier.

This mother was reconciling a debit card statement from a federal assistance program.

"You have beautiful children," Jenna remarked as she sat down.

"Thank you. I try hard to raise them right. It's so difficult here."

The children abandoned the swings and grabbed the grocery bag of toys, running behind the park bench to play on the grass, squealing, laughing, giggling, teasing.

Jenna talked for about twenty minutes with the children's mother, whom she took to be about thirty-five years old. Her name was Flora Washington. Her husband had died in a traffic accident a year and a half earlier. He had been a security guard. They were Baptists.

Jenna wondered if this was the right time to fulfill one of her key obligations to Eckhardt: the need to satisfy ultimate law, the Maker's law, concerning the poor.

Jenna reached into her fanny pack and pulled out the folded money order for three hundred thousand dollars: the correct amount of the poor tithe based on the Old Testament reckoning concerning the paycheck from Eckhardt. She hunched over to use the park bench as a writing surface. Flora was unaware of her actions.

Jenna began to put Flora's name in the payee block. As she finished writing Flora's first name, a soap bubble floated right by her face. She looked up and saw that the children were playing with bubble wands and soap bubble solution. The bubble kits weren't store-bought—the mother had mixed dishwashing liquid, glycerin, and water. The wands were broken. The children had to hold them near the ring, but didn't know any better, running and laughing and jumping through clouds of bubbles their siblings were blowing.

Jenna bent back down to finish writing Flora's name and saw that the money order had gotten wet, not from a bubble bursting on it but from a tear from her own eye.

"Flora, I've got something for you that you're probably going to have a hard time believing," she began.

The young mother looked up, wondering what Jenna was trying to say.

Jenna extended the money order to Flora. "This is for you and your children. This isn't a joke."

Flora took the money order and examined it skeptically. She didn't believe it, but Jenna kept rambling on about how she had been the recipient of a tremendous gift and how she was obligated to pass part of it on, that God's law required it. Flora turned the money order over to check the watermark, micro-optical security patch, and draft limit; she had once trained as a bank teller. The draft had been cut only yesterday, but everything about the money order actually looked right. Was the impossible happening right here in this park?

Flora interrupted Jenna. "How can this be real? You can't even afford to wash your clothes!"

Jenna flinched and looked down at her lab coat. "Let me tell you the story about this lab coat, which has something to do with why I'm giving you and your children this money order."

The cabbie, still seated in his cab nearby, was absentmindedly watching the two women sitting and talking on the park bench. He noticed the shoulders of the children's mother start to heave and shake, and the redhead reaching out and hugging her. He wondered what that was all about. He glanced at the meter. This lady was running up some pretty good cash for him at this park. A stray soap bubble landed on his windshield and burst.

On the way back to the airport, Jenna had a vague smile on her face. She had pocketed her glasses to just let the shadows cross over her closed eyes as the cab moved through the miserable traffic. She recalled parts of Eckhardt's conversation with her several days earlier.

"The Levitical tithe," he had said, "you can direct to wherever God's work is being done. You can also split the Levitical tithe any way you want. It's a tithe that *you* control.

"You'll be tempted to split the poor tithe because you'll feel guilty you can't relieve all the suffering in the world. If you tried to help a quarter million people, they'd each get about a dollar. That won't help them, and you'll still feel guilty. You need to see past the deception your guilt imposes on you. Because your income happens to be large, the tithe to the poor will also appear huge. If everyone with average incomes obeyed this law, we'd abolish poverty altogether. People *are* guilty who fail in this; the Scripture calls it *grinding the faces of the poor*.

"So," he concluded, "you will help just *one* person. Your choice is strictly voluntary, up to you. You're doing no wrong in passing by or not choosing others, because God alone has a claim on that money."

"Give it all to only *one*?" She still had a hard time understanding this idea. It seemed inherently unfair, but she realized he was prompting her to take off the distorted moral glasses she'd been wearing since birth.

"Jenna," he looked her straight in the eye, using her first name, "God moves one person at a time. In this matter, He does not deal with classes or groups. Groups and classes resent this. Jesus generated intense hostility when he pointed out that God bypassed the widows of Israel to help only one widow from Zarephath, had bypassed the lepers of Israel to heal one leper from Syria. That hostility against God working one person at a time lives on today. You must see this with new eyes. You must learn to work with one person at a time. You must *make* it personal."

He had then leaned in closer toward her. "That," he added with emphasis, "is because God, unlike the state, is not impersonal. There's nothing more personal than God, and His image bearers have no business being impersonal or institutional in dealing with the poor."

And Jenna had experienced the guiltless joy of visualizing the release from miserable poverty that one family would enjoy because Jenna had honored the ultimate law the Creator had laid down.

God moves one person at a time. The ultimate law of mercy.

She was learning her theology in ways the institutional church would have had trouble recognizing, let alone sanctioning. A member of no church, with no Bible of her own, having only a vague awareness of things like baptism ... and yet she was being used and moved upon for purposes far greater than herself, and she willingly submitted herself to her Maker and, as she had come to recognize, her Redeemer.

As the cab slowly made its way through the airport toward the drop-off, Jenna noticed large flashing security signs directing taxis into a single lane for inspection. The cab driver shrugged and glanced at Jenna through the rearview mirror.

"Was that here earlier today?" Jenna wanted to know.

"Nah, this is somethin' new," he replied. He craned his neck over to see farther down the line. "Looks like they're just checking ID cards and letting people move on."

Jenna nodded, collecting her cards and boarding passes to keep at the ready. It'd take a minute to work their way up to the inspection point. The smell of vehicle exhaust was already seeping into the cab, making her nauseous. She hated airports.

Once at the head of the line, the cabbie flashed his ID at the first security officer while lowering the power rear window for Jenna to pass her documents to the second. Jenna waited patiently, expecting to collect her papers and be on her way to the terminal. She glanced around and noticed that the inspection lane was being dismantled and the signs turned off. End of shift, she assumed.

"Open the trunk, please," the first officer ordered the cabbie.

Jenna swung around, realizing something wasn't right, but the second officer appeared at the back window with further instructions, none of which sounded friendly.

"We'll need to inspect your carry-on luggage too, ma'am." He pointed at her attaché case and purse. Puzzled but not yet alarmed, she passed them to the officer through the window. The first officer told the cabbie to follow him on his motorcycle. Jenna noticed two police cruisers, lights flashing, pulling up behind the cab.

"What did he tell you?" she asked the cabbie.

"Nuthin'. Just to follow him. Never heard of airport security pulling anything like this before." He put the cab in gear and joined the small impromptu motorcade as it made its way into the part of the airport that was off-limits to the public.

Jenna turned around to examine the police cruiser directly behind them, and a bolt of recognition struck her. The man next to the driver was the same corporal who had taken her and Hernandez to see Stall—and he was still in uniform.

"They're not airport security," she told the cabbie. "They're with the Pentagon."

The cabbie looked at her through the rearview mirror again, wondering if his redheaded fare had run afoul of the military. "Did you take photos of that place or somethin'? I know they hate it when people photograph the Pentagon. Maybe they saw you do something wrong."

"I wish that were the case," she sighed as the motorcade stopped at a huge motorcoach guarded by a half-dozen soldiers. "I'm afraid they want to see me because I'm doing something right, and they don't happen to like it." She watched as uniformed men brought her luggage and personal effects into the coach, figuring she'd be the next to enter it.

The motorcop, leaving his bike running, walked back to speak to the cabbie.

"We're taking your passenger off your hands, sir. Please follow me back to the main airport feeder road."

"What about my fare?" the cabbie asked, tapping on the meter.

"Give her your business card. She'll mail you a check."

The cabbie started to grumble, but the officer was insistent.

"Give her your business card *now*. Then follow me."

The rear door was opened, and Jenna knew it was time to face the person responsible for setting up the roadblock. She collected the card from the cabbie and stepped out of the cab to study the metallic motorcoach, which evidently served as a mobile command center. She hardly noticed the four soldiers surrounding her, nor did they have to urge her forward. Jenna wanted this over with. She heard the taxi motorcade departing behind her as she walked up to face the motorcoach door.

She grabbed the door handle and pulled it open, surprising the soldiers by stepping up into the motorcoach in one decisive movement and closing the door behind her.

Inside were six military guards, two of whom were tearing her luggage, purse, and attaché case apart to search through their contents. Seated behind a desk at the end of the coach was a heavyset man in his sixties, crew cut freshly trimmed, uniform rumpled, gripping a mug of coffee with one beefy hand and flexing Jenna's boarding passes with the other.

"You haven't learned to knock before coming in?" the man scowled.

"I believe I've given you far more courtesy than you've given me. I give you Exhibit A."

She pointed at the guards going through her lingerie. They stopped in mid-search, vaguely embarrassed. The big man harrumphed, and the guards quickly resumed the inspection.

His gaze bore down on her. "My men were to knock first and escort you in. You obviously preempted that. You just yank doors open recklessly without knowing what's behind them?" he demanded.

"I've yanked a disconnect module out of a safety-defeated power panel with my bare hands," she retorted, "so my threshold for recklessness is pretty high. Frankly, you don't even show up on my radar."

"Do you know whom you're talking to?" he warned.

"I can see you're a general," Jenna observed.

"And I can see you're a pain in the rear," the man shot back, waving the boarding passes in her face. "Why do you have five boarding passes for five different airlines?"

"Airlines overbook flights all the time. Is it a crime for me to overbook flights?"

"We'll see. If you want to make any of these flights, sit down and submit to a polygraph test, now." He pointed to the machine being rolled across the motorcoach floor toward Jenna.

She kept her eyes fixed on the general, barely blinking.

He snickered. "No argument from you? No debate about unreasonable search and seizure?"

"I'm guessing that everything you do is unreasonable, so let's get it over with." She sat down and let the polygraph technician wire her up, her gaze still fixed on the general's eyes.

Curiosity got the better of her and she ventured a question. "Don't you and General Stall answer to the same superior?"

"He answers to the president; I answer to the secretary of defense."

"Riiiiiight. Aren't the president and secretary on the same page?"

"They're not even in the same universe."

Moments later, the tech looked up at the general. "I have baseline lock. She's ready, General Melliton."

The general nodded back. Jenna didn't recognize his name, but was positive this boorish man was the opposite of General Stall in too many ways to count. She hoped to apply that knowledge during the interrogation.

"You're Doctor Jenna Wilkes?" he asked.

"Yes."

The general glanced at the tech, who gave a thumbs-up. The polygraph was working fine.

"Why do you have boarding passes for five different airlines?"

"Some airlines serve peanuts, others serve pretzels, some Coca-Cola, others Pepsi."

The general glared at her, but she met his angry gaze and then some. He glanced at the tech. "Well?"

"Uh, she told the truth, so far as the polygraph is concerned. But I don't think what she said was an actual answer to your question."

General Melliton rubbed his stubbly chin and tried again. "Which of these five airlines were you planning to fly on today?"

"None of them."

The tech nodded. She spoke the truth.

"Do you own stock in any air carriers?" The general walked around to lean against the front of his desk, folding his arms and looking Jenna in the eye.

"No."

"Maybe you should." He glanced backward at the stack of boarding passes on his desk. "So, which airline *are* you planning to fly on today?"

"Air Eckhardt."

"There's no such thing," he smirked.

"We kinda fly under the radar, because the fare is free. If we let word get around, we might have to let people like you fly on it. And there goes the neighborhood."

Melliton decided to cut the quibbling short. "Look, you don't want to be here, Doctor Wilkes, and I sure don't want you here either. So, let's just get down to what's important."

She nodded, but he still saw fire in her eyes.

"Go ahead," she answered.

"What exactly did you create in that isolator lab?"

"I don't know."

"How does it work?"

"I don't know."

"Do you know anybody who knows how it works?"

"Yes I do."

"Who might that be?"

"Me."

Melliton tilted his head toward the technician, who ran over the printouts once again. "Well?" the general demanded.

"I don't know how, sir, but all four of her answers are truthful."

"Test it again," the general insisted.

The technician turned toward Jenna, who took her eyes off the general to focus on him. "Do you like General Melliton as a person?" he asked her.

"Yeah, he's swell. He really bleeds red, white, and blue," she mocked.

The meters were going crazy on the polygraph. Melliton couldn't help but notice and pointed at the readouts. "What's that mean?"

The technician paused. "Down deep, I don't think she really likes you. Sir."

"Well, it's mutual." He circled back behind his desk, noticing that Jenna was no longer watching him but staring at the polygraph instead. He figured this was yet another way for her to show contempt for him.

"Doctor Wilkes, you're on the verge of making a very powerful enemy right about now."

The tone of Melliton's threat raised the hackles on the necks of the guards.

It also raised Jenna's ire. "You know, I cooperated with you, I let Igor here wire me up, I answered your questions even though you abducted me without a warrant, and *still* you're threatening me? Forget this crap." She started yanking the probes off her arms and head with pointed disgust.

Melliton paused, wondering whether to insist on continued questioning, but Jenna began striking up a conversation with the technician.

"Hey, do these things work correctly if the subject is suffering from severe post-traumatic stress disorder?"

The technician looked up at Melliton, who nodded his okay to answer the question. "No, Doctor Wilkes, in some cases of PTSD the polygraph results can be virtually worthless."

Jenna walked over to her luggage, quickly repacked her effects, and zipped everything up. The guards looked on, uncertain what to do since Melliton issued no orders but only stared at Jenna in silence. She slung her luggage over her shoulder, walked up to the general's desk, and quietly collected her boarding passes.

She surprised him by pushing her business card across the desk toward him. "Based on your technician's answer, you've wasted your time and mine with this polygraph stunt. Next time you want to know something, just call me."

There was a knock at the motorcoach door.

Jenna smiled at the sound. "Air Eckhardt," she explained. "Great door-to-door service."

The guards outside informed Melliton that Eckhardt's private limousine had somehow determined Jenna's location and was waiting outside for her.

Jenna stopped at the threshold to look back at Melliton. "General, do you know why I like Air Eckhardt best of all?"

He shook his head, figuring she'd get the last word in no matter what.

"Granola bars," she answered.

She closed the door, leaving Melliton to stew over the civilian who got the better of him in front of his own men.

That was a situation that Melliton would not allow to stand.

A quick consultation with the corporal who alerted him to Jenna's presence in D.C. prompted Melliton to redeploy the vehicle inspection points. There was enough time to catch a second fly in the web—Jenna's doctoral advisor.

34

After Jenna left the Pentagon, Stall called Riesen in to continue the meeting with Philip Hernandez. The discussion was sharp and divisive, with three agendas in bitter competition. But some things started to make more sense in the course of the debate.

"The problem," said Philip, "is that the energy flow behaves like lightning in one respect: it follows the path of least resistance. *That* is why the approach Jenna recommends is the only way to go on this."

"Philip," Stall intervened, "Why not just close the water gates feeding the turbines? Why drain the entire dam?"

"The grid will kick in, finding the shortest *electrical* path to avoid a switch to a different form of energy, in this case the mechanical rotation of the turbine rotors that generate the electricity. This is why Sexton said that nothing short of draining the dam could force the effect to leap energy between the mechanical and electrical domains."

"Where would we put the water?"

"Jenna suggested watering the desert with it."

Riesen all but laughed at Philip's statement. "Water the desert? What is she talking about? What a waste!"

"She said it wouldn't be a waste if watering made the desert fertile."

Riesen scoffed, but Stall found the idea interesting. It brought to mind some predictions in the Old Testament, ones he had not considered capable of being literally realized.

Had there not been six straight years of record snowfalls in California, Stall would have had no options in regard to the dam: the water behind it would have been too precious to risk. As things stood, there'd be no better time than the present to entertain the possibility of draining it. The general understood the importance of fortuitous timing.

Stall directed his next instruction to Philip. "Philip, look me now straight in the eye."

Philip complied.

"Tell me why you believe in any of this."

"Let's just say that Jenna and I spoke on the flight over, and she did another dissertation defense for me in private. As far as I'm concerned, she passed this time."

Riesen posed another question of Philip. "What would happen if we didn't drain the dam but shut down the entire North American power grid?"

"Jenna speculates that power would flow into the grid from a natural source, like the millions of lightning strikes hitting the earth daily. Normally, most lightning hits the oceans, but that might be what changes. Either way, the effect will stay electrical. The lightning would modulate to conserve the AC patterns feeding into Livermore to deliver those eight kilowatts into her device."

Philip's answer was simply unacceptable to Riesen.

Stall tried to walk through Jenna's proposition with Philip to make sure he understood it properly. "Philip, are you saying that if we drain that dam, the power flow won't be interrupted? That the entire region's power will still be at full capacity?"

"Yes."

"Are you expecting supernatural lightning bolts to fly out of the sky to feed the generators or something?"

"No, it will be completely unremarkable."

Stall thought about the story of Elijah and the destitute widow, whose tiny cruse of oil and small container of flour never went empty—also unremarkably, without an overt show of power. "What's the difference between shutting the valves to the turbines versus draining the entire dam?" the general asked.

"If you don't drain the dam," Philip answered, "the water still behind that huge wall has immense potential energy, pent-up energy due to the pull of gravity on it. The proximity of that energy affects the path of least resistance I mentioned. But if you drain the dam, that path shifts through the mechanical motion of the turbines. Water in the dam prevents the transition from electricity to mechanical motion."

Riesen shook his head. "I have a master's in electrical engineering, Dr. Hernandez, so forgive me for being critical, but do you have equations or measurements to back up these assertions? You're being so vague, it sounds like you're talking about auras, magic, or other nonsense. Can you quantify this alleged path of least resistance in a way meaningful to another scientist?"

Philip didn't lose a beat. "The effect is tied to the local energy density. Not too many scientists have dealt with that concept, but a few have assigned significance to it. In the twentieth century, I think Hoyle and Narlikar floated the idea that the vacuum speed of light was a function of the local energy density. They weren't necessarily correct, but at least they saw that the local energy density could have far-reaching implications. Those energy density terms appear in Jenna's dissertation, but are handled in a new and novel way."

"Sir Fred Hoyle?" Riesen mocked. "You can only cite dissident physicists in your favor?"

"I have an eight-kilowatt energy flow in my favor, coming out of nowhere. Right now, the only scientists who don't look like deer caught in the headlights *are* the dissidents."

"Is there any proof her equations are correct?" Riesen pressed.

"Jenna's equations predict the energy jumps we've already seen. They predict that the energy draw should remain electrical at the known jump points. And they have. There *is* no other scientist with equations on the table concerning these discoveries. She's at least seven years ahead of anybody else on this stuff ... maybe even decades ahead."

Riesen pointed at the green plastic bottle on Stall's desk. "You're telling me, General, that Doctor Wilkes demonstrated her invention by blowing bubbles in your face? How can you even *consider* draining a hydroelectric dam and jeopardizing the power grid on the word of a redhead with a fetish for children's toys?"

Stall drummed his fingers on the desk, considering how seriously Riesen took this issue.

Philip reached out for the green bottle. "You should be careful there," Philip warned Riesen. "Using kids' bubble wands to illustrate the principle was Eckhardt's idea, not Jenna's. Think twice before slamming a Nobel laureate, unless of course you're another Nobel laureate."

Riesen pursed his lips, now feeling stupid for throwing around his master's degree in front of Stall. "Fine, Doctor Hernandez, show me what I missed." He leaned back, unconvinced but attentive.

"As I understand it," continued Philip, "when you're standing still, measured time is undistorted and flat, like the film in the ring." He dipped the wand into the soap solution and held it up. The shape of the lights overhead glinted off the iridescent film of soap stretched across the plastic loop.

"When you move faster and faster," he said, waving the wand in a wide arc, "time distorts like this film, and dilates, slows down. It's a bad analogy, but you'll understand it better when I get to the point. If I wave the wand fast enough, bubbles are created. The bubbles correspond to traveling at the speed of light. The bubble's shape represents time that has stopped completely, as viewed from the rest frame.

"This is where Jenna's imagination comes in.

"Basically, modern science had concluded that the only way you can create bubbles is by waving your arm—the wand has to be in motion. But she figured out the other way to create a time bubble, as she calls them." Philip reloaded the wand and put it up to his lips, blowing a large bubble that floated toward Riesen.

"She was able to get that frozen time effect without pushing objects up to the speed of light. She got that result in a stationary setting. You can keep the wand motionless and create the same effect."

"How?" asked Stall.

"Well, it's complex for laymen, General. She talks about folded manifolds and overlapped frames. She's visualizing geometries others cannot even conceive. How she was able to grip *space itself*—able to discern its warp and woof interweave with the fields in it by extending Einstein's equivalence principle—defies explanation. That was what her dissertation committee ran aground on. It was unorthodox, it was all but heretical, and she did herself no favors seven years ago in defending it the way she did. Oh, wait a minute, I've got something that might help ..."

Philip pulled two coaster-size glass discs out of his briefcase. "It's an even worse analogy than the soap bubbles, but bear with me. These are polarized lenses, like you find in good sunglasses. If I hold them together aligned in the same direction, the light goes straight through them, right?

But as I rotate one of the lenses …" he slowly twisted the top lens against the lower one, "less and less light can go through and the two lenses appear darker. At ninety degrees rotation they appear black." The lenses behaved as Philip described.

"This analogy might help you grasp what Jenna is doing to space itself. Empty space normally lets everything pass through it, including time. It's almost as if the isolator rotates space against space, blocking time from passing through the core." He repeated the visual demonstration. "Jenna's equations include something akin to a polarization tensor for spacetime."

"All fiction," Riesen shot back. "Not even good fiction. Polarized lenses? I have more respect for the children's book where the ant walks across a folded skirt to illustrate a tesseract."

"Oh, you like your physics straight up?" Philip asked. "Fine. The tensors we use in physics, the Faraday tensor, the stress-energy tensor, et cetera, all give field components in terms of space and time. So this young girl, see, she figures out how to invert those tensors to express space and time as a function of those fields without omitting those pesky retardation potentials. That covers, oh, about the first half page of her work well before she applies her new geometry to spacetime foliation—she's just warming up, see. Keeping up with me, Colonel?"

Dialing down the sarcasm, Stall barred Riesen from responding. The general wanted confirmation on corroborating witnesses. "Eckhardt thinks she's right about all this?" he asked Philip.

"You can't argue with the results, Harry. No scientist in his right mind would have ever granted the possibility of her isolator doing what it does. None. That's probably why the dissertation committee rejected it … I'd have to say, mercilessly. Too much was at stake."

"What, exactly, was at stake there?" Stall wanted to know.

Philip ran his bronze hands through his black curly hair. He was guilty of the very thing he was about to expound against.

"Uh, well, scientists protect their turf. Orthodoxy. They rally around the prevailing paradigm. Sure, they've gotten fingered for it. Some thinkers have blown the whistle on that game. Kuhn. Popper. Bloom. Indicting refereed journals as self-reinforcing circles. Indicting scientists for bias, for inability to see past textbook definitions. The system kept out crackpots nicely, but also threw its share of babies out with the bathwater.

"It's why we rejected Jenna's work. Who'd burn an entire library of physics books on the word of a combative, rebellious twenty-two-year-old?"

Riesen jumped at the opening. "Doctor, *we* seem to be planning to drain an entire dam on the word of a combative, rebellious twenty-nine-year-old at this point. You are clearly admitting that the conservative thing to do would be to reject this proposal."

Philip returned the wand to the bottle and tightened the cap. But after he had placed it back on Stall's desk, the general reached over for it. Stall began expertly hefting it up and down about a foot in the air while speaking to Riesen.

"Colonel, I think you're hung up on the wrong thing."

Riesen looked quizzically at him.

Without warning, Stall tossed the bottle at him, and Riesen quickly snapped his arms up to catch it.

"Sir?" Riesen asked, taken aback.

"You weren't quite ready for that, William?"

"No."

"*Nobody's* ready for this technology, but here it is, being thrown in our face. It's potent, it's controversial, and we understand precious damn little about it. So ..." He put his elbows on the desk and interwove his fingers, leaning forward for emphasis.

"How would *you* deal with this technology, Colonel? Shove it back into a CryoMax lab, like a genie back into his bottle? Since when are we Luddites here?"

"But an entire dam, General ..."

Stall put the phone to his ear while answering Riesen. Philip warily regarded the exchange.

"It's just water, William," Stall reasoned. "A hell of a lot of it, sure, but it *can* be refilled. Why are you so sure the energy transfer won't leap to the turbines? It's been leaping everywhere else Zilcher has pushed it. Eckhardt, Hernandez, Sexton, Johanssen, Bartleby—they all to a man believe Wilkes is right. Where is the contrary evidence? Old-school thinking is coming up empty. Isn't orthodoxy cracking even as we speak because of Wilkes?"

Riesen sensed that, secular-sounding rhetoric notwithstanding, Stall's religiosity had robbed him of the objectivity needed to make the right call. So long as Stall was operating under color of authority as a general officer of the U.S. Army, he was expected to keep his personal convictions in check.

The colonel received confirmation that things had gotten out of control when Stall barked his next words into the phone.

"Get me the Army Corps of Engineers."

Philip stewed in the backseat of the cab, disturbed by the earlier clash between Riesen and Stall. Nothing good could come of it.

The traffic into the airport slowed, and Philip soon learned why at the vehicle inspection checkpoint. Minutes later, he was in General Melliton's motorcoach. Philip had more to lose than Jenna, and realized the quickest ticket out of Melliton's mobile command center was to play along and cooperate. Good intentions aside, he got off on the wrong foot as the polygraph was being wired up.

"Was Jenna here earlier?" Philip wanted to know.

"*I'm* asking the questions here, Professor," Melliton warned.

That told Philip what he wanted to know—she *had* been here, and they'd probably gotten nowhere with her. Interrogating Philip was their fallback position.

"Do you know what Doctor Wilkes built at CryoMax?" Melliton began.

"Yes."

"What is it?"

"An isolator."

"Really. Just a plain-Jane isolator."

"Well, it's got some extra bells and whistles, but it's an isolator all the same."

"Porter?" Melliton called the technician by name.

"All true so far, sir."

Melliton knew he'd have to be clever with this one. "Her isolator pulls power without being plugged in?"

"Yes.

"Do any other isolators do that?"

"Sure."

"Porter?" Melliton checked again.

"Still good," the technician replied.

"Does her isolator work the same way conventional ones do?"

"No. Is this twenty questions or something?" The quip was ignored.

"Do you know how her isolator works?"

"No."

"Who does?"

"Doctor Wilkes."

Melliton slammed his fist onto the desk in fury, teeth gritted, but said nothing. He would not reveal that Jenna had been there, even in a moment of anger. "Can her invention be turned into a weapon, Professor?"

"Absolutely."

"Do you know how it can be turned into a weapon?" Melliton persisted.

"Yes, it would be quite easy, in fact."

"Tell me how."

"Melt down the titanium and pour it into molds to make bullets."

"You trying to be funny?"

"Not at all."

"Porter?"

"He's still telling the truth, sir."

"Professor, let me be more specific," Melliton spoke as if to a child. "Apart from turning it into bullets or dropping it on someone's head, can the Wilkes device be weaponized?"

"No." Philip looked Melliton in the eye, not backing down.

Melliton leaned over toward Philip. "Listen, Professor, if I can't get what I need from you, I'm going to have to go and get it out of the girl. If you want to throw her to the wolves to save your own skin, that's your problem. I don't really care."

"Look, General, I couldn't protect Jenna when she was my student. What makes you think I can protect her now?"

Melliton wrote on his notepad, ignoring Philip's question.

Against his better judgment, Philip let his exasperation peek through. "You know, just because you have a hammer doesn't make every problem a nail."

"Maybe so, Professor, but you're forgetting one thing." Melliton kept writing.

"What's that?"

"I've still got the hammer." Melliton looked up at Philip. "It's big enough that I can mix metaphors like that with impunity." He set the pad down and tried a different line of inquiry. "Concerning Doctor Wilkes—does her dissertation research provide the answers I'm looking for?"

"Yes. You'll find the answers there."

"I don't think so," Melliton frowned. "I hired Doctor Brevard Mays to analyze her dissertation, and so far he's found nothing in it remotely relevant to what's going on in Livermore. You do know Doctor Mays, don't you?"

"Yes," Philip admitted, "he was my best student next to Doctor Wilkes." Philip found it ironic that he wouldn't have qualified that praise just a few months ago.

"Why would Doctor Mays be unable to see any connection between Wilkes's dissertation and these power flows?" Melliton pressed.

"I don't know."

"He's lying," the technician cut in.

Melliton snapped at the technician. "Nice to know the polygraph's plugged in, Porter. That's the first lie it's detected all day." He turned back to Philip. "Well, what of it, Professor?"

"Brevard is very bright. He would be able to figure out the connection, given enough time and information." True enough, Philip knew, but he kept his next thought to himself. *If you picked Brevard because you want to pit him against Jenna and fight fire with fire, you've achieved your goal, General—you're now officially fighting one loose cannon with another.*

The technician assured Melliton that Philip's statement was true. Melliton tapped his pen on his chin thoughtfully.

"Professor, I'm pretty sure there's something you're not telling me, something that would explain why Doctor Mays is drawing a blank."

Philip didn't want to mention the earlier versions of Jenna's dissertation, knowing Mays only had access to the final purged copy. He decided to take a big risk and put on a sarcastic air. "Okay, I'll come clean, General. It's hard to believe, but Doctor Wilkes, the one who wears the coat of many stains, is so damn smart we might as well burn the world's physics books. Hell, she's already built a half-dozen time machines. You should see the first itty bitty one she made: it's really cute and only cost $12,000. Such a deal."

Melliton stalked back behind his desk, livid. "Get this jerk out of my sight!" he erupted. "We'll get what we need from the girl."

The technician detached the polygraph wires as Melliton disappeared behind a steel door. Philip collected his briefcase, hoping he could still make his flight home. A military courier took him away.

As the technician powered down the polygraph to clean it, he found it odd that Philip's last comments showed no evidence of lying. He dismissed the anomaly, deciding the polygraph was due for another calibration.

General Conrad Melliton flopped into his desk chair steamed at the dismal progress his team had achieved. He'd interrogated two key principals and had nothing—*nothing*—to show for it. He believed more than ever that national security was at stake. It was clear that these people had something to hide; otherwise, why work so hard at trying to keep it hidden?

He reached for some bottled water he hadn't finished, took a sip, then poured the rest into a small potted plant he kept on his desk, a gift from his granddaughter. The plant was the only part of his private life allowed into his work environment. He was otherwise all business. The plant wouldn't even be here had his granddaughter not pushed the right buttons, but Melliton always kept his promises.

All but his promise to nail down what was going on in Livermore.

That's when a phone call he never expected came in, from a disaffected colonel who used to work under him.

35

The stopover at Eckhardt's Boston mansion was something Jenna was looking forward to. She made herself at home in the Valley of the Books, chatting briefly with Katherine while waiting for Eckhardt to arrive by helicopter. While waiting, she decided to go through her briefcase and put it back in order. She hated that Melliton's soldiers had violated her privacy so casually.

Flipping through the papers, she noticed something she had forgotten to give to Professor Hernandez. It was an envelope addressed to him, with Sexton's return address on it, wedged in the stack of papers Hernandez had given her to copy and relay to Eckhardt. The inclusion of the private note was obviously an oversight by Hernandez.

Jenna put the envelope back in her briefcase, wondering. The envelope was a bit mysterious. It had no stamp, had never been mailed, and was mixed in with Sexton's review of her dissertation. Did it have something to do with Jenna? Was it a cover letter to Sexton's analysis of Jenna's work? She pulled the envelope back out of the briefcase and stared at it.

It wasn't hers to open. It was a private message to someone else.

She opened it, hesitating before unfolding the sheet of graph paper inside. *Maybe it's about my doctoral work.* Her justification sounded lame even to herself.

Then Jenna read it.

Dear Philip,

Please forgive me for letting you take the blame for the garbled wording on the Wilkes Agreement. You should know that the wording was no mistake. I knew what the agreed-upon wording was, but I didn't want the committee to quash Wilkes's research. I also needed to know how willing she was to defend her ideas against opposition, to get a taste of what price the iconoclast pays. I therefore chose the wording in the Agreement deliberately. I don't know if you'll ever get this letter, but if you do come to read this, know that privately

I have always held you blameless. Science is too often done by cowards. No one could accuse your student of cowardice. She might end up shaming us all. Good for her.

Peace,

Wally Sexton

She got up and started pacing like a caged animal, one emotion being overtaken by the next in an angry cataract of resentment. *Get a taste? The price the iconoclast pays? He ruined my life! I can't believe he did this! All that suffering for nothing! A taste? It was a ton of bricks, not a taste!*

Furious, she called Metro Hospital on her cell phone and got through to Sexton's room.

"Hello?" he answered.

"You had no right to do this to me," Jenna exploded. "I just read your note to Professor Hernandez. All these years I thought it was an innocent mistake that couldn't be helped, but now I find out it was all done deliberately, with calculation! What gave you the right to go out and destroy me like that? Like a cat playing with a mouse? I'm a person, not a pawn! I can't believe you did this!"

"Miss Wilkes, I'm so sorry ..."

"You know, at the rotunda, I first thought you were a pompous jerk. Then, at the hospital, I start to think you're my friend, that I was wrong about you being a jerk. But you know what? You're worse than a jerk. I don't ever want to see you, talk to you, or have anything else to do with you, Doctor."

"But Miss Wilkes ..."

Jenna snapped her cell phone shut so abruptly it flipped out of her fingers and fell to the wood floor. She kicked it across the room in anger.

The phone slid under Eckhardt's wheelchair; he had entered the Valley unnoticed. He maneuvered over to pick it up.

"I heard everything," he rolled up toward her, his tone conciliatory.

Her chin jutted out defiantly, defensively, angrily, eyes roiling. He knew she had been hurt by what she learned about Sexton.

"Why?" she demanded of Eckhardt. "Why did he do it? Why'd he put me through hell like that? He had no right to do this to me! I lost the last seven years because of him!"

"Jenna," Eckhardt tried to calm her down, "I know this is painful news. But you have to think this through. Sexton had a lot to lose."

"And so it's okay to make me the loser instead?" she accused.

"No. I know this looks bad, but you have to open your eyes wider to see what Doctor Sexton did for you. Had he not adjusted the agreement, what do you think would have happened?"

"What?"

"You would have defended your revision zero dissertation the next day, the dissertation Doctor Hernandez was expecting you to present all along. The revolutionary aspect of your work had already been shut down that first day, completely rejected, no second chance possible. Sexton kept it alive for you, was letting you defend it. He let you live to fight another day."

"I don't buy it. He could have defended me, stood with me."

"You may have taken him down to defeat with you. You know how the committee treated you. The dean was already looking for reasons to retire elderly professors to make room for new blood. Should Sexton have ended his career defending your crackpot idea? That's a lot of what-ifs to put on an old man's shoulders, don't you think? You were young, resilient. He felt his time was coming to a close."

"Resilient?! Try *vulnerable*." She began pacing again as she railed. "Look what happened to me, Doctor Eckhardt. I couldn't hold a job. I was a Ph.D. working as a waitress at nights to keep from being evicted. My mother gloated that all the time and money I sank into Stanford was a waste. She laughed when I lost my chance at postdoc research. *Laughed.* I was a failure. She said it served me right for following the same dream my father followed."

Eckhardt's voice was measured. "Okay, fine, Miss Wilkes. Let's do that—let's look at what happened to you. You ended up at CryoMax, where you figured out how to realize your ideas, on the cheap, on the sly, with limited resources. Now you're on the verge of turning the entire world upside down. Had you stayed at Stanford, none of this would have happened, because postdocs work on other people's projects. Anything done on your own would have been strictly theoretical, suitable for obscure journals at best. You had no resources. CryoMax had the resources you needed, and you had the motivation to figure out how to use them."

"But I *took* those resources from CryoMax, Doctor. *Stole* them."

"I know. I know because I allowed that to happen. I got you hired, I kept you protected, I put you in a department I thought would spur you to see possibilities, and you didn't disappoint me. You figured it out. I saw that you were in a position to reach critical mass. You would *never* have had the impact, never built these devices, never pursued your dream, had Sexton not set these events in motion. Yes, that made life difficult. You should thank him that he made your life difficult. You wouldn't be here right now if he'd made your life easy. Nothing good comes easily. *Per ardua ad astra*: through adversity to the stars."

Jenna was shaking her head at his words. "You don't get it. I went incommunicado during those two weeks, Doctor Eckhardt. I shut out everything to rewrite that paper. No phone, no mail, no visitors. And guess what? My father *died* during that time, and *I didn't even know*. He never lived to see me get my doctorate. If Sexton hadn't meddled, my father would have seen his dream for me come true. And then ..." she hesitated, "and then Dad was supposed to be buried, but I wasn't around to object when my mother had him cremated, because I was hospitalized. So hearing that all this was actually *intentional* is—"

"Your father's dream was to see you cave-in before that committee?" Eckhardt asked softly.

Now tears filled Jenna's eyes. She knew the answer to that question better than she knew anything in the whole world. She looked away, feeling as if her father were somehow looking at her through Eckhardt's steady gaze.

"Sexton didn't have the right," she persisted, trying to evade Eckhardt's calm logic.

"Exactly. The only thing he had a right to do was to knock you down, then and there, force you to knuckle under, and turn you into a carbon copy clone of the other Ph.D.s the school was churning out. He had no right to keep the door open on your new ideas with an unwilling committee. What he had the right to do was prevent you from even defending that first revision, since you didn't have written permission to make the switch. Who initiated the questioning on your paper that morning, Jenna?"

"Sexton," she admitted grudgingly. "Sexton did. Carter really wanted to wait till Professor Hernandez arrived so the defense could be canceled according to protocol, but Doctor Sexton overrode her and began questioning me."

"There! See, that's what I'm talking about. Sexton had no right to do that. He violated Stanford policy right there. That's when he gave you your first chance to defend yourself. Do you think Hernandez would have let you present that revision had he known about it?"

"No. Definitely not."

"Right. You wouldn't be here today if it weren't for Sexton. He stuck his neck out as far as he could. He was responsible for pushing you up to escape velocity. I wouldn't have known about your work except for seeing all these rapid-fire revisions being pumped out under your name at the document center. Sexton put you on my radar. Maybe some gratitude and forgiveness would be in order. By your own admission, you had no right to steal resources from CryoMax. It's hypocritical to hold Sexton to a standard you yourself failed to meet, isn't it?"

Jenna's eyes were red and puffy, and she felt about an inch tall. The air in the room, saturated with unspoken accusations, throbbed dully in her suddenly hot ears. Nothing was said, but the roar of conscience forced her to see she had kicked Sexton when he was down—the very thing the committee had done to her.

"I have to go see him, Doctor. Right now. I have to apologize to him, in person. I treated him terribly."

"You don't have time for that. Seriously. You can call him back, or maybe write him an apology."

She stared at the note in her hands, re-reading it over and over in silence.

"I know what to do, then," she decided. "Can you send something to Doctor Sexton for me?"

"Sure. I'm heading out to the West Coast in an hour. What do you want me to take?"

"Hold a second." She thought through her words carefully as she wrote. "Please, please, *please* get this to Doctor Sexton as soon as possible," she begged.

"Gladly, Miss Wilkes. He'll have this today." Eckhardt looked down to see what Jenna had given him.

It was the original note from Sexton to Hernandez, handwritten on graph paper, that ended with Sexton's simple sign-off: *Peace, Wally.* Underneath Sexton's words, Jenna had added something else:

Dear Dr. Sexton,
Thank you.
Peace, Jenna

He looked up at her with a pleased expression, but she misinterpreted it.

"Is it too short?" she asked.

"No," Eckhardt answered. "No, Jenna, it's just right."

Part III

36

Several weeks later, Riesen was summoned to Stall's office. The colonel could see that Stall was seething. Stall bid Riesen to sit down, then handed him a sheet of paper. Riesen examined it and handed it back. No words had been exchanged.

Stall spoke quietly. "At first I was sure the leak was something Emmerich had done, or maybe one of his underlings had loose lips."

Riesen remained motionless.

Stall looked him in the eye and asked just one question of him. "Why?"

The simple word hung heavy in the air, as much an accusation of betrayal as a request for explanation.

Riesen both dreaded and welcomed the inevitable showdown. "I swore to protect and uphold the Constitution. That comes first, General, sir."

Stall nodded. He glanced down at the court injunction on his desk blocking the further draining of the dam. It had only been drained by twelve feet.

"Was the strategy behind this injunction your idea, Colonel?"

"Honestly, no. The ACLU figured out that angle on their own."

"I see." There was nothing but disappointment in Stall's eyes, but Riesen too had deep disappointment in his superior officer.

"Can I pose a few questions, then, William?" the general ventured.

Riesen noticed that Stall had used his first name, indicating at least a partial relaxing of the tension. "Please, go ahead, sir." Riesen maintained his outwardly calm demeanor.

"What makes you believe that draining that dam constitutes an establishment of religion? That draining it will knock a hole in the Constitution from which it can never recover?"

"I think Doctor Wilkes was quite open about the implications of her work. This operation would use public dollars in an experiment that provides a pretext to knock down the wall of separation between church and state. Court precedents are clear on this—a textbook, even a scientific one that omits deities and religion, establishes a religion if the ideas in it lead to or imply a god. The courts hold that such textbooks place our democracy at risk. And this dam experiment is more blatant than any textbook they've struck down."

"Let me understand you then ..." continued Stall. "If the dam were to break, the U.S. Constitution would collapse with it? The U.S. Constitution is safe only if the water stays behind the wall of that dam, and it's jeopardized if that wall were to be breached? That a piece of paper stands or falls with the water behind that wall?"

"It's a piece of paper, as you call it, that hundreds of thousands of Americans have died protecting."

"How many of those who gave their lives to protect the Constitution do you honestly think would oppose draining that dam if they were alive today?"

Riesen paused to think. The secularization of the country had really been a post–World War II phenomenon. Insofar as the vast majority of past soldiers' personal convictions were concerned, they may well have agreed with Stall were they to be summoned from the grave. But that was hardly relevant.

"Times change," Riesen answered. "We now know different. Their views weren't informed by a better appreciation of what the Constitution means. They also supported segregation, and if you go back far enough, slavery and worse."

"Maybe so. Sounds like you don't hold them in much respect—you cite their sacrifice to bolster your case, then trash their views as irrelevant." Stall rose from his chair.

"It seems to me," the general continued, "that whatever they died for is the thing they died for, and you can't come back in with your revisionist views and rewrite their epitaphs, Colonel.

"Further, it looks like the thing you're protecting is something of a moving target. That's pretty inconsistent, isn't it? Shouldn't the interpretation of the First Amendment also be a moving target? It shifted where it is today, why can't it shift somewhere else? But maybe it's not a moving target at all. Maybe it's a mangled victim of our penchant to twist things to suit our whims. Shouldn't you be defending the Constitution as originally written? Wouldn't that be more of a defense? If that document has been gutted, and you defend the gutted version, what kind of defense is that? Soldier?"

Riesen sat motionless. He didn't know whether to answer or simply leave. "It's a living document," he finally answered.

"Interesting," said Stall, still standing. "If I had a time machine and brought back some American soldiers from a hundred years ago, and they stood in this room, you realize what would happen regarding this matter?"

"What?"

"You and they would be trying to kill each other to protect the Constitution."

Riesen rose, preparing to put his cap back on. "General, I've been reassigned effective this morning to General Melliton's staff, at my request. I don't believe we can work together anymore." *Because you're willing to support a misguided Christian apologetics project with tax dollars.* Riesen thought it but didn't say it. He'd already said it five different ways and Stall wasn't listening.

"I'm very sorry to lose you, Colonel." Stall was sincere. "I'm even more sorry that you'd rather grovel under Melliton's boot than work where you're treated with respect. But I suppose you've already chosen your allegiances. One or the other of us is deluded, no doubt. But I'll stand with the former generations if you don't mind. They seemed to have a better idea of what they stood for. You're simply standing against something. You can't fight something with nothing, Colonel. Give my regards to Melliton." And Stall saluted, holding his salute.

Riesen returned the salute and waited for the general to drop his. Stall held the salute for an unprecedented minute and a half, his eyes boring into Riesen's.

Riesen found himself awash in thoughts: thoughts of betrayal of Stall, thoughts of Stall's betrayal of his oaths, thoughts about what Riesen was defending in the first place, thoughts of trading the benevolent oversight of Stall for the belligerence of Melliton. Stall was forcing Riesen to think all these through, not privately, but while being compelled by protocol to stare straight into Stall's penetrating gaze.

Stall finally dropped the salute and sat down, examining the injunction on his desk. Riesen let himself out of Stall's office, sure he had done the right thing. And not so sure.

37

It was the most heated meeting of the President's Committee of Advisors on Science and Technology on record. The Science Advisor to the President, Dr. Oren Hellman, had to use an iron fist to keep matters under control.

The quantum theory guys were in an uproar. The CryoMax isolator results jeopardized the long-dominant Copenhagen Interpretation of quantum mechanics while boosting the minority school of thought, the Stochastic Causal Interpretation. That minority view gained ground because the instantaneous propagation of the isolator effect couldn't be explained by appeals to photon entanglement.

The metaphysical implications were even worse. Many of the advisors feared the result of draining the dam. They grasped the significance of what Wilkes was predicting: this experiment could defy naturalistic explanation—and might do so in public view if the project couldn't be kept under wraps.

Up till then, they had all defined a miracle as a suspension of natural law, an intervention by an alleged divine being to briefly set aside natural law to make a point. Alleged cases of miracles were at least twenty centuries old, easily attributed to earlier primitive ignorance and myth-making.

Wilkes's work, if allowed to continue, would prove that there was external intervention necessary to support natural law and the cosmos in the first place. If that intervention, arguably divine in origin, would be withdrawn, the physical universe could not exist. There was no free lunch, not even for the universe itself. And she had somehow stumbled on it.

Hellman couldn't help but notice how similar this meeting seemed to be to the old McCarthy hearings he'd seen on a history videostick. It was a mental association he couldn't shake, making him increasingly hesitant about slamming the door on the Wilkes project.

Moreover, he respected Eckhardt as a scientist, despite having no patience for Eckhardt's rigid theological views. As far as Hellman could see, the only good coming out of Eckhardt's religious conceit was in the unrelated sphere of philanthropy—Eckhardt was anything but stingy with his earnings. Hellman knew his appreciation was strictly pragmatic, mirroring Voltaire's outlook on the social usefulness of religions he personally disdained.

More worrisome, this issue had the potential to inject the evolution-creation debate back into the public eye. The cold war between the camps had occasional hot spots break out. The creationists invariably lost in the courts of law, yet exercised disproportionate influence in the court of public opinion despite the media's depiction of evolutionism as the mark of an intelligent person.

Scientific evidence favoring evolution mounted because more researchers worked from that perspective, but the creationist counterflow of opposing ideas occasionally captured a scientist or two for its side. Thankfully, such gadflies remained in the minority. Until now, they'd all been stripped of any meaningful soapbox from which to speak.

Hellman had consulted with Philip Hernandez and Jonas Eckhardt in preparation for this meeting and received different accounts of the significance of Wilkes's work. The difference in their stories reflected the difference in their religious views. Hernandez was an atheist but was willing to go where the data led. Eckhardt was predictably theistic in his assessment. But both agreed that the cat had already been let out of the bag with the eight-kilowatt flow previously reported. They differed as to what breed of cat it was, though.

Hernandez was clinging to the multiverse theory to account for the energy flow. With a multiverse of innumerable universes, Jenna's device might be robbing the Peter universe to pay the Paul universe. Hernandez held this view despite the insuperable problems the explanation suffered (conservation interconnectivity, the resulting infinite regress, conflict with the causality-protecting wave collapse theorem, and neutrino shielding issues looming on the horizon). If the time-honored principle of Occam's razor were applied, Eckhardt actually made more sense: his was the simplest explanation that accounted for all the data.

It was an absolute mess.

That mess was spilling out into the conference room: scientists arguing about time travel, of all things. The group refused to adopt the redhead's loopy "time bubble" label for the singularity inside her isolator, but the honor of providing a new name incited an extended debate. The final winner was *chronopore*. Once approved, nobody bothered to use that term either.

Time travel was usually discounted using a causality argument, that effects and causes cannot be arbitrarily transposed. This debate was different. It centered on conservation laws. All the possible what-ifs were hotly disputed, involving the hole left in the present when an object was shifted in time. Up until the Wilkes discovery, a one-time placeholder of equivalent mass and energy would have been thought adequate to plug the hole, to balance out energy accounts and satisfy the conservation laws. Wilkes had driven a stake straight through that hypothetical idea with irredeemably hard data: a continuous eight-kilowatt flow that no existing theory could account for. It appeared that the universe didn't "just exist," but that something outside the universe was forcing it to exist. It was a materialist's nightmare.

Hellman *was* a materialist, one who up until now enjoyed discomfiting theists who crossed his path. But a mental picture that Eckhardt had painted for him earlier made his skin crawl.

"Man," Eckhardt began, "behaves like a little kid sitting on his daddy's lap, slapping his daddy's face. The kid can't reach the face without sitting on that lap."

Hellman recognized the simile, recognized that daddy represented God, recognized that the slaps were so many denials that God even existed. Hellman was about to dismiss the relevance of such blatantly circular reasoning when Eckhardt gave the story a disturbing twist.

"For decades," Eckhardt concluded, "most scientists have been successfully probing for new ways to slap that face. Jenna has dug down in a different direction to ask, *Hey, whose lap is this I just found?*"

It was a thought that caught Hellman in a mental vise so powerful, it distracted ... no, *vexed* him ... during the entire meeting. *Whose lap?* This wasn't a science debate anymore.

During a break in the proceedings, Hellman was pouring fresh coffee for himself when one of his colleagues, Dr. Roger Ferrier, approached him. Hellman nodded his unspoken acknowledgement as he sipped from his cup. Ferrier nodded back, glanced around at the milling scientists, and made an observation that hadn't been voiced in open session.

"Shame that Doctor Wilkes's discovery doesn't point to extraterrestrial intelligence or alien life," Ferrier lamented, shaking his balding head. "For something like that, the committee would have approved draining that dam in three minutes flat. Hell, most of these guys would have gone out there with buckets to help get it drained faster." Ferrier shrugged at the stray thought and drifted back into the sea of gray suits, Hellman staring after him in consternation.

Four hours later, Hellman called the president to inform him that the committee had deadlocked over the matter of draining the dam.

"How's that possible, Oren?" the president asked. "You're there to break a tie if one should occur. If I'm going to challenge the injunction, I need a consensus from you guys."

"I recused myself." Hellman loosened his tie, weary from the prior battle.

"Oren, this is too important for you to recuse yourself."

"Mr. President, sir, with all due respect, this is too important for me *not* to recuse myself."

And so Dr. Oren Hellman hung up the phone, brooding, never having intended to become a modern-day Gamaliel, and hating every minute of it.

38

Because her life had been marked by personal trials, she found herself attracted to the stories of others who understood personal sacrifice. Jenna saw how sacrifice was somehow fundamental and how it shaped the one who set aside self-interest, that love itself was bound up in sacrifice if one considered the kind of love of which there was no greater.

It was late, and she'd had her nightgown on for an hour already. She propped her head on her hands lying stomach-down across her bed, her legs crossed in the air behind her. She flipped the page and kept reading from the leather-bound book, her red hair often falling across its thin pages. Facing Jenna, Pinball assumed the regal posture of the sphinx, one paw stretched out farther than the other, her eyes satisfied slits.

Eckhardt suggested that the centuries-long attack on this book had its parallel in the attacks on her own work. That comment had been enough of a hook for Jenna to acknowledge that the caustic witnesses discrediting this book might also be mistaken. She recalcitrated when informed she had a closed mind, but finally realized it was in fact true.

When she had time to *study* the book, she went online for scholarly resources, becoming a closet seminarian in the process. She understood that such study was not to be neglected if she were to understand it. But when she wanted to *receive* what the book had to say, she pulled the leather copy off her nightstand and read it like this, lying on her bed.

Jenna felt she had found a sentence in it that she was ready to plant her life upon.

Her studies indicated that the sentence hailed from the most ancient part of the book. But the thought it contained spoke to her, and so she closed the book and considered the thought in its breadth and fullness.

Though He slay me, yet will I trust Him.

She wished her father were alive to see what was happening in her life. The thought saddened her. She pulled herself up and sat cross-legged, bidding Pinball to crawl into her lap.

She remembered the good times with her father. His unqualified support of her, even though she was the youngest of the three sisters, and often mistreated by them and her mother. She remembered ...

Her unwashed lab coat was slung across the bed and in reach. She put her hand on it and squeezed the fabric.

"*Though He slay me ...*" She couldn't get the thought out of her head.

Captain Michael Boudreaux was worried about dealing with Colonel Riesen's replacement, and more so when he learned there'd be no replacement, that General Stall intended to work directly with the two captains. Mike expected serious blowback given the unorthodox tactics they employed, but was gratified how easy Stall was to work with. That was good, considering the conflicting agendas warring over the stalled draining of the dam.

The working relationship with Stall also made it easier for Mike and Richard to convey Jenna's request to him. It involved a major retrofit to the UPS truck, but if Stall approved it, the mods could be made quickly.

Several days later, a UPS truck made a pickup at 3:30 AM at Jenna's home. A pickup that made the truck three tons heavier than when it first arrived. Only the guards, Jenna, Bryn, and the two captains knew of it.

The timing of the UPS pickup was none too soon. It wasn't long before legal steps were taken to nationalize the isolators, a draconian eminent domain play, to turn them over to the National Laboratory at Livermore for study.

At her polygraph test, Jenna told the interrogator that the isolators had already been given to the government, and she didn't know where they were. She answered no other questions as to details, but there was no doubt she was telling the truth about those two points.

She complained that intergovernmental agency communication failures were their problem, not hers. She hadn't lost the isolator, they lost it, so why were they holding her without cause?

The authorities had no choice but to release her. Had they bothered to compare notes with General Melliton, they might have known better than to let her go.

The night sky far from city lights was dominated by the Milky Way overhead. Richard glanced upward as he stepped out of the UPS truck and made his way to the campfire on the far side of their camp. He joined Mike, who was already enjoying the warmth of the fire from his lawn chair. As Richard sat down, he noticed Mike pressing some earphones into his ears.

"That doesn't look like your media player," Richard pointed out.

"It's not. This is Bryn's." Mike tapped the blue metal case.

"Where's yours?"

"We traded. He was criticizing the death metal music I listen to. Said it sounded like machine gun drumming and Cookie Monster vocals. Said I couldn't appreciate real music, classical stuff, so he challenged me to trade players with him."

"Let me hear what Bryn listens to," Richard asked.

Mike handed the earphones to Richard and hit the play button.

"This sounds exactly like your play list," Richard remarked.

"It is. I recorded my music over his. His music was boring as hell."

"I hope he appreciates all that you do for him," Richard pulled the earphones back out.

"He'd better. It took forever to erase that junk of his." Mike handed Richard half a deck of playing cards. Richard pitched a joker into the midst of the flames. Mike assessed Richard's toss carefully, compensating for the cool breeze, before flicking the eight of hearts in. They spoke more quietly as they depleted their stack of cards.

"Are you scared by any of this, Mike?" Richard asked, aiming his next toss carefully.

"Yeah. But I'm going to help her anyway." Mike's flick went wide.

"Why?"

"Because of what I see in her eyes when she talks about what's behind all this stuff."

"What do you see?" Richard asked.

"Trust." Mike shot another card into the flames and looked back at Richard. "Trust like I've never seen in anyone's eyes, ever."

"She might simply be insane," Richard suggested, the campfire reflected in his pupils.

"I dunno. She might be the only sane one here. You don't see her tossing cards into a campfire." Mike hurled the empty card box into the fire.

"Maybe." Richard's last card went in.

"What were we playing for this time?" Mike wanted to know.

"The right to throw the card box into the fire."

"Oh." Mike frowned. He pointed at the flame-engulfed box curling up in the embers. "Do you want me to fish it out?"

"Let me sleep on it." Richard opened a nearly empty bag of marshmallows and extended it to Mike. Mike took a handful out.

"What about you, Rag?" Mike asked, throwing a marshmallow into the fire.

"What?"

"Will you keep helping her?"

Richard thought about the question. "Yeah." He nodded. "I'll see you and raise you two." Three marshmallows arced into the campfire.

"Why are *you* gonna help her?" Mike persisted, tossing two more puffs into the flames.

"Different reason from yours." Richard crossed his legs and leaned back.

"Okay, why?" Mike wanted to know.

"Because she's gonna need it."

Richard inflated the now-empty plastic bag and tied it off. He nudged the bag over the fire; it gently floated upward on the heated air, glowing orange from the reflected flames. The two men watched it sail into the night sky, a luminous bubble briefly outshining the distant constellations.

Jenna met Eckhardt at the usual place, a tarmac near the Oakland charter flight terminal. She climbed into the jet and found him waiting on the leather sofa in the aft cabin.

She hadn't spoken to him for a month; they last met on the day she had her tumultuous reunion with Professor Hernandez. Jenna had then turned over copies of Sexton's papers to Eckhardt, and hadn't seen the chairman since.

It upset her to follow the CryoMax boardroom battles in the newspapers. It was small comfort indeed that the vote of no confidence against Eckhardt had failed to carry by only one vote; his opponents would surely be emboldened to try again.

She sat down across from him and adjusted her lab coat.

He carefully handed her a straight black staff nearly six feet long.

She examined it closely: it had the same outer surface as her cane. "Doctor Eckhardt, is this ... ?"

"Yes, Jenna. I think Wallingford Sexton would look at this one and say, Well, that's more like it." Eckhardt's eyes creased as he grinned.

"Is there a danger of the government trying to nationalize this staff or the cane you built? I'd hate for these devices to be confiscated."

He shrugged. "Honestly, Jenna, this is an old battle. It goes back a long way, centuries."

"You're going to say it's the battle to suppress the truth, right?"

Eckhardt nodded wearily. "The battle over the dam is a battle to suppress the truth. To hold it down, to choke its voice. It's an old battle. And I must confess to feeling like a *very* old warrior in that old battle." He leaned back and rested himself for a few moments.

Jenna was worried. "What's happening in the courts? Will we be able to finish draining the dam?"

"The problem in the courts," he began "is that some bad precedents have been set since the 1980s."

"Precedents?"

"Yes, during those old creationism trials. Legal precedent now allows a school textbook containing no religious references to be banned because it could still establish a religion. So textbooks were tossed, teachers reprimanded, superintendents fired, and worse.

"This is now happening with your dissertation. Ironically, you were something of an atheist when you wrote it. But precedent has caught up to your scientific work and cried foul because it could violate the wall between church and state."

"How?" she cried out. "It's nothing but equations!"

"Jenna, the *implications* of a statement determine its status as a religious utterance. We've drifted *so* far off our moorings ... and I'm very sorry."

She nodded, feeling the heft of the staff in her hands. Unlike the cane, it had a digital control panel on it. Jenna pointed to the panel and looked questioningly at Eckhardt. He took a deep breath and explained its purpose.

"This setting controls the aperture, the beam width. The second lets you program a cycle of ons and offs. The third setting lets you select, within limits, the beam's wavelength. Nothing dangerous like UV, mind you, just visible light. Strange, isn't it, that shunting creates electromagnetic waves only in the visible spectrum? As if it were *meant* to be observed. But you can mix in ionizing energy with the fourth control, which amplifies the harmonics." He tapped the staff in Jenna's hands, and she started to understand what he was getting at.

It was fundamentally meant to be observed.

"Who owns the water in the dam?" she asked Eckhardt.

"Technically, the people of California own it, although *I'd* take it one level further than that," he said, smiling broadly for the first time. "Those folks have an interesting initiative and referendum process. You might want to look into that. Interposition would be interesting too—the state standing between the dam and the federal government."

She nodded, vowing to research what he was talking about. His promptings rarely led to dry wells.

She rose to leave, and then turned to Eckhardt. "I owe you so much, Doctor Eckhardt, I feel I'd like to hug you good-bye for once."

"I can't get up, Miss Wilkes. My multiple sclerosis has progressed too rapidly."

"May I still try?"

He took her free hand in both of his and held it as he spoke. "There's an Old Testament idiom for people working together in unity. It's in Zephaniah 3:9, where the English versions speak of serving God shoulder to shoulder. The Hebrew really says *serving with one shoulder*."

She understood what he meant her to do. Holding the staff in her right hand, Jenna sat down next to him, her left shoulder touching his right. This was the most physical contact she'd ever had with Eckhardt, and even it was regulated by a text of Scripture. Her lip quivered because she could feel how frail his frame really was.

Eckhardt broke the silence. "It's time for you to go now, Jenna Angela Wilkes. You and that staff have work to be done."

She nodded and gripped the staff more tightly. Eckhardt leaned back and closed his eyes; his breathing wasn't smooth.

Karla was hurrying down the aisle. "Doctor Wilkes, I need to get the chairman strapped in now. Let me help you down the gangway."

Two minutes later, Jenna was on the tarmac. It was dusk. The light from the terminal outlined her in stark silhouette, while her shadow stretched far across the expanse of concrete runways and taxiways.

She stood watching Eckhardt's jet move onto the main taxiway, feet apart, her right hand having planted the staff on the tarmac, her red hair and lab coat waving in the wind. The airport was a noisy place, but there was a peaceful silence in her mind as she watched the jet recede.

A peaceful silence.

And an implacable resolve.

39

Niles Emmerich was talking with Bic Johanssen in the latter's office when Bartleby burst through the door, embedding the doorknob deep into the spackle that filled the previous hole he'd made in the drywall. Bic didn't react, but Niles jumped.

"What the *hell* are you doing, Bartleby!" he cried in surprise.

"Turn on the TV!" Bartleby yelled. "You've got to see what's on the TV! God, hurry up, you're missing it!"

Bic quickly flicked to the digital news feeds on his laptop, while Niles and Bartleby scooted around behind him to watch.

"Turn up the sound, Johanssen!" Niles ordered, "I can't hear anything."

They watched stunned as the scene unfolded before their eyes. The reporter's voice-over droned on and on about the situation at the dam generators, where a sea of news reporters and TV cameramen were crowding around the yellow police tape keeping them back.

Someone had built a makeshift ramp to the top of the generator building, which was apparently how the UPS truck ended up parked on the rooftop. Behind the truck, and looming up to the sky, was the enormous expanse of the main dam wall. And standing on top of the truck, wearing a headset she used to address the crowds over a small PA system, was a redheaded woman holding a black staff, standing barefoot in her flowing dirty lab coat.

"What's she saying, Ron?" Bic asked, unable to make out Jenna's words against the intrusive voice-over. "And why all those cameras around her? What's going on? Did she take someone hostage?"

"Well, *she* didn't actually say it, Bic, but people *think* she's taking the entire state of California hostage." Bartleby's breathing was labored. "At least, she's making it clear that nobody had better come near her, shoot her, or anything, or the core will overload."

"Wait," snapped Niles, "they're turning up her volume. Shut up."

Then they could hear what their former employee was telling the people of California, of the United States, of the world, from the Mount of UPS.

"You may not come up on this building's roof. I cannot guarantee the consequences if you do, and I cannot guarantee the stability of the core. If you try to take me out with a sniper, no one will know how to control the core, and the consequences may be dire for those downstream of this dam. If you use knockout gas, no one will know how to prevent the core from undergoing energy reversion."

She adjusted the headset microphone closer to her mouth.

"I want everyone in the state to watch what I'm going to do here, on top of this truck, at eight o'clock tonight, and then I want you to consider what you're going to do about the draining of this dam. In the meantime, I'd recommend that no airplanes or helicopters fly over this area because I can't guarantee their safety either. Approach closer at your own risk."

The voice-over resumed, talking about the device or weapon she had under her control that the military acknowledged was a potential threat.

Niles turned to Bic. "I've learned enough about your redhead to know that pretty much everything she was saying was literally accurate, meaning she actually poses no threat whatsoever. We're merely reading that into her words."

Bic and Bartleby stared at Niles, surprised at his insight.

"Do you plan to tell anybody that?" asked Bic.

"No, I figure she's been a burr up my behind long enough, let the state of California get a bellyful of her. This is too good to miss." Niles walked back around the desk laughing. "God, she's good. Those poor people have no idea what they're up against with her." He kept laughing as he left the room.

Bic and Bartleby exchanged worried looks.

"What's going to happen at eight o'clock?" Bartleby wondered.

"I don't know. Whatever it is, do you want be sitting here watching it on the tube, or over there in person?"

"I don't know," Bartleby hesitated. "Maybe they don't want people around there, especially if she's going to blow the dam up."

"Well, I'm going, damn it. There's no way I'm not going to be there."

After issuing her warnings, Jenna climbed down the ladder on the far side of the UPS truck, disappearing from the cameras. The truck was parked sideways on the rooftop of the generator building, the yellow police tape keeping about twenty yards between the gathering crowds and the concrete structure. A ring of orange traffic cones on the rooftop encircled the truck, interrupted at intervals by equally superfluous red hazard triangles.

The only thing that spectators could see were the feet of four people in the narrow gap between the roof and the underside of the UPS truck—four people seated at a table, with the smell of barbecue incongruously floating in the air. It was maddening how little of the scene could be viewed. The reporters speculated about the identity of the three unknown figures, two of which wore open-toed sandals.

There was no way to approach the side of the generator building to catch a glimpse behind it without breaching the area regarded as dangerous. No helicopters risked conducting surveillance from overhead. Sending anyone rappelling down the dam wall would be too easily detected.

Shielded from the crowds, Bryn, Mike, Richard, and Jenna settled down to try to enjoy an early dinner, but Bryn was worried about whether her threats would be taken seriously enough to keep intruders at bay. He knew that aligning with Jenna's cause had now put him in the line of fire, causing him to question his stated hunger for "exciting research." He was right where he wanted to be, or so he had thought before things had come to this.

"I wouldn't be too concerned about any of that, Brynster," explained Richard. "We've got some military guards out there on the line, and they seem to be *very* friendly with General Stall, if you catch my drift."

Mike looked up, a gleeful look in his eye. "That's right, nudge nudge wink wink. Unless there's a lone gunman out there, you're good to go."

Jenna looked up. "That doesn't sound all that comforting, Captain Boudreaux."

Mike shrugged, catching an alarmed look in Bryn's eyes. "That's the risk *you* took taking it to the public, Doctor Wilkes. There are pluses and minuses."

She nodded and tried to focus on relaxing so she could approach her cheeseburger without her stomach knotting up. She paused and held up a finger. "I know we've never done this before, but would you all mind if I prayed for us before we eat?"

The three men nodded. Her prayer was brief and heartfelt, both for the food, and for courage. She inwardly prayed for the strange dynamic that just barely held this team of literal misfits together. She had no idea her life would ever lead to anything even remotely like what was transpiring here today.

Moreover, she had never actually tested the new staff, but she had faith in Dr. Eckhardt ... and Dr. Sexton.

I hope Doctor Sexton is able to see this on his TV, she thought.

She didn't know it, but he *was* watching ... and smiling ... at home in his wheelchair.

Sexton couldn't wait for eight o'clock to arrive.

40

The President of the United States came on the air at 7:30 PM Pacific time to speak briefly to the nation, which had dropped nearly everything to consider the amazing drama playing out at the foot of a California hydroelectric dam.

"So far as we know," he calmly intoned, "Doctor Wilkes is interested in working within the system to get an initiative on an emergency California ballot. She has *not* unilaterally demanded that the dam be drained; she wants the voters to decide the matter. She advanced the money to pay for signature acquisition, computerized balloting, and the printing of manual ballots. She already has two sponsors lined up for her initiative in Sacramento. She assures us of her patriotism, but she will not cancel her demonstration. If Californians defeat her initiative, she will terminate her protest.

"You may have wondered, as I did, what's the rush? There are two reasons why the matter is urgent and needs to be decided quickly. First, California's governor advises me that right now his state can easily afford to drain the dam because the Sierra snow pack is at record surplus levels. It's safe to drain it now; it may not be safe again for years to come. Second, the dam needs to be drained before the winter rains begin. The draining must either be done very, very soon, or not at all. Which it'll be is up to the citizens of California.

"In the meantime, at the request of the governor, I've ordered the army to maintain order and keep the situation under control at the dam site. We are prepared to intervene if we need to.

"I recommend all Americans remain calm, particularly those in California who may be called to go to the polls to settle the controversy. Let us all pray for a positive outcome in this highly charged situation. God bless America. Thank you, and good night."

Riesen knocked on Stall's door.

"Come in," the general called out.

Riesen stepped inside and saluted. Stall returned the salute, wondering why Riesen had come.

The colonel was clearly disappointed. "Well, General, it looks like it's out of our hands."

"Why should it even be *in* our hands in the first place?" Stall asked.

Riesen didn't comprehend, so Stall elaborated.

"This may come to you like a brick between the eyes, Colonel, but in point of fact *we* actually work for people like Doctor Wilkes. It's easy to lose sight of the proper relation of civilians to military personnel. They are our bosses, and we exist for their benefit, not to control them or the outcomes of their honest work."

Riesen shook his head. "General, I don't know why the president insisted on having you handle the situation at the dam instead of Melliton or someone else, but I'm pretty sure you're tilting events the way you want over there."

"Just upholding the Constitution, son, just upholding the Constitution. She has a right to speak and to petition against grievances. Read that document again if you've since forgotten it."

"That woman is one giant walking grievance. Sir." And Riesen rose to depart.

Stall stopped him. "If her grievances are well-founded, she's a hero. At least, a lot of people watching her on TV seem to think of her as a folk hero already. The major insta-polls are favoring her protest about three to one. Oh, excuse my oversight, William, I didn't properly answer your question."

"What question?"

"About why the president insisted on having me conduct operations in the dam's spillway."

"Okay, why?"

"He gave me authority because he's the commander in chief and has the right to choose *anybody he wants* to conduct his operations for him. That's also in the Constitution. So, you can see how glad I am to learn how interested you are in upholding that document."

Riesen became bitter. The whole matter should never have gotten to this point. "We had this under wraps. Why did she go public?" he demanded.

"What did you *think* she would do, Colonel? Roll over and play dead?"

"You're implying that it's somehow my fault this happened?"

Stall slammed his palms on his desk. "That dam was being drained quietly, Will. We even had a great cover story about maintaining the valve inlets. Everything was on a need-to-know basis, but that wasn't good enough for you. You just *had* to go out and provoke them."

"She obviously doesn't play by the rules," Riesen stewed.

"Pfft. Open your eyes, Colonel. She called for a *vote*. She's not only playing by the rules, she's the *only* one playing by them." Stall shook his head and regarded Riesen with pity. "Face it, Colonel. You were *used* to force this thing out into the public eye."

"By Wilkes?"

"No, higher up than that."

"Eckhardt?"

"Higher."

Riesen knew where this was going. "General, no God has somehow used me to make this matter public."

"Oh, so you like General Melliton's counter-explanation better?"

Riesen hesitated uncertainly. "You heard what he said to me?"

"Indeed I did. He said security was blown because you were stupid."

Riesen was incensed. "I didn't think you bugged anybody's offices here, General."

"I don't," Stall corrected. "I don't and I won't. Ever."

"Then how did you know what General Melliton said?"

"He told me."

41

"Jenna, it's showtime!" Richard called out.

"Just a minute!" she shouted from the inside of the UPS truck.

Bryn set the ladder against the truck so Jenna could climb back up to the roof. He turned to Mike with curiosity. "I'm surprised the wheels of this truck can handle the weight of that big isolator straddling the rear axle."

"It only *looks* like a UPS truck, Bryn," said Mike, kneeling on his haunches to check the battery connections to the PA system. "It's a military vehicle. It could handle something twice that weight."

"I had no idea."

"You should have known it wasn't a normal UPS truck by the way the two drivers were dressed when you met them." Mike grunted out the last few words as he forcibly tightened the battery terminals.

"Right. You're right there. I obviously missed that." Bryn glanced at his watch and knocked on the truck wall.

"Coming!" she called back. And out she came, staff in hand, ready to storm the roof.

"Still barefoot? Any reason?" Bryn asked her.

"It's too slippery up there."

Bryn helped her up the ladder.

Jenna looked down at him and whispered, "Wish me luck!"

"Tell you what, I'll do more than that. I'll pray for you!" he whispered back.

Bryn, an atheist, praying? She chose to overlook the inconsistency, inserted her earplugs, and turned to climb into the darkness of the heavens.

For it had grown dark quickly, and that was her intent, to make her demonstration easy to see when it started. The timing was purely for visual effect because the demonstration would be impossible to miss sonically.

She had configured the staff, the new frame shunt, to repeatedly unleash a beam of stupendous photonic energy for thirty seconds followed by thirty seconds of inactivity. It would cycle on and off until stopped.

Before the isolator was collected from her home, she'd had Richard cut a hole in the truck's roof centered over the planned position of the isolator. *The place where you stick the toothpick through the top of the sandwich,* Richard had called his handiwork. Ten inches of hollow pipe positioned under the hole formed a sleeve to keep the staff safely aligned during insertion.

The optical show was one thing, but Jenna feared the sonic aspect the most, knowing the expected intensity of the sound blast. *Are the earplugs we're wearing up here even adequate?*

She feared because the beam, as she had configured one of its transient components, would do the same thing to the air in the sky as a lightning bolt does: ionizing it for a split second, causing a tremendous thunderclap. She would be standing right next to the beam's shaft, inside the shock wave zone, all but holding a lightning rod in her hand ... except no lightning in nature formed a perfectly straight beam piercing into heaven.

She remembered as a kid taking a flashlight and shining it straight up into the night sky. She had asked her father if other people could see her flashlight beam. He had smiled and said that if she could build a strong enough flashlight, the whole world might be able to see it.

And she had.

Jenna knew that once her head popped over the truck's roofline she'd immediately enter the living rooms of a billion people via the TV cameras trained on the truck. She closed her eyes tightly, asked her God for strength, and climbed out onto the truck's roof.

The crowds suddenly fell silent. She wasn't prepared for that—the effect was eerie. Never had so many people's attention been on her all at once. It momentarily brought back memories of her dissertation defense, but the comparison was utterly inadequate. *At least this won't take long,* Jenna realized. She'd only need to face them a few minutes before leaving the spotlight.

Jenna put the headset on and positioned the microphone over her mouth. She looked back at Mike and Richard, who were handling her sound system. They gave her the thumbs up. She turned to face the people, her eyes scanning the front row behind the yellow police tape.

Is that Ron Bartleby? She wondered. *Oh, Bic's with him.* She waved at them, momentarily unaware that thousands of people in front of her were watching her every gesture. About half of the crowd waved back.

She cleared her throat.

"I'm asking the citizens of California to go to the polls in a few weeks and exercise their God-given right to vote on whether to drain this dam or not. This is your water, your dam, your government, and you choose what you want to do with it. That means that if you choose not to drain it, that's the end of it, at least for me. I'm here to work within the system, to show you that great things can be done within the system if you have faith.

"If Californians vote to drain it, and the state interposes its authority against the federal government, this dam *will* be drained, and the most important discovery of the century will be accessible to the world. I'm here to give you just a taste, a small preview, of the awesome possibilities hidden here. I'll show you what my work has achieved, and what greater works are around the corner, for those of you willing to dream. The power of one person still means something. Every one of you matters. Prove you matter by voting on the initiative being prepared for your consideration."

The crowd murmured as she paused, all wondering what she meant, figuring the next event would be the pivotal one.

She held up her left hand to silence them, the staff still in her right, its business end resting on the truck's roof. She eyed the nearby hole in the roof and adjusted her grip on the staff.

"In a moment, it'll get too loud to hold a conversation. I'm going to unleash a tiny piece of the available energy. It won't harm you or the dam, but it *will* scare you, at least the first time. There'll be a huge thunderclap. It will repeat once every minute until all the votes are tabulated. Once the vote is in, I'll shut off the thunder. You will either drain this dam or send me packing. But I pray you'll choose victory and not choose to turn back the clock."

She raised the staff over her head to aim it, and loudly proclaimed, so all could hear, a line from the Book of Job.

"This is but a whisper of His ways, but of the thunder of His Power, who can know it?"

And she slammed the staff straight into the hole on the truck as hard as she could.

And the thunderclap threw her backward off the truck.

And an immense red beam shot straight up, splitting the heavens and bathing the entire dam wall in deep red, the color of Jenna's hair.

And all the people backed up and screamed.

And the Joint Chiefs of Staff stood in awe at what had happened as they watched on TV.

And Niles Emmerich and Jonas Eckhardt, observing from the CryoMax boardroom, watched silently, both smiling.

The beam continued to shine, the brightest beacon ever sent heavenward by man, a little girl's flashlight pulling every eye skyward.

It winked out thirty seconds later. The crowd had been backing away, but the hard-core videographers and reporters stood their ground, doing their job.

Bartleby started yelling. "She said it's going to come on again! It'll keep turning on and making thunderclaps every minute! Be prepared!"

The word spread quickly, and on schedule, the staff, sticking about halfway out of the top of the truck, again split the air and sky with a concussive, valley-shaking thunder blast and a red beam.

Sexton, watching the television, dropped his face into both hands, sobbing with huge spasms. He had no idea, could not have imagined, what that dissertation defense seven years ago, the rejected paper, would lead to. He was overwhelmed with emotion.

Jenna had fallen and broken her leg, knocked unconscious. There was no way any of her friends could have caught her in time: they'd all been knocked to the ground as well. They scrambled toward her and examined her leg.

Richard was prepared. "I have an army medical kit in the truck. Hold on—at least it didn't break the skin." He ran around the vehicle and disappeared inside it. This was the first time the crowd had seen anyone other than Jenna near the truck since the incident began.

Richard raced back out with a large white case with a red cross emblazoned upon it. The TV cameras caught that. Sexton blanched as he watched. Eckhardt and Niles dropped their jaws. Bic and Bartleby burst through the police tape, running up to the ramp.

The guards stopped them, ascertained they were Jenna's friends, and let them up the ramp to the building's rooftop.

Three thousand miles away, Eckhardt instructed Niles to signal the extraction team.

The beam had gone dark again. Bartleby and Bic had reached Jenna. Richard and Mike were splinting her leg by the light of the floodlights illuminating the makeshift camp behind the truck.

"What happened?" asked Bic diving to his knees. "Is she okay?"

"She's unconscious, but her signs are fine," said Richard. "Probably a concussion from the fall. Leg's broken."

But Mike interrupted Richard with urgency. "Look, no time for introductions, you're going to need these," he handed earplug packs to Bic and Bartleby. "*Everybody* around here had better get some of these."

The two CryoMax men had barely inserted the earplugs before the third thunderclap hit.

"That's going to keep going until the vote is finalized?" asked Bartleby in shock.

"That's her plan," said Bryn, his heart pounding in his ears at what had happened.

"We need to get her out of here!" shouted Bic.

Mike answered without looking up. "Already done. Look up."

Bic lifted his eyes skyward to see a dot of red light cross over the dam wall. A helicopter.

"Whose chopper is that?" asked Bartleby. "The army's?"

"No, it's Eckhardt's," Richard answered. "It's taking her to Oakland, but we didn't expect her to get hurt doing what she did." He looked back down at the injured woman, shaking his head.

The chopper stayed clear of the beam, moving over closer to the ramp. Since the beam winked off every thirty seconds, the pilot had to rely on memory to avoid drifting into its path.

The chopper was still letting down its flex ladder when the fourth thunderclap struck.

The TV cameras were taking the entire drama in. All of America was engaged in the events in the shadow of the dam. And not Americans only, but the entire world watched, astounded at the beam and thunderclaps. Awestruck descriptions by the reporters feeding their voice-overs to their networks could only hint at how loud the thunderclaps were.

The TV cameras captured Jenna being lifted, unconscious, into the helicopter, her leg already splinted. The world gasped in disbelief at what the redheaded, barefoot woman in the dirty lab coat had done with her staff, which continued to mark time with an in-your-face display that made Old Faithful seem like a toy squirt gun.

Eckhardt turned toward his associate. "Well, Niles?"

"To think I was going to fire her, Jonas. I was an absolute idiot."

The farther the helicopter flew from the dam, the more the distant thunder receded into inaudibility. The chopper was crowded. Everyone who'd been on the rooftop had crammed into it. Bic, Bartleby, Mike, Bryn, Richard, Jenna, the pilot, and two of Eckhardt's assistants. Having flown in the chopper before with his uncle, Bryn knew the crew and made some hasty introductions.

Jenna slowly awakened as Mike wiped her forehead with a moist cloth, checking her breathing and pulse.

"What happened?" she mumbled weakly. She had no idea, having been knocked unconscious at the first blast unleashed by her staff.

"You fall down, go boom," Mike quipped.

"Lots of booms," added Richard. "Warn us the next time you decide to turn the amp up to eleven."

She turned her head away and recognized Bartleby's face in the dim cabin light. "Ron ... you came to see me."

"Are you all right?" he asked worriedly.

"My leg really, really hurts." She winced and grabbed it, hitting the splint with her fingertips. "What's wrong with my leg, Ron?"

"You broke it during your fall. We're in Eckhardt's helicopter, heading toward Oakland. His plane is waiting for you."

"Can you make the pain stop? It's unbelievably bad," she winced.

Mike looked to Richard.

"Field medic time," Richard announced, digging up a hypodermic from his kit. "Jenna, keep in mind you may be woozy if I give this to you."

She was in severe pain. "It's worth it. Give it to me."

She was out several minutes later, sleeping peaceably, dreamlessly.

Bic rose, palms sweaty, still in disbelief at what had happened. "Well, everyone, I think the one thing we *can* safely say is that she definitely deserves to sleep."

All nodded.

Bartleby's eyes were glued to his digiscreen as he tuned in to catch the local TV coverage. "There's footage here of what happened, all from different angles. The networks keep replaying her slamming that black stick into the truck. God, I had no idea she was thrown off the truck with such force."

He looked at Bic, barely able to control his emotions. "This must be what she was talking about back when this whole thing began. She begged me not to throw that circuit breaker in the isolator lab because it might be dangerous. I saw it in her eyes, but pooh-poohed it. And now *she's* the one who ultimately got hurt by the damn thing."

"She'll be fine," said Richard. "In fact, I'd say she probably anticipated this happening."

"Why do you think that?" asked Bryn, finally recovering a measure of composure.

"Didn't you see it? She brought a cane with her."

42

The next evening, Katherine wheeled Jenna into Eckhardt's Valley of the Books. Jenna found the wheelchair awkward; the cast on her leg forced her foot straight out. The good news was the fracture wasn't total. She'd be able to lose the cast sooner than most people if she took care to obey Eckhardt's medical staff.

Eckhardt was waiting for her in the center of the Valley in his own wheelchair.

Jenna looked up at Katherine and asked a favor. "Katherine, please, let me push myself the rest of the way."

"Are you sure, dearie? You're still on pretty strong pain medication."

"It's okay, I'm fine. Thank you."

Katherine released the wheelchair's handles, telling Jenna to call if help were needed.

Jenna wheeled herself over to Eckhardt, doing something unexpected as he looked on. She steered her wheelchair behind Eckhardt, turned, and came up beside him. The two wheelchairs were aligned side by side. She leaned over and gently touched his shoulder with hers.

"Serving with one shoulder," she said in hushed tones. "Zephaniah 3:9. The original Hebrew."

His eyes flashed as he spoke. "I've got bad news. Tonight's Thursday night."

"Why's that bad?"

"Hard to reach the buffet from these wheelchairs, I've learned." A rueful grin crossed his face. "But we'll need to hurry because nobody can eat till you get there."

"Why is that?" She was puzzled.

"I told you the first time you visited here. Remember?"

"Honestly, I don't think so."

"I told you that the first shall be last. That's why I eat last."

"So?"

"The rest of the verse states the last shall be first."

"Yes?"

"You need to eat first, before anyone else can eat. *Katherine!*"

Katherine hurried to collect Jenna and wheel her into the kitchen area. She soon had a plate made up on her lap, balancing precariously on her cast, and was wheeled into the dining area …

… where she saw Bryn, Bartleby, Bic, Niles Emmerich, Richard, Mike, and General Stall. All were standing, the general and captains holding an intense salute. Katherine wheeled Jenna past them to push her in at the head of the table.

Eckhardt spoke first. "Thank you for your courage, Jenna. We won't know the outcome of what you've done, but however it goes, you've already changed the world, and I think for the better. My only regret is that in this room your praise is being sung by unworthy cowards."

She felt the lump in her throat swelling. The next thing she heard *really* startled her.

"That would include me."

She turned her head toward the unexpected voice.

Sexton! In his wheelchair, rolling forward!

He put his hands in hers, and she thought the corners of her face would tear off from smiling so hard at him.

"Turning the world upside down can be hazardous to your health, I see." He looked at her cast. "Can I sign it?"

"Sure."

"Plaster?" he tapped the cast. "Isn't that old school?"

"I'm allergic to the new composites," she explained.

Nodding, Sexton took out a marker and carefully wrote on the uneven white plaster, determined to guide his bruised hand by sheer force of will. In short order, everyone wrote messages on her cast, even Niles.

Dinner was marked by animated discussion over the prior evening's events. The general informed Jenna that the staff and isolator were safe from tampering. She learned that Hernandez had arranged to have Stanford University endorse the initiative, to stand behind its now-famous student.

That's not how they treated me when I was there, but better late than never, she thought. But she was disturbed to learn the Stanford vote was far from unanimous.

Bic explained the situation to her. "Many academicians oppose draining the dam. They're using the media to raise issues of a conspiracy. They want the government to take this technology out of your hands and give it to qualified researchers. The ACLU accuses you of railroading the voters with a threatening display. All we can say is, you're going to get a fair shake, but the outcome is far from certain. Courts have overturned initiatives in the past."

Mike piped up at that. "Makes ya wanna sneak your thunderstick into the Ninth Circuit Court of Appeals and fire it up, I'll bet!"

Jenna grinned at Captain Boudreaux's preference for "extreme diplomacy."

"What is Professor Hernandez doing?" she wanted to know.

Eckhardt fielded this question. "He's gone on television urging everyone to visit the dam. He suggested a schedule based on car license plates to avoid overcrowding. He's banking on people catching your vision by experiencing it in person. He said seeing—and hearing—is believing. The average person thinks you're a hero, the way you risked everything to do what you thought was right. It's bad that you fell and were injured, but that seemed to really capture the people's hearts. Those people who had hearts."

Sexton lifted up his glass and proposed a toast. "To Doctor Jenna Wilkes, creator of the eighth wonder of the world."

All glasses clinked roundabout, with cries of "Hear, Hear!"

And Sexton finished his toast. "... and of the ninth wonder, around the corner."

They all drank, knowing that the world had gone insane over the events at the dam, that special editions of *TIME* and *Newsweek* and *USA Today* were being churned out furiously, that Eckhardt had to bolster the guards at Jenna's home to over thirty men circling her small property. He had arranged to fly her cat here to Boston.

"Jenna," said General Stall.

"Yes, General?"

"Can I make one recommendation?"

"Please."

"I recommend you *not* watch any television or read newspapers or check on the internet to see how people are responding to what you did. Leave that to us. You need to be insulated from all that static so you can focus on your mission."

She nodded.

Eckhardt elaborated further. "General Stall doesn't want you to be distracted by the praise of those who think you're Wonder Woman, or by the criticisms of those who want to bring you down. Either way, you'll be distracted, and you need unbroken focus. The only person's opinion you need to worry about is God's."

Jenna noticed a frown flit across the faces of Bryn and Niles. Niles was about to object when Stall interjected.

"Amen, Jonas, Amen," the general solemnly added.

Jenna appreciated their concern. "Thank you, General. The last thing I want to be is a media hero—it frightens me beyond words. It took everything I had to climb up that truck in front of all those cameras, all those people ..." She shuddered involuntarily.

Eckhardt extended a bottle toward Jenna's empty glass. "More grape juice?"

"I'd *love* some more."

After dinner, Jenna asked if she could speak with Sexton in private. The two were rolled into the adjoining den and the doors were closed. They fidgeted for a few moments in their wheelchairs. Each was acutely embarrassed about what they had done to the other, and the words simply didn't come easily.

"Jenna ..."

"No, Doctor, let me ..."

"No, please ..."

"I shouldn't have made that phone call, Doctor Sexton. I flew off the handle."

Sexton looked away, the sting of her anguished call to him still ringing in his ears. "The guilt is mine," he concluded. "You were right. I treated you like a pawn." He drew out a familiar piece of graph paper and unfolded it. "It's right here in black and white. I'm sorry you had to see this."

"I'm not." Jenna reached over and took the paper out of his hands, carefully folding it back up. She gently kissed the paper and handed it back to him.

Sexton's voice wavered. "I read the note you added to this," he tapped the folded sheet. "You were so angry, so hurt … betrayed … I can't believe you could still forgive …"

"I guess, Doctor Sexton, that at first I didn't appreciate the difference."

"Difference?" he tucked the graph paper back into his pocket.

"I used to think it was all an innocent mistake, a random event that steamrolled me back at Stanford. But it's better knowing that someone was behind it. At least, better for me. Now I know the difference."

"What difference?" Sexton repeated.

"It's something Eckhardt quoted to me," her eyes gleamed. "The difference between chance and purpose. It was something about the difference between falling into the grinding power of a mindless machine versus falling into the loving hands of a father. Eckhardt said all the language of men fell short in explaining the difference. He was right."

"These are guilty hands, Miss Wilkes," Sexton raised his bruised hands. "Not fatherly hands. Not loving hands."

She disagreed. "I re-read your note a dozen times before I wrote on it and gave it to Doctor Eckhardt to return to you," she explained. "I read it enough times to finally understand it. You wanted to see me grow, to succeed, to fight and win."

"But …"

"That's what fathers do. That's what *my* father wanted for me. He wasn't here to see that through because he died. After he died, there was no one left who had faith in me. No one."

Jenna touched the bruised top of Sexton's left hand. "But you had faith in me. Otherwise, you wouldn't have risked putting me back in front of the committee like that. You wouldn't have opened up the questioning over their protests. You could have taken the easy way and gone home early that day. You didn't. You had faith in me."

Sexton dared to cup her hand between his own. She smiled warmly.

"Peace?" he asked. "Then you really meant it. Peace."

"Peace," she affirmed.

"What can I do for you, Harry?" Eckhardt asked as the general quietly entered the Valley of the Books.

"I'm troubled by what happened last night," Stall began. "A colleague of mine sees Jenna's injury as proof the beam can be weaponized. He knows that saying so publicly would make the situation unmanageable, so we're off the hook for now, but for how long, I can't say."

"She was injured by the fall from the truck," Eckhardt reminded the general.

"Yes. True. What's it going to take to prove it can't be weaponized? It sure sounds like a weapon, even acts like a weapon."

"I know how to prove it, but at the moment there's a tactical advantage in leaving things where they stand."

"Understood." Stall turned to leave, then pivoted back toward Eckhardt. "Excuse me for being direct like this," the general apologized, "but I have a personal question, Christian to Christian. About the girl, Jenna Wilkes."

"Yes?"

"She considers herself a Christian?"

"I'd say yes."

"Wasn't her conversion pretty unconventional, Jonas?"

"Is there such a thing as a conventional conversion?" Eckhardt leaned back in his wheelchair. "Maybe that's an idea we've manufactured. We've turned it into a mechanical process, it seems to me. As if conversion were a follow-the-formula commodity."

"Pretty risky to leave things to chance like you've done, isn't it?" Stall asked.

"I didn't leave it to chance at all," Eckhardt replied. "I simply left it to God to keep His promise."

"Promise?"

"It's a pretty radical promise to our ears, Harry. People usually say, I'll obey the Bible once I have a rational basis to believe it's true. Knowledge and understanding precede obedience, they'll say. Rational man always puts rationalism first."

"Sounds entirely reasonable to me," Stall shook his head. "Who'd argue with that?"

"It's a shock, I know, but the Bible turns that whole concept on its head," Eckhardt replied. "The person who obeys, who does God's works, will come to understand that the doctrine is true. In the Bible, obedience precedes understanding, comes before knowledge. God promises understanding to those who do His will first. Seventh chapter of John, verse seventeen."

Stall walked over to the Bible on the coffee table and quickly looked up the reference. He nodded slowly, closed the Bible and walked toward the doors, turning around at the threshold.

"Going by the Bible. That's pretty unconventional too, Jonas."

"Don't get me started."

Jenna was propped up in bed in the guest bedroom, writing on a pad by the light cast by the nightstand lamp. Someone knocked tentatively at the door.

At this hour? she thought. "It's okay, I'm awake," she called out.

Niles Emmerich slowly opened the door. "May I come in, Doctor Wilkes?" he asked.

She nodded, wondering why he had come.

He walked over to her wheelchair and, seeing nowhere else to sit, settled down uncomfortably into it and turned to face her.

She spoke first, without emotion. "You tried to remove Doctor Eckhardt from the board."

He looked genuinely surprised. "Not true, Doctor Wilkes."

"You didn't initiate that, what was it called… ?"

"Vote of no confidence?"

"Right. Vote of no confidence."

"No," he answered, shaking his head, "that was a motion by Davapolous."

Jenna stopped, uncertain of herself now. "How did you vote on the motion?" she asked.

"I voted to support Jonas."

"I don't believe it!" she scoffed.

"Ask him yourself. Doctor Eckhardt will tell you."

Jenna realized his claim would be too easy to disprove—Niles *had* to be telling the truth, as unlikely as that seemed. Then she remembered something Bic had told her, that everything Niles did was done because it was good for Niles. Apparently, Eckhardt was the key to his accession to the chairmanship: that was why Niles protected Eckhardt. She nodded and decided to reply graciously rather than question his motives.

"I didn't expect that, Director Emmerich."

He folded his hands, and then his face softened—a rarity, she realized. The words didn't come easily for Niles. "Doctor Wilkes, I must say what you did last night was positively ... Mosaic."

She continued to regard him with puzzlement, nodding for him to go on.

He spoke more quietly. "There's something I need to know from you."

"Yes?"

"Do you know what we do in our San Diego facility?"

She shook her head, and he explained it to her. She caught on quickly.

"So...," he concluded, "I need to know: can your isolator do what those San Diego cryotubes can't?"

She thought a moment. "No, it can't. Even if you had a core cavity large enough to fit a person inside, the only way back to the present causes the body to age as it makes up for lost time. The core catches up to our clocks. The progress of a disease then pushes forward also. The core only moves one way—it's not a time machine in the popular sense of the word. Anyone inside would be asphyxiated as the core resynchronizes. And you can't crack an active core open like an egg; nature won't let you. The manifolds reorient themselves to prevent it."

Niles was clearly shaken, wringing his hands slowly, repetitively.

Finally forcing a smile, he rose from the wheelchair and thanked her, wishing her a good night's rest.

Before he reached the door, Jenna called out to him. "Director Emmerich!"

He turned around wordlessly.

"Director Emmerich, are you asking me this because someone you know has a terminal illness?"

He paused uncertainly and licked his lips.

"Is it you?" she persisted.

He shook his head. "No, it's my sister," he admitted. "She has late-stage leukemia."

"Bryn's mother?"

He nodded almost imperceptibly. "Regina." There was resignation in his face. "She's hospitalized, but they'll transfer her to hospice care. She's a widow. My brother-in-law died of lung cancer several years back."

She shook her head sympathetically. "Director Emmerich, there's nothing I can do for her. Except pray."

"Nothing?" he asked one last time.

She didn't feel competent to explain such difficult matters but thought she'd at least try.

"The Bible says that all our times are in His hands. *Teach us to number our days, that we may apply our hearts unto wisdom.* The clock is ticking on all of us. My invention doesn't cheat time; it doesn't postpone the inevitable. It manipulates the synchronization between the core and the normal world. I think that God, who sees all of time at once, notices no difference between the core and real-time."

He looked up at her, relaxing a bit more. "Sounds like Jonas has turned *you* into a theologian as well. Anyway, time synchronization is not what makes your work controversial. It's the energy differential and what *that* means. Against you, Pandora ranks a distant second." He started to close the door behind himself again, shoulders hung uncharacteristically low.

"Wait!" she called out again.

He paused and turned his head around.

She addressed him, her concern clearly genuine. "Do you have a picture of your sister?"

Niles walked back to her bedside, pulling his digiscreen out as he approached. He fiddled with it a bit and handed it to Jenna. She looked hard at the smiling face on the screen: also a redhead, mid-fifties, sun-worn, dark eyes full of life.

"Bryn's hair isn't red," she remarked, her gaze still fixed on the image.

"He picked up his dad's hair color," he answered. But now Niles became curious. "Why did you want to see a picture of Regina, Jenna?"

She paused a moment, wondering *was that the first time he's ever used my first name?* She explained her interest to him. "I wanted to have an image of her in my mind when I pray for her … and for you, and Bryn. It seems too impersonal just praying over a name. I hope you don't mind."

She handed the digiscreen back to him. He looked at the image for a few moments, powered off the device, nodded at her, and left her bedroom.

She watched after him as his pensive form disappeared from sight.

Stall stuck his head into the kitchen, waving a large Thermos bottle he'd retrieved from his car.

"Katherine," he asked, "Any chance I could trouble you for some coffee to go? I've got a long drive tonight."

"Absolutely, General Stall," she answered, drying her hands on her apron. "It'll take a few minutes. Have a seat while I get it ready." She took the Thermos from Stall and began to rinse it out in the sink.

The general sat down at the kitchen table and watched as household staffers entered and left the kitchen. The coffee smelled fabulous as it brewed.

"Katherine," Stall finally asked, "do you ever talk with Miss Wilkes?"

"Oh, all the time," she answered cheerfully. "She's a beautiful person, isn't she?"

"Yes. Tell me, has she ever gone to church?"

"Of course. She's been to, what, eight or nine so far? It's been very challenging."

"For Miss Wilkes?"

"For the churches."

"The churches? I don't get it."

"Well," Katherine sat down across from Stall, "they're looking for buzzwords from her, but God's interested in her heart. The outside means more to some churches than the inside. She doesn't fit their expectations.

They keep trying to slow her down, turn her into one of them. I think her zeal makes others look like they're standing still. Despite being so new to it, she believes the Bible more intensely than they can imagine ever believing it or obeying it. And that's hard for some people. If she were boastful, they'd have a right to complain, but she's so quiet and humble."

Katherine arose to check the percolator. "Ah, nice and hot. Nothing worse than lukewarm coffee." She filled the general's Thermos, tightened down the cap, and handed it to him with a warm smile.

"Thank you, Katherine," Stall tucked the Thermos under his arm. "I still find it hard to believe that churches would have trouble dealing with someone who's simply burning the candle at both ends."

"Oh," Katherine turned back to the sink to keep working. "You're quite right. Good churches do make room for someone who burns the candle at both ends."

"So? What's the problem then?"

"She doesn't burn the candle at both ends, General Stall." Katherine continued working without turning around. "I thought you knew. For Jenna, the entire paraffin factory is on fire."

It was late in the evening, but Wolf Borse felt he needed to speak to Eckhardt about his findings. Eckhardt hadn't yet retired, but was in the Valley of the Books seated in his wheelchair. Wolf approached him with some fresh printouts of significance.

"I think they're going to notice *this* at the neutrino detectors," Wolf told Eckhardt. He handed the printouts to the seated figure. The graphs showed regularly spaced spikes that Wolf had circled in red. "Every sixty seconds, Doctor Eckhardt. A burst of neutrino activity."

Eckhardt flipped through the printouts from the three detector installations. "Yes, they'll see this pattern started last night, about 8:04 PM Pacific time."

Eckhardt nodded for Wolf to continue, declining to make use of the downstairs decorrelator chamber. Wolf trusted Eckhardt's judgment on this and explained the second problem openly.

"There's no way they won't compare notes between themselves with such an obviously nonrandom result. They'll expect the amplitudes to match, thinking the neutrinos are coming from a galactic source. Once they realize the amplitudes don't match, they'll know it's local. They'll triangulate on the intersecting wave fronts and trace it to the West Coast."

"Cat's out of the bag now, Wolf, isn't it?" Eckhardt shook his head.

"Doctor, they'll assume the source is nuclear, even though it's not." Wolf looked worried.

Eckhardt pondered this before answering. "That could be good or bad. If she's accused of making an illegal nuclear device, her only defense may be to explain the actual principle of operation."

"A dissertation defense in front of the whole world, Doctor?"

"Maybe. Let's hope not. But her enemies are going to exploit this for all it's worth."

Sexton appeared suddenly at the entryway and rolled his wheelchair into the Valley, his eyes glowing. "I overheard you two," he winked. "I have an idea, one that's very simple."

Eckhardt prevailed on Sexton to use a secure method to communicate.

Sexton tried to write the words the best he could on Eckhardt's pad, allowing Wolf and Eckhardt to consider his notion. *Have the NRC approach the isolator with their most sensitive radiation probes. Where there's no smoke, there's no fire. Get them on* your *side and preempt this attack.*

Eckhardt spoke after crumpling up the paper. "That would definitely take the wind out of their sails, Wally. I'll communicate with Oren."

Wolf had started writing now, and shared his pad with Sexton and Eckhardt. *Those Geiger counter guys aren't going to like going near something that unbelievably loud. That valley is the closest thing to Mount Sinai since Mount Sinai.*

Eckhardt felt comfortable speaking his reply openly. "If they're less courageous than our redhead, let them send a robot up to the truck."

43

Philip Hernandez watched from across the street, his eyes following the two gray-suited attorneys, leather cases bulging as they hurried down the steps of the courthouse. He glanced at his watch and looked up again. He was expecting something …

And he wasn't disappointed. Another attorney was hustling up the stairs toward them, waving some papers, acting distraught. The three intercepted each other in the middle of the steps, the newcomer conveying the news. One of the first two dropped his case in disbelief at the other's report. After some brief discussions, which Philip couldn't possibly overhear, all three suits slowly reentered the courthouse.

That's what I wanted to see, Philip thought. *Go and withdraw that motion.*

He knew the bad news his opponents just received involved the *amicus curiae* brief filed by the Nuclear Regulatory Commission, the one that declared Jenna's beacon to be non-nuclear, and therefore exempt from the injunction just filed against her. But her enemies wouldn't cease to find new, creative ways to impede her cause, pursuing parallel paths with plenty of backup plans along the way. Could Jenna and her advocates stay one step ahead of her detractors forever? Philip honestly didn't know.

He *had* been exposed to some of the other strategies mounted against her. The press conference he had just held was still fresh in his memory.

The primary strategy of the scientists opposing drainage of the dam was to seek to move her experiment somewhere deep inside a national laboratory, out of the public eye. Philip had to patiently walk through the facts with his interrogators, explaining why this wasn't an option, that the energy path only moved laterally, never upstream. This isolator's path was now irrevocably tied to the generator building at the dam, like a conductive path etched into an insulator that suffered dielectric breakdown.

Philip himself was a quick study in the specifics of Jenna's isolator and the peculiar phenomena associated with it, having been briefed by Jenna during their flight to Virginia several days before.

That flight had an uneasy beginning, where student and advisor had their first meeting since her last dissertation defense. Given how she behaved at Stanford, Philip expected her to drive the knife deep, especially in light of the vindication her rejected ideas had received.

However, Jenna was inexplicably humble and forgiving, even asking forgiveness from Philip for the difficulties she caused him seven years earlier. She expressed genuine gratitude for his mentorship (which he maintained at Stanford against the urgings of his colleagues) and took full responsibility for what happened to her. This was definitely a far more mature Jenna than he had known, and he wasn't exactly sure how to deal with her. But he knew to revise his expectations to avoid misjudging her again.

More to the point, for every loose end being tied up, several hundred more threads were being ripped apart in Jenna's wake. And things were going to get worse before they got better.

A few victories were chalked up, however. Philip still marveled at General Stall's facile outmaneuvering of the ACLU just two days before.

The ACLU had filed to remove the U.S. Army guards who answered to Stall from the dam site. Stall had waited for the court ruling to come in, a ruling that declared that such federal invasion of state property was illegal. This was what Stall was waiting for: his men immediately went on official leave but continued to guard the dam on their own time in uniform. When Riesen spurred General Melliton to send troops out to the dam, Philip successfully secured a restraining order against Melliton using the exact ruling the ACLU used against Stall.

The ACLU didn't hesitate to pit state law against federal incursions, and use federal law to overturn state law, as their needs dictated. It was more important to win than be consistent. In that spirit, they exploited the court of public opinion, arguing on one hand that *state's rights* was a code word for racism and bigotry, then labeling federal acts favoring Jenna's protest as being fascist, painting the specter of the blatant *usurpation* of state's rights.

Philip could not but muse over the ironies his own involvement in the matter had ignited. After a seven-year hiatus, he had resumed his representation of Jenna Wilkes, except now in the courts of law and public opinion rather than in academia. His status as a noted Hispanic scientist resonated with the majority of Californians who listened to him speak on television, while his status as a card-carrying atheist immunized his advocacy of Jenna's initiative against the most virulent attacks from that angle.

Philip walked calmly across the street with the motion he had come to file on Jenna's behalf, and hoped that Eckhardt's legal team would continue to have their act together, unlike the ACLU attorneys who had just been forced to tell the court clerk, "Never mind."

While Professor Hernandez waged battle on Jenna's side, crossing the supposed "hard line" in the sand between theists and atheists, the President of the United States was shaking his head at a group whose criticism of Jenna's initiative was the most vocal. He watched a news conference where a representative of the World Conclave of Churches condemned Jenna and her initiative, with dozens of major religious figures standing behind him in tight-jawed solidarity. It was clear that the tactic of using amassed religious authority, of driving a wedge between conservative and liberal Christendom, was going to be effective. Perhaps decisively so.

If I hadn't heard this news conference with my own ears, I'd never have believed it, he thought. *To hear them tell it, the most unwelcome visitor in their churches would be God Himself.*

All manner of Biblical warnings were cited against her. She was reviled as a false Christ and a false prophet who brandished miracles and lying wonders to deceive the people.

The fact that Jenna never claimed to be a messianic figure, that there was no miracle inherent in the beam's operation, that she simply didn't fit the warnings in the Bible, meant nothing to critics trying to shoehorn her into the devil's boots.

None of it made any sense to the president. *All Wilkes ever tried to get across is that we live in a moral universe. Why would religious leaders fight for an amoral one? That's like calling for Barabbas to be released.*

He cinched up his tie and went into a cabinet meeting that, he was grateful to say, involved something less divisive: the three-decade-long crisis in North Korea.

Seven of the nine Supreme Court justices took the time to visit the dam site, doing so privately, without fanfare. After internal debate concerning the matter, the chief justice forwarded a note to the president revealing the court's intention to not hear any challenge on the matter of interposition, letting stand a 2013 decision on interposition in Massachusetts.

Prior to 2013, interposition had been considered a dead maneuver, last utilized in the nineteenth century, but Massachusetts used the tactic to sidestep marriage legislation passed that year in Congress. The Supreme Court had ruled in the state's favor 7-2, creating a precedent that was now crippling federal efforts to obstruct the draining of the dam.

The president crumpled the note, thinking about this turn of events. *It all depends on whose ox is gored,* he figured.

Eckhardt hadn't counted on *this* strategy by his well-funded opposition.

Jenna's detractors bought virtually all the airtime in California for the three days leading up to the vote. Attack ads were being emailed to Californians, were printed in California newspapers, were broadcast on California radio, were offered as free downloads on iTunes, were placed as front-page advertisements on Yahoo!, Google, MSN, and DellNet, all without leaving any room, time, or opportunity for Jenna's side to respond.

It was a virtual lockout. Since the Wilkes Initiative wasn't considered political, the media strategy couldn't be challenged using the fairness doctrine.

44

Jenna was surprised by her visitor's sudden appearance.

General Stall let himself into her room, dressed in civilian clothing. She was propped up on her bed, her good leg crossed over the cast-bound one with a pillow wedged in between for comfort. Lab books were scattered over the comforter; she had just been writing in a fresh one. Doing her work in longhand had become second nature.

After exchanging brief pleasantries, Stall got to the point. "Doctor Wilkes, I'm afraid there's only one way you'll be able to raise a defense against the smoke screens being used against your initiative. People can't see the issue through all the dust being thrown up in their faces."

"What needs to be done, General?" Concern was etched onto her face.

"You need to appear on television," he began. "You need to make a final appeal. We can announce a news conference, and the media will cover it. You'll have a chance to make sure Californians aren't swayed by the propaganda campaign against your initiative.

"I'd recommend you draft a speech ..." he began, but she cut him off.

"I can't do it, General. There's nothing left in me."

"It could make a big difference," he added calmly.

She shook her head. "I can't do it."

He nodded, and went on. "They've asked me to share something else that we just learned a few hours ago. You're aware that Doctor Sexton was flown home a few days back?"

"Yes, he said he was going to see his sons." But she instinctively tensed up at the change in Stall's eyes as he continued.

"Yes, that was a good idea. I'm glad he got to see them. I'm sorry to be the one to tell you this, but Doctor Sexton passed away earlier this morning."

Her eyes widened. "Doctor Sexton?" her voice cracked.

The general put his hand on her shoulder as she diverted her eyes downward. They filled with tears. Her shoulders heaved as she grieved the loss of her advocate. Stall waited with her, gently squeezing her shoulder every so often. When she had finished sobbing and collected herself, he stepped back from the bed.

"I'll let myself out now, Doctor Wilkes. I'm sorry about Doctor Sexton. I understand you two had recently become friends."

Her lips again trembled at his words.

"I need to get back to the Pentagon," he added, and walked toward her doorway.

Jenna uncrossed her leg and tossed the pillow to the floor, bending over to examine the wording Sexton had inked onto her cast weeks before. She found it, trying to read it through still-tearing eyes.

They can only beat you if you let them. You've been a walking example of this for me. God bless you, Wallingford Sexton.

She ran her fingers gently over the words, something she-knew-not-what being kindled deep inside her. Before the general reached the door, Jenna called out to him to stop. He turned, mildly surprised.

"On one condition," she said, her voice trembling with determination.

"What might that condition be?" he asked her.

"I speak from on top of the UPS truck at the dam."

This time it was his eyes that widened. He pointed at her broken leg. "You're in no shape to travel, Doctor Wilkes."

"That's my condition. I need to be on top of that truck. I want that spillway filled all the way to the main road with people when I start talking. I'll need a much bigger PA system and portable lighting for the entire spillway. Can it be arranged for tomorrow night?"

The general thought about her intentions. "It can be done," he answered, "but I advise against it. Strongly advise against it. You're putting yourself in harm's way out there. The risks are huge."

"It's worth it, General Stall."

He nodded grimly.

It was late at night. Jenna knew not to be up and about at this hour, but she had climbed into her wheelchair and made her way to the Valley of the Books to do something she'd been warned not to do. She wheeled up to one of the computers and pulled up an internet news feed.

The first half-dozen adults she heard being interviewed about the dam only made her feel angrier and more self-righteous. She thought she was in the right place spiritually now, fired up with righteous indignation, congratulating herself for ignoring the warning not to watch.

The cameraman dipped his camera down as the reporter bent over to speak with an eight-year-old girl who'd come with her parents to the dam spillway.

"What's your name?" the reporter asked her.

"Brianna Dixon," the diminutive blonde girl responded.

The thunderclap hit, and sheer terror gripped the girl, her eyes reacting to the vicious slap inflicted on her body. She was shaking.

Jenna, mouth hanging open, shuddered at the girl's reaction.

"Brianna," the reporter continued, "you wanted to say something?"

"Um, yes," the girl was nervous. "I just …"

"Go on," the reporter urged gently.

"I just wanted to ask a question for the lady who put the stick up there." She pointed at the UPS truck forty yards behind her in the out-of-focus background of the video. "Will she hear me if I ask?"

"I don't know, Brianna. Why don't you ask it anyway?"

The girl shuffled self-consciously, then put her hand on the microphone to pull it toward her mouth.

"I just wanted to know, didn't God put that water in the dam for *us*? Why is the lady telling us to throw the water away that God gave? Why is she scaring us? Nobody wants to come here with the noise. My friends and I used to play around here. It's a terrible, scary place now. Why did the lady make it that way? She scares me."

"Do you think she's a bad lady?" the reporter pressed.

Brianna shuffled again and didn't answer.

"Do you know the name of the lady who put the stick up there?" the reporter asked.

"They call her Doctor Wilkes, don't they?" Brianna blinked quizzically at the camera, then back at the reporter. "But I thought doctors make sick people better, so they don't worry anymore. But my mom and dad and friends can hear the noise all the time in our houses. And they're worrying more and more. Is that lady a real doctor?"

"So you think we should leave God's water in the dam?" The reporter led the girl on.

"I dunno," Brianna backed up into her father and pulled his hand around her. "The lady is very brave. Maybe God is making her brave."

The next thunderclap caused the girl to cringe against her father, desperation in her eyes.

"I'm *not* brave." Brianna's lip quivered and she clapped her hands over her ears. The girl closed her eyes tightly and spun around in her father's arms to hug him; his face never once appeared on camera.

Jenna logged off the computer. "But you *are* brave, Brianna," she answered the now-black screen. Her gaze dropped to the floor. "How could I be so thoughtless? How could I do this to innocent children?" A sickening wave of guilt, then numbness, passed through the self-appointed daughter of thunder, but at long last a profound sense of compassion quenched the fire smoldering in her heart. She looked up at the cast on her leg with deepened respect, and then she dared to turn her head upward to whisper into the dimly lit ceiling space above her.

"You're also using that little girl to keep me humble, aren't You?"

The internet bogged down with news of the press conference Jenna had scheduled for 7:00 PM the evening before the vote. She had been out of the public eye since television cameras captured her dramatic departure from the generator building. Jenna was news, and her opponents saw this as a classic political tactic: the last minute hit-and-run that couldn't be answered. They did everything to minimize the impact it might make, especially since Jenna's initiative was headed toward easy defeat. The downward trend had even accelerated, and the opposition refused to yield momentum to the redhead.

The preparation for her appearance was spearheaded by Bryn and the two captains, all mindful of how badly Jenna's initiative was being hammered. Eckhardt paid for the traffic control, lighting, and extended PA system needed to insure she would be heard throughout the spillway. The extra notice made it possible for TV cameras and correspondents to be better situated, although most set up their equipment and left guards to protect it. Until zero hour, there was no point waiting near the thunderclaps that ceaselessly beat upon that valley like waves on a beach.

The crowds began accumulating hours ahead of time, since first-come, first-served was the rule enforced by traffic control. Once the safe capacity of the spillway was reached, the road was closed and entry barred.

A few minutes before the appointed hour, a helicopter appeared over the dam wall, all but retracing its approach a few weeks earlier when Jenna had been airlifted out of sight. The chopper avoided the beam, clearly visible in the twilight.

The chopper stabilized about fifteen feet off the top of the generator roof and sent its flex ladder cascading down. The two captains and Bryn descended first, the former verifying with the guards that the rooftop had remained secure. The TV cameras were taking in the entire scene, and once again the world was transfixed by the drama unfolding before their eyes.

The huge crowd came to witness what they hoped might be history, braving the clockwork concussions of the thunderclaps. They pressed forward now that Jenna's appearance was imminent.

Inside the helicopter, Jenna was shocked by how loud each thunderclap was—and she wasn't even on top of the UPS truck yet. She'd never experienced that sound while conscious.

She was helped to the chopper's ladder, her leg still in its heavy plaster cast, and carefully made her way down, Captains Green and Boudreaux monitoring her while Bryn prepped her headset. She was unconsciously counting the seconds to the next thunderclap, fast becoming aware of how frightening this was actually going to be. Her crutch was handed down the ladder to Richard, who assisted her behind the UPS truck, hiding her from the TV cameras once again. Another thunderclap struck as the helicopter gained altitude to depart.

Bryn came up to her, and they stood looking at each other. There wasn't much point in talking, since their group had donned protective earplugs before getting within earshot of the beam. But his eyes spoke for him. *You'd have to be insane to get up close to that beam,* he thought. That bright red beam, those ear-splitting booms, the faint smell of ozone, made the scene nightmarish. He could never bring himself to crawl up the ladder to the truck's roof in perfect health, let alone with a crutch and a leg in a cast.

He gently placed the wireless headset on her head and adjusted the microphone for her. He dusted some dirt off her unwashed lab coat and forced a brief smile, looking right at her. She nodded at him, indicating she was ready, and Bryn and Richard guided her to the ladder against the truck. Climbing up the ladder with the cast on was slow going, and she hoped she could navigate the actual arrival onto the truck's roof with the awkward deadweight the plaster represented.

When her head peeped up over the roofline, the crowd went silent, as it had done a few weeks earlier. She noticed that the crowd noise would well up between thunderclaps, only to be driven into silence once the shockwave of the blast hammered the air.

After some effort, she had gotten herself disentangled from the ladder rungs and was standing on the UPS truck when the next thunderclap hit, nearly knocking her down. She regained her balance and looked out at the crowd, then closed her eyes to draw on strength from somewhere, from Someone, else.

She limped over to the staff, sticking nearly four feet out of the top of the truck. The bottom of the staff, she knew, was embedded in the titanium top of the isolator and had contacted the core. The shunt was being gated by the controls Eckhardt had built into the sheath-like cladding of the device.

She stood only one foot from the staff, then faced the crowd resolutely, throwing the crutch forward and off the truck. A murmur rose from the crowd for a moment, but quickly subsided, all eyes again on Jenna as she regarded the multitudes.

At the next thunderclap, she winced as if an explosion had gone off next to her, which was disturbingly close to the truth, but she rose again to full height and stood looking at the crowd again. The sixty seconds ticking off to the next thunderclap seemed like an eternity, with a billion pairs of eyes around the world all glued to her, wondering what she was doing.

While the cameras watched, Jenna scanned the crowd. She didn't react to the next thunderclap but stood her ground, immovable, unperturbed, yet still watching the crowd closely. This was becoming unnerving for everyone, even those watching on television or on internet video.

It was meant to be unnerving. It felt like she was judging them with her eyes alone.

She bent over slightly and wrapped her fingers around the staff, still not releasing the gaze of the crowds nor pulling out the staff. The next thunderclap struck while she was holding the staff, the beam being emitted only inches above her grip. The cameras caught the effect of the shockwave on Jenna's forearm, the muscles and tendons jarring as her clothes shuddered. She looked like a puppet daring to pull on its strings to yank the puppet-master down. As the thunder reverberated down the valley walls, the crowd's murmurs grew audible.

She remained motionless, hand still on the staff, for three more thunderclaps. The drama heightened to the breaking point. Jenna's steady gaze held the crowd captive.

A few seconds after the fourth thunderclap, she tightened her grip and pulled the staff all the way out, causing the crowd to gasp. They didn't know what to expect, and although she now held the staff across her waist horizontally, like a weightlifter about to do a military press, they feared her turning the staff toward them.

She began to speak, her words echoing down the valley through the massive PA system.

"You're all afraid of this staff? Me more." She patted her leg cast with one hand before placing it back on the staff.

"The courts would have gone easier on me had I painted a giant cross on this dam, apparently because a cross is easier to ignore. I had a hard time believing that the people of Israel could see thunder from Mount Sinai and hear God's voice and then forget everything they had seen a month later. But you turned your back on this wonder while it was *still in front of you*. It looks like the Israelites showed amazing restraint in waiting several weeks before diving back into darkness.

"I pray you'll recognize how crucial your vote tomorrow actually is. You people of California, out of all the world, have been given the right to vote concerning the shape of the future. Other countries would take that right from you.

"I want you to see how precious this right, one we all have in common, is to me personally, so I'm now going to walk to my new polling place, a twelve-mile walk, to cast my ballot. Funny that my polling place is an elementary school, where the life-long process of seeking the truth begins. I'm taking my staff, I'm going to vote, then I'm going home, and I'll discover what kind of people Californians truly are when I read the next day's newspaper.

"Think about the emptiness that now broods over this valley and whether you had any part in muffling the marvels of God."

Jenna made her way to the ladder and was aided down from the truck's roof by her friends, disappearing behind it. She soon reappeared next to the truck, staff in hand, ready to move toward the ramp leading to ground level. A cadre of Stall's men formed a protective ring at the bottom of the ramp, awaiting her.

Before beginning her trek, she turned off her headset and patted the side of the UPS truck with her free hand. She addressed the vehicle in words only Bryn and the two captains could hear.

"Thanks for holding together so long, my friend. I've put you through a terrible beating. The good news is, since you've been on TV, UPS stock has gone through the roof. It's publicity you can't buy."

She looked at Richard and Mike with a weak smile, glancing down as Bryn slipped a walking shoe on her one bare foot. Once it was securely tied, she yanked her earplugs out and turned to face the ramp, a determined expression spreading across her face.

Bryn reactivated her headset mike, and she began her slow walk down the ramp to be received in the center of the circle of guards. Before she reached the circle, Jenna had one last thing to say over the PA system.

"Up until now, I've only asked you to vote, but I have one last thing to ask of you people gathered here in this valley. Please allow me to walk out to the main road in total silence. That's all I ask of my fellow citizens, to not speak, to let me pass by you in silence. Please honor me in this one thing."

And so she started moving toward the crowd at a slow, strained pace, leaning on the staff with both hands to pull herself forward, the cast on her leg being impossible to miss. The soldiers encircling her were keeping about three yards between her and the crowd on all sides. Her progress was slow and difficult, but the TV cameras remained focused on her, while cameramen she had passed by hustled to take up new positions in her path, keeping her staggering figure center stage on the world's video screens.

The effect of thousands of people in the valley watching her walk in silence was even more profound than the thunderclaps had been. As Niles watched the TV in Eckhardt's home, Eckhardt leaned over to him.

"Now that it's so quiet, the people can't help but hear their own conscience."

Niles nodded. "Reminds me of Tennyson. *But over all things brooding slept, The quiet sense of something lost.*"

"I didn't know you read Tennyson."

"I don't. That's an internet quote of the day."

They watched the lone form trudging oh-so-slowly away from the generator building through the dry brush speckling the spillway, the crowds parting for her while photojournalists scrambled to anticipate the best camera angles to capture her march. The spectacle now played out against the haunting backdrop of silence rather than clockwork thunderbolts—reminiscent of a still, small voice that once dwarfed thunder, earthquake, and whirlwind so long ago.

The silence spoke to the heart. A vague sense of remorse was suffusing the crowd, an awareness of having treated with contempt something that was genuinely wonderful beyond words.

Even the TV coverage honored her request, horizontally scrolling the comments of the correspondents at the bottom of the screen. Although she only intended her words for those who could vote the next morning, the world itself was moved as she took one step after another, focusing her eyes straight ahead toward the main road at the mouth of the valley.

Niles turned to Eckhardt. "Jonas, she's really going to walk all twelve miles like *that*?"

"Yes, Niles, she's going to try. If she falls down, we'll be there to help pick her up."

"This whole thing was her idea?"

"All of it. I couldn't talk her out of it."

"Why didn't she just force them to drain the dam? That's what I would have done."

"I know. She's not doing the easy thing, she's doing the right thing."

Niles looked hard at Eckhardt, his head shaking slowly in disbelief. "Why do you think your God chose a woman?"

"God uses the weak to confound the strong. Women being the weaker vessel, perhaps it's not so unusual for Him to use a woman to confound His enemies."

Niles watched Jenna marching fitfully on the screen. "Well, *somebody* sure took you seriously for once, Jonas. Either that, or you've created a monster."

Eckhardt adjusted in his wheelchair painfully. "That's the entire point. From the other side of the aisle, she *is* a monster, lurching toward Gomorrah. I won't even try to deny it. That young lady," he pointed a now-shaky finger at the TV screen, "is showing the people that there can be no neutrality. With every step she takes, she crushes that comfortable lie under her feet."

"The talking heads say she's nothing but a meaningless pawn," Niles reminded Eckhardt.

"Funny thing about pawns," Eckhardt pointed out. "They cross the chessboard to become queens."

Viewers who tuned in late encountered a scene that defied reason: a crippled redhead in a dirty lab coat trudging through the crowds and the brush. The only sound came from the spectators parting in front and reuniting behind her as Jenna pushed forward, punctuated by the irregular *thonk* of her staff. Only by reading the scrolling marquee at the bottom of the screen could newcomers gather what had happened.

It took two hours for her to reach the main road, and she stumbled more than a half-dozen times throughout the ordeal, but the crowd maintained its silence. When they saw her turn right to press forward on the shoulder of the highway, the murmurs rose up from the masses. Within moments the crowd was in a roar, talking to itself about what they had witnessed. The impact on television viewers was just as intense.

The two-hours notice allowed the Highway Patrol to clear the highway in advance of her departure from the valley, and they forced all exiting people and cars to detour left while Jenna limped to the right, circled more loosely by the guards now that they were out of the crowd.

Only TV cameramen and other media were permitted to track her progress. The cameramen alternated short shifts, some resting while their coworkers took over, but Jenna had only her staff to lean on.

All the airtime purchased by the opposition was preempted by her march, which was deemed too newsworthy to terminate. The few stations that tried to put on the prepaid attack ads found their viewership rapidly collapsing to nothing. Nobody wanted to miss what the woman in a cast was doing as she marched to, of all places, a simple polling place.

The next morning, people awoke to the spectacle of Jenna's march, the TV caption still reading *Live Coverage* indicating it was still in progress. She was stumbling more frequently after walking all night. The cameras never left her face, which was streaked with sweat and dirt and pain and conviction. Viewers learned she never really stopped walking, only accepting a few cups of water from Captain Richard Green as she marched forward. The live shots of Jenna were occasionally intercut with archive clips of the UPS truck on the roof, the eighth wonder of the world having fallen silent.

The networks used archive clips of the truck because the valley had been completely cleared by the local authorities around 2:00 AM, several hours earlier. Waiting with their night vision goggles on their heads, Bryn and Mike made a one-word cell phone call to Eckhardt's people once the vicinity had been vacated and the lights and PA system removed.

"Ready."

In the darkness, another UPS truck, headlights off, turned into the dam spillway from the main road and made its way to the generator station. Mike had backed the original truck down the ramp, while the replacement truck with the aluminum fake isolator was put into position. The new truck's appearance was carefully matched to the original, inside and out. The license plates were quickly switched.

Bryn hefted a black staff in his hands, bemused. "Mikey, I'd love to be there when those guys try to insert the fake staff Jenna has with her into the wrong isolator."

"Fake isolator, fake staff, fake truck." Mike laughed. "She thought of everything. Pretty smooth how she handed the real staff to you behind the truck and went out marching with a fake."

"You know what she told me about that tactic?" Bryn asked.

"What?"

"She said she was being gentle as a dove but clever as a serpent."

"That's in the Bible."

"You're kidding."

"No, I'm pretty sure."

"Huh." Bryn turned the staff over in his hand to study the control panel. "Well, the real staff is no good without a real isolator, that much is certain. Anyway, we've got unfinished business inside the turbine room."

"All ready for ya," Mike confirmed. "Everything's ready to install. Should only take a half hour, and then we can put the real isolator where nobody will think to look for it."

"I hope Jenna's got that figured right," Bryn commented. "To put it in plain sight like she wanted. Anyway, let's deal with the generator room."

The two men were quite adept at being clever as serpents themselves.

45

She had traveled nine of the twelve miles to the elementary school polling place when she had fallen over completely, splitting her lip and gaining a large raspberry on her left elbow. The billion people watching her all gasped.

She'd allow nobody to help her, pulling herself up to her feet and dusting her sweaty lab coat off. Beyond exhausted, she looked around to get her bearings, nodded in the correct direction, and planted her staff another foot in front of her.

The march resumed. And the viewers were pulled even deeper into the drama they were watching.

The networks realized there'd be no way they could all get their cameras into the polling place, so after figurative straws were drawn, video feeds were arranged for two networks to share their live footage with the competition. Those two networks took over coverage from the entrance to the school to the interior of the polling place.

As she limped into view of the elementary school, a gathered crowd of nearly four hundred people cheered. The networks had kept her on the air, nonstop, for nearly twelve hours, and she was clearly showing the strain with every raising of the staff, every lifting of the heavy cast-laden leg, every strained breath from her burning lungs.

It took her nearly ten minutes to reach the steps, which she negotiated one at a time, resting on each step for a few seconds. She was almost there.

And what nobody in the world knew except Jenna herself was that she had remained completely focused on her march for twelve straight hours. Her mind didn't wander once but became subservient to her will, becoming more focused and powerful than it had ever been. The trial weakened her outwardly but strengthened her inwardly.

Richard approached and whispered a quick explanation as she mounted the final step. "These people are waiting for you to vote first before they cast their ballots. It's a very small community. This place is kinda remote, so they're using manual ballots here."

She nodded at the captain and continued to plant the staff in front of her, pulling herself along with aching arms and screaming leg muscles. Two soldiers held the door open for her. Jenna didn't notice the cameraman backing down the hallway to keep her in his viewfinder as she approached.

Jenna heard someone running, and without warning found a small girl standing in front of her, breathless. Their eyes met.

"Brianna," Jenna rasped in recognition.

The girl's eyes widened. "You know my name?" she asked in surprise.

Jenna tried to clear her throat. "Yes. I heard what you said to the reporter."

Brianna reached up to touch Jenna's split lip with a tentative hand.

"You kept falling down," the girl said, withdrawing her hand and looking at her fingers.

Jenna nodded. "I did."

Brianna looked at all the writing on Jenna's cast. "My brother had a cast too. I drew some flowers on it." She looked back up into Jenna's eyes, then her gaze fixed upon the staff. "That stick scares me," she pointed.

"It's just a stick," Jenna answered, eyes weary but glowing. "Touch it and see."

Brianna tapped it with her fingers, a faint smile forming as she realized the staff wouldn't hurt her. She looked back into Jenna's face. "Are you going to take God's water away?"

"It'll always be God's water," Jenna replied. "Maybe we'll use it to water some of God's plants. I don't know."

"Why did you make the noise so scary?" Brianna asked, turning around curiously at the cameramen who approached.

"If you want to feel safe in a dangerous place," Jenna asked, "would you want to have a lion as your friend or a caterpillar?"

Brianna thought about Jenna's question. "Have a lion for my friend."

"Right. A lion. Because the bigger your friend—the more powerful he is—the safer you'll be. He'll scare away anything that will hurt you, right?"

Brianna nodded attentively, her foot-shuffling habit in full swing.

"Do you understand, Brianna?" Jenna asked gently, her voice still ragged.

"The noise was loud because you have a really big friend who keeps you safe. Bigger than a lion." Brianna's eyes darkened as she reached back up to touch Jenna's injured lip. "You still got hurt."

Jenna nodded. "I still got hurt."

"Is God your friend?" Brianna asked.

When Jenna nodded, Brianna seemed satisfied and abruptly walked away, but stopped to address the startled cameraman in the knowing tones of innocent youth. "*That's* why it was so loud and scary!" The girl ran back into the crowd.

Jenna resumed the final leg of her journey as she passed through the door. Her staff made a hollow metallic sound as it struck the tiled flooring inside the building. The setting was modest: nothing fancy at all. Nothing remarkable, no outward show, just like Jenna's discovery of what she wanted to call the Sexton Effect.

She klonked along, stopped to put on her glasses, squinting through the dirty lenses at the signs pasted to the three tables manned by polling place volunteers. A–L, M–R, S–Z. She continued toward the rightmost table. Seated behind it, a cheerful retiree in a checkered shirt and a Cleveland Indians cap looked on.

When she tried to speak to him, her voice croaked from hoarseness brought on by twelve hours of labored breathing. "Jenna Wilkes," she wearily told the poll worker.

"I know. I've been watching you," he responded, pointing to a small portable TV on a nearby school desk. He spun the registry around and pointed to where her name appeared. "Please sign here, Miss."

She wedged the staff under her left shoulder and tried to bend over, taking the pen from the poll worker. Her hand shook so terribly that her signature was utterly illegible.

"I'm afraid I'm having a little trouble writing," she tried to tell him. "Is this good enough, or did I ruin it?"

He examined her jagged scrawl, then looked up into her exhausted eyes, considering the dried blood on her lip and chin. "I'll vouch that's your signature. Here's a ballot. You can vote in those curtained booths a few steps behind you."

He pointed just behind her, but it looked like a mile away to Jenna.

The cameras caught everything, dialogue included. Richard maintained his vigil nearby.

She entered the booth and focused all her energy on marking the ballot as steadily as she could, adding a note across the top of it. Content that she accomplished what she purposed to do, she took a deep breath, closed her eyes, and prayed that God would open the eyes of her fellow citizens.

But her strength was finally spent, and she collapsed, taking the entire row of curtained booths with her to the floor in a sickening crash of metal and wood and human body.

The cameras caught her fall, and kept recording as Richard, his fellow soldiers, and the poll workers rushed to Jenna's prone form. The cameramen approached as well, still capturing the live footage. She still had her ballot in her hand, so a camera moved in on it to let the viewers of the world know how she had voted. The note she had written in a wobbly hand was legible enough to read, and appeared on the video feed to the nations.

God, give this great people strength today.

46

The ACLU cried foul at the entire thing, attacking the "contrived" march and her illicit manipulation of the ignorant. They insisted she was an unwitting pawn, a stalking horse being used by that billionaire Eckhardt. Several newspapers hit upon the same derisive headline: *Speak Softly but Carry a Big Black Stick.* The smears did them no good and even backfired: by evening, the exit polls revealed that 78 percent of the voters approved the measure, while the percentage of eligible voters participating was the highest it'd been since before World War II.

But Jenna was unaware of the results, recuperating from her self-imposed ordeal at Metro Hospital, where she had been flown partway by Eckhardt's helicopter. Her absence once again created a problem, as the scientific community moved to quickly take over her project and frustrate Jenna's intentions regarding the draining of the dam.

Her black staff was found in the ambulance that transferred her from the chopper to Metro; it was quickly confiscated. The UPS truck was impounded and spirited away to Lawrence Livermore National Laboratory, where the isolator mounted in it was moved to an underground facility.

Jenna had accounted for those two possibilities in advance, and also for a third: the lockdown of the turbine rooms, choreographed by General Melliton through Colonel Riesen. Her technology was redefined as a matter of national security. The vote required the dam to be drained, but never mandated public access to the results of the draining.

Only Lawrence Livermore personnel would explain what was happening inside the generator building. From the viewpoint of the scientists who took control of the turbines, Jenna's project smelled like the second coming of cold fusion, a long-discredited idea that misled scientists when neutron counters operated too close to their noise floor to give meaningful results. The scientists characterized Jenna's work as having no more merit than cold fusion. In her absence, the press could only focus on her gainsayers.

The government scientists had prepared a list of counter-explanations they intended to float to the general public, explanations that made perfectly good sense so long as nobody could see the turbines. Anything Jenna, Philip, or her associates might say about what was going on inside the building would be swiftly denounced. It was their word against hers, and she wasn't allowed inside, while scientists with access to the interior assured everybody that Doctor Wilkes must have lost her sanity on that pointless march.

A week later, the draining of the dam was nearing completion. Riesen kicked himself for not thinking of his "national security" solution earlier, but it had looked like Jenna's initiative was destined for defeat up until the morning of the vote. But he discovered the way to prevent the drained dam from confounding the clear categories of the U.S. Constitution.

The day the dam became empty, the authorities said the extra power had to be fed in from the North American power grid to take up the resulting slack. Nothing special was happening inside the generator room. By these firm statements, Jenna's long march looked like self-destructive folly.

General Melliton gestured for Riesen to sit down. He had summoned the colonel to his Pentagon office for a debriefing.

"Well?" asked Melliton.

"Mission accomplished. We've outmaneuvered them on all fronts. General Stall's tactics have gotten him nowhere." Riesen couldn't resist a faint smile.

Melliton glared at Riesen.

"What's this you're saying about General Stall?"

"We prevailed, sir. He lost."

Melliton stood up angrily.

"What do you mean, talking trash about General Stall? Was this all about getting back at Stall in some twisted way, Colonel? Just so there's no misunderstanding, know this: he's ten times the man you are. If all you can do is salute the uniform and not the man, that's your business, but you will say *nothing* disrespectful about Harrison Stall in my hearing again."

"But he's on the wrong side of this issue, sir."

"Maybe, maybe not. None of your business either way."

Riesen thought it *was* his business; that was the whole reason he had asked to be reassigned to Melliton. The colonel dared to ask Melliton why he thought so highly of Stall, and was silenced by Melliton's answer.

"Colonel, General Stall and I might be working different angles on this, but let me tell you something about him. He's the *only* general I know who's more interested in his men than where his next star is coming from. The only one. Just because I'm fighting tooth and nail against him doesn't mean I wouldn't salute him with my dying breath. At least he stands for something."

Riesen was dumbfounded. He started to apologize, but Melliton held his hand up to stop him.

"Colonel, just secure the intel like you're supposed to. Keep your editorials to yourself. Make sure Doctor Mays gets what he needs at the National Laboratory to figure this device out."

"Yes sir." Riesen's words were clipped.

"Most important, let's see how well you can hold the line on unwanted publicity on this thing before you dream of criticizing a man of Stall's caliber. Understood?"

"Yes sir."

"Let me make myself absolutely clear on this. Once upon a time, Martin Luther nailed ninety-five theses to a church door and set most of Europe on fire. I'll be damned if I'm going to let this woman nail up a ninety-sixth one on my watch. Dismissed."

Riesen departed in confusion. He had switched sides but where had he ended up? Being chewed out by Melliton was even worse than the insanely long salute Stall had made him hold weeks before. His conscience pounded within him.

Were his stated motivations merely a pretext for his real ones? Was he guilty of the very thing he had repudiated in Stall, nursing a hidden agenda?

He wouldn't let himself believe that.

Riesen promptly collided with General Stall in the hallway. The two saluted.

"You look distracted, Colonel," Stall observed.

"Yes sir."

"I'm curious about something, if you don't mind me asking," Stall continued. "A squad of soldiers was sent out on a mission similar to yours about twenty centuries ago. They were supposed to guard a tomb and make sure nothing out of the ordinary happened there. I've always wondered how those men felt about that assignment."

"Why should I know anything about that?" Riesen asked.

"Just a hunch," Stall replied, his concern genuine. "You don't have to reply, Colonel. I think I've already gotten my answer. I can see it written in your eyes."

"The latest test results on the staff," the technician announced, handing over a digital key to the lead researcher, who rose from behind his computer screen to accept it.

"Thank you, Russ," the soft-spoken young scientist answered, plugging it into his computer to download the data.

"Can I ask a question, Brev?" Russ inquired.

"You can ask … I may not have an answer for you," Brevard replied.

"Well, we're all wondering …" Russell Pierce gestured toward the other technicians milling around the isolator dominating the center of the hangar-like security laboratory.

"You're wondering why mainstream science can't explain this device." Brevard finished.

"Yeah."

"You all believe this device represents a problem that needs to be solved."

"Of course. That's why we're here. That's why *you* are here." Russell thought this was all self-evident.

"I'll tell you what I think," Brevard sat back down to resume his work. "I think mainstream science can't find a solution because it's actually part of the problem."

"What?" Russell was caught off-guard.

"Just kidding," Brevard waved him off. "A bad joke. Blame the instant coffee."

"Sure thing, Brev. But we are going to solve this thing, right? This lockdown is driving us all crazy."

"Sure, Russ, consider it solved." Brevard's friendly smile encouraged Russell, who circulated back toward the group surrounding the isolator.

Brevard reflected on his friend's reaction to his unguarded comment. There was science here, no doubt, but there was something more basic than science here too. Something these technicians weren't ready to hear.

Brevard turned back to the monitor, pretty certain that Dr. Wilkes had done the same thing he was now doing: analyzing bogus data. At least he was in a position to keep the other researchers in the dark, although he marveled that no one else had caught on.

He knew the isolator was fake the second he watched the forklift pull it out of the UPS truck days earlier. The angled cant of the lifting rack, groaning with the weight of the unit, was all wrong: this isolator was too light to be made of titanium. When no other scientists noticed the subtle effect, Brevard swiftly barred the team from weighing the cube or chemically testing the metal.

He had also glanced through the truck's windshield to memorize its Vehicle Identification Number. A quick online check against the license plate told him everything he needed to know: this wasn't the truck the world had seen on television. He ordered it quarantined to bar others from learning the same thing.

Brevard hadn't been hired to conceal what he learned, yet he now found himself in Jenna's shoes. The two had never met, but he felt a vague sense of camaraderie with her. But he knew a day of reckoning with Riesen was imminent because Brevard was deliberately leading Project Wardenclyffe into a ditch. The oddball name the army gave the project didn't help matters any: named after Tesla's ill-fated tower, it only triggered stronger associations between Wilkes and Tesla in Brevard's mind.

When Riesen had once asked him how he had voted on Jenna's initiative, Brevard said he voted against it. Riesen was openly relieved to hear that.

But Dr. Brevard Mays had lied about his vote.

A vague sense of camaraderie had gotten in the way.

Jenna begged Nurse Takashi to allow all five guests into her room. Takashi finally relented, figuring she was no match for the redhead who marched twelve miles just to cast a ballot. Jenna's hospital room quickly became crowded.

Richard started in on her first. "You know, for someone who criticized Mike and me for not looking our best at the power station, you sure look like hell."

She smiled, and had an apt reply. "Frankly, Raggedy Andy, I was surprised you even kept up with me during my walk." Mike elbowed Richard in the ribs.

Jenna looked up at Bartleby. "So, Ron, when will I get to see your vacation photos?"

He handed his iPod Peta to her without a word being spoken. She examined its display screen: a clear real-time video image of the turbines still running, the dam's logos easily visible in the foreground.

"These look kinda personal," she noted. "You wouldn't want to go public with these, would you?"

Richard and Mike let her know that *those plans were stalled.*

Despite speaking in obscure allusions, the team felt a pent-up energy in the room, knowing that Jenna's anticipation of the opposition's strategy had saved them from embarrassment, suppression, and worse.

"Well," she observed, "I do know a little bit about having one's vacation photos disdained, after all."

Bryn looked at Bic and then back at Jenna. "The Eagle has landed."

"Good to know Pinball is okay," she answered cryptically. Her expression turned serious. "Should I have a news conference and concede my defeat?"

"That'd be awful big of you to confess your errors," Bryn suggested. "Tell the people you meant well, but got caught up in your own delusions."

"Okay," she nodded, "Let's do this today. Set it up. Nurse Takashi will wheel me out to the front steps of the hospital. Have a lectern ready for me. I want to get this over with and go home and forget all about that dam. When you leave, ask the nurse to help me get my shower started."

She glanced at her lab coat slung over the hook on the bathroom door. "It's important to have closure, to clear the air of misunderstandings."

The scene of the news conference outside the hospital bustled with reporters. Even in defeat, an appearance by Doctor Jenna Wilkes was newsworthy.

The hospital's automatic doors opened. A nurse pushed the wheelchair-bound redhead toward the microphone-studded lectern. Nobody applauded; only the news services were alerted to the news conference, the location of which was kept secret from the public. A few pedestrians stopped to indulge their curiosity but moved on, not knowing who was going to speak at the lectern—probably a hospital administrator dedicating a new children's wing.

Her team was ready, so Jenna was going forward with her plan.

Takashi stopped the wheelchair ten yards short of the lectern, allowing Jenna to walk the rest of the way with a crutch, still dragging her cast-clad right leg. The brief walk to the lectern reminded the viewers, nearly five hundred million across the world, of her dramatic march a few days earlier.

She settled in behind the forest of microphones and spoke without notes.

"My fellow Californians *did* drain the dam. I'm saddened that the world has been unable to see what is happening with the turbines because a cowardly darkness fell while I recovered my strength. So I'm going to show the world what is happening inside the turbine room."

She lifted her hand up, palm outward, and closed it into a tight fist: the signal for Richard to substitute the live data stream from the turbine room for the television camera video feeds. The networks were expecting a pretaped concession speech to appear, but that's not what materialized on the monitors.

The world's first look inside the turbine room clicked into sync. The spycams scanned the operation, revealing the current date and time on the wall clocks, and the familiar faces of Lawrence Livermore spokesmen the world had recently come to know.

The spycams continued rotating, a slow rotisserie cooking some reputations as the turbines came into view.

The spokesmen had all insisted that once the dam was drained, the turbines ground to a halt and remained motionless ever since. The turbines evidently didn't get that memo—they were clearly spinning at full speed.

Jenna resumed talking over the stunning video streaming into cyberspace from the dam's generator building.

"This is what is being hidden to keep you in the dark," she began. "This is real-time video from inside the dam's generator room. Seeing is believing. These turbines are running without any water in the dam, supplying energy to nearly a million people."

She gained momentum as she spoke, her eyes flashing behind her glasses with growing intensity.

"When I became a scientist, I never dreamed my colleagues would suppress scientific information. What an ugly word *suppression* is—it means others deciding what's good for you to know, shaping what you think. Did you enjoy being fed lies about these turbines days on end?

"Bottom line, science is now the search for naturalistic explanations. Non-mechanistic explanations need not apply. But there's a lot more to the universe than what's inside it. It has the impress of something external upon it, and you're seeing it in this video feed.

"These turbines spin without water turning their blades because the natural laws governing them stand on top of a more fundamental law. My research peeled back natural law to peek underneath. Was there an infinite regress of natural law, what scientists call *turtles all the way down*? Or was there an ultimate backstop, but one still based in natural law? Or is there something more to what we see? These turbines show there's something more here."

She tried to clean her glasses on her lab coat, to no avail. She decided to pocket them. The networks went to split screen: Jenna's face on the left, the feed from the turbine room on the right.

"Something might be controversial because it's false and conflicts with what everybody knows to be true. But consider this: it might be controversial because it is true, but everybody believes something that's false.

"I've been accused of promoting the supernatural. That's the wrong word to use. *Super*natural implies that the world we know is the basic reality and something insubstantial floats above it … maybe. My work points to something *infranatural,* underneath nature, something *more* foundational, substantial, fundamental, than the world itself, the bedrock underneath reality. A Word, a Law, a Chief Cornerstone that the builders, like the men in this video feed, have rejected. God upholds all things by the word of His power, and that's not a miracle, it's a hard, inconvenient fact."

She swallowed, realizing she was getting caught up in her own preachiness. She wanted to get through this without breaking down.

"I'm a private person, not a political crusader, not a prophet, not a theologian. I want my privacy back. Do not harass or stalk me. You may be curious about me, but there's nothing to tell. I'm just like any of you, and if you were in my shoes," she glanced down at her bare feet, "you'd want the same." She brushed her hair out of her eyes once more, then spoke more evenly, with utmost gravity tinged with hope.

"There's an invisible hand spinning these turbines. I would wish for the people of the world to look from the hand, to the arm, to the face of the One who keeps His covenant for a thousand generations, His covenant with the night and with the day, His covenant with time itself.

"I believe none of these turbines will need to be maintained. They'll spin at full throttle, suffering no wear and tear, even without lubrication. But you should hope I'm wrong about that. When the Israelites wandered for forty years in the wilderness, their shoes didn't wear out, and they were fed manna from heaven. If you're receiving electricity from turbines that can't wear out, you should be very, very concerned about that similarity."

She looked up to see Eckhardt's helicopter landing on the roof of the hospital. "I promise you one thing, though. My work is just beginning."

The prompt confirmation by individuals as high up as Oren Hellman and Jonas Eckhardt that the video feed was genuine meant that nothing could be done to undo "this unfortunate leak," as the opposition had labeled it.

Jenna limped back to where Takashi waited with the wheelchair. The nurse wheeled her into the hospital, and Jenna wasn't seen in public again for a long time.

The micro videocams were quickly discovered and removed from the turbine building. Too late, Riesen realized, but at least the phenomenon could be studied in private again. He leaned over the catwalk railing to watch the immense central turbine spinning below. Brevard Mays joined him, leaning over the railing as well.

"Pretty big turbines," Brevard commented. "You can't appreciate the scale of what's happening in here on that leaked video at all."

Riesen was still bitter. "Small comfort, Mays."

"Maybe," Brevard replied. "But can you imagine what people might think if they were actually standing inside this building? You're lucky the turbines and generators aren't open to public view."

"Not good enough," Riesen complained.

Brevard hesitated. "How did General Melliton handle seeing the Wilkes press conference?"

Riesen glared at Brevard. "Apart from saying he wouldn't even trust me to guard a latrine at this point, I think he took it rather well." The colonel turned around to resume his vigil.

After a minute of silence, Brevard started to wonder why Riesen spent so much time brooding here. "Does it bother you, watching them spin like this?"

"Should it?" Riesen didn't look up.

"Depends," Brevard answered. "Depends on what's causing them to spin, doesn't it?"

"I don't appreciate the direction you're taking this conversation," Riesen turned toward Brevard. "Don't appreciate it one bit, Doctor Mays."

Brevard shrugged. "I don't know, Colonel. When I watch these huge turbines roaring like this without a drop of water in sight, it makes me wonder if we're playing with fire. Whatever is making them turn *must* be here, inside the building. Doctor Wilkes called it the "invisible hand" that's spinning the turbines. Don't you sometimes wonder whether *it* appreciates you hiding its activity from the people?"

Riesen turned to lean back over the railing, ignoring Brevard's question.

"Doctor Mays," Riesen changed the subject, "are these generators stoppable? Could we stop, say, *one* of them?"

"There are nine turbines here. If you stop one, the others will simply spin faster. Stop another, the remaining seven go faster yet."

"If I stop all nine?"

"You mean, try to pull the invisible hand off all the turbines?"

Riesen looked back at Brevard. "If that's what it takes."

"What about all that campaign talk about protecting the power grid, blah blah blah?" Brevard asked suspiciously.

"No options are off the table," Riesen replied. "If *you* can't figure out how to shut the isolator off so these turbines can go back to normal, I'll do whatever's necessary to—"

"Colonel, listen to me," Brevard interrupted. "Let's say you stop eight of the turbines, and then you reduce the magnetic field of the last generator to zero. What's going to happen?"

"What?"

"The only magnetic field left is the earth's field. To induce the necessary current, rotor and stator will switch roles while either the turbine and generator rotate at unthinkable speeds, or the earth's field strength goes through the roof, or both. And I'm not even considering heating in the wires. See, nature is filled with limits. There's even a limit to how much power can be radiated by gravitational waves—just under ten-to-the-fifty-third-power watts. The fabric of space can't handle a power flow beyond that limit."

"So?"

"What I'm trying to tell you is, when push comes to shove, what we're facing here can shove back harder than you can push. It can shove back harder than the universe itself can be pushed. Maybe showing a little respect for what's happening in this room would be a healthy thing."

Riesen shook his head. "There's nothing to respect in *this* room, Doctor Mays. We'll figure this out; we'll control it like we've controlled every other aspect of the physical world, and that'll be the end of the matter."

"You've got an awful lot of faith in science, Colonel."

"We're paying you scientists enough, Mays. You'd better deliver."

Brevard nodded curtly and started to leave.

"Mays," Riesen stopped the scientist.

"Yes, Colonel?"

"There's no basis to her prediction that these things can't wear out, is there? You *did* test for that, like I asked, yes?"

"We tested for it," Brevard acknowledged uncomfortably. He had hoped to postpone this discussion till later, but Riesen was forcing his hand.

"And?" demanded Riesen. "The test results, Mays?"

"The turbines *won't* wear out. On that count, Doctor Wilkes nailed it on the money."

"Impossible! You handpicked three experts in tribology to help debunk her prediction!"

"Colonel, wear comes from friction, from things rubbing against each other." Brevard pointed at the generator to the right. "See the sensors we attached near the shaft of number six?"

"I see them."

"Fact. There's no vibration traceable to the shaft anymore. Fact. Everywhere we sample the gap between the shaft and sleeve, we find the shaft perfectly centered. It never makes contact, never rubs against its mounting sleeve. That rotational precision extends to the turbines underneath. The mechanical centering is accurate beyond belief. Tribologists study things that move against each other. My guys have nothing to work with down there. Nothing's in contact."

"But all the noise in the room!" Riesen objected.

"Sympathetic resonance in the outer cowls excited by blade periodicity," Brevard replied. "It has no impact on the rotation. There's no metal-to-metal friction because whatever is turning the rotors is also keeping them suspended in perfect alignment. Those bearings were to be replaced this year, but as things stand, that's unnecessary. Water turbulence is no longer a factor, and aeroelastic loading of the blades—"

"You're saying something is preventing the moving parts from touching each other by keeping the rotors perfectly centered as they spin?"

"You've got the picture, Colonel. Of course, you could always spread disinformation about needing to send maintenance crews in here and then denounce Doctor Wilkes as a liar. That worked so well before, did it not?"

"Where's the centering force coming from?" Riesen ignored the barb about Jenna.

"Where are *any* of these forces coming from, Colonel?" Brevard was exasperated. "Anyway, you're missing the point. The centering force, while small, creates the biggest problem of all."

"Explain."

"The biggest problem is, knowing *how* to apply the centering force to insure zero differential stress. You'd need to know the physical configuration of each shaft down to the atom to keep them perfectly centered while rotating that fast. Remember, humans can't build perfectly symmetric parts—they're always out of round a bit."

"What are you trying to say, Mays?"

"I didn't try to say it, I *said* it. You'd need to be omniscient to keep these shafts from touching the sleeves and mounts."

"Nonsense."

"Russell Pierce already demonstrated that the shifting Reynolds numbers for the air-blade interfaces for just *one* turbine are too complex for all mankind's computers combined to calculate. The invisible hand in here runs that calculation in real time for all nine turbines without breaking a sweat."

Riesen smirked at Brevard. "That's because *you* guys aren't sweating hard enough."

"You're not listening, Colonel. Your demands on human reason aren't reasonable."

"But you keep insisting this phenomenon violates natural law!"

"Absolutely false. This phenomenon isn't breaking natural law, it's *applying it.* And applying it far more perfectly than humans could ever hope to do."

Riesen scoffed. "Your research is headed in the wrong direction, then."

"Research goes where the data goes, Colonel. If you have a predetermined goal in mind, I advise you to pull the plug on the project now. You'll achieve your goal faster using fiction."

"That's not your call, Mays."

"Fine," Brevard countered. "I'll tell you what *is* my call, then. I'm supposed to report directly to Melliton, but you won't let me talk to him. You even rewrite my reports before he sees them."

"That's the way we're going to play it," Riesen answered. "I control the lockdown and decide what's pertinent to release. Melliton trusts me on this."

"Looks to me like he shouldn't. You're taking this situation personally. You've lost perspective. I'd say you're suffering from worldview shell shock."

"Stow it," Riesen barked.

"Suit yourself. I'm taking the transport back to the lab. Thanks heaps for treating us all like prisoners of war. That's the last time I voluntarily sign up for a research lockdown."

"Mays, who said you'll have any choice the next time? Scientists are a state resource. The state calls the shots."

"No, Colonel," Brevard pointed down at the turbines. "I think you'll find that whatever is turning these nine generators is calling the shots. Good night." Brevard left Riesen alone on the catwalk.

Riesen knew he'd have to do something about Mays. The scientist was proving to be a liability. Riesen was wise to cut communications between Melliton and the maverick researcher.

The colonel pondered the roar of the turbines, the power churning through the generators, all sounds that should never have been audible in the building under these circumstances. The building was supposed to be quiet, silent. There shouldn't have been a peep coming out of this hydroelectric plant so long as the dam remained empty.

"What's it going to take," he whispered to the central turbine directly below him, "to shut you up?"

47

Later that evening, Jenna ran her hands over the surface of the large isolator, lightly tapping its titanium shell with her fingertips.

"Soon we'll release your core from its cocoon," she cooed softly. She wondered how many more wonders of the world were lurking behind the dark metal. Wonders that weren't universally welcomed.

She knew that the World Conclave of Churches was denouncing her appearance, citing passages from Deuteronomy they interpreted as teaching that ore must be painstakingly dug out of the earth, that a surplus of energy was inherently ungodly and violated the principles of religion. *They quoted Deuteronomy?* she marveled.

Environmentalists who favored simpler lifestyles dreaded new sources of cheap energy, thinking that high-priced energy promoted their goals best. Most conservatives called her a new Deborah, most liberals labeled her the new Jezebel, but there were notable exceptions to the rule—some atheists supported her while many religionists didn't.

But they're all missing the point, she sighed. *My work isn't about energy. I can't believe they're so shortsighted. So self-centered.*

The pundits still warred over her march, which dominated the airwaves for days. Her opponents claimed it was fair game to block Jenna's ads with their own, but not fair for her to block theirs by being newsworthy. They sought to reverse the same fairness doctrine ruling they had used against her. Some accused her of creating a new form of terrorism to block the democratic process. The record-breaking turnout was irrelevant—for her opponents, *democracy* simply meant they alone retained control over the manipulation of voters. When one bitter pundit complained that his group couldn't get its ads on the air, his fed-up counterpart asked why he didn't just break a leg and walk for twelve miles too, like the girl had done.

Jenna learned that hecklers were sent to the dam but were too afraid of her black staff to deride her openly. Another group wanted to block her progress toward the polling place using their bodies as a human shield. That group called off the dogs once they sensed the parallels with white segregationists blocking African-American students from entering a public school decades earlier.

Jenna was glad to be back at her old desk. She sat and wrote busily into a notepad, briefcase wide open, staff and cane laid next to it. The titanium isolator was right behind her, exactly where it had been months before.

The lab door swung open and Bartleby and Bryn walked in. She signaled for them to grab some rolling chairs and approach. After settling down, Bartleby reached curiously into her briefcase and lifted something out of it.

"A blonde wig, Jenna?" he asked. He dropped it back in and pulled out a carefully folded, immaculate white lab coat.

She smiled, looking down at the lab coat she was actually wearing, the stranger to the inside of a washing machine. "That's about all the disguise I could muster," she pointed to the wig and coat, "but those things work remarkably well."

She folded her legs, feet once again bare, *no more cast, thank God,* pumps shoved under the lab table. She had leaned the freshly cut cast, now empty on the inside but covered with friends' messages on the outside, against the isolator frame. Sexton's handwritten lines faced outward, embellished with the blue ribbon she had purchased for the cane what seemed like an eternity ago.

"I make a pretty realistic ditzy blonde," she added mischievously.

"You also give ditzy redheads a run for their money," Bartleby observed.

"Bryn," Jenna turned serious, "I'm told you've managed to clear the bugs out of this particular room. Is that true?"

He nodded. "It was the one time we had most of the people who do bugging working together, sharing information on how to mount countermeasures against their own devices. That may be the first and last time such information may be shared."

"I hope not," she smiled knowingly. "I'm thinking that the age of sharing information won't wink out quite that quickly."

"Good news," Bryn added, and she noticed Bartleby nodding up and down with excitement. Bryn also caught Bartleby's reaction and asked him, "Do *you* want to tell her?"

"Sure!" Bartleby began. "The stock price for CryoMax is doing great. Niles had no reason to come down here and throw management weight around this quarter. That's probably more a miracle than getting industry and military cooperating to debug your lab."

She nodded again, taking in the news. She recognized that not all the news could be good, but her quiet joy at the news that *was* good to hear washed over her, and she enjoyed it while she could.

"Ron, would you mind if I speak alone with Bryn for a few minutes?" she asked.

"No problem. I need to meet with Bic anyway. Oh, I almost forgot." He pulled a wadded up newspaper from his back pocket. "Today's front page." He handed it to her.

The headline read *Sexton Effect Still Strong*. The subhead alluded to the million households relying on it for their electrical power. Editorials argued over whether or not those households should have to pay the state for that power, and pictures of Sexton and Wilkes graced the right column.

She pursed her lips considering the assessment, then tossed the paper into her briefcase. "Thanks Ron. We'll talk later too, okay?"

"Sure."

"Say hi to Bic for me."

"You bet. But I'm stopping by the commissary first."

Bryn and Jenna were soon alone.

"Your mother ..." she began, but Bryn held up his hand.

"Some more good news," he said, and she could see hope in his eyes.

"Yes?"

"Because of her late-stage status, she was admitted to a trial program for a new therapy. She's only been on it three weeks, but she's showing some improvement in her blood counts. The new treatment works in one out of four patients tested so far, but she seems to be in that category. We're crossing our fingers."

"Niles came to me one night about your mother," Jenna told him.

Bryn found that surprising. "Niles? He never even speaks to my mother, his sister—they had a falling out years ago. If she had her druthers, I wouldn't be working under him at all."

Jenna considered this circumstance. It mirrored her relationship with her own mother, which was abysmal, and the strained relationship with her sisters, which was fed by friction with Mom over what happened to Dad. Jenna had received voice mails from her sisters and mother—none of the messages were supportive. The sisters needed to stay on Mom's good side. Mom was livid that Jenna had dragged the family's good name into the mud by becoming a media hog.

Jenna didn't return any of the calls, yet knew she'd eventually have to. She looked back at Bryn.

"I didn't know that about Niles and Regina. Your uncle came to me deeply concerned about her one night at Doctor Eckhardt's home. Asked me to intervene somehow. Even showed me a picture of Regina on his digiscreen when I asked."

"I had no idea," Bryn said. Was there a dimension to his uncle he had failed to notice? "Honestly, that's not like him."

"Maybe we're all at our best when we're not really like ourselves, but rise above ourselves," she answered. "Okay, different topic."

"Go," he prompted.

"The turbines."

"Yes?"

"All the religions are claiming the God of the Turbines for themselves."

"You can't help but notice that, Jenna. You're the Little Red Hen, after all."

"That's not the biggest issue," she answered.

He crooked his head at her. "What, then?"

"There's some liberty in interpreting the God of the Turbines while the turbines are feeding power to a million people. A success has a thousand fathers, but a failure is always an orphan."

Bryn had to figure out what Jenna was saying, and then it dawned on him. He started in with a hushed breath. "If the turbines were to fail, leaving a million people without power, nobody would conclude that the God of the Turbines was good or benevolent."

"Right," she replied. "Undermine His goodness, and the situation changes completely. We're either facing unknown forces of chaos, or a malevolent God who doesn't care about people."

"How'd you work this all out?"

"People haven't changed in four thousand years, Bryn." And she walked him through the story of Israel in the wilderness, who questioned and insulted God's benevolence and paid so heavy a price for their murmurings.

"So," he concluded, "you think modern man is wandering in the wilderness trying to find his way out?"

She paused before replying. "Something like a postmodern wilderness that the God of the Turbines has rendered untenable. But man is pretty resourceful. If he's dead set on not being ruled by God, he'll be sure his alibi is airtight." She looked back briefly at the isolator. She knew exactly what it would take for her opponents to pull that off—and she'd be ready for them.

"What's the answer then?" he pressed.

"People need to see that God only delivers *good* gifts from on high, that whatever moral evil is coming our way comes strictly from humans themselves." *Translation: I'll need to turn the tables on them when they seize the real isolator.*

"You realize I'm not a Christian," he pointed out.

She nodded.

"But," he continued, "I know when something's a raw deal or not. You'll let me help you?"

"Of course. I won't be able to go it alone. I was proud to be part of a team that set aside its differences to work together. It reminded me of how a Jewish zealot and a tax collector ended up on the same team once.

"One thing's for certain," she resolved as she picked up the staff and regarded it closely, "the scene at the dam was nothing compared to what's coming around the corner."

She was referring not only to releasing the core from the titanium, but to the most momentous idea in part six of her dissertation concerning inertial frame counterflow, which she now likened to an Old Testament description of a river that flows in two directions simultaneously.

As Bryn departed, Jenna quietly thought about her signature verse: *Though He slay me, yet will I trust Him.* She now understood the verse may be more relevant to her immediate future than she had previously expected.

Especially ...

Especially because she had discovered something on the rooftop of the truck the night she pulled the staff out of the core ... something about the core that could only be noticed if you were directly above it. No one but Jenna had ever been in that position, so nobody knew of it but her.

And the discovery troubled her immensely. It was the reason she had kept her hand on the staff as long as she had, thinking about the discovery while focusing on the crowd and her words to them concerning the vote the next morning. It had taken a superhuman effort to hold herself together, to focus on her intended plan and put the distracting discovery out of her mind.

But she had never stopped thinking about it thereafter. Never stopped while awake, and couldn't stop even while asleep, because she relived those minutes on the truck's roof over and over again in her mind when she dreamed.

Because once she had reached out toward the staff, the most disturbing thing about standing on the truck's roof hadn't been the thunderclaps pile-driving their molar-cracking shock waves deep into her bones, knocking her joints loose.

Not even close.

Her theory hadn't predicted it. She didn't think anybody had predicted anything like it. In fact, virtually everyone predicted against it.

But it was incontrovertible.

When she had reached out over the core, the soccer-ball-sized cavity deep inside the large titanium cube, there was something wrong—very wrong—with her hand. It had taken her a little while to figure it out, to realize what was going on with her hand as she gripped the staff.

The part of her hand extended directly over the core—and that part alone—was weightless.

When she had pulled the staff out, it was weightless for the brief moment she held it over the core, exhibiting only inertia due to its mass, gaining back its weight once pulled away from the hole. When Jenna had held the staff horizontally from its midpoint, balancing it in her hands, she had discreetly rotated the right end of it over the core while talking to the crowd, and the staff overbalanced to the left in her grip. How she could multitask enough to keep her speech straight while testing the effect, she had no idea … but she had.

And Jenna had forced the distraction out of her mind while she marched because she couldn't afford to divert her focus.

But ever since her recovery in the hospital, she realized that this distraction would deal a lethal blow against the status quo, and more disturbingly, against the primary foundations of her own research. Doubly so if rotating the isolator showed the effect had a tetrahedral shape: four different orientations 109 degrees apart, with one null-gravity axis per overlapped manifold.

It was disturbing because Jenna's research had been unashamedly built on Einstein, and Einstein's work had bestowed life and shape to hers—she owed him everything. Moreover, she absolutely revered him and his seminal contributions to science.

And how was Jenna going to repay her enormous debt of gratitude to Einstein's greatest work, to general relativity, to curved spacetime?

By driving a black staff through its heart.

The laws of nature required it.

48

Jenna's guests had flown in from three different states on her dime, which had grown thin enough for her to start rationing her remaining monies. But this was important to her.

She wondered if she should have separated these guests, entertaining them on different nights, but decided that this arrangement, although peculiar, made the most sense to her heart. For her, everything was tied together, even if it wasn't evident to an outsider how that could be.

She was gratified the huge turkey she had roasted appeared to be tender and juicy. It was the first one she'd ever made; her sisters were the true cooks in the family. Jenna had refused any assistance in the kitchen from her guests, wanting to be the one to prepare and serve this meal.

She'd never really met some of her guests before tonight, and the two she did know personally were recent acquaintances.

She pushed her way through the swinging kitchen doors into the dining room, holding the turkey on a platter. Some oohs and aahs went around the table. Two Caucasian couples, each with one child; an African-American lady with four wide-eyed children trying hard not to fidget; and Hitomi Takashi, a nurse at Metro Hospital on Thanksgiving leave this year: all beamed at the feast, the aroma, the bright candles. Looking at the table, Jenna was glad she had remembered where the leaves were to stretch it out enough to seat twelve people. She recognized that this feast completed her obligation regarding the poor tithe, but she didn't regard it as an obligation but an honor upon her house.

She still remembered meeting the two couples at the door a half hour earlier. They had arrived about five minutes apart. David Sexton, his wife Julia, and their thirteen-year-old daughter, Milla. Then Fremont Sexton arrived shortly thereafter, with wife Pat and their nine-year-old son, James Wallingford Sexton. They spoke fondly about Doctor Sexton, the sons expressing gratitude over Jenna giving credit to the late professor emeritus for a significant aspect of her revolutionary work. Jenna shared news from her last meeting with Eckhardt: announcement of his funding of the new W. E. Sexton Building at Stanford's extended campus, housing a new Institute for Advanced Studies, with Philip Hernandez appointed as acting director.

When Flora Washington arrived, Jenna learned that the children expected her to remember their names, but only Michael, the youngest, had stuck in her memory. Jenna apologized to the three and relearned their names quickly: Freeman, Rachel, and Leila.

Saying grace at the table was still new for Jenna, but Flora interrupted her before she began.

"You start, and I'll finish the prayer," Flora instructed.

Jenna smiled appreciatively. Her prayer was only three short sentences, but Flora had more on her mind that she wanted to thank God for. As she listened to Flora, Jenna found herself once again tearing up, her hands tightly folded on the Thanksgiving table.

Jenna could hardly speak, she was so broken up by what Flora was saying. *Why am I always falling apart like this?*

Jenna recognized Flora's allusion to the prophet Joel, where God promised to restore what the years of locusts had consumed. She'd expected Flora to apply it to her own family's circumstances, but she hadn't. Flora's prayer had applied the promise to Jenna's life instead, and Jenna's heart had seen the connection.

Hitomi Takashi reached down into her purse and pulled out a green surgical cap, extending it across the table to Jenna.

"I'm supposed to wear this?" Jenna asked, cracking a smile through her tears.

"You blow your nose with it," Takashi laughed.

Jenna blew into it. All smiled, but the youngest children wondered how Jenna got away with ruining a perfectly good cap like that.

"Jenna," Flora asked as the food was being passed around, "I know it's a very private thing for you, but will you let me tell the Sextons and Hitomi here the story of your lab coat?"

"You'll have to be the one to tell them," Jenna's voice cracked as she tried to dry her eyes with her napkin, "because I won't be able to get through it."

Four-year-old Michael piped up at the mention of the lab coat. "Mama says we're not supposed to wear dirty clothes. Normally. But she says your coat is different, that it's okay for you to wear something you won't wash."

Jenna tried to smile through the new tears again welling up in her eyes, reaching out to put her hand on Michael's head as Flora began to tell the story behind the lab coat.

The rest of her guests had already left, but David Sexton wanted to speak with Jenna privately while his wife and daughter waited in the car outside. He had brought a package with him and insisted on delivering it to Jenna in person.

"I'm the executor for my father's estate," he explained, as they sat down on the living room couch. "He wasn't able to get this to you before he died, but he left instructions for me to see this through." He handed her a gift-wrapped box. "My father had originally given this to Doctor Hernandez but changed his mind and asked me to return it to its rightful owner. I have no idea what it means, though."

Jenna's eyebrows were knit in concentration as she tore the wrapping paper off to reveal a gorgeously framed document, one covered up by a note taped to the cover glass. She looked up at David, who shrugged, equally mystified.

The note was in Doctor Sexton's handwriting.

Dear Jenna Wilkes,

I initially gave this to Doctor Hernandez to give to the Smithsonian, but I think you should be the one to put it out on loan to them when you're good and ready.

Might I suggest the German phrase Sieben auf einem Streich for the placard?

God bless you,

Wallingford Sexton

Jenna read the German words out loud, butchering them, and asked David if he knew what they meant.

"It's from a well-known fairy tale, Jenna. It means *seven with one blow*. Taking seven opponents down with a single strike."

"What could your father mean by that?" she wondered, carefully peeling the note off the glass to see what was underneath.

She couldn't believe her eyes.

It was the original agreement she had signed with the seven Stanford professors so long ago. Stunned, she hugged the picture frame tightly to her chest, squeezing her eyes shut and trembling with emotion. It seemed as if she were trying to hug the very words themselves, sheared free of the limitations of glass and paper.

David was embarrassed, not knowing what to say or do. "Did my father do something to upset you?" he ventured at last.

At first she shook her head no, but then nodded up and down. She looked up at the ceiling, tears unstoppable, and hugged the frame more tightly.

She finally managed an answer. "Yes, David, he did something to upset me." Her throat was so tense her words were barely audible. "And I'm so grateful to God that he did."